KU-021-109

'Really **enjoyed** this one. Lost quite a lot of sleep!'

'**Brilliant read!!!!**'

'Yet another **brilliant** book by Mark Sennen
The final page left me open-mouthed'

'Mark Sennen is a **master** thriller writer'

'Had me **hooked** from start to finish'

'Felt like I'd lost a friend when I **finished** it'

'**Five stars** just about sums up the novel'

'I read this book in 2 days because I just **couldn't** put it down'

'**What a fabulous find**'

'The Charlotte Savage series just gets **better** and **better**'

'One of my all-time **favourite** fictional characters'

'Real **intense**, gripping **page-turning** stuff'

'**DON'T READ ON YOUR OWN!**'

THE DI CHARLOTTE SAVAGE SERIES

Mark Sennen was born in Epsom, Surrey, and
later spent his teenage years on a smallholding
in Shropshire. He read Cultural Studies at the
University of Birmingham. Mark has had a number
of occupations, including being a farmer, drummer
and programmer. Now his hi-tech web developer's
suite, otherwise known as a shed in the garden, has
been converted to a writer's den and he writes
almost full-time.

A DI CHARLOTTE SAVAGE NOVEL

TWO EVILS

One of you must die...

MARK SENNEN

avon

This novel is entirely a work of fiction.
The names, characters and incidents portrayed in it are
the work of the author's imagination. Any resemblance to
actual persons, living or dead, events or localities is
entirely coincidental.

AVON

A division of HarperCollins*Publishers*
The News Building
1 London Bridge Street
London SE1 9GF

www.harpercollins.co.uk

A Paperback Original 2016

2

Copyright © Mark Sennen 2016

Mark Sennen asserts the moral right to be identified as the author of this work

A catalogue record for this book is
available from the British Library

ISBN-13: 978-0-00-758788-9

Set in Minion 11/14 pt by
Palimpsest Book Production Limited, Falkirk, Stirlingshire

Printed and bound in Great Britain by
Clays Ltd, St Ives plc

MIX
Paper from
responsible sources
FSC™ C007454

FSC
www.fsc.org

FSC™ is a non-profit international organisation established to promote
the responsible management of the world's forests. Products carrying the
FSC label are independently certified to assure consumers that they come
from forests that are managed to meet the social, economic and
ecological needs of present and future generations,
and other controlled sources.

Find out more about HarperCollins and the environment at
www.harpercollins.co.uk/green

All rights reserved. No part of this publication may be
reproduced, stored in a retrieval system, or transmitted,
in any form or by any means, electronic, mechanical,
photocopying, recording or otherwise, without the prior
permission of the publishers.

Acknowledgements

Two Evils was a bit of a monster to write. Many-headed and with a vicious sting in the tail. Thanks must go to Katy Loftus for being the first to attack the beast I had created. She was followed by two other fearless souls prepared to go into combat in the name of narrative cohesion, namely Natasha Harding and Polly Lyall Grant. Last, but definitely not least, my editor Caroline Kirkpatrick, oversaw the whole battle from the first cut to the coup de grâce and managed to keep a smile on her face amid the carnage. Thank you!

Enough with the metaphors.

I'm grateful to everyone else at Avon/HarperCollins who worked on the book. There are dozens of people behind the scenes who never get a mention but without whom the pages in front of you would be blank. They too deserve a shout out.

My agent, Claire Roberts, ensures I can afford the occasional dollop of pickle to go with my working lunch of cheese sandwiches. Thanks, Claire!

Finally, thank you, as always, to my wife and daughters for their love and support. Without them Charlotte Savage would never have got past the front doors of the police station.

For M

Chapter One

Creepy, creepy, creepy-crawlies. Little black ticks running over my naked skin. Flies swarming in the air. I slide onto my front, burying my face in the softness of the pillow, but it's no good, I'm awake now and can't settle. I roll over. I realise there's only one fly, not a swarm. Just one fly buzzing against the window. One too many. I don't like flies. They give me nightmares. Flashbacks. I can recall every last detail. The smell of the sea. The sound of the surf. The blood on my hands.

I blink. The fly is still hurling itself against the window. I stare at the insect and wonder. Something isn't right. I push myself up from the bed and swing my legs down onto the rough wooden floor. I walk out onto the landing and down the corridor. I knock on the door.

No answer.

I knock again and then turn the brass doorknob. The hinges creak as the door eases open. Inside, the window is unlatched, swung wide, the white net curtains billowing like waves breaking into a sea of foam. Sunbeams flicker in through the window and across the floor to the bed where she lies unmoving. I creep to the bed and where the sunlight strokes her face I bend and brush her cheek with my lips.

Nothing. I try again, this time pressing harder against the dry, cold skin. No reaction, not a twitch. Her eyes remain resolutely shut as if she is determined not to be disturbed by anyone ever again.

Day Two

This time the creepy-crawlies are real. A dozen flies swarming in the air. I open all the windows hoping they'll go away. No such luck. More come, following their noses, the promise of decay drawing them in.

She's begun to smell now, the weather warming, the summer heat growing by the day. Pieces of flesh lie loose on her face and her bare flabby arms and her room is full of insects. Droves. Swarms. Hordes. An odour of rotting cabbage, urine and meat gone bad permeates throughout the house. I sit at the foot of her bed and cry.

Day Three

The next day I rip up a dozen oak floorboards in her room. I fashion a coffin from the ancient planks. I'm good with tools. Woodworking. Metalworking. I kiss her on the lips one last time, aware as I do so of her cheek twitching and rippling. Maggots beneath the skin. Consuming her.

I roll her in a sheet and pull her from the bed and into the coffin. Slip, flop, thud. The coffin is heavy and I slide it from the room and down the stairs. Outside, I balance the coffin on a wheelbarrow and weave my way out to the orchard. Then I dig down into the soil and rock and bury her beneath the apple trees. A leaf flutters from above and falls into the grave like the first flake of snow in winter. Inside my chest my heart has turned to ice.

Day Four

Breakfast is a gruel of cold porridge served with a wooden spoon in a cracked bowl. A drop of honey sweetens the goo, but not the day. On the table beside the bowl is a notebook. My diary from years ago. I found the book in her room. Why she kept it I don't know, but perhaps in some small way what was within helped her to understand where things went wrong.

I stare down at the book. I know I need to relive the events inside, but not now, not here.

Day Five

I knew I would return. The place has too many memories for me to stay away. I park my car and walk across fields, the notebook clasped tight in my right hand. There's a copse in the distance. Green leaves in a sea of waving corn. I wade through the corn and reach an old fence which hangs between slanted posts. Within grows hazel and scrub and a huge tangle of laurel.

I step over the fence into another world, wandering the woodland until I find my secret place. As a young man I used to come here to meet my best friend. I'd talk to him about my problems, speak of my hopes and aspirations, tell him of my sorrows.

As I grew and matured I gradually weaned myself from my obsession. Life went on and I forgot about my secret place.

And yet here I am, looking for my friend, once more seeking help.

I kneel in the shadows, place the notebook on the ground, and begin to scrabble in the dirt. The brown covering of dead laurel leaves gives way to mulch and soil. My fingers reach down, pushing into the soft material and scraping away until

I've dug a shallow hole. There it is, shining in the light. A hemisphere of bone, long ago cleaned of flesh and polished to a gleaming white. I pull the skull from the ground and hold it in front of me. In the right eye socket a large marble twinkles. A double cat's eye whopper. There used to be a marble in each eye, but one dropped out and was lost.

'Hello, Smirker,' I say. 'It's been a long time.'

I kiss the wide bone of Smirker's forehead and then I place him on a nearby brick so we can have a talk.

Smirker smiles at me with his perfect teeth and winks at me with his one good eye. I beam back at him. I can see he's spotted the diary.

'Ssshhh!' I say, picking up the book and turning to the first page. 'This was just a dream, right?'

Smirker smiles again, but I can see he doesn't believe me.

To be honest, I'm not sure I do either.

The Shepherd sits in his rocking chair. He moves back and forth, the rocking soothing, almost as if he is once more a child in the arms of his mother. There's a creak from the rockers on the bare boards of the floor. No carpet. The room is sparse with no floor covering except for a small hearth rug. Aside from the rocker there are a couple of wooden chairs with straight backs. A monk's bench. A table, the surface much worn. To one side of the room stands a huge dresser, plain with no frills. There is a fireplace but no fire. Hasn't been for years. Cold is something you get used to if you experience it for long enough.

From somewhere across the fields a bell chimes. Twelve strokes. Midnight. A new day beckoning.

The Shepherd nods to himself, the movement of his head matching the rhythm of the rocking chair. There is something mechanical about the action. Purposeful. Like the clock in the church ticking off the seconds. God marking the time until the sinners must face their day of judgement. The final toll of the bell fades and he realises that in the moment between yesterday and today something has changed. There's been a subtle alteration in the ether. Perhaps the change is merely something physical, meteorological. Then again, perhaps the slight ripple in the air is something quite different. Perhaps it is the voice of God.

He puts his feet out to steady himself, to stop the movement of the chair. He sits in the silence of the night and listens.

God, he knows, doesn't always announce Himself with a bang. His voice is sometimes not much more than a whisper. Only those prepared to listen can detect His presence.

The Shepherd pushes himself up from the chair and stands. He walks across to where the velvet curtains hang heavy. He draws one back and peers out into the small hours which lie like a suffocating blanket of silence across the valley. The air is still, not a branch or a leaf moving, the treetops reaching for a sky filled with crystal lights.

Just on the edge of perception he can hear singing. Two young boys performing a duet, their voices as clear as the night.

Oh, for the wings, for the wings of a dove
Far away, far away would I rove . . .

He closes the curtains, returns to the rocker and eases himself down into the chair. The music continues to play in his head until the final line.

And remain there forever at rest . . .

The last note hangs in the darkness before the terrible black of the night snuffs the sound out.

The Shepherd blinks. He knows the truth of it now. He realises that God has spoken directly to him. Those who have abased the pure of heart must be judged. Memories may fade but crimes are not lessened by the passage of time. The evidence must be weighed and the sinners must be punished.

And, the Shepherd thinks, the punishment must fit the crime.

Chapter Two

Derriford Business Park, Plymouth. Monday 19th October. 3.30 p.m.

A throng of reporters clustered round the entrance to the coroner's court as Detective Inspector Charlotte Savage emerged. Rob Anshore, Devon and Cornwall Police Force's PR guru, drew the reporters' attention to the person following close behind and ushered Savage away.

'Let the Hatchet deal with this, Charlotte,' Anshore said. 'She's prepared a statement in response to the inquest verdict with the official line. You know, sadness, condolences, and all that crap to start with, moving on to the utmost confidence in her officers bit to finish.'

The Hatchet. Otherwise known as Chief Constable Maria Heldon.

Heldon was a replacement for the previous Chief Constable, Simon Fox. The *late* Simon Fox. Fox had killed himself using a vacuum cleaner hose, his fifty-thousand-pound Jaguar, and a one-pound roll of gaffer tape. Savage had been the one to find him sitting there stone dead, a cricket commentary playing on the car radio an unlikely eulogy for a man whose idea of fair play had been to try to kill her.

Inside the courtroom she'd presented her own account of

the events leading up to Fox's death and her testimony had, thankfully, been accepted at face value. The coroner had listened to all the witnesses and weighed the evidence and after due consideration he'd arrived at a verdict of suicide. Summing up, he'd said Fox had been living a tangle of lies and deceit which had included friendship with a corrupt Member of Parliament who himself was involved with a group of Satanists. Ultimately Fox's precarious mental state had led him to believe there was no way out other than to top himself.

Savage and Anshore stopped a few metres to one side of the entrance and they turned to watch as Maria Heldon dispatched the reporters' questions with curt, defensive replies.

'Chalk and cheese,' Anshore said, gesturing at Heldon. 'Simon Fox was a media charmer. Knew how to play the game. He was a decent man. Pity he's gone.'

Crap, Savage thought. The real reason for Fox's troubles was that he'd been prepared to break the rules, ostensibly to shield his son, Owen, from prosecution. Some years ago Owen had been involved in a hit-and-run accident which had killed Savage's daughter, Clarissa. Fox had used his position as Chief Constable to obscure his son's tracks, but Savage reckoned he'd done it more out of concern for his own career than any love for his son. She'd discovered the truth thanks to help from a local felon by the name of Kenny Fallon and some out-of-hours work by DS Darius Riley. She'd confronted Owen Fox and foolishly put a gun to his head. The lad had confessed it hadn't been him driving the car, but rather his girlfriend – now wife – Lauren. Owen had also told Savage it had been his dad who'd decided to cover up the accident in the first place.

'Simon Fox was a disgrace to the force,' Savage said, trying to remain calm. 'He let power go to his head.'

'Really, Charlotte, I'm surprised.' Anshore wagged a

finger. 'Don't you have any sympathy for the man's mental condition?'

Savage didn't answer. Clarissa's death had badly affected her and her family. Jamie, her son, had been little more than a baby at the time, but Samantha – Clarissa's twin – continued to feel Clarissa's absence as much as Savage and her husband, Pete, did. Fox's actions had compounded the misery. His death had brought about a resolution of sorts, but nothing would bring Clarissa back. The moment when Savage had seen her child lying broken in the road would stay with her forever. The worst of it was that Savage had had to keep everything bottled up. Aside from herself, Fallon and Riley, no one knew the real truth behind Fox's downfall or Savage's unorthodox investigative approach. Nevertheless, Maria Heldon could smell a rat.

'You know what they'll say,' she'd said when she'd questioned Savage about Fox's death. 'No smoke without fire.'

Well, there was fire, plenty of it, but Savage wasn't about to tell Heldon anything of the spark which had set the flames alight.

'Anyway, bet you're glad the whole thing is over,' Anshore said, sounding conciliatory. 'Can't have been pleasant finding Foxy in the car like that. All gassed up and turning blue.'

Anshore was a media guy, so he could be forgiven for not knowing about the finer details of carbon monoxide poisoning. Fox hadn't been blue, in fact he hadn't even looked dead. Just a trail of drool trickling from his mouth alerted Savage to the fact something was wrong.

As for pleasant? Well, worse things had happened.

They walked away from the court towards the car park and as they approached her car Savage turned back for a moment. Maria Heldon had finished speaking and the reporters had shifted their attention to the next group to emerge: Owen

Fox, his wife, Lauren, and their solicitor. Owen had jet-black hair like his dad, but his facial features were softer. Lauren was blonde, her hair matching the curly locks of the baby in her arms. Both parents were early twenties, not far off the age Savage had been when she'd had the twins.

'A difficult time, hey?' Anshore said, following Savage's gaze. 'Tough for the family.'

'Tough?' Savage held herself stock-still, bristling inside once again. She wished Anshore would shut up, wished she was away from here. 'I guess you could fucking say so.'

With that she wheeled about and headed for her car, leaving Anshore standing open-mouthed.

Detective Superintendent Conrad Hardin had been at the inquest too. He'd listened to three days of evidence replete with a myriad of unwholesome revelations about Simon Fox. Now, back in his office at Crownhill Police Station with a cup of tea and a plate of biscuits, he could finally relax. The past few weeks had been a nightmare, but at least, he thought, his own officers had come through with flying colours. DI Savage in particular had handled the situation with a coolness he'd rarely seen in a woman.

Hardin reached for his tea and slurped down a mouthful. A stack of mail formed an ominous pile next to the plate of biscuits. He took the first piece of mail from the pile, promising himself a biscuit once he'd dealt with three items. The white envelope had been addressed in block capitals, with his full name – without rank – at the head. A first-class stamp sat in the top right corner and was franked with yesterday's date. The letter had been posted in Plymouth.

He noted the details without really thinking about them, the result of half a lifetime as a detective, but when he opened the envelope his interest was piqued. The letter inside had been handwritten in a Gothic script with eloquent curls and flowing lines. The Fs, Ps, Qs and Ys were nothing less than calligraphic perfection. This, Hardin thought, was somebody who thought presentation was as important as content.

Having read the first few lines, he was swiftly disabused of the notion. The content was waffle and he'd barely skimmed through half the letter before dismissing the message as the mad ramblings of somebody who needed psychiatric help.

Hardin stuck his tongue out over his bottom lip, as he always did when he was deep in thought. The letter had been addressed to him personally and began in an overly familiar fashion.

Dear Conrad . . .

He paused and started from the beginning again, once more struggling to make any sense of most of the content. However, towards the bottom of the page a line stood out.

How about your sense of duty, PC Hardin? What about your sense of respect? Do you have any left? Are you ready to repent?

PC Hardin?

It was a long time since he'd been a police constable. For a moment Hardin smiled to himself, memories flooding back. He looked up from the letter, his eyes drawn to the map of Devon on the wall. He'd started out at Kingsbridge nick, what – twenty-five, thirty years ago? Things had been very different then. He'd patrolled the town on foot, the lanes and nearby villages on a bicycle. If he was lucky he went out with a colleague two up in a squad car. Stopped for lunch in a sunny layby with a view of the sea. Back in the eighties the area had hardly entered the twentieth century. A few drunks, the occasional burglary, some Saturday night argy-bargy after closing time. So different from the inner-city problems he had to deal with now.

He stifled the smile and bent to the letter again.

You probably won't recall me, but you must remember what happened all those years ago. When you were just a bobby on the beat. Before you became a DETECTIVE. Who could forget that face in the photograph?

Of course he remembered. The event was imprinted on his memory. He'd pushed the details as far back into the recesses of his mind as he could, but every now and then an echo came sliding to the surface, like a body rising bloated from the depths of a lake.

How about your sense of duty, PC Hardin?

Duty? He'd done his duty back then. Ever since, too. What was this joker hinting at? Were they trying to scare him? Was this some kind of blackmail scam or a threat, even? He'd put away dozens of criminals in his career, many of them dangerous, and yet it seemed unlikely the letter was from one of them. No professional felon would act in such a way.

A prank then. A prank or a madman.

He read the final paragraph.

Last time you failed them and you failed me too. Back then you obeyed your superiors and followed orders, but now we're going to start afresh. We're going to play a game, PC Hardin, and this time we're going to play by my rules.

Hardin shook his head and then refolded the letter and placed the piece of paper back in the envelope. Really he should report this, get John Layton and his CSIs up here to examine the thing. By the book was Hardin's motto. He tapped the envelope with a fingertip and stared at his name, wondering how he could possibly explain the circumstances to Layton. He shook his head once more and sighed. Then he opened one of his desk drawers, popped the letter in, and slid the drawer closed.

As a young kid, Jason Hobb had liked playing out on the mud next to the old hulk. His grandad had told him the wreck was a pirate vessel which, one dark night, had foundered in the shallows as the crew argued with the captain about the division of their loot. While they bickered, the falling tide left them stranded and by the time dawn broke the game was up. They were arrested by customs officers and, after a quick trial, five of the crew were hanged and the rest thrown into prison.

Now, eleven and a half years old and somewhat wiser, Jason realised the story was entirely made up. After all, according to his grandad, the pirates had been hanged from the Tamar Bridge, their bodies dangling for days until the seagulls had picked the corpses down to the bone. By the time Jason had discovered the bridge had been built in the 1960s, his grandad had passed away, the little wink the old man gave whenever he told Jason something outlandish just about the only thing he could remember about his face.

Right now, Jason leant on his spade near the wreck. He didn't play so much nowadays, not since his dad had gone away. The area around the old ship was no longer a place of adventure. More often than not he came to the mud to dig for bait. He sold the ragworms to the local fishing shop in nearby Torpoint, the few quid he earned clattering down on the kitchen table and bringing a hint of a smile to his mother's face.

'You're a good boy, Jason,' she'd say, pocketing the coins and sometimes handing a couple back to him. 'If only your old man had been as thoughtful.'

While he was sad he no longer got to see his grandad, he couldn't care less about his old man. His father, Jason had come to realise about the same time he began to doubt his grandad's stories, was nothing more than a lazy, drunken fuckwit.

Water began to slosh around Jason's boots, the incoming tide sweeping over the mudflats. If he wasn't careful he'd be getting wet. He pulled the spade from the mud and picked up his bait bucket. A dozen raggies wriggled in amongst the silt, no more. Hardly enough to make a journey round to the fishing shop worthwhile. Jason scanned the shoreline. Usually around this time there'd be a couple of fishermen setting up their gear in advance of the rising tide. Today there was no one. Jason sighed, wondered about tipping the bucket's contents back into the sea. Then he caught sight of the old houseboat moored a couple of hundred metres along the shoreline. Larry the lobster fisherman lived there. As dusk fell, Larry liked to hunt for young boys. He'd capture them, keep them overnight in a huge crabbing pot, and then in the morning he'd slice them thinly and fry them in a pan with a few langoustines for his breakfast. At least that's the story Jason's grandad had spun him.

Jason squelched towards the shoreline. In Torpoint the streetlights had begun to pop into life. This time of year, night fell quickly and in a few minutes it would be dark. As he reached the harder ground where the mud mixed with shingle, a car pulled up. Two men got out and sprung the boot of the hatchback. They began to unload fishing gear. Jason quickened his pace and arrived just as one of the men

14

was lighting a cigarette. He nodded at the man and pointed at his bucket. Did they by any chance need some bait?

'No, lad,' the man said. 'We're sorted, ta.'

Jason trudged away along the shoreline. Another hundred metres and he'd cut up into town and head home. Over at the old houseboat a light flickered in one of the windows. Looked as if Larry was in. The lobster man wouldn't pay him anything, but perhaps Jason could swap the worms for a brace of crab. Despite his grandfather's tales, Jason figured the man was worth a visit. It was the only way he might get a reward for his hard work. In another couple of minutes he was at the narrow gangplank which led from the shoreline to the boat. On one side of the gangplank a rope hung from a series of rickety posts. Jason stepped onto the wooden slats and walked out to the boat. Larry's accommodation was a jumble of marine plywood nailed onto uprights and resembled a floating cowshed. Jason reached the end of the gangplank. He edged around the side deck of the boat until he found what he guessed must be the front door. He knocked. There was no reply. Either Larry was asleep or he wasn't in. Jason shivered in the damp night air and turned away. He hurried across the gangplank and back to the shore, strangely grateful Larry hadn't answered.

'I've been looking for a boy like you, Jason.' The voice hissed in the darkness as a shadow stepped from behind a concrete groyne. 'Want to come along with me?'

The shadow jumped forward and Jason felt a hand across his mouth. Then there was a grunt and something slid around his throat, a thin strip of leather tightening across his windpipe. Jason slipped to the ground, aware as he did so he'd let go of his bucket, the worms slithering free and disappearing into the soft mud.

Chapter Three

Something woke Savage early. There'd been a bang from outside, a splintering noise. She reached out to prod Pete into consciousness. He stirred, mumbled something, but then turned over. He'd been out at an official Navy dinner the night before and the meal had turned into a serious drinking session. Disappointed Pete hadn't been around to discuss the inquest, she'd opened a bottle of wine for herself. Half a glass had been enough to make her realise alcohol wasn't going to help and, after she'd put Jamie to bed and checked on Samantha's progress with a history project, she'd read for a while and then called it a day.

Savage got out of bed, strode to the window and peeled the curtain back to reveal an ethereal predawn, a mass of dark clouds tinged on their undersides with a violent red. In the garden below, a fence panel had launched itself across the lawn and smashed into the corner of the house. The previous evening there'd been a strange calm with barely a breath of wind, but now a full gale blew.

September had seen something of an Indian summer and the warm weather had lingered well into October. While most people had been glad the onset of autumn had been delayed, Savage had been eager for the first storm. She wanted a break in the seasons, something to mark the end of the events concerning Simon Fox. Today, she supposed, signalled that. Now it was time to move on.

Once dressed, Savage headed outside. Their house stood in an isolated position on the east side of Plymouth Sound, clinging to a sloping garden at the far end of which cliffs tumbled to the sea. The place wasn't much to look at. A succession of owners had added their mark, leaving a hotch-potch of building styles, the whole lot covered in white stucco and resembling a multi-tiered wedding cake. The location made up for any architectural failings though, and the view across the Sound and out to sea lifted Savage's spirit, no matter the weather conditions.

She stepped away from the house and into the full force of the gale. The wind howled across the lawn, buffeting her clothing and snagging her long red hair. At the end of the grass a hedge marked the boundary of the garden and on the other side lay an area of scrub. A rhythmic boom came from beyond the hedge every few seconds, accompanied by a wall of spray as waves smashed into the base of the cliffs. She stood for a moment and looked across the Sound, tasting the salt in the air. Then she got to work. She pulled the broken fence panel away from the house and weighed it down with several old bricks. Next she moved over and examined the rest of the fence. The remaining panels had adopted a forty-five-degree angle to the wind, but they wouldn't remain standing for long. The storm had broken several of the posts which had held them up, the posts having rotted in the ground. The whole lot would need renewing.

Savage returned to the house to fix breakfast. Being out in the wind had been exhilarating. Usually, something like the broken fence would have depressed her, the destruction

17

a sign of decay, of change. Today she had a different feeling. That area of the garden had always been a bit of a mess. Having to replace the fence meant she could clear away some of the old shrubs and start afresh.

'All right, love?' Pete came into the kitchen. He tousled his hair and shook his head. 'The kids won't get out of bed and I've got one heck of a hangover.'

'The fence is bust. We'll need to replace the whole thing.'

'Great.' Pete opened a cupboard and fumbled inside for painkillers. 'Any more bad news?'

'No,' Savage said. She moved across to Pete and reached past him into the cupboard. Extracted some ibuprofen tablets from the top shelf. Kissed him on the shoulder. 'None at all.'

Savage was snug in her tiny office at Crownhill Police Station by eight thirty, leaving Pete to do the school run. Since the frigate he'd commanded had been decommissioned, he'd had much more time to be a proper parent. She remembered when, a dozen years before, he'd been away for great chunks of the year. As a newly qualified detective constable she'd somehow managed to juggle the day-to-day family routines and the demands of the job. With toddler twins the task had involved running on little sleep and copious amounts of black coffee. These days she got more sleep, but hadn't kicked the caffeine addiction and a full cup sat on the desk beside her keyboard. She reached for it and took a sip before getting down to work. This morning she had to prepare for a presentation. A management meeting had been scheduled for later and DSupt Hardin wanted her to come up with some pointers for, in his words, 'adding value' to their detection strategy. An hour into the task, the coffee long gone, she was starting to make real headway when there was a knock at the door.

'Ma'am?' The voice had a strong South-West accent and

came from a young woman who'd peered into the room. Twenties. Blonde bob. Big smile. DC Jane Calter.

Calter was a junior detective but enthusiastic. While DS Darius Riley was the closest thing Savage had to a confidante, it was Calter whom she often worked alongside. The DC's quick thinking and have-a-go attitude had saved Savage's bacon on more than one occasion.

'Yes, Jane?' Savage glanced up from her notes.

'Misper,' Calter said. 'A kid from over Torpoint way.'

'And?' Savage wasn't usually so curt, but she needed to finish her work for the meeting. A missing child surely wasn't anything to do with Major Crimes. Uniformed officers and other agencies should be dealing with the issue. She said as much to Calter.

'Yes, ma'am,' Calter said, holding out a sheet of paper, a mugshot of the missing boy top right. 'But the mother's got a new squeeze. The guy has previous for assault. We informed the woman, but she went with the man anyway.'

Calter went on to explain that the woman's own mother – the kid's grandmother – had contacted the police requesting information regarding the new boyfriend. When the police had alerted the woman, she'd taken the warning as interference from her mother and ignored the advice.

'And this man, the boyfriend, where is he now?'

'That's just it, ma'am. He's missing too.'

Savage sighed. She turned from the screen and reached for a pad and pencil. 'From the top then, Jane.'

'Jason Hobb. He's eleven. According to his mother, Jason went digging for bait yesterday afternoon. He usually does that on the shore alongside Marine Drive.'

'Time she last saw him?'

'She says she gave him some lunch around oneish and then he went off.'

Savage raised her eyebrows. 'Lunch? But it was Monday. Shouldn't the lad have been in school?'

'Yes.' Calter looked down at her notes. 'According to one of the local PCSOs, he's a well-known truant.'

'Right. Go on.'

'When it began to get dark and Jason hadn't returned home, the mother began to get worried.'

'And she called us?'

Calter sighed. 'No. She rang round a few of Jason's friends but she didn't report him missing until this morning.'

'Jesus.' Savage shook her head. In any investigation, but especially one involving the disappearance of a vulnerable individual, time was of the essence. 'Other agencies?'

'Mobilised first thing, as soon as we got word. PCs on the ground plus the lifeboat, coastguard and the MoD Police launch. So far the only sign of him is a blue bait bucket found at the high tideline next to Marine Drive.'

'OK.' Savage pushed back her chair and reached for her jacket. 'Let's organise a door-to-door and get over there. What's the name of the boyfriend?'

'Ned Stone. Thirty-nine. Originally from down near St Austell but living here now. Beat up his wife a dozen years ago. Ex-wife now, of course. Got three years inside for his troubles.'

'Other offences?'

'A couple more assaults.'

'Right. So he's a bit of a bad boy, but I've known worse.'

'Yes, ma'am, but I've got a theory. This kid's in the way, right? He's a gooseberry in Stone's tasty new pie. Say the kid does something to annoy Stone. He loses his rag with the kid, lashes out and accidentally kills him. Then he panics and takes the body somewhere.'

Savage cocked her head. She had to admire Calter's keen-

20

as-mustard attitude, but in this case the DC was wide of the mark. 'Hang on, Jane, we're getting way ahead of ourselves. First, let's get some officers doing the door-to-doors. Second, we find Stone.' Savage paused. Computed what Calter had told her. Made a judgement. 'Single mum with new boyfriend trying to muscle in and be the boy's new dad? I reckon the lad's probably just run away.'

As mornings off went, Tuesday, Detective Sergeant Darius Riley thought, was turning out to be pretty decent. Some time after eleven in the morning and here he was doing what he liked doing the best. A little R and R. In bed. With his girlfriend, Julie. Decadent, she'd said. The luxury of several hours between the sheets while the rest of the world was out earning an honest crust.

Decadent, maybe, Riley thought as he poured Julie another cup of coffee from the pot and then went back to massaging her feet. But what was wrong with enjoying yourself?

'I could get used to this,' Julie said, as she sipped her coffee and then lay back, her dark hair spreading across the fluffed-up pillows. 'The goddess treatment.'

'Fine by me,' Riley said. 'As long as the goddess dishes out a few favours now and then.'

'Well, there's no time like the present, is there?' Julie smiled and placed her cup on the bedside table. She kicked her feet free from Riley's grasp. 'And, unless you've developed an over-riding foot fetish, I'm sure there's other parts of me which might interest you.'

Riley grinned, but before he had a chance to move up the bed his mobile rang. He stared across at the phone, willing the bloody thing to stop.

'I thought you had the morning off?' Julie said.

'The morning, yeah, but I'm on call from twelve.' Riley

21

looked over to the bedside clock. Eleven twenty-seven. By rights he was off duty for the next thirty-three minutes, but as a sergeant on the Major Crimes Investigation Team he couldn't simply ignore the call. He tumbled off the bed and padded across to where his phone sat on the windowsill. 'Darius Riley,' he said.

'Sounds like one of my bad jokes, sir.' The voice came with an Irish lilt and a couple of laughs. 'There's a coffin with a body in it on a beach. Oh, and an ice cream. A ninety-nine has a big part to play in all of this, I kid you not.'

'Patrick,' Riley said, recognising the caller as DC Patrick Enders. He stared out of the big floor-to-ceiling window. His flat had a good view of Plymouth Sound and the grey sea bristled with whitecaps. The October day didn't look hot enough for ice creams. 'Where's this?'

'Jennycliff. You know, the place over on the—'

'I know where it is, Patrick.' Riley shook his head. Enders was one for over-explaining. If something could be said in ten words where one would do, Enders would oblige. Riley looked to his left across the water. Lying on the east side of the Sound, Jennycliff was a small open area with sloping grassland and a path which led down a cliff face to a stony beach. 'In fact I can see the cafe from here.'

'I'm waving, sir. Can you eyeball me?'

'Don't be stupid, I haven't got binoculars. Get to the point, would you?'

'I got a call that there was a body on the beach and that the circumstances were suspicious. I went over there and found the body down on the foreshore in some sort of coffin or box. The coffin's on a raft. I reckon the whole thing must have floated in on the tide, pushed up by these strong winds.'

'Male or female?'

'Female, sir. But I only got a peek at the body for a second

22

or two. There was a crowd of people and the PC with me slid the lid back on sharpish. Then we moved the lot of them back up the path and away from the beach. The PC is standing at the top of the path now, stopping anyone going down. I've—'

'Fine.' Riley turned away from the window. Julie shook her head and waved one finger in a playful manner. 'I'll be right there, Patrick. Thirty minutes, OK?'

'Naughty boy,' Julie said, as Riley hung up. 'Just when things were getting interesting you're off.'

'Sorry,' Riley said, as he watched Julie trace a line on her stomach. 'But don't do anything without me, OK?'

Savage and Calter boarded the car ferry for the journey over the Tamar to Torpoint. The trip only took five minutes or so, but every time she made the crossing Savage liked to get out of her car and climb the steps to one of the raised deck areas. Calter accompanied her. Half a mile away to the south, the wide expanse of the river turned east through the Narrows and ran into Plymouth Sound. Torpoint lay ahead, on the west bank of the river, cut off from Devon by the Tamar. To reach the town you had to use the ferry or take a twenty-mile detour via the Tamar Bridge.

'Over there, is it?' Savage pointed to the far shore. 'Behind the ballast pound?'

'Yes, ma'am. Marine Drive. Jason was out on the mud apparently, but the RNLI and the MoD boats haven't found him.'

'Christ, I can't imagine what the mother's going through. Let's hope my theory's correct and he's just bunked off somewhere and ended up round a friend's house.'

The rhythmic clanking of the chain slowed as the ferry neared the far side of the river and Savage indicated they should return to the car.

Ten minutes later and they'd parked up at the top of a slipway on Marine Drive. A row of houses stood on one side of the road, while on the other lay the estuary, a vista of Plymouth over the water. The tide was out, the beach a mixture of shingle, seaweed, rock and mud. A dozen officers – a mixture of detectives and uniforms – awaited Savage's briefing. They'd been assigned a list of roads to work along and all Savage needed to do was gee them up a little. She gave her standard talk on the importance of procedure, on how seemingly tiny details could turn into major pieces of evidence, and sent them on their way.

After they'd gone, she decided to walk along the foreshore. The main part of the Tamar estuary turned to the east, leaving a vast area of mud to the west. The shoreline curled round to a little bay at the head of which was a boatyard. Before that, some fifty metres from the shore and half submerged in the mud, lay the hulk of an old wooden ship. The curving timbers of the frame resembled the skeleton of a whale and inside the whale stood a real life Jonah. Savage stared across. She couldn't make out much about the figure poking in amongst the timbers except that he wore a Tilley hat.

John Layton, their Senior CSI.

She moved along the shoreline and then walked down to where the shingle turned to mud, watching Layton struggle across a patch of brown towards her. The CSI had an almost obsessive eye for detail and order which, when it came to crime scene management, proved invaluable. His obsession didn't stretch to his appearance though. Sludge smeared his thigh-high waders and covered much of his clothing. There was even a splodge of sticky gloop atop his hat. Layton reached Savage and with one hand tilted the hat in greeting and then used his little finger to scratch his nose. The nose was Roman, shaped like a ski jump with the end chopped off, and the finger deposited a blob of muck right on the tip. Layton's other hand held up a plastic evidence bag.

'What the hell are you doing out there, John?' Savage said. 'If you'd slipped over you'd have been in a spot of bother.'

'Going to do me for not running a risk assessment, are you?' Layton said. 'Only, if I hadn't gone out there I might never have found this.'

Layton passed Savage the bag.

'Right.' Savage took the bag and peered at the contents. Water and mud sloshed around inside, but there was something else in there too, something wooden and bent in a J-shape. 'What is it?'

'Dirty habit. Mind you, somewhat out of fashion these days.'

'A pipe.' Savage could see now as she moved the object around in the bag. 'But what's it doing out there and how did you know to look?'

'The boy's mother said Jason used to play around the wreck.' Layton waved a hand at the expanse of mud. 'I knew he'd been digging bait down here, but to be quite honest I didn't know where to start searching. It's an impossible task, so I figured I'd just take a quick look at the old ship.'

'And what could the pipe have to do with Jason's disappearance?'

'Somebody was digging out there. Although there's been a couple of tides, the water hasn't entirely removed the evidence. You can see spade marks.'

'The pipe could belong to the bait digger.'

'Or the pipe could belong to somebody who was out there when Jason was digging bait.'

'And how the hell do we find out who that was?'

'Our best bet might be over there.' Layton pointed along

25

the shore to where some sort of houseboat sat on the mud, a zigzagging gangway leading from the structure to the shore. 'Whoever lives in that old thing would have a good view, wouldn't they?'

Chapter Four

I'm starting to write in my notebook again. Yes, again! The last time was way back in January and now it's July. In June a cowboy president visited Britain and a concert for Nelson Mandela was held at Wembley Stadium. England were knocked out of the Euros after finishing bottom of their group. Still, the Seoul Olympics are just a couple of weeks away. Did I mention that I'm now thirteen years old?

Today is Saturday and the weather was fine so we all played football in the afternoon. Jason and Liam weren't there though. Jason was sick in bed and Liam was doing extra work in the vegetable garden. I should say that Jason and Liam are my best friends. They're both eleven and I'm thirteen. The age difference doesn't bother me because the pair of them are bright and clever. Not like the other boys. To be honest, Father doesn't like me to play with any of them, but given the situation there's not much he can do about it. Mother doesn't care one way or another. She's usually too drunk to notice or off with one or another of the various men she likes to entertain.

When I say they're my best friends, I suppose I mean my only friends. Although I go to school, the kids in my class don't like me much. I guess I got off on the wrong foot when I busted this lad's nose on the first day I was there. Ever since then most of them have steered clear. I'm not bothered and, besides, living *out here I wouldn't get to see any of them except in school time. I tend to keep my head down and try to stay out of trouble. Break times and lunchtimes I go to the library and study. At parents' evening my form teacher told my mother and father she was concerned I was a bit of a loner, but other than that she said there was nothing to worry about.*

Jason and Liam don't go to school of course. They have their own private tutors who come in. There's a psychologist too. Isobel. She's supposedly an expert in child behaviour. She visits on a Wednesday and talks to the boys one-to-one. The older lads like her a lot. She's very pretty and has long dark hair and a smile which makes them blush. Her breasts stick out and all the men apart from my father stare at her as if she's Samantha Fox. I asked Jason what she does and he said she makes him look at abstract pictures and asks what he sees in the patterns. Gobbledygook, my father calls it. If he had his way he'd stop her from coming, but she's part of some government scheme so he can't do anything about her. Mother doesn't like Isobel either, but that's for different reasons. Recently Mother has been getting friendly with this man from the Home Office and I think she's worried this man and Isobel might meet and hit it off. She needn't fret. He comes on a Friday, usually in the evening, and I don't think he's interested in women like Isobel. To be honest, despite what he gets up to with Mother, I don't think he's much interested in women at all.

The Shepherd isn't at home this morning. He's in a high-ceilinged room in a barn on the moor. He rented the barn for a song and paid a year's money in advance. The place is isolated. Nobody comes here. No one's going to disturb him. For the Shepherd's purpose the barn is perfect.

He breathes in, his nostrils assaulted by an odour of grease and oil. In front of him, on a workbench, an array of tools lie in neat rows. Pliers, hammers, wrenches, saws, screwdrivers, spanners, punches, clamps. Tools for making. Tools for breaking and holding. For cutting bits of metal, bending bits of metal, drilling bits of metal.

He stands back from the bench and turns to the centre of the room. There. A shiny creation of gleaming metal and stainless steel and cogs and wheels and rods which turn or slide round and round or back and forth.

God's altar.

The Shepherd gasps. His creation is both beautiful and terrifying, the implications profoundly disturbing. Right now the sight is too much; he must escape the confines of the room. Fresh air is what he needs.

Outside he leans against a wall and slumps down, his shoulder snagging on the rough stone of the barn. He slips to the floor and sits there, exhausted. He lets out a long breath and the air clouds in front of him, the vapour drifting up into the brooding sky. Finally, after weeks of toil, his work is complete.

For a moment he lets his mind wander to the man with the skull. You see, he knows all about the man who buries things in the dirty earth.

The boy who digs in the grubby soil . . .

Yes, that's what this is all about.

The Shepherd holds his hands out, clasping them together in prayer.

'Please, God. Don't forsake me now, give me the strength to carry out your wishes.' As he says the words he feels a rush of adrenaline. There's a part of him which fears what is to come, fears the eventual outcome, but he knows he has to fight against his demons in order to succeed.

And with God's blessing he will.

He presses his back against the stone wall of the building

and looks at the streaks of mist scudding low across the moor. Earlier, the dawn had been veined with skeins of vermilion, the undersides of the clouds patterned like the web of some giant spider.

'Red sky in the morning,' he mutters to himself, smiling. 'Shepherd's warning.'

He struggles to his feet, a gust tousling his hair. He turns and looks west to where a sheet of rain marches across the landscape. The first drops reach him, spattering in the mud at his feet and then wetting his face.

Soon the storm will sweep over the hills and the valleys and rush through the villages and the towns. The wind will scour the sinners until they are naked. Then the Shepherd will lead them to the altar and there they will prostrate themselves before God and beg for forgiveness. And at the end will come the boy who plays with the skull.

And he will be judged too. And he will not be forgiven.

Chapter Five

At Jennycliff, Riley turned off and drove down the access road to where the wooden cafe sat at the top of the cliffs. He spotted DC Enders standing by the path which led down to the shore. Enders wore a high-end red Berghaus, the hood raised against a light drizzle swirling in from the sea on a gusty breeze. A tangle of brown hair poked out of the hood above his boyish round face. The DC was a good few years younger than Riley and already married with three kids, but despite their differences, he felt an affinity with Enders. Perhaps it was because Enders' Irish roots were, in a way, similar to his own distant Caribbean heritage. Perhaps it was because he just liked the lad.

Enders stood next to a PC, the officer explaining to a dog walker with a lively border collie why she couldn't go down to the beach.

'No access until further notice, ma'am,' the PC said. 'In police jargon, it's what we call an ongoing incident.'

'Nicely put,' Riley said, as the dog walker moved off.

The PC shook his head. 'Never seen anything like it, sir. She's naked down there. Butchered. God knows who would do such a thing. Horrible.'

31

'Right.' The PC was working himself into a frenzy, Riley thought. 'Well, you remain up here and DC Enders and I will go and take a look, OK?'

'Yes, sir!' The PC swallowed. Nodded enthusiastically.

'Do you remember your first body?' Enders asked as they negotiated the tortuous path down the cliff face to the beach. 'Mine was a homeless guy down under the flyover at Marsh Mills one January. The poor bugger had frozen to death over Christmas, but by the time he was found the weather had turned. Terrible stink. Yours?'

'A stabbing,' Riley said. 'Never would have believed anyone could bleed so much.'

'That way.' They reached the beach and Enders indicated off to the right. 'She's over in the next cove.'

The gravel crunched under their feet as they trudged along. Little waves came up over the gravel and sucked at the stones as the water fell back. The tide, Riley thought, was on the way in. But he might have been wrong about that.

'What a beauty,' Enders said, gesturing out into the Sound. A large yacht slid by a couple of hundred metres offshore, the crew on board well wrapped up in oilies and obviously returning from some serious sailing out beyond the break-water. 'Beats London, doesn't it?'

Riley thought for a moment. 'Sometimes.'

'Only sometimes? Don't tell me you'd honestly swap this for a crowded, polluted city?'

Riley pondered the question. He'd been down in Devon for a couple of years now. He'd got together with Julie and recently she'd moved in with him. He knew he should feel settled and content. Yet being a black officer in a white force, a London lad in a provincial city, he did sometimes feel like a fish out of water. He missed the vibrancy of London, the diversity of people, the clubs, bars, the fact that twenty-four hours a day something was happening.

'Maybe on Saturday night, but come Sunday morning I'm quite happy here.' Riley glanced at the yacht. 'I'd be even happier if I could afford one of those things.'

'Yeah, right. Fat chance on a police salary.'

They rounded a rock promontory and there, halfway up the beach, was some sort of raft. The thing atop the raft was more of a box than a coffin. Rectangular. Like a crate used to ship goods. The box lay on two eight-by-four pieces of plywood, the plywood supported by a criss-cross of wooden beams. Beneath the frame, a dozen plastic barrels provided the flotation.

'The question is,' Riley said as they approached, 'how long has it been here?'

'No idea.' Enders pointed to the yacht again. 'We need someone who knows about tides and stuff. DI Savage or John Layton.'

They stood next to the raft now. Riley clambered up onto the structure and Enders joined him. The raft creaked and shifted under their weight and then settled. Riley pulled out a pair of latex gloves from his pocket, took a gulp of fresh air and reached out and lifted the lid of the box.

She was naked, just as the PC had said. The right arm had been severed above the elbow, the amputated limb lying neatly alongside the torso. The left arm was still attached, but the hand was missing three fingers. On the stomach a series of burn marks patterned the surface like zebra print, while near the breasts there was evidence a cutting device had been used. The head was the worst. Where the eyes should have been there were nothing but gaping holes where some kind of drill had twisted its way in and the mouth was nothing but a froth of bubbled plastic.

Riley reached in with his hand and flicked the right arm with a fingertip. The limb made a hollow ringing sound.

'Oh,' Enders said, a smile spreading across his face along with a tinge of red as he stared down at the mannequin. 'Sorry, sir. If I'd known, I wouldn't have called you out. I took the PC at his word and I only caught a glimpse before he whipped the lid back on. That's where the ice cream came in. There was this kid up on the raft with a ninety-nine. The whole thing was about to fall off the cone and land on the body.'

'Never mind,' Riley said. 'It's one for the canteen. The lads at the station will be joking about this for months.'

He looked down at the raft. The structure had been painstakingly constructed with dados and lap joints on the subframe, the pieces of plywood on the top had had the edges rounded over and the surface given a coat of wood stain. Somebody had spent time and money on building the thing.

'It's a lot of trouble to go to,' Enders said, following Riley's line of thinking. 'Unless the raft is some sort of publicity stunt.'

'Publicity?'

'Yeah. A promo for a soft drink or a movie.' Enders gestured at the structure beneath his feet. 'You set this lot up and hope someone might film a video which will go viral and get hundreds of thousands of views. Isn't that how it works?'

Riley had no idea. Since Julie had moved in there hadn't been much time for movies.

'I'm right, sir.' Enders had picked up the disembodied arm and was running a finger up and down one side. 'There's a message engraved here, look.'

Enders held out the arm. Hundreds of little indentations peppered the surface and spelt out a sequence of letters:

TB/PS/CH/BP

'A game, I reckon. Xbox, PlayStation, that sort of thing. This is a code. Maybe it's a set of keystrokes to a secret level or an Easter egg.'

Riley looked down at the rest of the mannequin. Perhaps the raft *had* been constructed in a special-effects workshop. That could explain the high-quality joinery.

'Where's the press then?' Riley said. 'And why here, why not somewhere a bit more glamorous? Seems to me if this was a clever publicity stunt then the budget's been wasted.'

'Someone got their timing wrong. Couldn't read a tide table.' Enders dropped the arm back into the box with a clatter and patted Riley on the back. 'You know, London types.'

'Very funny, Patrick.'

'They've probably chartered a big motorboat and are waiting out at sea with a bunch of journos and hampers full of hospitality food and plenty of booze.'

'Well I hope they brought enough to last them a while because they'll be waiting a long time.'

'Are we going to impound the raft then?'

'No, that's not our job. We'll leave it to the coastguard or the harbour master or whoever's supposed to deal with this type of thing. Come on, Patrick, we've got better things to do with our time.'

'Hang on, sir.' Enders was peering down at the arm he'd just dropped. Something had fallen from the hollow interior. He bent and picked the item up. 'More trickery?'

Enders showed Riley a cylindrical aluminium tube around six inches long. A rubber bung had been pushed in at each end. Enders began to ease the bung from one end of the tube. The bung popped out and Enders tipped the tube slightly. A small piece of rolled parchment fell out and into the box, something wrapped inside.

'What's that?' Riley moved closer. The parchment was

stiff and translucent, a scrawl of ink on the uneven surface. 'Unroll it, Patrick.'

Enders reached for the roll and gently teased it open. Wrapped within was a small piece of something like china or white plastic.

'God-bod Biblical stuff,' Enders said, peering down at the writing. 'Hellfire and damnation. Sinners will burn in the fires of hell sort of thing. Me being a good Catholic boy, I should recognise exactly where in the Bible this comes from, but I don't.'

'What's the white thing?' Riley asked.

Enders picked up the object and let the parchment fall back into the box. 'Looks like porcelain or some kind of fine china.'

Riley stared at the parchment as the light material rocked back and forth in the wind. Was this part of the publicity stunt? If so, they'd certainly made an effort with the paper prop. The piece of broken china was another matter.

'Nothing else in the tube then?' Riley asked. Enders picked up the tube and stared inside. He shook his head. Riley pulled out his phone and held it out level in front of him. 'Put the piece of china on there, would you? I want to look at it more closely.'

Enders placed the little white object on the glass screen and Riley held the phone up close to his eyes. The surface wasn't uniform, nor was the shape. It was around half an inch long and bulbous at each end.

'This isn't china,' Riley said. He gestured at the item. 'It's a piece of bone.'

The water was creeping round the edge of the houseboat when Savage arrived. A series of scaffold boards had been fixed to uprights sunk deep in the mud and rope hung between the uprights to provide some sort of notional security. She placed a foot onto the first board, feeling the wood strain beneath her, and walked out to the boat. 'Boat' was rather a grand title for what amounted to a bodge job of plywood, old window frames and off-cut timber. Beneath the superstructure lay the remnants of an ancient barge, black with layer upon layer of a tar-like antifoul. The boat didn't look seaworthy and Savage doubted it could get anywhere under its own power. Likely as not this would be the barge's last resting place and when the owner was dead or gone the boat would rot down to the frame in the same way as the one along the shore had.

She stepped onto the deck. In front of her, a regular house door in white PVC plastic and glass stood incongruously between two pieces of salvaged teak. She was about to knock on the glass when she saw something move at the far end of the boat. Somebody was back there.

'Hello?' she said.

The figure glanced up for a moment before disappearing from view. Savage edged along the side deck until she came to what she guessed must be the stern. Lobster pots and crab creels lay strewn about a large platform. To one side a dozen marker buoys stood in a jumble amid a nest of rope, their flags fluttering in the wind. Nearby there was a stack of white crates and a figure in a huge black cloak was sorting crabs from one crate to another. An unlit wooden pipe stuck out from a full beard.

'If you're after a lobby, you're out of luck,' the man said, the pipe jerking up and down as he spoke. 'Shrimps I've got, or else one of these nice spiders.'

'Police, Mr . . .?' Savage moved from her precarious position on the side deck and onto the rear platform. 'Just a few questions.'

'Larry.' Larry laughed to himself and then held out a huge spider crab towards Savage. The legs wiggled helplessly in the air while the claws snapped open and shut, searching for something to clamp onto. 'Larry the Lobster.'

'Detective Inspector . . .' Savage leant back, avoiding the creature as Larry moved the crab nearer to her face. 'Detective Inspector Charlotte Savage. We're investigating the disappearance of a young boy. He was out digging bait next to the wreck.'

'Gone under, has he? Should have learnt to read the tide tables. Can't help idiots, I'm afraid.'

'We believe he made it back to the shore. We found his bucket. We also found a pipe out in the mud.' Savage pointed at Larry's mouth. 'You're a pipe smoker.'

'When I can afford it. And yes, I lost one out there the other day.' Larry shook his head and then sneered. 'You think I've got him, do you? Down below confined in a giant creel with the others?'

'Larry, this isn't a joking matter. The boy is eleven years old. He's a kid.'

'When I was only a couple of years older, I was working for a living out on the blue.' Larry held up his right hand and Savage saw it had only fingers, no thumb. 'That was how I lost this. Caught on a trolling hook as the line went over the transom. Right into the bone. Wireline it was, so the skipper had no choice but to cut my thumb off, else I'd have been dragged down to the deeps.' Larry turned to the crate of spider crabs. 'That lot would have been eating me, instead of the other way round.'

'He was out there late yesterday afternoon. Some time about five or six o'clock. Did you see him?'

'Seen nothing. Around then I was probably cooking my tea.'

'We have a couple of witnesses who saw him hanging around on the shore near here.'

'Really?' Larry's voice was deadpan, wholly disinterested. 'Told you, I saw nothing.'

'Here.' Savage reached into her jacket and pulled out the misper leaflet she had of Jason. 'This is the lad. Maybe you didn't see him yesterday, but can you tell me if you recognise him? His name's Jason.'

Larry held out his hand, the one with no thumb, his first two fingers open like scissors in a rock-paper-scissors game. The fingers clamped shut on the picture. Like crab claws, Savage thought.

'Jason you say? Interesting.' Larry stared down at the image as if the name would allow him access to some secret hidden in the ink. 'Jason. I have seen him before, but I didn't know his name, more's the pity.'

'When did you last see him?'

'I swapped some bait he dug for a couple of crabs. Some time a few weeks ago. Maybe before that too. Good lad from what I remember. Polite.'

'He came here? Onto your boat?'

'Yeah. Stood right where you're standing now.' Larry smiled and then glanced down at the deck. A pile of fish guts sat near a pool of blood up against a hatch in the deck. Larry nodded at the hatch. 'I invited him in for a cuppa, but the lad said no. Was something in his eyes. I didn't push it. People talk, love, don't they? A man and a young boy? Doesn't bear thinking about what folks would say. Mind you, when folks do talk, you lot don't do anything, do you?'

'What are you getting at, Larry? Do you know something?'

'Lass, I know a whole lot more than I'm telling, but not about the boy. Seen this sort of thing afore, years ago, but nobody believed anyone then. I'd be looking closer to home if I were you.'

'What do you mean?'

'He was unhappy. I told you, I could see it in his eyes. Deep down.'

'Thanks for the advice.' Savage turned to go. She didn't need help from a crazy old fisherman turned psychologist. His pipe may well have been found out near the wreck, but the man knew nothing. 'If you think of anything else give us a call. The number's below the photo.'

'No good to me, love,' Larry said. 'I ain't got no phone. If I need to, I'll come in and see you, right?'

'Yes,' Savage said, visualising a horde of spider crabs crawling over the desks in the crime suite. 'You do that.'

Pete was doing his impression of a pizza chef as Savage came into the kitchen at a little after six thirty, a sing-song of mock-Italian words in a heavy accent accompanying his antics. Jamie, Savage's seven-year-old son, laughed uncontrollably as a circle of dough spun in the air, flying dangerously close to the ceiling.

'Mamma mia, Mummy's home!' Pete said as the pizza base fell just beyond his reach and folded into a pile on the floor. 'Shit.'

'Daddy swore, Mummy!' Jamie said. 'He used the S word.'

'He said "shovel it", sweetheart.' Savage walked over to Pete and cast him a stern look. 'As in shovel the pizza off the floor.'

'He didn't! He said sh . . .' Jamie paused. 'You know. The same as the C word.'

'The C word?' Savage stared at Jamie, thinking that having a fourteen-year-old sister wasn't altogether a good thing for the lad. 'Spell it.'

'C. R. A. P.'

'Oh.' Savage stood next to her husband and stared down at the mess on the floor. 'Well I'm sure I don't know that C word or the S word, but I do know I'm hungry.'

'There's more.' Pete pointed to a large mixing bowl containing a huge hunk of dough. 'Might even be enough for you too.'

'Thanks. I do live here.'

'Yeah, I know.' Pete switched his focus to the radio. 'But I heard on the news a kid had gone missing. Didn't realise you'd be back.'

'Yes.' Savage looked across to Jamie. He was already bored of the conversation and his head was deep in a *Beano* annual. 'An eleven-year-old.'

'Suspicious?'

Savage sighed. 'The kid regularly plays truant and the mother's got a violent partner. Plus she didn't seem to think it worth telling us he'd gone missing last night until this morning. So yes, deeply worrying.'

Pete put his arm out and held Savage around the waist. He glanced over to Jamie. 'Well, you're home now. Let's have something to eat and a drink and you can forget all about it for a few hours, can't you?'

Savage half turned to the window. A reflection of their little family tableau shone back at her. She refocused and stared beyond the pane to where the lights of Plymouth flared in the growing darkness across the inky black water. Jason Hobb was out there somewhere. Face down in the cold sea. Battered to death by his mother's boyfriend. Abducted by some pervert. Or perhaps, as she'd said to DC Calter, the boy had just run off and tomorrow he'd turn up, safe and sound and everyone would live happily ever after.

'Forget about it?' Savage said. 'Yes, of course I can.'

41

Chapter Six

Crownhill Police Station, Plymouth. Wednesday 21st October. 9.22 a.m.

Wednesday morning and there was still no sign of Jason Hobb. The door-to-door officers had come back empty-handed and the various search and rescue teams were winding down their operations. There was as yet no evidence a crime had been committed but everyone involved was becoming increasingly worried.

The first piece of good news came at ten o'clock. Ned Stone, the mother's boyfriend, had been located. Apparently he was back at his digs in Devonport. A ground-floor bedsit on Clarence Place. Savage grabbed DC Calter and they headed over there and rendezvoused with a local PC.

'Spotted his car, ma'am,' the woman said. She beamed at Savage, pleased with herself. 'Wasn't there when we went round late last night nor first thing this morning.'

'Well done,' Savage said as they strolled up the narrow pavement. 'And you think he's in?'

'I stood to one side of the window. There's a telly on full blast.'

Savage nodded and slowed as they reached a dark blue door. 'This it?'

'Yes.' The PC pointed across the street to a battered red Corsa. 'And that's his car. As I said, it wasn't here earlier and there was no answer when we knocked.'

'So he's been away.' It was a statement, not a question. Savage didn't need to bring up the obvious implication.

'Told you, ma'am,' Calter said, moving forward. 'Let's get in there and find out what he knows.'

'Yes.' Savage put a hand out. 'But we play it straight, OK?'

They approached the door and Savage enquired about other exits. Not from the bedsit, the PC said. Savage looked at the three bell pushes to the right of the door. Flats one, two and three. She pushed the button for number three and then, after there was no reply, number two. Almost immediately there was a sound, somebody descending the stairs and then a figure behind the glass panel. The door opened a fraction, coming up against a security chain. A woman's face appeared in the gap. Elderly, looking concerned.

'Police.' Savage kept her voice low and proffered her warrant card. 'We've business with Mr Stone. If you could let us in that would be great.'

The woman looked back over her shoulder and then nodded. She released the security chain and was already scuttling down the corridor and up the stairs as Savage and Calter entered the hallway. Halfway down on the right a bicycle leant against the wall. Beyond the bicycle a door with a Yale lock. Savage walked down and knocked on the door.

'Police, Mr Stone,' she said. 'Open up, we'd like a chat.'

There was movement from within the bedsit and the noise from the TV ceased. Somebody stumbled behind the door and then the lock clicked open. The man who answered the door had a chiselled face and a short haircut. A tattoo ran up one side of his neck and on the hand which pulled open

43

the door was more ink: *F. U. C. K.* She wondered how that worked. Did the other hand have only three fingers?

'Ned Stone?' Savage held up her warrant card so there could be no confusion. 'Police. We'd like a word please. You can invite us in or you can come down to the station.'

'Hey?' Stone blinked and then rubbed his eyes. He was wearing a pair of loose-fitting grey tracksuit bottoms and a white T-shirt, the latter inside out. He shook his head. 'I've just woken up and I don't know what the hell you're talking about.'

Stone turned from the door and walked back into the room. On the far side a mattress lay on the floor against one wall. A duvet had been rucked up on the bed and now Stone went over and slumped down on top of it.

'Late night, Ned?' Calter said as she moved past Savage and entered the room. 'Burning the candle at both ends? Well, we've got plenty of beds down at the custody suite and the rooms are a darn sight cleaner than this one.'

'What's your problem?' Stone said.

'Jason Hobb is our problem. Yours too.'

'He's gone missing, Mr Stone,' Savage said. 'I understand you're with Angie, Jason's mother. Is that right?'

'With?' Stone looked up and grinned, but the smile wasn't friendly, more like a dog baring its lips. 'I wouldn't say that exactly. I've seen her a few times, yeah.'

'Seen her?' Calter said. 'What does that mean? You're having sex with her. Eating her food. Using her toilet. You're probably not paying her bills, but hey, she can't have everything, right?'

Stone kept silent. Shook his head.

'Do you know where Jason is, Ned?' Savage said.

'How the fuck should I know? I haven't seen him since I was round Angie's place on Saturday.'

44

'Are you sure about that?'

'Of course I'm sure. What's happened to the lad?'

'We're trying to find out. He vanished Monday evening while digging bait.'

'Gone in the water, has he?'

'Why do you say that?'

'No reason. Just from what you said.'

'You've got several convictions, Ned.' Calter again. 'One for beating your ex-wife black and blue.'

'It wasn't like that. She went off with another guy, the two-timing bitch. She didn't realise how lucky she was to be with me.'

'Lucky?' Calter huffed. She cast a glance around the room. 'Yeah, I guess you're quite a catch. If you're fishing for worms.'

'Look, bitch, what's your problem?'

Calter stepped towards the mattress. She raised a hand. 'Nobody—'

'DC Calter!' Savage moved across to Calter. 'Enough. Wait outside.'

'Ma'am, I only—'

'Out! That's an order.'

The DC shrugged and lurched from the room. Savage sighed. Calter had taken an understandable dislike to Stone and the man had got under her skin. That was all very well, but confrontation wouldn't work here. Subtlety was needed.

'Let's get back to the subject of Jason,' Savage said. 'Are you sure you haven't seen him?'

'Of course I'm sure.' Stone stared at the open door after Calter, shaking his head. 'I haven't been over the river since the weekend. I was in Plymouth all day Monday and in the evening.'

'How well did you get on with Jason, Ned?' Savage dropped to the floor in a crouch so she was at the same level as Stone. She wanted to change the parameters of the interview. Become the man's friend. 'Did you ever go digging bait with him, fishing maybe?'

'Fishing?' Stone had sat upright now. He glared across at Savage. 'You've got to be fucking joking. I'm not his dad, am I? The kid's all right, but he stays out of my way and that's how I like it.'

'So if you're not in the relationship for an instant family, why exactly are you with Mrs Hobb?'

Stone cocked his head and half opened his mouth as if Savage had lost the plot. 'Why is anybody with anyone? It's a laugh, isn't it? Angie turns me on. She might have had a kid but she's got a great body.'

'So it's about the sex, is it?'

'Yeah.' Stone smiled. He stared at Savage as if he fancied his chances. 'When we met she hadn't been with anyone for a couple of years. She was gagging for it.'

'I bet she was.' Savage returned Stone's smile. 'And you gave her what she wanted, right?'

'Yeah. She loved it. Still does. Can't get enough, know what I mean?'

'Yes.' Savage nodded. 'So you think you've got a long-term thing going with Angie? You'll move in, make an honest woman of her. Contribute to the household. Pay the mortgage.'

'Nah, don't think so.' Stone paused. Cocked his head. 'Haven't you heard that expression? Treat 'em mean and keep 'em keen? I don't want to go getting all lovey-dovey.'

'Nice. You should write a book on the subject, Ned. You'd make a fortune. And that's what this is all about, isn't it?'

'Hey?'

'I believe she owns her own house. Most of it, anyway. OK, so Torpoint isn't exactly Salcombe, but with a little

46

work the place is worth a couple of hundred K. But Angie's mum sussed you out. You told Angie you had a job in the Navy dockyards, but you don't have a job at all. What's more, you did three years for assaulting your ex.'

'Fu . . .' Stone paused and said nothing for a moment. 'You've got it wrong. I love Angie. We're made for each other.'

'Right.' A few seconds ago Stone had said he didn't want to get lovey-dovey; now, apparently, she was his soulmate. Savage stood. She walked across to the door. 'You should know she's worried sick. Angie. We are too, to be honest.'

'And me.'

'Really?' Savage shook her head as if she didn't believe Stone. 'If you mean that then I suggest you tell me what you were doing Monday so we can eliminate you from our enquiries.'

'I was out in town drinking all day. Various pubs. Had a right skinful.'

'On your own?'

'Yeah. Sad fucker, ain't I?'

'And then you came home?'

'Yes.' Stone paused. 'No. I kipped round a mate's flat in Stonehouse.'

'You'd better start thinking about the pubs you visited. We'll want a list. The name of your mate too.' Stone nodded as Savage stood in the doorway for a moment. 'And don't think about doing a runner either, OK?'

'A runner?' Stone cocked his head on one side. 'Why on earth would I do that?'

Savage didn't stop to give an answer. She went outside and found Calter peering into the rear of Stone's car.

'We should have this in, ma'am,' Calter said, tapping the rear window. 'The CSIs should be giving the vehicle the once-over in case the boy was in there.'

Savage thought for a moment. She glanced back at Stone's place. The curtain twitched, Stone's face visible for a moment before he ducked back from view.

'I don't think so, Jane. Not yet at least.'

The wooden raft was all but forgotten by Wednesday. Riley had arranged for the coastguard to take care of its disposal, while he'd handed the aluminium tube, complete with contents, to the Scientific and Technical Services Unit. His concern now was coordinating some intel on a forthcoming drugs raid. A pet grooming parlour in the Stoke area of the city was doubling as a distribution centre for cannabis. Bring your pooch in for a shampoo and leave with a quarter of resin hidden in a bag of dog treats. The place had been under surveillance for the past week and alongside the regular clientele the visitors had included a number of unsavoury characters who wouldn't normally bother to wash themselves, let alone their mutts.

Riley sat at a terminal in the crime suite and peered at the screen. The surveillance logs, he hoped, would show some sort of pattern which might indicate the best time to make the raid. The last thing they wanted was a dozen dogs scampering out the front door and onto the main road. Mayhem. It didn't bear thinking about.

'Darius?' The voice came from Gareth Collier, the office manager. Collier was ex-military and his voice always had a smidgen of the tone of a sergeant major layered within. His appearance, with a severe haircut and a couple of tats on each forearm, gave no doubt as to the world he'd once inhabited. Collier's investigations always ran on rails, but unlike with trains, tardiness was something he didn't allow. 'Can I have a word?'

'Sure,' Riley said as Collier came over. 'What's up?'

'This guy is what's up.' Collier slid a piece of paper onto the desk in front of Riley. 'He's gone missing on Dartmoor.'

'What's this?' Riley said, as he looked at the thumbnail photograph and digested the information on the sheet. Perry Sleet. Forty-one. An animal drug salesman. In the photo, Sleet was wearing a rugby top and a cheeky grin. God's gift. 'Déjà vu?'

'Yeah, you might say so. All over again.'

Riley nodded. A while back he'd been involved in a missing persons case concerning a prison officer from HMP Dartmoor. The man had vanished on his journey home, turning up some days later at the bottom of a mineshaft in a remote part of the moor, a bullet in his brain for good measure.

'Isn't this one for mountain rescue?' Riley looked up at Collier. 'It's not as if I'm some kind of expert on moorland disappearances.'

'Not an expert, no, but the right man for the job undoubtedly.' Collier nodded at the piece of paper on the desk in front of Riley. 'You see, there are problems.'

'Problems?' Riley said, hoping he'd be able to deflect whatever Collier was trying to push his way. He gestured at his monitor. 'Only I'm bit stretched for time on this one.'

'All taken care of, mate.' Collier turned his head and indicated a couple of young DCs three desks over. 'Tweedledum and Tweedledee. Keen as the proverbial. You can brief them when I've finished with you.'

'Gareth, I—'

'Sleet's car was found yesterday evening up on Dartmoor. Door open, radio still on, a cup of coffee in the drinks holder on the dash. There's been a cursory search of the area but no sign of the man. This is a guy who, according to his wife, is not an outdoor type.' Collier nodded over to DC Enders.

49

'Not like our man over there. Sleet didn't have any walking gear. No GPS. No waterproofs. He had some wellies for traipsing across muddy farmyards, but they were still in the boot with the rest of his things.'

'The drugs?'

'Sleet carries samples only. Food supplements, that sort of thing.' Collier shrugged. 'We've got some right smack-heads in Plymouth, but I think topping someone for a mineral lick is beyond even their stupidity. Anyway, if this was about the gear he was carrying, then where's Sleet?'

'So what's your hunch?'

'Hunches aren't my job, they're yours.'

'Huh?' Riley looked up at Collier. The man's eyes narrowed and there was a thin smile on his lips. The office manager was teasing him, of that Riley had no doubt. He'd fed him a little nugget of information. Bait to see if Riley would bite. 'There's more, isn't there? Tell me.'

'Sleet's married with two kids. Just bought a nice new house in Plymstock. Playing at happy families. Only I'm wondering if it's an act. See, we've found Sleet's mobile. At just after one o'clock he received a call from a particular number. The name listed alongside the number in his address book is "Sarah". Just the woman's first name, no other contact details. The call logs show that was the only call from or to the number.'

'The wife found out then. Blew her top and went a little OTT. Or maybe it was this Sarah's other half.' Riley thought of his own girlfriend. Wondered about the kind of jealousy he'd feel if he discovered she'd been having an affair. 'Do we know who this Sarah is?'

'No. As I said, there's no other details on Sleet's phone and all calls to the woman's number go through to voicemail. The phone is a pay as you go, but we're working on tracing it.' Collier shrugged and pointed down to the sheet of paper on the desk. 'Meantime, see what you can come up with.'

As Collier strode away, Riley glanced down at the paper and took in the full details. Perry Sleet had disappeared some time on Tuesday afternoon. He'd been up Tavistock way in the morning and kept two appointments. He'd had lunch at the Elephant's Nest, a mile or so from the village of Mary Tavy – the receipt was in Sleet's wallet in a jacket on the back seat – but had failed to turn up for a three o'clock meeting. His car had been found at the end of a little-used lane a few miles to the north-west of his lunch stop. A walker, suspicious that the door was open and nobody around, called 101. By six the local policing team had become concerned enough to send for the Dartmoor Rescue Group.

Riley turned to the next sheet where Collier had helpfully added a couple of photographs harvested from Sleet's Facebook page. The Sleet family on holiday. Catherine – the wife – with two young kids; Perry himself, grinning as he rode a jet ski. Riley focused on the picture of Catherine Sleet. High cheekbones, brown eyes matching her wavy shoulder-length hair, a see-through shift over a bikini revealing full breasts. This, he thought, wasn't a woman you'd want to cheat on. Was she, though, somebody you might kill for?

Jason woke to a night so dark that there was nothing but black. He opened and closed his eyes but it made no difference. If anything, the grey milkiness when he scrunched his eyes tight shut was more comforting than the blackness. If the absence of any light was frightening, so too was the lack of any sound. When he shifted his body he scraped on some kind of wooden floor, but that was the only noise.

He lay still, listening, His heart thumped, but the thud, thud, thud was a sensation rather than anything audible.

Silence. Deathly silence.

Jason stared as hard as he could but the blackness was still absolute. This was a dream, he thought. He'd wake up soon. Then he reached down and pinched himself on the thigh, his fingers slipping on his jeans before he managed to catch a bunch of skin underneath.

Ouch!

This was no dream. Even though there was nothing to see, he was wide awake. He quivered slightly. Recently, he'd stayed up watching movies with Ned Stone. Not Disney though. These had been horror movies. Zombies, vampires, dead things which came in the night and dragged you screaming from under your duvet. Now he wished he'd listened to his mother who'd kept telling him to go upstairs to bed.

He pushed himself up and sat for a moment or two. He tried to recall what had happened. The last thing he could remember was being on the shoreline with his bait bucket. He reached up and touched his neck. Sore. Somebody had grabbed him. Was it Lobster Larry or some other pervert? Perhaps his grandfather's stories had a ring of truth about them after all. Still, it was no good worrying now. Wherever he was, he needed to escape. He'd watched enough of Stone's movies to know that at some point they always came back. The perverts, the zombies, the grey ghouls frothing at the mouth.

Jason tried to stand and promptly smashed his head on something above. Fuck! He tried again, feeling his way with his hands. Shit. He was in some sort of tunnel, probably no more than a metre high. He began to crawl instead, but his hand came up against wood.

What the . . .?

He spun round in the darkness, feeling in all directions. There was a side wall. And there. And there. And there. He ran his hands over the surface. He rapped with his knuckles.

Wood. The same as the floor and the ceiling. He was trapped in some sort of box or crate. A metre high by one and a half wide by two long.

He moved to one side of his little prison and tried kicking at the wooden wall. A dull thump was the only result.

'Help!' Jason shouted as loud as he could, but his voice came back to him muffled in the same way as his kick had. 'Help! Heeelllppp!'

All of a sudden he had trouble breathing. He gasped, but each breath seemed to draw in less and less oxygen. He moved to one side and bashed the wooden wall with his fists. Bang! Bang! Bang!

It was no good. He was trapped. Trapped in something resembling a coffin.

A coffin?

In the darkness he thought he heard some kind of groaning and then his nostrils caught a whiff of decay, of rotting flesh.

The dead were coming to get him. The zombies, the ghouls, the vampires.

Jason crawled into one corner of the box and began to cry.

Chapter Seven

It took Riley forty-five minutes to get to the remote piece of moorland where Perry Sleet's car had been found. He brought Enders with him, aware the DC had an innate sense of direction and knew his way around the moor. Still, even Enders had trouble navigating to the exact spot, confessing that the northern part of the moor was pretty much unknown to him.

'Pure wilderness,' Enders said as they turned up a lane which climbed the side of a steep valley. 'If matey boy's gone a-wandering out here then he might not turn up for days.'

As they crested a rise, Riley's eyes followed Enders' hand gesture. The moor spread out before them in a splurge of greys and browns, not a tree or a building in sight. The terrain lay in great folds like a series of soft pillows plumped up and placed in a near endless succession as they tumbled into the distance.

'Jesus.' Riley shook his head. 'According to Collier, the helicopter was out this morning. Didn't spot anything.'

'Doesn't surprise me. Unless he was wearing some kind of high-visibility clothing, they could fly within a hundred

54

metres and not spot him. Imagine he's face down in a stream bed or at the bottom of a tor. Maybe he's even gone down a mineshaft like that prison officer we found earlier in the year.'

'His death wasn't an accident, remember?'

'And this is?'

Riley didn't say anything. He just stared ahead as the lane curled left around a small hill and then ran down to a five-bar gate where a blue Audi A3 Sportback sat on the verge, a big 'Police Aware' sticker plastered over the windscreen.

'Dead end.' Riley eased the car to a stop twenty metres from the Audi. 'And no farm or anything beyond that gate.'

'So what was he doing here?' Enders clicked open his door and a gust of wind instantly cooled the inside of the car. 'Bit exposed for a spot of al fresco sex, I'd have thought.'

'Takes all sorts,' Riley said as he got out too. He pointed at the Audi. 'Anyway, perhaps they did it in the car.'

'They?'

'Sleet and this Sarah woman.'

'And then what? Her hubby arrives at an inconvenient moment and boshes Sleet?'

'Something like that.' Riley began to walk down the lane towards the gate. 'If Sleet hasn't turned up by the end of today, the car's coming in for a good going-over. We'll know more then.'

As Enders began to complain about their trip being a waste of time, Riley tried to focus on the surroundings. While remote, this wasn't a good place for an assignation. You were out in the open and it would be pretty obvious what you were up to should anyone come along. On the other hand, who *would* come along? He asked Enders whether this was a good spot for walking.

Enders laughed. 'Does it *look* like a good spot for walking?

No. Too bleak. There's no tors, nothing of interest. I doubt anyone but the most hardened would bother coming here. Besides, you've got ranges all around. Live firing. Weekdays most of the moor round this way would be off-limits.'

'Army?'

'Yes.' Enders gazed around at the dreek weather. A thin mist of rain curtained sideways in the wind. 'And much as I love the outdoors, I don't think I'll be signing up to yomp over this part of the moor any time soon.'

Was that it? Had Sleet somehow got mixed up in something he shouldn't have? Had some Royal Marine training exercise gone horribly wrong? Riley put the thought from his mind and moved across to the Audi. Collier hadn't said anything about the keys, but then, even if Riley had had them, he wouldn't have risked opening the car for fear of contaminating the inside. He peered in through the driver's window. As noted on the sheet of information, there was a cup of coffee in the drinks holder, the flask the cup had come from sitting on the passenger seat. It seemed unlikely Sleet had been indulging in a bout of passionate sex. More likely he'd poured the cup while waiting for somebody, or perhaps he'd simply come up here after his lunch at the pub in order to pass the time until his next appointment.

There didn't seem to be anything untoward inside the car. Sleet's jacket was lying on the rear seat. A briefcase poked up from the rear footwell. The report mentioned that the boot contained several boxes of samples and Riley recalled a wallet had been found in the jacket. There had been no blood or any sign of a struggle.

He straightened. If something had happened, it had happened away from the car. Riley looked to the sides of the lane. There was plenty of room to pull off the road, but none of the indentations in the grass appeared fresh. If somebody had arrived after Sleet then they had made sure their vehicle remained on the hard tarmac.

He peered back towards their own car. Imagined Sleet sitting drinking coffee and spying a vehicle in his rear mirror. He'd have placed the cup in the holder and got out of the car. He'd left his jacket behind, so he'd either expected the rendezvous to be over quickly or his emotions had overcome any thoughts about getting cold. If it had been a woman, perhaps Sleet had leapt from his seat and run to meet her.

Riley paced back up the road a few metres. He examined the verges again. Nothing except some pieces of litter. No, not litter. Confetti. Confetti?

He moved to the side of the road where several pieces of yellow and pink paper lay on the verge. Sodden with rain, they'd stuck to the sparse vegetation. He tried to get his head around what might have occurred here. Confetti suggested a birthday or some kind of a celebration. Then Riley thought of a present on a nest of the little pieces of paper. An item of jewellery? He imagined a woman opening a velvet case and seeing a sparkling ring, Sleet scattering a handful of confetti in the air as some kind of symbolic gesture.

'Patrick?' Riley knelt and beckoned the DC over. 'What do you make of this?'

Enders strolled up the lane and hunkered down next to Riley. He picked up a couple of the pieces of paper.

'From a hole punch, sir?' Enders placed the pieces on his hand and examined them. 'That's my guess.'

'Hey?'

'They've been cut from a sheet of paper. Look, there's letters on the surface.'

Riley stared down at Enders' hand. Not letters, letters *and* numbers. And not from a hole punch either. Shit, he had it

57

now. He glanced down at the ground and picked another piece from the grass.

'Know what these are, Patrick?' Enders shook his head as Riley showed him the pink dot on the end of his finger. 'They're AFIDs. Anti-felon identification tags. They're ejected whenever a Taser weapon is fired. Each carries a code to identify the particular Taser which was used.'

'Are you telling me this guy was *Tasered*?'

'Look. Over there.' Riley pointed to a clump of heather where a flash of yellow lay amongst purple flowers. Still on his knees, he shuffled closer, feeling the damp of the moor seep through to his skin. The sliver of bright yellow plastic looked something like a piece of disposable packaging. 'That's part of a Taser cartridge. Totally illegal for private use of course.'

Riley didn't pick up the plastic. Instead he stood. This put a whole different slant on the situation. Not only would Sleet's car need to be gone over by the CSIs, now they'd need a team up on the moor too.

'So Sleet's . . .' Enders stood as well and turned his head back and forth. 'Where?'

'Fuck knows,' Riley said.

The day had been long and largely fruitless, Savage thought as she traipsed across the car park about to head home in the gathering gloom. There'd been some excitement when it turned out Jason's father, like Ned Stone, also had several convictions for assault, less when he was tracked down to a cell in HMP Exeter. As for Stone, he was certainly an unpleasant piece of work, but she remained to be convinced he had anything to do with Jason's disappearance.

'Ma'am!' The shout came from DC Calter, half tripping down the steps from the entrance to the station. She jogged

58

across the car park and stood next to her, shoulders down. 'It's the boy, ma'am. A body. Sorry.'

'Oh.' Savage put out a hand and steadied herself against her car. For a moment anger welled inside, but she was surprised how quickly the feeling was replaced with resignation. As if, deep down, she'd known the probable outcome all along. She stared past Calter towards the concrete monstrosity of the station. 'Sometimes I wonder why we do this job.'

'Me too.'

Savage shook her head. Focused on Calter. 'Where?'

'On the Drake's Trail cycle path. The Shaugh Prior tunnel. In there.'

'Get back inside the station,' Savage said as she opened the car door. She ducked in. 'Find Gareth Collier and start setting things in motion. I want Ned Stone brought in and questioned too. Oh, and if no one else has, then you'd better call the DSupt as well.'

'In hand, ma'am. Apparently he's heading out to the crime scene himself.'

'Hardin? Great, that's all we need.'

Savage slammed the door, started up, and swung the car out of the station car park. She headed north up the Tavistock Road, swept along in the dwindling traffic of the rush hour. She then turned right down past Bickleigh Barracks. After passing the entrance to the army base, the road narrowed and turned left and then right before crossing over the disused railway line, now a cycle trail. The lane followed a strip of woodland and then crossed back over the line at the entrance to the Shaugh Prior tunnel. She pulled over to the left-hand side of the road and parked behind a marked police car. The lights on top flashed, each flash painting the surroundings with a blue-grey streak. As she got out, the door to the car opened and a uniformed officer emerged.

'Evening,' he said. He nodded into the car where a woman officer sat in the passenger seat half turned so she could watch the middle-aged man slumped in the rear. 'PC Dawson, ma'am. I'll take you down to the scene while Lisa here stays with the gentleman who found him.'

'No one remained with the body then?' Savage said.

'Er, no.' The officer reached up and scratched the back of his neck. 'Bit nippy. Plus somebody had to stay up here with this fella.'

'Both of you?'

'Yes. Backup in case he got nasty or tried to do a runner.'

'I see.' Savage peered in the window again at the man in the back. He appeared too shell-shocked to do anything much. She gestured to where a narrow path led from the road down to the cycle track. 'Shall we?'

PC Dawson nodded and then tramped along the road and down the path. Savage followed. The path curled round and down into the railway cutting. As they reached the bottom a cyclist swished past, the taillight on the bike blinking into the distance in the near dusk.

'Jesus!' Savage said. 'We need to close this as soon as possible. Where's the body?'

'Way up in the tunnel,' Dawson said, pulling out a penlight torch and handing it to Savage. 'Our witness says he found it when he stopped halfway to take a leak. I left a fluorescent safety vest next to the boy.'

Savage moved forward, Dawson just behind her. Deep in the cutting the light was fading and Savage wanted to get her bearings before night came. She'd been up and down the cycle path many times with her children. On most of the route the gradient was easy and with several tunnels and viaducts there was always something for the kids to get excited about.

A graceful horseshoe curve of granite blocks marked the

entrance to the tunnel, the surface of the stones covered with moss and ivy. Inside the mouth, a strip of concrete stretched into the darkness, ballast to either side. Water dripped from the ceiling and splashed on the floor.

'Looks as if the lights are out,' Savage said. When she'd been in the tunnel before, there'd been lights every fifty metres or so. The lights had been strong enough to dispel the slight sense of unease as she'd ridden through. Now there was nothing but inky black. Savage made a mental note to check whether the failure had been reported and then pushed on, the torchlight swathed in the darkness, picking out the rough walls. They'd gone a hundred metres when something glowed bright in the beam.

'There,' Savage said. 'The reflective tape on the safety vest. You stay put.'

'On my own?' Dawson said.

'Stop wittering. I'll only be a few steps away.'

'Yeah, but you've got the torch.'

Savage stayed in the centre of the tunnel and walked on, leaving Dawson trying to get some illumination from his phone. Beyond the flare of light from the fluorescent jacket something lay up against the wall, seemingly half buried in the stonework. As she got closer she could see whatever it was had been pulled into a small recess. A few more steps and she stood next to the safety vest. Now when she flashed the torch into the recess she could see the tumbled form of a body. A boy, naked apart from Y-fronts and a pair of wellington boots on his feet. The body lay face down, dark fluid glistening on the ballast beneath the boy's right hand.

'Shit,' Savage whispered to herself. She'd seen many bodies, some in the most appalling of states and circumstances, but she'd never become immunised to the shock. Here was somebody who a day or so ago had been walking

61

and talking, feeling happy or sad. They'd been laughing or crying. Taking in the world through their eyes, nose, ears and fingertips. For the short time this boy had lived he'd been different from the soil and the rocks and the inanimate objects which were no more than a collection of atoms. Now he was just that. A bunch of decaying cells. Ashes to ashes. Dust to dust. A life gone, the poor kid's consciousness extinguished forever.

'You found the body then?' Dawson's voice brought her back to the tunnel. His words echoed off the stonework for a moment before being choked to nothing by the mass of rock around them.

'Yes.' Savage remembered to breathe. She slowly exhaled. She tried to suppress her anger and emotion and instead focused on the scene around her.

'Why here?' Dawson said. 'They must have known the body would have been discovered fairly quickly.'

'Maybe. Maybe not. Other cyclists must have passed through the tunnel today. It was just fortuitous that ours decided to stop and relieve himself next to this hole.'

'It's a refuge for railway workers,' Dawson said knowledgeably. 'If a train came, they could shelter as it passed.'

'Don't tell me you're a railway nut, PC Dawson.'

'No, ma'am. There's an information board on the cycle route. Tells you all about the old line. Did you know that—'

'No, and I don't want to know either.' Savage stepped away from the body and then turned and walked back to the PC. 'Get along to the far side of the tunnel and stop any more cyclists coming through.'

'Hey? Must be a couple of hundred metres and it's pitch black, ma'am. I'll probably brain myself. That's if the killer is not waiting for me. I'd rather not.'

'Don't be stupid. Here, take this.' Savage handed Dawson

the torch. 'I'll make my way out and secure this end. I don't want to think about what our chief CSI is going to say when he arrives.'

Dawson huffed but reached out and took the torch. 'You'll be OK, ma'am?'

'Yes, now go before anyone else comes through.'

The PC shuffled off, his shadow dancing away in a circle of light. Savage turned to where a faint glimmer marked the edge of the tunnel. She took tentative steps on the concrete surface as utter blackness folded in around her. As the sounds of Dawson walking off grew fainter, she heard the drip, drip, drip of water falling from the ceiling. She tried not to think about the killer nor about the hundreds of tonnes of rock balancing overhead. This was a strange place to bring the body. Did the killer come here merely to dump the corpse or was this where some sort of assault took place? Did the tunnel have a special meaning or was the place just convenient?

Lost in her thoughts for a moment, she stepped off the central concrete slab and onto the rough ballast at the side. She put her hands out to steady herself against the tunnel wall. The stones were rough, damp and slimy. She moved away from the wall, stumbling on something at her feet. She crouched and felt around in the darkness. There. A rustling. A plastic bag containing something soft.

Savage put her hand in her pocket and pulled out her phone. She pressed a button on the side and the screen flashed into life. She turned the phone so the screen pointed downward. The bag contained a bundle of fabric. She used the phone to prod the bag open. Clothing. Tracksuit bottoms, a T-shirt, and a hoodie. Too much of a coincidence to belong to anyone but the boy.

She stood and moved back to the concrete path. The whole tunnel would need to be fingertipped from end to end. They'd need arc lights, generators, dogs and God knows what else. Never mind, that would be down to Layton. It was just the sort of logistics problem he loved.

'Maaaaaa'am! Are you in there?' The echoing voice belonged to DC Calter.

'I'm coming, Jane. Stay where you are.' Savage moved forward again, aware of lights up ahead. Activity. The rest of the team. 'What took you?'

'The boss man.' Calter stood at the entrance to the tunnel dressed in a high-vis jacket and wielding a large rubber torch in her right hand. She jerked a thumb behind her. 'He insisted on coming but I had to wait for him to phone the Hatchet.'

Savage peered up the railway to where a large round figure barrelled down the path from the road and staggered onto the track. Detective Superintendent Conrad Hardin.

'That you, Charlotte?' The voice boomed across to Savage and then echoed down the tunnel. 'Couldn't have made it any more difficult, could you?'

Hardin brushed some debris from his trousers and marched towards them, shoulders hunched, as if he was still playing front row forward for the Devon Police First Fifteen. Sadly, Hardin's glory days on the rugby pitch were well in the past and 'First Fifteen' was now used as office banter, referring to the DSupt's penchant for finishing an entire pack of chocolate digestives single-handed and at one sitting.

'Sir,' Savage said. 'You didn't need to come. You could have coordinated things from the station.'

'Of course I needed to bloody come,' Hardin said, puffing from the exertion. 'The CC is keeping tabs. Next thing you know she'll have a security tag around my bollocks.'

When Maria Heldon had taken up her post, she'd instigated a full-scale, force-wide audit of operational procedures. The audit was yet to be completed, but Heldon had already

64

decided there was a lack of leadership due to senior officers spending too much time in meetings and not enough time on the ground. Hence Hardin's presence at the scene.

Savage shook her head. The last thing she wanted was the DSupt poking his nose in.

'Well?' Hardin gestured into the tunnel.

'Bad news I'm afraid, sir. He's in there. Jason Hobb. And we're not talking accidental death.'

'Bugger.' Hardin stared into the blackness as if he had some kind of superhero night vision. He shook his head and there was silence for a moment. Then he stuck his tongue out over his bottom lip before speaking again. 'Where the fuck is that John Layton?'

It was early evening before Riley managed to make his way over to Plymstock to interview Perry Sleet's wife. Getting the CSIs organised and up onto the moor had seemed to take forever and by the time he'd returned to Plymouth and dropped Enders off at the station the streetlights were on and the rush hour over.

Sleet lived in a new-build just off the A379 to the west of the River Plym, the estate set in a huge quarry. A sign announced to Riley that he'd arrived in Saltram Meadow, although the estate had been built in the old quarry workings and was next door to what had once been the local tip. Still, Sleet's property wasn't bad, a three-storey townhouse with what looked like a pretty decent garden out the back.

Riley pulled up outside and stared at the house. These days property developers provided you with a ready-made dream, the garden with a front lawn and little flowerbeds, inside everything fully fitted. He wondered if that included the family. Except in this case, just a few months into their new life, it appeared as if things had gone very wrong for

65

the Sleets. Would the developers be honouring their money-back guarantee if the dream soured?

The woman who opened the door introduced herself as Catherine and she was even better looking in real life than in the Facebook shot Riley had seen. She smiled at Riley and ushered him in and through to the living room, the furnishings within almost exactly as he'd expected, right down to the white leather sofa with double recliners. One of the recliners had been tilted back, a fleece blanket thrown to one side, the TV flickering on the far side of the room with the volume muted. On the arm of the recliner sat a box of tissues.

'Any news?' Catherine asked as she walked across to the sofa and touched a button on the side. The recliner moved into an upright position and the woman sat. She gestured at Riley to do the same. 'He's usually so reliable and nothing's been bothering him. I can't think why he would have left the car and set off onto the moor.'

Riley nodded. He hadn't asked any questions yet, but Catherine Sleet seemed keen to give answers. He took one of the armchairs. This woman appeared at first sight so cool and in control that he wondered if the box of tissues was part of an act.

'I know what you're thinking,' Catherine continued. Riley still hadn't said anything more than his name and rank but he nodded. 'You're thinking why isn't she blubbing her eyes out. Well, I'm trying to hold it together for the sake of the kids.'

'I'm not here to judge you,' Riley said. 'Your husband is missing and it's our job to find him. Besides, people have varying reactions to stress. We all cope in different ways.'

'Well, I'm struggling, if you must know. It's been over twenty-four hours without a word. That's not like him.'

66

Catherine shook her head. 'Shit, what am I saying? He's never done anything like this before. Not been missing for a minute, understand?'

Riley nodded. 'Perry was up Tavistock way on business, right?'

'Yes.'

'And he's a rep. Animal health. Visits farms and the like?'

'Uh-huh. He drives all over Devon and Cornwall selling drugs and supplements to farmers. Not that he carries the stuff around in his car, only samples. He gets the farmers to sign up to trials, that sort of thing.'

'And you knew where he was going yesterday?'

'Yes. I gave the schedule to one of your officers. Perry is very meticulous. If he makes an appointment for eleven o'clock then he's there on the dot.'

Riley looked down at his notebook. 'It seems he kept his meeting at Lydford Gorge before lunch, but not his next over at a farm near Mary Tavy. The appointment wasn't until three and it appears as if Perry drove onto the moor to wait. Would you say that was unusual?'

'No. Perry always insists the client is the most important person in the loop. If he had to kill a couple of hours then he'd do it.'

'Yes.' Riley tried not to wince at the unfortunate expression. 'You said when I came in nothing was bothering Perry. Are you sure?'

'Yes.' Catherine swung her eyes to the sideboard where there was a sequence of family photographs in multicoloured frames. Kids on slides, in the sea, at a birthday party. 'We mean everything to him.'

'So there's no reason he might have run off? Nothing at all which could be worrying him? Nothing he's keeping from you?'

'I told you . . .' Catherine paused and then stared hard at Riley. 'What are you implying?'

'Could he have gone up to the moor to meet somebody?'

'Who? You mean a client? I can't see why he'd . . .' Catherine shook her head and then froze. She spoke flatly. 'You mean a woman.'

'We have reason to believe someone else was up there on the moor with Perry. Does the name "Sarah" mean anything to you?'

'Sarah?' Catherine's mouth dropped open for a second. 'No it doesn't. Perry loves me, loves the children. He wouldn't do anything to threaten our family.'

'I'm sure he wouldn't, but we need to explore all the possibilities. To your knowledge has Perry ever had an affair, Mrs Sleet?'

'No he bloody well hasn't!' Catherine pushed herself up from the sofa. Her body language suggested the interview was over. 'Why don't you get out there and look for Perry instead of asking stupid questions?'

'Thank you for your time.' Riley stood too. He tried to sound conciliatory. He wanted to end the interview on a good note. 'We'll find him, don't worry.'

He strode out into the hallway and opened the front door, aware of the woman's eyes at his back. He turned on the step, about to say something else, but Catherine Sleet slammed the door shut in his face.

Chapter Eight

Near Shaugh Prior, Devon. Wednesday 21st October. 6.48 p.m.

'That John Layton', as it turned out, had been delayed by an RTC which had blocked the Tavistock Road.

'Nightmare,' Layton said as he supervised the unloading of equipment from a van up in the lane. 'You lot go blazing off at one hundred miles an hour but by the time I head out there's an accident involving a bus and a car. Coincidence? I think not.'

'Get on with it,' Hardin said. 'That poor lad's probably been lying in a tunnel for the best part of twenty-four hours.'

'Right you are.' Layton shrugged. 'Still, can't do much until the pathologist gets here.'

'Give me strength. If this farce continues much longer, the CC will have tags for the lot of us.'

'Hey?'

Layton didn't get an answer because Hardin turned and walked away. The CSI looked at Savage for an explanation.

'Let's just say that since Maria Heldon took over, the DSupt has developed a castration complex. Now, shall we get down to the scene so we can at least be ready when Nesbit arrives?'

Ten minutes later, suitably attired in her PPE kit, Savage

returned to the tunnel. The darkness of earlier had now gone, banished by a number of halogen lights set atop a series of tripods. She found Layton a little way in, hunched over the bag of clothes, the whole area bleached with white light. Beyond, several more sets of lights led up to the body, while, even deeper in, shadowy figures wielded spotlights and head torches as they searched the rest of the tunnel.

'What do you think?' Layton said as Savage approached.

'I think this is a dump site,' Savage said. 'Whatever went on, it happened somewhere else. Hence the bag containing the clothes.'

'Bloody sicko.' Layton stood and held a hooded tracksuit top in his gloved hands. 'You know, when I started in this job I was quite liberal. Rehabilitation, understanding, treatment not punishment. Over the years my left-leaning political outlook hasn't changed much, but my views on what should happen to these kind of people has.'

'You're not the only one.' Savage patted Layton on the shoulder. 'Seeing this sort of thing hardens us, I suppose. And I'm with you. Hanging's too good for them.'

'Yeah, you're right.' Layton bagged the top. 'I just hope you're there at the bust.'

'What's that supposed to mean?'

'Savage Justice. Haven't you heard the banter at the station?' Layton paused, a wry smile on his lips. 'That Harrison guy, he burned to death in a car you were tailing. Those twins who killed women on Midsummer's Day: one committed suicide while the other fell down a mineshaft and broke his neck. Then there was the Chief Constable: you discovered him sitting in his car with a vacuum cleaner hose attached to the exhaust pipe.'

'Bloody hell, John, you're kidding me, right? Is this sort of stuff going round the canteen?'

70

'It's not malicious, Charlotte. They're saying it in admiration. They probably don't quite believe the stories themselves, but they'd like to think they were true.'

'Well, they're not, OK?'

'No, of course not. Still, I don't think the rank and file would be too bothered if they were.'

'Well I *am* bothered. You don't know—'

'Here he is. About bloody time.'

Savage turned to see a thin, stick-like figure silhouetted against the glare of the lights. Dr Andrew Nesbit, the pathologist. As he moved closer, the details on the silhouette filled out. Like Savage and Layton, Nesbit was wearing a white coverall, but as he walked towards them he was struggling to close up the front, the zip having snagged the tweed jacket beneath. Without the white PPE, Nesbit would have resembled an elderly actor who'd come to audition for the part of Sherlock Holmes, although he was sans deerstalker and pipe and wore a pair of half-round glasses.

'Charlotte. John.' Nesbit jerked a thumb back over his shoulder and then managed to free his jacket and zip up the coverall. 'These crime scenes will be the death of me one day. Nearly broke my leg coming down the path to the railway line.'

'You're not the only one, Andrew,' Savage said. 'I think the DSupt is thinking of installing a stairlift. Although a forklift might be more appropriate where he's concerned, don't you think?'

'I couldn't possibly comment.' Nesbit paused and peered at Savage over his glasses. Then he turned his head, his bushy eyebrows arching as he stared deep into the tunnel. 'Shall we?'

Savage, Nesbit and Layton moved on until they reached the last set of lights. The body was lit on three sides by an elaborate series of tripods holding an array of halogens. Now there was no hiding from the horror. The boy's pale white skin contrasted with the dark stones of the ballast he was lying on. Apart from the Y-fronts and boots, he was naked. He lay on his side, arms stretched above his head, legs slightly bent. Savage tried to swallow a sudden rush of nausea which rose in her throat. At most crime scenes there'd be something to ameliorate the horror. In a woodland setting there'd be flowers or the sound of birds in the trees. In the city you could hear a constant background noise, reminding you that although you stared down on death, elsewhere there was life. Here in the tunnel there was nothing but the dank smell of the underworld.

Savage and Layton stopped a few metres from the body and allowed Nesbit to approach alone.

'Do we know the boy's name and age?' Nesbit said.

'Jason Hobb,' Savage said. 'He was just eleven.'

'Just eleven? That says it all, doesn't it, Charlotte?'

'Yes. He'll never be anything else but eleven and a head-line in the papers.'

'Quite.' Nesbit put his bag down on the concrete and then stepped over and surveyed the body. 'There's wounding on the hands. Cut marks. Not much blood though. I think he died somewhere else. The body was brought here afterwards.'

'I wondered if that was the case,' Savage said. 'What we can't quite work out is his attire.'

'No? Well, we'll leave his underwear and boots in place until the PM.' Nesbit moved closer to the body and knelt. He touched one of the arms and then bent to the head. His gloved fingers examined the boy's neck. 'Seems the killer used a ligature. Did the boy have a belt?'

'No. From the clothing in the bag it appears he was wearing tracksuit bottoms.'

'Then I'd say the killer may well have used his own. Look, there's more bruising on the back. I think the belt was used like a choke chain. The killer pulled up with one hand on the belt while pushing down with the other. The boy would have been powerless.'

Powerless. Savage shook her head, not understanding how anyone could gain pleasure or satisfaction in subjugating another person, let alone killing them.

'This one's dangerous, eh, Charlotte?' Layton pointed at the figure of Nesbit hunched over the body. 'And I've got a bad feeling in my waters.'

'I thought you were like Dr Nesbit, John? Scientific enquiry, evidence, reason.'

'I'm just saying I'm uncomfortable with this. I can't quite place my finger on it, but something's not right here.'

'Andrew?' Savage said. 'How say you?'

'Well, there is something odd here.' Nesbit was peering at one of his hands, holding a gloved finger up and rotating it. 'There's a substance on the surface of his skin. Something sticky.'

'Sticky?'

'Perhaps more slippery than sticky. Possibly grease. Perhaps it's something from the tunnel. Oil from the trains maybe?' Nesbit bent to the body again. He lifted one of the legs. 'Of more importance is the fact he's still in rigor. I'll take a rectal temperature reading to establish time of death. Give me a few minutes and I'll have an answer for you on that.'

'OK, doc,' Savage said. She turned away and walked back to the tunnel entrance, leaving Nesbit and Layton arguing over the ambient air temperature. She walked along the track and climbed the little path to the lane. She found Hardin standing in a pale circle of light cast by the mobile incident room van.

'Layton and Nesbit any good?' Hardin said. 'Because if those two can't find anything, we're buggered. There's nothing yet from the wider search and little chance of any witnesses.'

'The barracks at Bickleigh. They're not far away.'

'A bloody squaddie? That's all we need. They'll close ranks, deal with it internally.'

'No, sir. I meant cameras. They have them at the entrance. Perhaps they filmed a vehicle passing late at night. Possible a sentry also saw something suspicious.'

'Good idea. I'll get someone on to it.' Hardin paused and cocked his head. 'What's it like in the tunnel, Charlotte? Grim, I'll bet?'

'Very.'

'Well, I'll go in when Nesbit's finished.' Hardin looked over Savage's shoulder into the lane. 'Before that lot take the body away.'

Savage turned round. A little way up the road a white coroner's van eased onto the muddy verge, hazard lights flashing. Jason Hobb would soon be going from one cold grey place to another.

'Ah, here's Nesbit,' Hardin said.

'Conrad. Charlotte. It's as Charlotte suspected.'

'What is?' Hardin snapped.

'He was killed somewhere else and brought to the tunnel. The lividity shows he died in a different position from the one he's in now. Looks as if the killer used a ligature to asphyxiate him. Rigor is still present and this and the body temperature indicate to me the boy has been dead for around twenty-four hours.'

'I suppose that's good news,' Hardin said. 'Unlikely anything we could have done since we heard he was missing would have made any bloody difference.'

That, Savage thought, was one way of putting it.

Savage pushed through the double doors into the crime suite at a little after ten. The tunnel had been sealed and officers

74

stationed at either end. A thorough search of the surrounding area would take place come daylight. The post-mortem was due first thing in the morning as well, an event she was not looking forward to.

Collier had left for the day, but he'd scribbled bullet points on one of the whiteboards beneath the name for the operation: *Lacuna*. One, initial lines of enquiry would be discussed at a meeting of the team scheduled for directly after the post-mortem the following morning. Two, Ned Stone had, so far, not been located. According to a neighbour, he'd left his bedsit in the morning, shortly after being questioned. Three, DC Calter had been sent to Torpoint to interview Mrs Hobb.

Savage pondered the last point. Calter would need to conduct the interview with sensitivity, but they had to get to the bottom of why Jason's mother had failed to report the boy missing on Monday night. Was it because she was trying to protect somebody? On the other hand, perhaps there was some kind of genuine misunderstanding.

She was putting together her thoughts into a brief summary document when Layton came through the double doors carrying a plastic crate. He plonked the crate down on a table with a crash and waved at Savage.

'Got anything from the mother yet?' Layton said.

'No. DC Calter is over there at the moment. I'm thinking the delay in reporting Jason as a misper is down to her hiding something. She's a single mum and there's a boyfriend and – get this – the boyfriend's got form.'

'Nice theory, but it's a dead end.' Layton flipped up the lid on the crate. He delved inside and pulled out a number of plastic bags. Each held an item of clothing. 'Because unfortunately there's a problem. A big problem.'

'Go on.'

'These are the clothes you found in the tunnel. Likely they

belong to the dead boy.' Layton picked up one of the bags. Inside was a hooded sweatshirt. 'But they don't belong to Jason.'

'*What?*'

'I've checked the misper details. Jason was wearing an Argyll top, jeans with a belt, and some kind of cag with an inner fleece. Nothing like this. I've taken a look at the crime scene pictures. It's no surprise we made the mistake since the dead lad is around eleven too, certainly no older. But we've fucked up big time because wherever Jason Hobb is, he isn't lying dead in the Shaugh Prior tunnel.'

'Christ.' Savage stared at the other plastic bags. A T-shirt, a pair of socks, boxer shorts, some tracksuit bottoms with a rip in one knee. How had she missed this? She wondered about the inquest. Was she still too wrapped up in her own problems, even though she'd told Pete everything was fine? 'You're saying this is entirely coincidental? That Jason could be safe and sound somewhere?'

'Be nice to think so.' Layton pursed his lips and then pressed them together into a thin smile. 'But as you well know, happy endings are hard to come by in this business.'

'Shit.' Savage was already reaching for her phone. She needed to call DC Calter. Right now.

Calter was buzzing when she left the crime scene and, despite the lateness of the hour, was not displeased to be dispatched to interview Angie Hobb. The woman, Collier reckoned, needed to give them the full lowdown on her relationship with Ned Stone.

'Preferably before you break the bad news,' Collier had added. 'That way she'll be more responsive.'

Over at Torpoint the front door cracked open to reveal the angelic face of Luke Farrell, a family liaison officer. Farrell reached up and ran his fingers through his blond mop, looking something like a cross between a scarecrow and a teddy bear. He showed Calter into the hallway.

'News?' Farrell said. Calter nodded. 'Bad, I take it?'

'The worst. A body in a tunnel on the Drake's Trail.' Calter paused at the entrance to the living room. Kept her voice to a whisper. 'But I just want a couple of minutes before I tell her, OK?'

'Sure, but go easy.'

'You know me,' Calter said, smiling. 'When do I ever *not* go easy?'

Angie Hobb filled an armchair in the living room, legs pulled in underneath her, a cup of cold tea on a table to one side. Bare arms showed a healthy tan, but her face was devoid of colour. She barely glanced up as Calter and Farrell entered and sat on the sofa. Calter pulled out a pad and pencil.

'DC Jane Calter, Angie,' Farrell said. 'She's got a few extra questions for you. Nothing to worry about.'

'I'm sorry to press you, Angie,' Calter said with a half glance towards Farrell. 'You told us Jason failed to return home Monday evening. That he'd been digging bait in the late afternoon. Why didn't you report him missing straight away?'

'I said, didn't I?' Angie snapped. Her hands sat on her lap, tightly clenched. 'I thought he was round a friend's house.'

'But you didn't worry, didn't feel the need to check?'

'No. He often stays out late.'

'But all night, Mrs Hobb? An eleven-year-old?'

Angie said nothing. Shook her head and stared down at her hands.

Calter tried another line of questioning. 'Monday was a weekday. Why wasn't he in school?'

'He was upset about being bullied, so I let him stay home. Please, you've got to believe me.'

Calter felt a buzzing in her pocket. She pulled out her phone and silenced the call.

'Can anyone else corroborate this? Because the headmistress at . . .' Calter glanced down at her pad, 'Torpoint Community College says Jason's missed a lot of school this term. Nothing about bullying. She says there are concerns about family life.'

'Concerns?'

'Ned Stone. Your boyfriend.'

'Ned? He's got nothing to do with this.'

'Did you know Ned has a conviction for assault?'

'Yes, of course I did. You lot told me.'

'When did you last see him, Angie? Not Monday night, was it?'

'No, not this week. Ned was last round Saturday.'

'You need to think hard about this. Whether you want to cover up for this man. He's a violent offender, Angie.'

'Ned? He wouldn't hurt Jason, would he?' Angie looked hard at Calter and then glanced at Farrell.

'Has Ned ever got angry with you?' Calter said. 'Got angry and lashed out?'

'No, he hasn't.' Angie shook her head and then brought her hands up and hugged herself. 'I don't understand. You're confusing me. Why would Ned hurt Jason?'

'I told you, Angie,' Calter said. 'He's got a record for violence.'

'Ned loves me. Jason will turn up, you'll see. He's run away before and always come back.'

'He has?'

'Yes. In the summer shortly after I met . . .' Angie's words trailed off.

'Ned Stone.' Calter nodded. 'Suppose Ned had an argument with Jason and the argument got out of hand. Suppose Ned went too far.'

'What do you mean "suppose"? Have you . . .?' Angie looked again at Farrell, her mouth dropping open. Farrell stood and moved across the room. 'No! You haven't?'

'We don't know yet, but we've found a body.'

Now Angie was standing too. As Farrell reached her, she put her arms up and began to beat him across the chest.

'No! No! No!'

Farrell caught Angie as all the energy went out of her and her legs buckled. He moved her back to the armchair and lowered her down.

'My Jason! How can this happen? Noooooo!'

Calter almost put her hands to her ears to shield herself from the scream. She was surprised to see that in the turmoil Farrell had answered his phone. He stepped across the room away from the wailing. Calter got up from her own seat. She had to do something, to try to comfort the woman.

'Angie?' Calter moved to the armchair. She put her hand out and touched Angie on the shoulder. 'We need you to be strong. We need—'

'Fuck!'

Calter looked across at Farrell. He was Mr Goody Two Shoes and she'd never heard him swear before. He shoved his phone in his pocket and glared across at Calter.

'What is it, Luke?' Calter said.

'It's not Jason,' Farrell said, shaking his head. 'The body in the tunnel belongs to some other poor kid.'

'Oh, thank God!' Angie looked up, mouth agape. 'Jason, my Jason. He's alive!'

Chapter Nine

Friday again. I haven't had much time this week as I was given extra homework on account of getting into a fight at school. Thank goodness it's the weekend. When I mentioned this to Jason earlier, he shrugged. Something is bothering him. I know Father gave him the cane on Wednesday for some misdemeanour, but I don't think that's it. I'm beginning to wonder if it's to do with Bentley.

Bentley is Mother's fancy man. The guy from the Home Office. Of course, Bentley isn't his real name – it's the make of car he drives, or rather his chauffeur drives the car while he sits in the back and does his paperwork. Bentley, you see, is a minister. Not a religious minister though, Bentley is a Minister of the Crown.

The first time I saw him he jumped from his car and swept up the front steps with a number of aides in tow. The visit was routine, some kind of inspection, nothing much to worry Father though. Father keeps a tight ship and there's rarely anything amiss.

Lately though, Bentley's been coming alone or with just his bodyguard and chauffeur, slipping down the lanes to the home under the cover of darkness. Sometimes I'm in bed and I hear the big car crunching across the gravel car park, the headlights sweeping the coastline as the car turns in. Upstairs footsteps pound on the floorboards as boys scamper from room to room, while downstairs there's a banging of doors as staff jump to please him.

Tonight I met him face-to-face for the first time. He arrived a little earlier than usual and when I came into the living room in our private apartment he was sitting in Father's armchair, head down in a newspaper. As I entered, he looked up and asked me my name, almost as if knowing what to call me would give him some sort of hold over me. I shook my head and kept silent. As I stood there, Bentley smiled a lipless grin and nodded, as if accepting my right to challenge him. Then he returned to his newspaper.

I'm back upstairs now, snuggled down under the covers with a torch to help me to write. A few minutes ago I heard the familiar sound of boys on the move. I wonder about Bentley. What's he up to? Why does he come here?

While Mother is in thrall to Bentley, with Father it's different. Bentley has some kind of hold over him. It's the only way I can explain their relationship. You see, my father isn't a weak man, but Bentley walks all over him. He arrives whenever he likes, drinks my father's whisky and does things with my mother I'd rather not think about. Father just takes it. I guess Bentley, being in the government, could close the home with a snap of his fingers. Perhaps he could even get Father in trouble, considering the kind of punishments used here at the Heights. One word from Bentley and Father would be facing unemployment or even prison.

I've just looked at the clock and it's late, nearly twelve. Bentley is still here. I peeked out from the curtains and the car is still out front. The chauffeur is sitting in the driver's seat with the window open, smoking a cigarette. Bentley is somewhere downstairs and just what he's up to I have no idea.

*   *   *

81

The Shepherd jerks awake in the darkness. He holds himself still for a few moments until he has fully come to his senses. A dream, he thinks, it was only another dream.

Lately there have been many dreams. The Shepherd has seen them as some sort of test. God wants to know he can stay strong. Only those with the resolve to serve Him through the darkest hours and the harshest pain can enter the Kingdom of Heaven.

'I have sinned,' he says aloud into the grey air. 'But if I repent I will be forgiven. If I carry out the tasks God has set me then Good will prevail. If I stay faithful until the Very End then He will reward me with Eternal Life.'

He knows he won't sleep now so he pulls himself from his bed and heads downstairs. He prepares breakfast which he eats in the kitchen while listening to the radio. The news is full of the missing kid from Plymouth and a body found in a railway tunnel. The tunnel is just a couple of miles from the barn, the location too close for comfort. The Shepherd wonders if this is another test or if God is trying to tell him something.

He dismisses the idea and his mind turns from the boy in the tunnel to the other boy, the one who plays with the skull. The world is full of sinners, he thinks, and all of them deserve to be punished.

After breakfast he goes into the living room. Either side of the fireplace are bookshelves, the shelves bare apart from one particularly heavy volume. The book is old and leather-bound, the title on the spine embossed with gold. He takes the book from the shelf and sits in the rocking chair. He's broken his fast but now he needs sustenance from God's words.

His long fingers slide between the pages, ruffling the thin paper until he finds the passage he is looking for.

. . . as for the cowardly, the faithless, the detestable, as for
murderers, the sexually immoral, sorcerers, idolaters, and
all liars, their portion will be in the lake that burns with
fire and sulphur, which is the second death.

The Word of God is unambiguous. Sinners must be
punished. The Shepherd leans back in his chair, the ancient
text fuel for his mind. He allows himself to relax for a moment.
The last few days have been hectic. He has not only completed
his work in the barn, he's also tested the altar and the raft.
The altar performed admirably and the Shepherd was only
sorry that a mannequin was standing in for the true sinners.
The raft, too, had worked like a dream and as he'd watched
it float out to sea with the mannequin aboard he'd felt a
moment of catharsis. This was the beginning of the end.

Still, all his hard work on the altar and raft would be for
nothing without the attendance of his first guests.

Judgement is mine, saith the Lord.

Yes, but even God needs help to bring the accused to his
courtroom.

The Taser he'd purchased mail order from the States,
where apparently they were perfectly legal. Initially he'd been
uneasy about the device, seeing the thing as a necessary evil.
After having used the gun on his first guest he'd changed
his mind. The weapon was heaven-sent, instant justice
administered much like a lightning bolt from above. Sleet
succumbed to the weapon in the same way as his first guest.
The man had gone down instantly and then quivered like a
jelly as he received shock after shock.

He'd bundled Sleet into the boot of his car and driven
him to the barn. At the barn the man had been ready to fight

until he saw the Taser again. From then on Sleet had complied willingly and allowed himself to be locked in a cell.

Fool.

The Shepherd thinks of the passage from the Bible once more.

. . . as for the cowardly . . .

A coward is the worst kind of sinner. By failing to have courage and conviction, the coward spits in God's face and denies His existence. Cowards must experience the love of God and repent before Him.

The Shepherd returns to the kitchen to make himself a cup of tea. It's half past six and the radio station is repeating the story about the body in the tunnel. Poor lad. The Shepherd can't help but think the Lord has missed a trick. The pure evil which the boy faced is still out there, free to wreak havoc.

He reaches across and switches the radio off. It isn't his duty to question God. He merely has to carry out His wishes. And His wishes are clear.

Dead clear.

Chapter Ten

Near Bovisand, Devon. Thursday 22nd October. 6.30 a.m.

The alarm on her phone went off at six thirty, Savage reaching across to silence the crescendo before the noise could wake Pete. She blinked in the darkness and then got out of bed and stumbled to the bathroom. Peered at herself in the mirror. She hardly recognised the eyes which stared back. The past few months had changed her, she thought, and maybe not for the better. She'd come close to killing Owen Fox, a young man who, it turned out, was innocent of anything but protecting his girlfriend. If it hadn't been for the timely intervention of Kenny Fallon, she'd have pulled the trigger on the gun. Would she be feeling better if she had? Would she be staring at herself in the same way?

An hour later and the melancholy was subsumed by the usual pre-school hell and the need to get the children ready. Samantha had lost her phone and was refusing to leave home without it, while Jamie had – in his own words – 'bastard growing pains'. Savage had dosed him with Calpol but was more concerned with his ever expanding vocabulary of bad language.

'I'm innocent, officer,' Pete said, holding his hands up before scouring through the debris on the kitchen table as he searched for the phone. 'He didn't get the word from me. Must be on the National Curriculum list.'

'Right.' Savage replaced the bottle of Calpol in the cupboard and put the spoon in the dishwasher. 'Sam?'

'Huh?' Her daughter looked up from a pile of schoolwork and shook her head. 'Not me, Mum.'

Samantha gathered up her things, stuffed them into her bag and left the room.

'You all right?' Pete said. 'This kid and all?'

'Not really.' Savage shook her head. She'd told Pete about finding the boy in the tunnel when she'd crawled into bed in the small hours. 'I've got to attend the post-mortem this morning and you know how I hate them.'

'But it's not just that, is it?' Pete moved across the room and stood beside Savage. 'Love, you've either got to let go of Clarissa or accept you can no longer work these type of cases. Tell HR it's affecting your health. Any sense they might have to pay some sort of compensation and they'll move you like a shot.'

'But there's the rub, I don't want to be moved. I want to get the bastard sicko who's responsible.'

'Bastard?' Pete grinned. 'Well there's one case closed at least.'

'What?' Savage managed a half smile. 'Oh, right.'

'Look, however many nutters you bang up, she's never coming back, is she?'

'No.' Savage remembered the look on her face in the mirror that morning. 'I thought things would change after . . .'

'After what?'

'After . . .' She sighed. Pete knew nothing of her involvement with Simon Fox and his son. Perhaps one day she'd need to come clean. But now wasn't the time. 'After the girl on the moor.'

'Which one? You saved that Russian woman from the

Satanists. Then there was the lass captured by those twins. Not to mention the girl you pulled from that psychopath's freezer. How many does it take before the guilt's gone?'

Savage shook her head. She didn't like the way the conversation was heading.

'Face it, Charlotte. There was nothing you could have done to prevent Clarissa dying and however many cases you solve, however many kids you save, it won't make any difference.'

'It makes a difference to them, doesn't it? And to me.'

'Sometimes I wonder if it does.' Pete stood for a moment, staring at her intently as if he didn't want the conversation to end on a negative. But then he turned and stomped from the room.

An hour later Savage stood in the anteroom at the mortuary thinking the white lights had taken the colour from DSupt Hardin's face. He looked – appropriately – like a corpse.

'Hate these bloody things, Charlotte,' Hardin said, both his hands wrapped around a paper cup of coffee as if the warmth from the liquid inside might take away some of the chill in the air. 'So early in the morning too. Didn't even have time for breakfast.'

'Maybe that's a good thing, sir,' Savage said.

'Nonsense. Line the stomach. The old-fashioned way. The only way.'

No, Savage thought. The only *real* way was to avoid attending post-mortems at all. She'd never been to one which she could call 'nice'. The experience always lay on a continuum from horrible to downright appalling. She was not looking forward to seeing the victim from the tunnel dissected, and the argument with Pete hadn't improved the prospect.

'Mind you,' Hardin said. 'I wouldn't be here at all if it

wasn't for that bloody woman. At least I'll lose some weight from all this running around.'

'People.' Nesbit emerged from the main PM room. 'We're ready for you now.'

Hardin huffed and then poured the remainder of his coffee into a nearby waste bin. 'Ladies first,' he said, gesturing to Savage.

Savage followed Nesbit into the room, Hardin shuffling along behind her.

Nesbit had once told her they were 'blessed' in having three post-mortem tables. 'A conveyor belt of corpses,' he'd said. Savage could see nothing good about it. At least today the only body in the room was that of the boy. He lay on the central table, the others nothing but gleaming stainless steel.

At one end of the table a small block held the boy's head. At the other the wellingtons now looked even more incongruous than they had in the tunnel. Aside from the footwear, he had on a pair of Y-fronts and nothing else, and in the glare from the overhead lights Savage could see the lividity in his buttocks and thighs where the blood had pooled by gravity. In addition, every inch of exposed skin glistened with the slick, oil-like substance Nesbit had noted in the tunnel. Several deep cuts criss-crossed the boy's palms. The light also made a mockery of their mistakes of the previous night. Even allowing for the poor mugshot, there was no way this boy could be confused with Jason Hobb.

'Do you have a name for him yet?' Nesbit said as he came over to the body. 'Or is he still John Doe masquerading as Jason?'

'Moot bloody point,' Hardin said. He looked across at Savage. 'The confusion caused us a lot of problems.'

'Quite.' Nesbit turned to Savage, bent his head and looked

at her over the top of his glasses. 'And since I know the two people involved, I think I can say that misidentification was understandable, given the circumstances. Now then, shall we?'

The pathologist reached up and turned on the overhead microphone and began to make some initial observations. He noted the boy's height and weight and made a guess as to his age.

'Somewhere around eleven or twelve years old, I should think. Similar to Jason.'

'Which raises a question,' Hardin said. 'We've no other missing children of this age, as far as I know. Not here or nationally.'

'Not that we know of, sir,' Savage said. 'But it's possible reports might not have reached us yet.'

'Speculation is for another place,' Nesbit said. 'You know my motto: facts not flights of fancy. So we can start with the fact that this boy died from asphyxiation. Those cuts on the hands, while serious, would not have caused death. A ligature, most likely a belt, was placed around his neck and tightened.' Nesbit placed his hand against the boy's throat where there was some grazing and redness. 'Two fingers in width. Approximately three centimetres. There are several distinct marks from the ligature and I suggest the attacker alternatively tightened and loosened the belt, perhaps to try and elicit some sort of response or reaction.'

'A nutter,' Hardin said. 'I knew it.'

'That's not for me to say, Conrad.' Nesbit moved his hand to the boy's right arm where encrusted blood surrounded the knife wounds. 'At some point shortly before he was asphyxiated he received wounds to both hands. Possibly he was trying to defend himself from a knife attack. Nasty, but the cuts wouldn't have killed him.'

'Do you think that was deliberate?' Savage said. 'By not

killing him it meant he could continue to play some sort of game with a live victim.'

'Possibly.' Nesbit paused for a moment, head cocked to one side in contemplation. 'Bruising around the wrists suggests the victim being held firmly or tied up. The good news, if I can call it that, is I don't believe he was sexually assaulted.'

'No?' Hardin appeared disappointed. Sexual assault could have meant a sample for DNA analysis and that sort of evidence made an arrest and conviction far more likely. 'Pity.'

'Don't worry, there's the grease I talked about. I'm not sure what the substance is, but Layton sent off a sample. He fast-tracked it last night while you were sleeping like a baby.'

Nesbit took a scalpel from a nearby bench. At the same time he nodded to his assistant who held an electric cutting device. In one swift movement the pathologist sliced a Y-incision in the chest of the cadaver. He folded the skin back neatly and then moved aside. The mortuary assistant switched his cutter on and approached the body. The whirring sound increased in pitch as the blade began to slice into the ribcage.

Savage looked away.

It wasn't until a couple of hours later, the post-mortem almost concluded, that the subject of the wellington boots arose. The mortuary assistant was replacing the cap of bone on the boy's skull. He deftly folded the scalp back in place over the top and began to sew up the skin.

'The boots, Andrew,' Savage said. 'Can you get them off for us?'

'Hey?' Nesbit turned his attention away from the needlework of his assistant. He glanced down at the wellingtons as if seeing them for the first time. 'Let's see, shall we?'

He held the boy's knee in one hand while the other grasped the heel of one of the wellingtons. He began to pull.

'Jammed on. They seem way too small for the boy.' Nesbit stopped pulling and instead moved his fingers to the top of the wellington and tried to slip them inside. After a moment he gave up. 'It's no good, I'll have to cut them off.'

'He's not going to bloody need them, is he?' Hardin. Gruff. He sounded like he'd just about had enough. 'Get on with it so we can get the hell out of here.'

Nesbit took a fresh scalpel and sliced into the green rubber around the calf area. This time he was able to slip a finger into the opening. He cut again and then put the scalpel down and removed the right wellington. For a second he looked at the boy's foot and then shook his head.

'Nothing out of place here as far as I can tell. I'll take the other one off and then bag them for Layton.'

As Nesbit began to work on the other wellington, Savage moved closer. The first boot lay on the post-mortem table, flapping open where Nesbit had cut the rubber. There was something written on the material lining inside. Two words. For a second Savage thought of her own children. She'd sewn numerous name tags into their clothing. You couldn't do that with a welly so instead she usually took an indelible marker and wrote their names. That's what was written in the boot. A name. But not the name of the victim, not unless he'd been wearing boots much too small. Savage turned her head to read the writing. It was smudged and faded but the name was unmistakable.

'Oh fuck!' Savage looked across at Hardin. 'Sir, take a look.'

'Charlotte?' Hardin moved around the table and stood by her side. 'No. We don't need this. Oh God.'

'What is it?' Nesbit had finished removing the other boot and now he turned his attention to Savage's discovery.

Savage looked at the name again. 'Jason Hobb. These boots belong to him.'

Thursday found Riley pretty much left to his own devices. The discovery of the boy in the tunnel had meant Collier's attention had been deflected and a missing sales rep – albeit one who'd gone AWOL in suspicious circumstances – was way down the list of priorities.

The scene at the station was grim. The jokey banter gone. Every last copper had his or her head down working hard. The boy had been stripped and then strangled and what's more he wasn't even the lad everyone had been looking for.

Mid-morning, DI Savage came into the crime suite, back from the post-mortem on the boy. Riley gave Savage a smile, but she didn't return it.

'Ma'am?' he said, as she came over. 'Everything OK?'

'No.' Savage shook her head. 'Turns out the killer of the kid is likely the same person who's taken Jason Hobb, and Hobb – as you'll have heard – is still missing.'

'Christ.' Riley looked at Savage. Her pale, washed-out face told the whole story. 'Anything I can do? I mean. . .'

'I'll be fine, Darius.' Savage tapped Riley on the shoulder. She managed a half smile as she turned away. 'But thanks all the same.'

Once Savage had gone, Riley knuckled down and tried to focus on his own case. The mobile phone data hadn't arrived so he had nothing yet on the mysterious Sarah. He did have a result on the Taser though. The part of the cartridge Riley had found turned out to be from a consumer model – the X26c – not available in the UK but readily purchasable in the US. He'd contacted Taser International and requested sales data on the weapon. The felon identification numbers should theoretically mean he'd be able to find out when and where the gun had been bought. They might even give him the purchaser's name.

Meanwhile, he gathered background information on Sleet. The man seemed to be well liked at work and was one of the drug company's top salesmen. He'd grown up in Devon, gone on to study animal science at university and then worked for a time in the Midlands. In his early thirties he'd returned to work for the animal health company. There was nothing to suggest he'd made any enemies, nothing to hint at a reason for him to go missing. By all accounts Sleet was a happy-go-lucky type of guy, but perhaps under the surface there were darker issues even friends and family didn't know about. Riley had come across such cases before and, if it hadn't been for the Taser evidence, he'd have suspected some kind of depression had taken hold. The pretty little pieces of confetti put paid to that theory.

There was also the wife to consider. Catherine Sleet had at first seemed cold and distant, but by the end of the interview Riley had been left wondering what her temper would be like if she got really angry. The woman obviously didn't suffer fools gladly. Suppose her husband had been a fool, an idiot? Most men were, Riley thought. Even when you were with a woman like Catherine Sleet, the grass might appear greener somewhere else. If Perry Sleet had strayed, was it possible his missus had arranged a little surprise for her husband?

Riley shook his head. He was entering the realms of melodrama. The Sleets were most likely happily married and Catherine's reaction to his questioning had been nothing more than the signs of understandable stress.

Dissatisfied by his work so far, he pushed his chair back from the desk and got up. He needed a break, but as he went to leave the crime suite, John Layton pushed open the doors, coming the other way.

'You in a hurry?' Layton said to Riley. 'Only I've got something on the raft you and DC Enders found.'

'Yeah?' Riley looked down at the plastic tray in Layton's hand. At the mention of his name, Enders looked up from a nearby terminal. 'Show us then.'

'Sure.' Layton put the tray down on a desk. The tray was laden with several evidence bags, one of which contained the aluminium tube they'd found next to the mannequin. 'To be honest, I thought this stuff with your mystery raft would be the least of our worries considering, but it turns out you were right.' Layton pulled out one of the bags, inside a sliver of white material. He turned the bag over in his hands. 'It's a finger bone. From a child.'

'A child? We figured the raft could be part of a publicity stunt, but I guess we were wrong, not with a real bone.' Riley pointed at the bone. 'Anywhere someone could legitimately get their hands on one?'

'Nice pun.' Layton chuckled. 'I guess it's not impossible, but it seems a lot of effort to go to if this was some sort of promo. And most people wouldn't realise what it was anyway. You might as well have used an animal bone.'

'So where could it have come from?'

'A medical school or a museum. They're the first two places which come to mind. Perhaps more sinisterly, a morgue or a funeral parlour. None of the options are what you'd call legitimate.'

'And if not one of them, then where?'

'A grave, possibly?'

'I'm just trying to get my head around what's going on here. If it's any of the examples you've given me then this isn't really something for Major Crimes. However, if we discount those, then we're looking for a body, aren't we?'

'Are you thinking this is the Hobb boy?' Layton shook his

94

head. 'Doesn't compute I'm afraid, Darius. You can see from the state of the bone it's been buried in the ground for some time. Definitely historical, although not archaeological, if you get my drift.'

'Somebody else then.' Riley gestured at the aluminium tube on the plastic tray again. 'And what about the paper? Looks like something quite specialised to me, something we might be able to track down easily.'

'Ah, the paper.' Layton replaced the bone on the tray and picked up the third bag. Inside, the parchment had been flattened, the writing visible. He held the bag up to the light. The material was translucent with hundreds of little perforations. Shook his head. 'This is where things get a whole lot more interesting. You see, this isn't parchment; in fact it's not any kind of paper.'

'Well, what is it then?'

'Skin.' Layton put the item down and stared grimly at Riley. 'Human skin.'

Back at Crownhill the news about Jason Hobb's footwear caused a visible change in atmosphere in the crime suite. The misidentification of the previous night had been bad enough, this was far worse.

'Not good,' Collier said when Savage told him as he stood next to a whiteboard. 'Not good at all.'

The office manager wasn't usually so understated and Savage could see from his reaction he was deeply shocked. The boots linked Hobb with the murder in the tunnel and almost certainly meant they were dealing with a serial offender. What might possibly have been put down to a one-off had now turned into something very different and very scary. Operationally, the case would be a nightmare, but Savage could see from the way Collier was shaking his head that this had affected him on a more profound level.

'Anything from the scene?' Savage said, trying to break the silence.

'No.' Collier shook his head, downcast. 'Layton, for once, is sanguine about the lack of evidence. Says the fact he's come up empty-handed on the tunnel search must be the exception which proves his rule. There's also nothing from the army guys at Bickleigh. Their cameras cover the entrance gates apparently, but don't take in the road. Nothing suspicious reported either.'

Savage nodded. Collier had plainly been hoping for something to kick-start the investigation.

'Need to think this one through, Charlotte,' he said. 'The *Lacuna* meeting's scheduled for midday but this thing with the wellington boots puts a whole new perspective on the case.'

Savage left Collier with his marker pens and moved across the room to where Hardin was giving several detectives a good bollocking about the lack of leads. Once he'd finished, he turned to Savage.

'DCI Garrett,' he said. 'He'll be my deputy SIO on *Lacuna*. You're to help out.'

'*Garrett?*' Savage said. 'But—'

'But what, DI Savage?' Hardin said. 'Mike Garrett is a very experienced detective and on this case I want some clear and unemotional thinking. You boobed with the identification of the body and we can't afford any more mistakes.'

'Experienced? He's that all right. Sir, Garrett's retiring next month. His last few cases have been, to put it politely, lightweight. This is ridiculous, sir.'

'Ridiculous or not, that's the way it's going to be.' Hardin flicked his eyes up to the ceiling. 'This has come from the top, I'm afraid, Charlotte. The Hatchet has instructed me to make sure you keep a lower profile until the fallout from the inquest of Simon Fox has blown over. With one murder and a missing boy, this case is going to attract a lot of media attention. She wants you away from the limelight, understand?'

'No, sir, I don't understand. Hunting killers like this one is in my blood. I've got a track record on these sorts of cases. I—'

'Oh, you've got a track record all right. Usually your methods lie at the edges of legality. You're a potential liability, DI Savage, and right now the Chief Constable doesn't need your kind of officer.'

'You can't be—'

'Shut it! One more word out—'

'Sir!' The shout came from the far side of the room. Savage and Hardin turned as one as DC Calter replaced her phone on the desk. 'Possible on the body. A missing child from Newton Abbot. The misper was reported locally yesterday but the details have only just reached us. A young lad by the name of Liam Clough.'

'Liam?' Hardin's mouth dropped open. He looked at Calter and then cast a glance at Savage. He put out a hand and steadied himself on a nearby desk. 'Liam? It can't be a Liam. Get your facts right, girl. This is impossible!'

'Sir?' Savage moved closer to the DSupt as his face whitened. 'Is everything all right?'

'Liam? I . . . I . . .' Hardin shook his head. 'I need my medication. In my car. I'll be fine.'

Hardin pushed himself away from the desk, weaved across the room and barged out through the double doors.

'This new girl of his will be the death of him,' Calter said as she came over to Savage. 'Maria. She's a problem we need to work out how to solve, right?'

Savage didn't laugh at Calter's joke. Something was wrong with Hardin. Very wrong.

Chapter Eleven

Hardin stumbled out of the main entrance and walked across
to his car. He pulled the door open and collapsed into the
passenger seat. He opened the glovebox and fumbled inside
until he found a smoked plastic container. There was a small
bottle of water in the glovebox too. Hardin took a couple
of gulps and swallowed three of his pills. He leant back in
the seat.

Liam? Had he heard the name correctly or was he going
crazy? No, there was no mistake. Liam and Jason. The names
of the two boys were surely no coincidence. Hardin stared
through the windscreen at the station. Being a police officer
meant everything to him. Sure, he had his family, a wife and
two grown-up children he loved dearly, but they knew it
was in this concrete hunk of a building where his heart lay.

Hardin blinked and then shook himself. This was no good.
The last Chief Constable, Simon Fox, had killed himself.
Depression. The man had let personal issues get to him. That
wasn't the problem here. This wasn't personal. Quite the
opposite.

Hardin put the pills and the water back in the glove

compartment and flipped the hatch closed. His eyes moved up to the windscreen again. An envelope lay flattened against the glass beneath one of the wipers. He jumped out of the car and lifted the wiper blade. Another letter. He recognised the block capitals which spelt the address. He grabbed the envelope, ripped up the flap and pulled out the piece of paper within. He unfolded the sheet to reveal a series of pencil lines forming some kind of picture. Neat and precise and with numerals next to the lines, some cross-hatching and a shaded area. Hardin turned the piece of paper ninety degrees and then saw what the lines represented. A scale drawing in two parts. Something like an architectural plan on the left side and a cross-section on the right.

'No.' Hardin shook his head and bit his lip. 'Please, no.'

He placed the piece of paper on the car bonnet, both hands flat on top. He glanced towards the station again. Thirty years' service and the whole lot came down to this. He wouldn't count his time in the police as distinguished, he wasn't a brightly burning star, but there were other ways of serving. He was solid and dependable, reliable and honourable. And yet . . .

How about your sense of duty, PC Hardin?

He recalled the words from the previous letter. Was he honourable? Bearing in mind what he knew, could he really say that? Yes, Hardin thought, sometimes honour came from serving, and in one particular instance he'd obeyed orders rather than done what he thought was right. In the end the police force relied on the chain of command. Break the chain and chaos would follow. Besides, all he'd done was ignore a photograph. Two men seated at a table, a bottle of whisky, a couple of tumblers, a clock on the wall. Nothing to get excited about, nothing incriminating. Except for two things. One, there was something in the photograph which had made

Hardin, just a lowly PC at the time, feel distinctly uneasy. Something about the clock. Two, there was a word written on the back of the photograph, a word which only added to his disquiet. He'd reported both worries to his superior who'd handed the photograph over to a man from Special Branch.

'There's a simple explanation, lad,' the officer who'd made the journey down from London had said, pointing to one of the figures in the photograph. 'He's a good man, him. An honourable man.'

That word again. Honourable.

'But—' the young Hardin had protested, seeking a more meaningful answer.

'This isn't anything for you to be concerned about. Still, you say nothing about it, right?'

And that's exactly what Hardin had done. Obeyed orders. Said nothing.

Hardin stared down at the drawings once more. They were quite meticulous, and it was obvious what they represented. A box. According to the plan and cross-section, the box measured two metres long by a metre and a half wide and was ninety centimetres high. The cross-section showed a hole in the ground, gravel at the base for drainage. The box lay at the bottom of the hole, a tube ascending to the surface for air, the hole backfilled with earth. And in the box was a stick-figure drawing of Jason Hobb.

A sound brought Jason blinking into consciousness. Scrabbling. Something like a rat. Then from above came a small shaft of light. He opened his mouth to scream, but then stopped himself. Somebody was out there.

He moved across to the light source, an opening set into the roof of the box. A smooth plastic tube ran upwards from the opening and at the far end he could see daylight.

100

'Boy!' The light was abruptly snuffed out. 'Are you awake down there?'

A gust of bad breath wafted down and Jason jerked back. He cowered into one corner.

'I said, Jason, are you down there?' The voice came again, this time with a mocking, sing-song tone to it. 'I know you are. Don't be frightened. I do so want us to be friends.'

The man had used his name, Jason thought. Was this somebody he knew? He bit his lip. Best keep quiet, best not say anything.

'Stand clear of the opening, Jason, I've got some presents for you.'

A second later something slid down the tube and fell from above, thudding onto the wooden floor. Then something else. Again and again.

'If you're a good boy then you'll get some more. Oh, and this will bring a little brightness into your life.'

Another object clattered down, a beam of light spinning round and then hitting the floor and shining towards one wall of the box. A small torch!

Jason reached forward and grabbed the penlight. He gasped now he could see the true extent of his prison. He was in something resembling a packing case just a couple of metres square. Plywood walls, floor and ceiling on a wood frame. The opening which the torch had come through was an orange waste pipe which jutted from the roof a couple of centimetres. On the floor directly beneath the pipe lay three Mars bars and a can of Coke.

'You'll need this and these too. And don't keep the torch on too long, will you?'

An empty plastic bottle came clattering through the opening and then a toilet roll and a bundle of plastic bags.

'I . . .' Jason forgot his thoughts about not talking. 'Please, let me out.'

'Oh no, I couldn't possibly do that. Later, maybe. When I'm sure you won't try to desert me. Until then I need you to be a good boy and stay down there. It's all part of my plan, you see?'

'Noooooo! Heeelllppp!'

Something scraped up above and the light shining down the tube diminished to at first a faint glimmer and then faded completely. Jason clutched the torch in his hands and shivered.

As Savage came out from the front entrance of the station, she spotted Hardin leaning on the bonnet of his Freelander. The DSupt was staring downward and shaking his head, muttering something under his breath. She wondered what was up with him. He'd had a health scare a while ago but she'd thought he was over it. Unlikely this was a family matter though, since Hardin's marriage was rock solid. Which left work. The case with the two boys was harrowing, but she'd known worse. Much worse.

She jogged across the tarmac until she reached Hardin. 'Sir? Is everything all right?'

'No.' Hardin didn't look up. He seemed to be considering a piece of paper he was holding against the bonnet. 'Thirty years, Charlotte. That's how long I've been in the force. I've never put a foot wrong, always done things by the book. You know me. Tick boxes, risk assessments, everything written up in the policy book, nothing dodgy, rules obeyed to the letter. I don't think many other officers in this station could say the same, do you?'

'No, sir, I don't think they could.'

Now the DSupt did look up. He smiled at Savage. 'I didn't

mean that as a criticism of you, Charlotte. We do things differently, you and I. You've crossed the line on more than one occasion. If you want to go any higher in the force then you'll need to change your ways.'

'Sir, I'm sorry about the stuff up in the crime suite. It's just I'd sort of assumed I'd be the deputy SIO. It's what I do. Catching these pervs, right? Obviously I'll take whatever role on the team you want me to.'

'Enough.' Hardin stood upright, folding the piece of paper he had in his hand. 'Give me ten minutes and then come to my office, OK?'

A quarter of an hour later Savage was sitting at Hardin's desk. Hardin stood over to one side of the room, where he was fiddling with his new coffee machine. Something resembling the waste water from a dishwasher dribbled into a cup. Hardin stared down at the drink for a moment before passing the cup across to Savage.

'You're not going to like what I have to tell you any more than this muck,' Hardin said as he took his own cup and sat behind his desk. 'My words will be as bitter and hard to swallow.'

'Really, sir?' Savage picked up the cup and took a sip. Made a face and smiled. 'I doubt it.'

'You haven't heard what I've got to say yet.' Hardin glanced at his cup and then sighed. 'But promise me you'll listen before you jump down my throat, OK?'

'Yes, sir.'

'Right. There's no easy way to say this. You're off the Jason Hobb investigation.'

'Bloody hell, sir, you can't!' The words came out before she remembered her promise of but a moment ago. 'I mean . . . I . . .'

'There's a cold case.' Hardin nodded across to a cardboard

box on the floor. 'I'd like you to look into it for me.'

'No way. I'm not going to be shunted aside because Maria Heldon's got it in for me. First I'm not your deputy on the Hobb case and now I'm off the whole thing. The fucking cow won't stop until I quit the force. Bitch.'

'Charlotte!' Hardin raised his voice. 'I should reprimand you for that remark. It's insubordination. However, you've misread what's happening here. This has nothing to do with the Chief Constable and the case is important.'

'It's *cold*, sir. Frozen, I expect. You just said so yourself. Boxes full of files, files full of paper, paper full of witness statements which have been gone over time and time again. I know what this is. It's some sort of review. Just to say an ancient investigation is still active, when really we all know there's not a hope in hell's chance of an arrest, let alone a conviction.'

'I'm surprised at you. I thought you'd welcome the chance to get out on your own.'

'I want to be working on proper stuff, sir. You know, catching criminals. I want to find Jason Hobb and catch the killer of Liam Clough.'

'This *is* proper stuff.'

'But why me? Somebody else could do this work, surely?'

'I wish that was true.' Hardin looked at the box. 'If you need some help you can call on one of the junior DCs if they're not too pushed. DC Calter, perhaps.'

'Too pushed?' Savage sighed. Shook her head. 'It bloody sounds like the case is an afterthought. Doesn't really give me much confidence.'

'Charlotte, I said this is important.' Hardin reached down and pulled a file from the cardboard box. He placed the file on the desk. 'And you're the best person for the job. This is not a punishment.'

'Yeah, sure.' Savage looked at the file. Operation *Curlew*. The words were stuck on the front of the folder, the print from an old dot matrix printer for God's sake. 'Anything else I should know?'

'Just look through the file.' Hardin glanced at his cup of dishwater. 'And I'll get us some better beverages, hey?'

Savage pulled the manila file across the desk and flicked open the cover. Her eyes were drawn to the top of the first sheet of paper. Two small mugshots had been stapled into the document. The colour in the pictures had all but leached away but the expressions on the faces were timeless. Two young boys, each grinning at the camera, the picture from a time when having your photograph taken was still an event, not simply an everyday occurrence.

She searched the page for a date, to see if her hypothesis was correct. Yes, the document had been marked January 1990, the time of an annual case review. She scanned the synopsis and discovered the original incident had taken place nearly a year and a half earlier, on 26th August 1988.

Now she settled down to read through the file. The case concerned the disappearance of two boys who'd been residents at Woodland Heights, a secure children's home on the coast over near Salcombe. The two boys – Jason Caldwell and Liam Hayskith – had gone missing . . .

Jason and Liam?

The names jumped from the page, quickening her heart for a moment. As a coincidence the identical names seemed improbable and, whether happenstance or not, was cause for comment. Was this what had made Hardin react in such a strange way when the identity of the boy in the tunnel had been revealed?

Savage looked back at the photographs. Jason Caldwell

was the lad on the left. Blond hair cut in a pudding-basin style, light blue eyes, and a smile which belied the fact he'd spent most of his childhood in care. Liam Hayskith's smile was no less wide, but he had brown eyes and matching hair, the hair a mass of natural curls. She paused for a moment. Now she remembered the incident. She'd been at primary school back then and recalled some playground gossip, remembered too a warning from her mother to be careful. Never mind that the two boys were, in the terminology of the time, juvenile delinquents, and the initial suspicion was that they'd run away. Talk later was of somebody preying on young children, even that someone at the home might be involved.

Gossip. Suspicion. Rumour.

That's all it was back then, but Savage wondered about the truth. Maria Heldon had told Savage there was no smoke without fire. Was that the case here?

She read on, working her way through the brief biographies of the boys and on to the summary of the case. The first inkling anything had been wrong was when Jason and Liam hadn't come down to breakfast. A window in a storeroom had been found broken, although a forensic report seemed to cast some doubt on how and when that had happened, a finger of suspicion pointing to the caretaker. In the days following, there were some unconfirmed sightings across Devon, but nothing concrete. Staff were extensively inter-viewed and the rescue services conducted a three-day search of the coastline. There was evidence the boys might have been down at a nearby cove where several sets of footprints were discovered in the sand above the tideline, but nothing else was found and neither of the boys was ever seen again.

She moved on beyond the summary, working her way deeper into the document. All the pertinent facts were here:

106

names, dates, places, key witnesses, details of events, analysis. She began to read some of the witness statements. The home had been run by a Mr Frank Parker and his wife, Deborah. The Parkers said they'd heard nothing in the night and Mr Parker surmised the boys had made good their escape in the small hours. In another statement, the housekeeper reported the disappearance of a large kitchen knife. Detectives concluded the missing boys had likely stolen the knife, possibly for protection on their travels. However, later on, the housekeeper had changed her mind, insisting the knife had been missing for months.

Savage read on through dozens of other statements, some from the other boys. One interviewing officer described one boy as reticent, another as nervous, but the overall impression seemed to be that the young residents of the home were obstructive and not at all helpful.

'To put it bluntly,' a statement from one of the staff members said, 'they're a bunch of wrong 'uns mixed up with worse 'uns with a topping of nasty little shits.'

Savage shook her head, not quite believing what she was reading. Today, thank God, police attitudes had changed. What back then may well have been viewed as obstructive behaviour would nowadays be interpreted quite differently. More probing questions would be asked. There'd been too many mistakes in the past not to investigate cases like this properly. With Operation *Yewtree* and the events in Rotherham, the police had become a little bit wiser.

Hardin returned a few minutes later, furnished with some proper coffees from the canteen. He leant back in his chair and stared at the wall.

'Operation *Curlew*. Over twenty-five years ago it was. Half a lifetime for me.' Hardin shook his head and then rocked forward and looked at Savage. 'What do you think?'

107

'The names, Jason and Liam, can't be a coincidence. Is that why you want me to review the case?'

'Yes. I don't believe it's chance the two boys we're dealing with today are called Jason and Liam. I spoke with the Chief Constable a few minutes ago and she agrees. She wants to begin her watch with no skeletons in the closet.'

'I thought you said this had nothing to do with Maria Heldon?'

'It doesn't, this is my decision. All Heldon said to me was she didn't want anything swept under the carpet. In my mind that means you're just the person for the job.'

Savage's eyes were drawn again to the top sheet of paper in the open file. The photographs of the two young boys. They were either dead or living somewhere far away. The latter seemed unlikely after all these years. She looked back at Hardin. A crease had appeared on his brow and she noticed a slight shake of his hand as he lifted his coffee cup to his lips again.

'But there's more, sir,' Savage said. 'Isn't there?'

'That's where it gets tricky, Charlotte.' Hardin took a gulp of coffee and put the cup down. 'And where it gets personal too.'

'Sorry, sir?'

'In 1988 I was a young PC over in Kingsbridge. I was there.'

'You were part of Operation *Curlew*?'

'Initially, yes. But only for one day. Something else came up and I was transferred to more pressing business.' Hardin sat back again. He shook his head. 'Charlotte, I need you to look into this, but I need you to be discreet. If anyone asks, just say there's a review. That's all they need to know.'

'And what happens if I find out some uncomfortable truths?' Savage pointed at the bundle of papers. 'Because, to be honest, I think there was something missing from the investigation.'

'Go on.'

'The staff members' statements appear to have been taken at face value. I don't reckon that would happen today. I was just a child, but I remember there were rumours about the home and yet the possibility of abuse doesn't seem to have been raised at all. According to the review, the home closed down following the incident and that seems to have put paid to any further work on the case. The boys were consigned to history, forgotten.'

'Then I think it's time we made amends, don't you?'

Savage sighed and then reached for the file. She flipped the cover closed. She didn't want this case. She wanted to be out there looking for Jason Hobb. Orders were orders though and there wasn't much she could do about it.

'Yes, sir,' she said.

Chapter Twelve

The skin, Riley knew, changed things completely. The finger bone had had him worried, but there may well have been a plausible explanation for it. Not so for a piece of skin the size of a large envelope which, according to Layton, had come from the back of somebody's head. There seemed little doubt in Riley's mind that a crime had taken place, but what crime? Murder, perhaps? Unlikely. Far more probable was grave robbery or failure to report a death. Serious crimes, yes, but victimless.

That left the actual writing on the skin. The text was unambiguous and disturbing:

AS FOR THE COWARDLY, THE FAITHLESS, THE DETESTABLE, AS FOR MURDERERS, THE SEXUALLY IMMORAL, SORCERERS, IDOLATERS, AND ALL LIARS, THEIR PORTION WILL BE IN THE LAKE THAT BURNS WITH FIRE AND SULPHUR, WHICH IS THE SECOND DEATH.

110

The female mannequin in the box on the raft had been burned and hacked about. The arm had been severed. Could the damage be illustrative of what might happen to the cowardly and faithless mentioned in the text? If so, then was the whole set-up a message or a threat? On the other hand, perhaps Enders' initial hunch had been correct and the thing was some kind of prank.

'We need to impound the raft as evidence,' Riley had said to Enders once Layton had gone. 'Get the CSIs to work over it to see what else they can find.'

A phone call to the harbour master revealed the final resting place for the raft. The makeshift craft had been towed round to a boatyard up the Plym. There it had been craned from the water and broken up.

'That was the deal.' The harbour master sounded apologetic as he explained. 'If they took the raft off our hands they could do what they wanted with it. Boatyards always have a use for this sort of stuff. Odd pieces of wood, plastic barrels, sheets of ply. I daresay bits and pieces of it are stacked up somewhere, if you want to take a look.'

Riley did and an hour later he stood in the boatyard with Enders. The yard sat on the west side of the Plym, tucked between the Laira Bridge and a scrap metal merchant. Boats of all sorts stood on the shore in various states of disrepair, while others floated on the river tied up to a couple of long pontoons. This, Riley could see, was the other end of the market from the posh marinas with their huge gleaming yachts; G and Ts and tanned women lounging on spotless aft decks were in short supply.

The yard hand who'd accompanied them coughed and Riley brought his mind back to the job. He pointed at the pile of wood stacked up against a rusting shipping container.

'Is that the lot?' Riley said.

'Yup. Apart from the barrels.' The yard hand gestured over to a skip. 'I opened one up and didn't like the smell of what was inside. I was going to wash them out but then thought better of it.'

'Why?'

'Contamination.' The man turned and looked towards the estuary. 'Doesn't bear thinking about. We put anything in the river which causes problems and we'd have all sorts of environmental fines slapped on us.'

'And the stuff in the barrels, any ideas?'

'Some chemical. None of the barrels had any labels, so it wasn't worth taking the risk.'

'We'll need to take a look at them and get a sample for the lab.' Riley pointed at the pile of wood. 'And all this, it's not to be touched, understood?'

The man nodded and then stared at Enders. The DC had pulled a roll of blue and white police tape from his pocket and was draping great streams of the stuff over the remains of the raft.

'Crime scene?' the yard hand said, reading the words printed on the tape. 'What crime's that then?'

Riley thought for a moment. He wanted to make sure the man knew this wasn't a trivial issue, but he didn't want to give anything away.

'A serious one,' he said.

After lunch and another skim through the *Curlew* summary file, Savage headed to Woodland Heights. The children's home sat in an isolated position on the coast between Salcombe and Hope Cove, some fifteen miles east of Plymouth. A long driveway passed a static caravan park and ambled down across several fields, curling round to arrive at the big old house. Savage drove along the track, pausing to open and close a gate on the way. As her car bumped the final quarter of a mile down the pothole-strewn drive, the coastal panorama opened out and she could see the home stood close to a jagged outcrop a little to the west of Soar Mill Cove. Farther to the east, cliffs staggered round and into the Salcombe estuary in a series of dramatic rock abutments.

She pulled her car onto a large gravel area to one side of the building and got out. Situated just a few hundred metres from the high cliffs, the house had a commanding view to the south, where Savage could see several huge ships riding the horizon. Closer in, the strong breeze disturbed the sea, and the sunlight made the surface sparkle like a million blue diamonds.

She walked round to the front of the house, where a grand stairway led up to the entrance porch. Looking at the facade, she guessed the place must be Victorian, although later additions to the house had been cobbled onto the side and rear. Now there was an air of decay about the structure. Plywood panels had been nailed over the lower windows, 'Keep Out' stencilled on each in spray paint. The first-floor windows had no such protection and several had been broken. Above that there were a number of dormers poking from the slate roof. Considering the size of the house, she was surprised the place hadn't been snapped up by developers.

The property sat plumb in the centre of a large field and, aside from a small patch which looked like it had once been a vegetable garden, the area was down to grass. In the summer this would have been a great place to be. She closed her eyes for a moment and imagined groups of boys running free, playing football, making their way down to the nearby beach and swimming in the sea. Perhaps she was painting too idyllic a picture. Perhaps the freedom this place offered had turned into something else. There were no other dwellings in the vicinity, nobody to see anything untoward, no one to hear the screams.

Savage opened her eyes and shook her head. She was jumping to conclusions. Possibly nothing had happened here and the two boys had just run away. But if so, where had they been for the past two and a half decades?

She climbed the steps. White paint peeled away from the surface of the front door, revealing dark oak beneath, while a huge brass knob in the centre had tarnished green in the sea air. On the floor of the porch lay a plastic estate agent's sign: Marchand Petit, Salcombe. There were marks on the surface of the front door where the sign had been stapled to the wood. Somebody had torn it down.

She knew the home had closed the year after the boys had gone missing. The building had already been in quite a state and the council had sold it for a song. Over the intervening years there'd been talk of the place being turned into a hotel. The property was an eyesore, but Savage could imagine a developer reworking the inside into a number of luxury apartments. Second-homers would fall over themselves to buy a slice of seaside living. So far though, it didn't look like any sale had taken place.

She looked again at the door. There was splintering around the lock. The door had been forced. She grasped the brass knob and pushed. The door opened.

Inside, a long hallway led to the rear. On the floor, dust and debris lay scattered across red quarry tiles. A pile of bird droppings sat against one wall, black and white streaks leading up to a light fitting where a bundle of sticks marked an old nest. The air was damp, the scent heavy with mildew and mould. Savage stepped in, avoiding a large lump of plaster which had fallen from the ceiling. Both to the right and the left, huge portals opened to large reception rooms where there were more signs of decay. In one room, great swathes of wallpaper had peeled away from the walls, while in the other, part of the floor was missing, a dark, dank hole revealing some sort of cellar beneath.

She moved down the hallway to the rear of the house where she found another set of rooms: a kitchen, a dining room complete with several tables and benches, and a number of smaller rooms obviously once used for storage. She also found the door to the cellar, steps leading downward, a faint light from the hole in the floor of the room above.

Savage thought about going down there but then changed her mind. She had a torch in the car. She'd do the rest of the house first and then get the torch. Now she was inside though she couldn't imagine what she might find which could help the investigation. In fact, she began to wonder what on earth she was doing here at all. There wasn't going to be any evidence, not after all this time. Anyway, the police had presumably been through the property back when the boys had gone missing.

She returned to the hallway and climbed the stairs, placing each foot tentatively on the steps, worried about rotten floorboards. At the top, a landing ran in two directions, a number of corridors leading off the landing. She took a look in several of the rooms. Two had one or more bunk beds in. The others were empty. There was also a separate suite of rooms which looked as if it could be living accommodation for the staff. Although she was getting a sense of what the place must have been like, so far nothing struck her as out of the ordinary.

At one end of the landing a narrow staircase climbed to the attic rooms. Savage tested the stairs and then went up. The stairs curled round and ended at another landing, several doors opening into three small box rooms. Who slept up here? Savage wondered. Was it a privilege to be placed high under the rafters or possibly a punishment? She went into each room in turn. In the first two there was nothing of interest and the rooms seemed to have been recently inhabited by pigeons. There were droppings everywhere, feathers too. On one of the windowsills the skeleton of a bird sat next to a broken pane. In the third room there were two single beds, barely space to walk between them. Each had an old mattress, but mice or rats had been at the material and not much remained other than torn-up shreds. Savage stepped over to one of the beds. On the headboard she could see the boys had carved their names into the wood. When the mattress had been in place the carvings would have been hidden. Now the mattress had rotted away the list was a roll call of boys who'd slept in this room. Savage bent and looked at the names. There amongst them was Jason Caldwell.

The boy had been up here, but presumably the police had known that. When the boy had run away they'd have examined the attic rooms and questioned his roommate. There couldn't be any evidence here to help her now, could there?

She knelt by the bed and peered underneath the frame. There didn't seem to be anything under the bed. She put her hand beneath the bed and ran her fingers around the underside of the frame. There was nothing concealed there but she did feel a rough patch of wood on one of the legs. She lowered her head further. There, carved in the bed leg, were some more words. Not names this time but a sentence.

JASON CALDWELL WAS MURDERED

Savage let out a long breath and bit her lip. She quickly examined the rest of the frame and then moved to the second bed. Nothing. She crawled back across the floor and looked at the words again. There was something wrong here, she thought. She peered at the bed for a moment and then she had it. The wood of the frame was dirty, covered in dust and here and there smeared with bird droppings. However, the leg with the writing was clear, as if it had been cleaned, possibly prior to the name being carved into the wood.

Savage stood, not knowing if this was evidence or not. She moved to one of the dormer windows and stared out at the view. Was it possible somebody had got wind of the case review and had come here to leave her a clue? She didn't know but, since Hardin had only decided to investigate not more than a couple of hours ago, it seemed unlikely.

She was about to step back from the window and head for the stairs when something caught her eye. A car coming along the track. The car pulled into the car park and stopped next to Savage's vehicle. The driver's door opened and a man got out. Early fifties, cropped brown hair and rough-shaven, an old jacket over a lumberjack shirt, a muscular builder's physique bulging beneath the clothing. The man stood by Savage's car for a moment before spitting on the ground. He went to the rear of his own car, sprang the boot and pulled something out. Then he turned towards the house and glanced up at the attic windows. Savage jumped back, her heart pounding. She moved her head slowly forward and looked out again. The man was heading for the front door, a long metal bar in his right hand.

After visiting the boatyard, Riley and Enders headed across the Plym and round to Jennycliff for another recce. It was a little after two thirty when Enders pulled the pool Focus into the car park. A dozen other vehicles sat in a line on one side of the gravel expanse, windscreens glinting in the low winter sun. Several of the occupants were having a late lunch break.

Fish and chips in a cardboard tray. Cheap junk food bought for a few quid. But, Riley thought, the view across Plymouth Sound was priceless.

'We could grab a bacon butty while we're here,' Enders said as they got out. He pointed at the cafe which stood at the bottom of the grassy slope below the car park. 'A cup of tea would be nice too.'

Riley shook his head. 'Is there ever a time when you don't think about food, Patrick?'

'When I'm asleep,' Enders said. Then he grinned. 'No, scratch that. I dream of food too.'

'Well, if you could spare a minute or two for this investigation I'd be very grateful, as I'm sure would the taxpayer.'

They strolled down past the cafe and Enders made to head for the path which led down the cliffs to the beach. Riley tapped him on the shoulder.

'No.' He gestured over to a concrete area with a couple of benches and a coin-operated telescope. 'Let's take a gander over there. We'll get a better view of the Sound from up here.'

Riley walked across to where a large piece of polished granite stood at one end of the concrete. The stone was engraved with a representation of the horizon, interesting points shown with distances to each.

'What are you thinking, sir?' Enders said.

'I'm trying to get a handle on where the hell the raft came from. Here.' Riley pulled a little booklet from his pocket. 'Tide tables. Layton told me the wind was from the south-west on Tuesday. His theory is that the raft was launched from somewhere around the Sound or upriver. The tide ebbed and the south-westerly blew the raft across to this side of the Sound. It was pushed up the beach on the incoming tide and stranded.'

'From over there then?' Enders said, pointing across the

water to where a patch of green sat surrounded by sea. 'Down the Tamar, past Drake's Island and across to here. Seems an unlikely journey.'

'Whatever.' Riley ran his hand over the piece of granite, looking at the points of interest marked on the surface. 'The question is, what is the purpose of the raft and, of course, where the hell do the finger bone and skin come from?'

'I think the question,' Enders said, nodding his head to where the path went down to the beach, 'is what the hell is *he* doing here?'

Riley turned and followed Enders' gaze to where a tall man in a beige raincoat stood gazing out across the Sound.

'Dan bloody Phillips.' Riley shook his head. Phillips was the *Plymouth Herald*'s crime reporter and he had an uncanny knack of sniffing out a story using his rat-like nose to detect even the tiniest thread of evidence. 'You're right, what the hell *is* he doing here?'

At that moment the reporter paused. His head moved from left to right as he scanned the seascape.

'I swear I can see him sniffing,' Riley said. 'Uh-oh. He's spotted us.'

Sure enough, Phillips turned around on the path and began to walk towards them, a huge grin on his face.

'So, I *am* on to something,' Phillips said as he reached them. 'Good to see you, Darius.'

'On to what?' Riley said.

'Well.' Phillips smiled again and then gestured to the cafe. 'You don't appear to be here for lunch, there's no sign of a pooch, and as for that other canine-inspired pastime – dogging – I think you'd be better off once darkness sets in. And I'd lose your sidekick, he just doesn't hack it.'

'Dan,' Riley said as Enders glowered. 'We're just taking

a break. About to get something to eat. So if you don't mind . . .'

'Bacon butties all round?' Phillips began to walk away. 'My shout. And if you're good I'll tell you why I'm here. You're going to be interested, I promise. Very interested.'

'Sir?' Enders whispered. 'We really shouldn't.'

'You're probably right, but he's on to something,' Riley said. He turned to follow Phillips. 'And I want to know what it is.'

They strode up the slope and sat at a picnic table outside the cafe. Phillips appeared a few minutes later with a tray, three bacon baps and three cups of tea.

He plonked himself down and they tucked into their food.

'Right then, to business,' Phillips said after a few mouthfuls. He reached for a tissue and wiped some tomato sauce from the side of his mouth. 'You're here about that raft, aren't you?'

Chapter Thirteen

Near Bolberry, South Hams, Devon. Thursday 22nd October.
2.45 p.m.

Savage moved from the box room to the little square of landing and peered down the stairway. Somebody was moving around two floors below. A door banged shut and a crash reverberated through the house. Then she heard the man on the stairs coming up to the first floor.

'Where are you then?' The voice had a rough quality to it and was full of menace. 'Think you can come in here and do your drugs and your dirty business, do you?'

'Hello?' Savage hollered down the stairs. Better her presence didn't come as a complete surprise. 'Police officer up here.'

Footsteps shuffled on the first floor below. 'You won't trick me like that, you little bitch.'

The man came into view at the bottom of the stairs. He glanced up, a sneer across his round, pudgy face.

'Detective Inspector Charlotte Savage,' Savage said, taking out her warrant card. 'Here on police business.'

'Right, love. Sure you are. Now hold on there, I'm coming up to sort you out.'

'If you look closely you'll see I really am a police officer.

My colleagues know exactly where I am and if anything happens to me it won't be long before they track you down.'

'Hey?' The man ascended several stairs and then stopped and stared at Savage's outstretched hand. 'OK, suppose you are a police officer, what the hell are you doing here? This is private property.'

'The door was open. Anyway I'm investigating a crime.'

'What crime is that then? I've reported the vandalism many times and no one's ever bothered to come out here.'

'This is an old crime. From years ago. The missing boys.'

'Hayskith and Caldwell?' The man shook his head. 'You're wasting your time. There's nothing here, nothing I tell you.'

The way the man had said the names sounded odd to Savage, almost institutional.

'And you are, Mr . . .?'

'Samuel. Elijah Samuel.'

'Well, Mr Samuel, I have to warn you that, vandals or no vandals, you can't go around attacking people with iron bars.'

'This is my property and you're trespassing. You need a warrant to search this place.'

'There's nothing to search, is there? I just wanted to get a feel for what the home was like.'

'A *feel*?' Samuel's hand tightened around the iron bar. 'You can't imagine the hell this place was, sweetheart. Those boys didn't run away. They were too scared to do that. They knew they'd eventually be caught and brought back here. No, Hayskith and Caldwell got up in the middle of the night and walked down to Soar Mill Cove. Then they paddled into the water and swam. Straight out. Even in summer it wouldn't have been long before their bodies would have been numb. An hour or so and they'd have got hypothermia. Do you know what that does to you?' Savage shook her head. 'Ex-forces, me, and I saw it on training once. In the Cairngorms. We were in deep snow, six of us, whiteout conditions. Two lads became hypo and refused to go on. They were gone, in a dream-like state; we had to leave them or succumb ourselves. A week later, when the weather cleared through, we sent a helicopter to pick up the corpses. So, you see? For Hayskith and Caldwell the pain ended there in the water. They went to sleep rocked by the waves and woke in a better place.'

'You were here then, at Woodland Heights?'

'I was no more here than Hayskith and Caldwell. We were ghosts, all of us. Look.' Samuel held his free hand out to the side, palm facing Savage. 'You can see right through me. I'm nothing, a shell of a man.'

'What went on here, Mr Samuel? You need to tell me, tell someone. There's a case review going on and if any crimes were committed here we need to find the people responsible and put them away.'

'A review?' Samuel shook his head, half laughed, and then sneered at Savage. 'We had those sort of things in the army too and they're bollocks, right? You tick a box, make a comment and then shelve the file for another ten years. As for crimes, the crime was nobody took any notice and we weren't believed.'

'"We"? So you were a resident here?'

'Resident? Prisoner, more like. Only prisoners had more rights than us lot.'

'Things are different now. Post-Operation *Yewtree*, every agency is much more sensitive to historical abuse. Your story will be believed and if at all possible charges will be brought.'

'No, love. My story won't be believed and there won't be charges because you'll get nothing more from me. You think I want the tabloid press round here dredging up the past? No, it's history. I bought the place a few years ago, mistakenly thinking owning the home would somehow make things better, but it didn't. Now I'm selling. I want shot. I've discovered there's other ways of dealing with my personal issues.' Samuel knocked the iron bar against the banisters. One of the uprights shattered. 'Now if you don't mind I'd like you to leave.'

Savage nodded. 'OK, but remember what I said. If anything happened here, then people will be charged, got it?'

'Out!'

Savage slipped past Samuel and moved down the stairs. Samuel didn't follow. She carried on down to the ground floor; she could hear Samuel raging up in the attic as she pulled the front door open and went out onto the porch. She nipped down the front steps and one of the dormer windows smashed as she did so, the sound of Samuel destroying the bedroom echoing from inside.

Riley took a bite of his bacon roll. Chewed for a few moments to stall Phillips. How the journalist had found out about the raft or why he was interested, Riley had no idea.

'You know, four letters. Huck Finn's boat.' Phillips half turned towards the sea. 'And it was found down on the beach, wasn't it?'

'Might have been.' Riley followed Phillips' gaze. 'To be honest though, there's not much of a story for you.'

'Really? I think you're wrong there.' Phillips took a gulp of his tea. 'But put that aside for the moment. There's something else.'

Riley waited, but the journalist said nothing. 'Go on.'

'A Mr Perry Sleet. That name ring a bell?'

'A US chat-show host?' Riley said nonchalantly. 'Or perhaps a Republican party presidential candidate?'

'You're either stupid or you think I am. Perry Sleet lives

in Plymstock and his car was discovered abandoned on the moor on Tuesday evening, since when you've had people out looking for him.'

Riley sighed. 'OK, so a bloke's gone missing. Do you know how many mispers we deal with on an annual basis?'

'Hundreds, I expect, but that's not the point.'

'So what is, Dan? I really haven't—'

'Listen, DS Riley,' Phillips interrupted, his voice tinged with an edge of excitement. 'I've got something on Sleet. You might even say I've been doing your work for you.'

'OK.' Riley put down his bap purposefully, wondering if Phillips was playing some sort of game. Riley nodded at Enders. Enders pulled out a pad. 'Tell me. But if this is some kind of wind-up you're in a lot of trouble. Bacon roll or no bacon roll.'

'No wind-up, promise.' Phillips had abandoned his food and now he pulled out a tablet. His fingers slid across the surface and then he passed the tablet across to Riley. 'Read this.'

Riley took the tablet and peered at the image which filled the screen. It was the front page of a local newspaper – the *North Devon Gazette*. The paper covered the area around Bideford and Barnstaple. Phillips prodded a finger at a headline in the side bar: *Concern for Local Vicar Missing for a Week*.

'And?' Riley said. 'What's this got to do with Sleet or the raft?'

'At first sight, nothing.' Phillips took back the tablet and his fingers brought up a fresh image. 'My editor alerted me to the story and asked me to write a piece on the stresses of being a vicar in a rural parish. Wanted me to show things weren't always so green and pleasant. When I started researching I found something far more interesting. The missing vicar is a man named Tim Benedict. He's in his sixties.

The local police up in Barnstaple are working on the theory that pressure of work has got to him.'

'I still don't understand—'

'Here.' Phillips passed back the tablet. 'There's a picture you need to see.'

The screen now showed the raft. The image wasn't a good one. Light flared in from the side and the angles were all crooked.

'So you know all about this,' Riley said as he started to hand the tablet back to Phillips. 'Big deal.'

'Not so fast.' Phillips put out his hand and pushed the tablet away. 'A bystander took this photo before you lot turned up, so I apologise for the quality. Never mind though, the picture's good enough. Zoom in at the head end of the box, where the arm is. Tell me what you see.'

Riley took the tablet back and then placed his thumb and forefinger on the screen. Separated them. The wooden box swelled and the picture became pixelated. Still, he could see the engraving on the forearm of the mannequin, the letters which he and Enders had struggled to understand.

TB/PS/CH/BP

'So?' Phillips sat up and folded his arms, a smug grin spreading across his face. 'Am I on to something, or what?'

'No, I . . .' Riley shook his head. Wondered what sort of mind Phillips had which could lead him to spot the connection. 'Shit, I don't believe it. This must be a coincidence, surely?'

'If you say so.' Phillips sat back. 'Methinks not.'

'Sir?' Enders had stopped munching on his bap and craned his neck sideways to see the screen. 'TB/PS/CH/BP. I don't understand.'

'Work it out, Constable, it's bloody obvious,' Riley snapped, wondering how he was going to explain to Hardin

126

that the crime reporter had found something they'd over-looked. 'The first pairs of letters stand for Tim Benedict and Perry Sleet.'

Thirty minutes later Savage was standing on the cliffs above Soar Mill Cove. She'd left Woodland Heights, driven to the nearby National Trust car park and walked along the coast path for half a mile. Now she was looking down on a rock-fringed sandy bay. Despite its inaccessibility, she imagined the little beach would be packed in the summer. This time of year there was no one to be seen. She took the path which zigzagged down to the cove, passing a rock outcrop and cutting through bracken and gorse. At the bottom she stumbled down a concrete ramp to where a mass of seaweed tangled with flotsam and jetsam had been deposited at the head of the beach. She stepped over the debris and onto the sand. The tide was low and at the mouth of the narrow bay white water frothed around rocks as the waves came crashing in.

Out to sea a yacht rolled in the heavy swell as the crew worked their way downwind towards Salcombe, while closer to shore a pot boat headed in the opposite direction, a column of gulls wheeling in the air above, the solitary fish-erman aboard well wrapped up against the weather.

The two boys had gone missing in August. The water temperature would have been around seventeen degrees. Not the Arctic, sure, but survival time would have been only a few hours and that was without factoring into account the boys' ability to stay afloat in what, according to the report, had been a rough sea. Was Elijah Samuel correct? Had they made some sort of suicide pact and waded out into the ocean under a night sky? If they had, then why hadn't the bodies been found? Of course tidal currents may have taken them far along the coast, but it seemed unlikely to Savage that nothing would ever have turned up. Plus there was the message inscribed in the bed frame to consider. That suggested a very different story to the one Samuel had told her.

She walked out to where the surf was gliding over the sand. A wave rushed in and Savage had to skip back a few paces. Her footprints filled with water and the outlines softened. She had a sudden notion. Memories of Jason Caldwell and Liam Hayskith had faded in the same way. Blurred at first and then ultimately wiped from the surface by time. They'd left nothing behind but marks in the damp sand, soon washed away. Dying young, they'd never got the chance to grow to adults nor to make anything of their lives or to have children. It was the same with her daughter, Clarissa, she thought. Her footprints only existed in a few people's memories and one day they'd be gone forever.

Savage shook her head, frustrated and angry. This was why she should be part of the *Lacuna* investigation and not on some wild goose chase. Caldwell and Hayskith were long past saving, but Jason Hobb was another matter.

She turned to go. As she wheeled around she glanced at the marks she had made on the beach. Another set of prints bisected her own and ran parallel to the tideline. They led to one side of the cove and disappeared into the water, as if the person had rounded the rocks and was now trapped in the next bay by the rising tide. Savage's heart quickened for a moment, but then she saw a figure standing on the cliff side, as if they'd clambered up from the sea. Savage stared hard at the figure, the shape black against the sky, features indistinct. A man though, she thought. Thin, definitely not the bulky form of Elijah Samuel. And he was watching her.

For several seconds nothing happened. Then the man raised a hand as if in greeting before moving away up the slope and disappearing over a ridge. Savage turned and raced up the beach. She stumbled across the seaweed and then went through the narrow gap to the coast path. She began to run up the hill, but within seconds her lungs were bursting and her legs depleted of energy. It was no good, he was too far away, too high up. Savage stopped with her hands on her hips, breathing hard, wondering exactly what she'd seen, what the mysterious man had been up to.

Jason had no way of keeping track of the time. Day and night went unnoticed. The only thing which marked the passage of the hours was the occasional sound of a car coming and going. At some point – two days, perhaps three days after he'd first been taken – the stone up top scraped once more and the voice called down.

'Oh, Jason, are you down there?' A glimmer of light came down the tube. 'I'm up here with my old pal Smirker. We're both hoping you'll become my old friend too. You see, I'm all alone these days and Smirker isn't really much company. To be honest, he doesn't do any more than listen.'

Jason kept still. Perhaps if he pretended to be dead the man would open the box to see what was going on.

'Jason, come on now. You're really not being any more entertaining than Smirker. It's most disappointing. Especially as I've brought you some more presents. There are some breakfast bars and a pasty. Oh, and several cans of cola.'

Jason bit his lip. He *was* so thirsty and his stomach hadn't stopped rumbling for hours. The last Mars bar had gone ages ago and if he didn't get something to eat soon he was sure he'd pass out.

'Oh, Jason! You've got ten seconds to say something otherwise I'm off. One, two, three, four . . .'

Jason hugged his knees to his chest and let out a low moan.

' . . . eight, nine, t—'

'Stop! Please! I'll be your friend, just give me something to drink.'

'Good boy.' A bag rustled at the end of the tube and then a cascade of chocolate bars slid out. 'Mind your head, I'm dropping down some cans and a bottle of water.'

Jason moved out the way as the cans clattered down the tube. He grabbed one and popped the ring pull, a huge *fizz* coming as the sticky liquid sprayed everywhere. He put the can to his lips and gulped.

'Now then, I'm going to tell you a little bit about myself and then you'll do the same, OK?'

'OK,' Jason spluttered between mouthfuls of cola.

'Great!' There was a pause and then the voice lowered to a whisper. 'Do you keep a diary, Jason? You know when I was a lad, I did!'

Chapter Fourteen

It's Friday and Bentley's here again. He arrived as dusk fell on a balmy evening. We'd been playing footie out the back, all of us. Mother's away somewhere for the weekend and I'd assumed she was up in London with Bentley. Her absence meant Father was in a good mood and he let all the boys stay up late. But then we spotted the car. Father came roaring out of the house and ordered us inside. He told me to go to my room. Once there, I peeked out the window and saw him meet Bentley at the bottom of the steps. Father seemed angry and I heard him raise his voice. Bentley just shrugged his shoulders and a thin smile graced his lips. He said something I couldn't hear and then the two of them came inside, Bentley first and then Father following, his head bowed.

I waited a while and then crept from my room. Along the hallway the door to our apartment stood open and I could hear voices echoing from downstairs: my father and the care-taker, one of the other night workers as well. I went to the rear of the house. There's a sash window on the landing and just outside the window a cast-iron drainpipe. I eased up the window and clambered out onto the sill. I shimmied down the pipe as I'd done many times before, and a few seconds later I was standing in the concrete yard outside the kitchen.

The kitchen was dark, but through the window I could see

a rectangle of light. The cellar door stood open. The cellar is where Father takes boys for punishment, but I'd just heard Father talking. I moved round the house, away from the kitchen, to the yard at the back. I knelt down on the ground next to where an airbrick provides a view of the cellar. When I peered in I saw Bentley! And, beneath him on the bed, a boy.

Bentley had removed his belt and wrapped it around the boy's neck. He rode him as if he was atop a horse, the belt like reins. As the boy struggled, he twisted and pulled until the boy became still. Then he released the pressure until the boy moved again. He repeated the procedure over and over as he took his pleasure. Struggle. Pull. Comply. Release. Struggle. Pull. Comply. Release.

As much as I wanted to, I couldn't look away from the appalling tableau. Bentley resembled a white rhinoceros. Black hairs on a white scaly skin. Great folds around his waist. He snorted and growled and then he was done. He collapsed on the bed for a moment before heaving himself off. The boy sobbed and rolled into a ball and for the first time I noticed the blond hair.

Jason!

The Shepherd returns to the barn to check on his captives. His car pulls up in front of the gates and he unlocks the padlock securing the heavy chain. He squelches through the mud and across to the stone steps. He stands for a moment. To the right is a boarded-up farmhouse in need of serious renovation. To the left, beyond a stone wall, the moor heaves its way to the horizon in great rolls of green and brown.

He shrugs and climbs the steps. A sliding metal door is secured by another padlock. He unlocks the door, opens it and steps inside. There's a corridor with white walls and a concrete floor. On the ceiling, fluorescent tubes provide illumination. Electric cables run in armoured trunking and near ceiling height a ventilation tube hangs down. At first sight the place resembles an intensive pig or poultry unit, maybe a slaughterhouse.

At the end of the corridor there's a small hallway. A passage leads deeper into the building to a further sliding door. He gazes down the corridor and through the door to where a vast chamber opens out. In the centre stands the altar, complete with its array of blades and hydraulic rams and wires. Airlines run up to a welded gantry above and connect to brass control valves. To the casual observer the altar looks like something from a meat processing unit, but, the Shepherd thinks wryly, it's unlikely the machine would pass a health and safety inspection.

He turns to where there are two more doors. Behind each door is a tiny cell. Exposed blockwork. Two paces by one. The floors are concrete with a thin scattering of straw. Light comes from a mesh-covered bulkhead fitting. The Shepherd moves to the left-hand door. There's a little pop-hole and he slides it to one side and peers in. An old man is curled on the floor shivering with either cold or fear. A light knocking on the door brings no response.

He steps across to the next cell and looks in there too. Perry Sleet is sitting with his back against the rear wall, but as the pop-hole opens he springs to his feet.

'What the hell is going on?' Sleet yells at the door. 'I don't know what your game is, but you're fucking crazy. Let me outta here!'

'This is not a game and I am far from crazy,' the Shepherd says. 'Don't waste your energy trying to escape. Better to pray for forgiveness. I know I have.'

'Look, I've got money. Savings. Cash if you take me to a hole in the wall. You can have it. I've got an ISA with near thirty K in. It's yours. All of it.'

'Money means nothing,' the Shepherd says flatly. 'You cannot buy the gift of God. Money is the root of all evils.'

'Who the fuck are you?' Sleet stands in the centre of the tiny cell. 'At least tell me that.'

'My name is not important, but with my help you will come to know the love of God.'

The Shepherd flips the pop-hole down and shakes his head. Like the other man, Sleet doesn't yet realise what he's done. Soon, however, they will both understand the extent of their guilt. And soon they will be made to pay.

Chapter Fifteen

Crownhill Police Station, Plymouth. Friday 23rd October.
9.07 a.m.

First thing Friday morning found Savage sitting in her office surrounded by several cardboard boxes. While she'd been out on Thursday afternoon the boxes had been retrieved from the document store. Back in the eighties some of the material had been put on the nascent Police National Computer, but most had not. Sorting through this lot, she thought, would take half a lifetime. And what was she likely to find that others had missed?

She decided to start with a list of the primary witnesses and soon found a familiar name: Elijah Samuel. He turned out to have been a resident at Woodland Heights in the early eighties and then, bizarrely, considering the abuse he'd talked of, had been employed as the home's caretaker. Fast forward to the present and he now owned the place. Back when the boys had gone missing he'd been interviewed three times and on each occasion he'd come out with the same story. The one about the boys going down to Soar Mill Cove and swimming out to sea. Savage flicked through the statements from the other boys. None of them mentioned the suicide pact which Samuel said Jason and Liam had made. Perhaps they'd only told Samuel. Or perhaps the pact was a fiction created so Samuel could rationalise the situation.

After an hour or so she took a break, grabbing some coffee from the canteen. Other officers she knew nodded at her in passing but appeared too busy to talk. *Lacuna* was being ramped up and additional resources deployed, the team now working flat out to ensure no stone was left unturned in the hunt for Liam Clough's killer. Still, no one was holding out much hope of finding Jason Hobb alive.

Savage took her coffee to the crime suite. Over at the whiteboards, DCI Garrett was nodding sagely as Collier explained something. Garrett fiddled with a piece of grey hair which had settled on his lapel, concerned about the blemish on his immaculate suit. He was a detective from another era, Savage thought. Past it. She had nothing against his age, but his methods were stuck in a straitjacket every bit as constraining as the collar on his pristine shirt. In the last few months he'd been a time-server, counting down the days until he received his pension. Savage wondered if she'd be as disillusioned after thirty years' service.

She drank her coffee and then crushed the paper cup and threw it in a nearby bin. She was pissed off. However much Hardin had stressed the importance of the *Curlew* case review, it was as nothing compared to the urgency of *Lacuna*. The link between the cases could at best be tenuous, at worst the fact the names were the same just a sick coincidence. If there was a serial killer out there she should be the one trying to catch him. Garrett didn't have the feel for this type of case. He was as rule-bound as Hardin. *Lacuna* was all about getting into the mindset of a deranged beast and Garrett didn't have a clue about how to do that.

She returned to her office and began to work through the witness statements once more. Woodland Heights had been

136

run by Mr Frank Parker and his wife, Deborah. They had lived in and made use of a self-contained apartment within the house. The Parkers had a thirteen-year-old son who lived with them and there was Samuel – the caretaker – and two schoolmasters. There was also a housekeeper – Miss Edith Bickell – who came in to cook and clean. Both Samuel and the schoolmasters had lived in a shared house in a nearby village. If foul play had been involved in the disappearance of the two boys then one or more of these people knew about it.

Savage looked again at the report concerning the window in the storeroom. Samuel had claimed Frank Parker had asked him to come and repair the window, but in his own statement Parker had denied the fact. Additionally, the forensic analysis suggested the window had been broken from outside and not in. Samuel, it seemed, was lying.

Parker appeared, from the statements at least, to be somewhat of a tyrant. Investigating officers described discipline as akin to that of a nineteenth-century workhouse and his attitude to the police one of muted and reluctant cooperation. Even so, nothing had been found to incriminate anybody at the home and the investigation had soon come to a dead end. Within six months of the incident, Woodland Heights had been closed down after direct intervention from the Home Office.

She decided Parker would need to be first on her list of interviewees and was surprised to find he lived in the village of Hope Cove, not much more than a mile from the home. A phone call to arrange a meeting was answered by a brusque woman and lasted barely thirty seconds. Nevertheless, an interview was scheduled for late morning, Savage pleased DC Calter was free to accompany her.

* * *

137

It took Riley and Enders the best part of two hours to drive to a picturesque village which lay in the North Devon countryside close to the border with Cornwall. A local officer met them at the entrance to Tim Benedict's house. PC Paul Sidwell was plainly out of his depth. He was mid-thirties, with a friendly manner, the archetypal village policeman, but he hadn't considered Benedict's disappearance as anything other than something which had been inflicted by the man himself.

'His car's gone,' Sidwell said, indicating a garage to the side of the detached property. 'And his wallet too. Although I've done a trace on his credit cards and none have been used.'

'So you're thinking he's topped himself?' Enders said. 'Closer to God?'

'I don't know where he is,' Sidwell said, casting a glance at Enders. 'I'm hoping he'll turn up.'

'Sure.' Riley nodded. On the phone he'd only told Sidwell they had a similar case. Nothing about the raft or Perry Sleet. 'Can we go in?'

Sidwell pushed through the garden gate and up the concrete path. The house was modern but with white uPVC bay windows in a mock leaded style. Two steps led to the front door, which the PC opened without a key.

'The cleaner's here,' he said by way of explanation. 'Didn't seem much point in cancelling.'

Sidwell stepped in to the hallway and Riley and Enders followed. A laminate floor resembled oak, but nothing else seemed anything like Riley's preconception of what a vicarage should be. A table stood next to a coat stand and stairs ran up one side of the hall. The interior was from a Barratt show home.

'You boshed the place already then?' Riley said. 'Before the cleaner arrived?'

'Boshed?'

138

'Forensics. Fingerprints. Signs of a break-in.'

'No.' Sidwell shook his head. 'But there was no break-in. The door was unlocked.'

'And that didn't strike you as strange?'

'Well . . .' Sidwell paused and bit his lip. 'To be honest, at first it did, but then I'm from Bideford. Out here people often do leave their doors unlocked, open even, if the weather's fine. Besides, this is a vicar's house. People wouldn't steal from him. Not in this part of the world.'

'I see.' Riley half smiled. 'And we're what . . . ten, fifteen miles from Bideford? I guess the internal combustion engine has reached these parts, so it's not out of the question that somebody could have driven here, is it?'

'No, I suppose not.'

Enders let out a silent whistle. 'I might retire up here, sir. Sounds idyllic. Must be a better class of people than that lot of scrotes and skanks we've got down south.'

Sidwell led them into the living area. A table sat down one end, a sofa and two armchairs at the other, the room divided by a mock archway. A bureau against a wall was loaded with paperwork, a laptop to one side of the papers. Sidwell moved across.

'I've been through this lot,' he said. 'Nothing out of the ordinary. No work issues, no debts, no love letters from a secret admirer. Not much on the computer either. I've spoken to various parishioners and none of them could offer any explanation for his disappearance. Neither could the diocese. They're worried, of course. I understand the bishop is going to ask congregants to pray for Benedict on Sunday.'

'That'll help,' Riley said.

'You think?' Sidwell began to leaf through the documents on the bureau. 'I can't fathom it myself. As far as I can tell the man is a saint.'

'Look, this is a bit of a long shot, but we've got a misper down in Plymouth. He . . .' Riley paused. There was a hum from the hallway. A distant whooshing sound. Riley turned for a moment and then looked back at Sidwell.

'The cleaner,' Sidwell said. 'I told you she's in on a Friday. I know nobody's been here in the past week but—'

'She was here *last* Friday too?' Riley said. Sidwell nodded. 'Which means she cleaned after Benedict went missing?'

'Yes, but I don't see—'

'Wait here.' Riley rushed from the room. In the hall the sound of a vacuum echoed down from above. Riley climbed the stairs to find a middle-aged woman pushing an upright Dyson back and forth at one end of the landing. He coughed.

'My God!' The woman turned and, seeing Riley, she let go of the vacuum. 'Please, don't—'

'Police, madam,' Riley said. 'Detective Sergeant Darius Riley. I'm with PC Sidwell.'

'Oh.' The woman laughed. 'I thought you—'

'Never mind that.' Riley dismissed the casual racism. 'I just want to ask you something about last Friday.'

'But I've been over that with Paul. There was nothing amiss. Tim hadn't put his breakfast things away, but apart from that there was no sign of anything wrong. Nobody realised he was missing until Saturday.'

'Sure, but the cleaning?' Riley pointed at the vacuum. 'You cleaned last Friday morning?'

'Yes. Top and bottom.'

'And there wasn't anything different?'

'No, I told you.'

'And the bag which is in the vacuum now, is that the same one?'

The woman shook her head. 'There is no bag. It's one of

140

those cyclone ones. But I haven't emptied the vacuum if that's what you mean.'

'Do you mind if we take a look?'

'Of course not.' The woman bent to the vacuum and clicked a catch. The cylinder came away and she passed it across to Riley.

'The bathroom?' Riley said. The woman indicated a door across the landing. Riley walked over and went in, the woman following. 'Did you notice any mess anywhere? Specifically bits of paper?'

'Now you come to mention it, I did.' The woman peered down as Riley emptied the contents of the vacuum cylinder into the bath. 'Tim had accidentally spilled the contents of his paper punch. There were pieces all over the living room.'

Riley smiled to himself, feeling his heart start to beat a little faster at the woman's words. He stared down at the grey mass of hair and dust now lying in a pile on the white surface of the bath and probed the pile with a fingertip. In amongst the mess, he spotted what he was looking for: several pieces of confetti. Pink and yellow and covered in tiny numerals.

The village of Hope Cove faced due west, a concrete break-water and the promontory of Bolt Tail providing the residents with some small protection from the sea. Savage and Calter drove through, passing a motley collection of houses clustered around the beach area and the inn. A coastal road skirted the beach and then climbed away from the sea, hairpinning up from the village to a number of imposing properties situated high on a hill. Frank Parker's place sat in vast grounds and was reached by a rough track. Savage turned up the track and parked outside the entrance. A pair of large iron gates hung from brick pillars and a tall wooden fence surrounded the property.

'Obviously doesn't care for visitors, ma'am.' Calter pointed at the 'Private Keep Out' sign. 'Sure you don't want me in there with you?'

'No. Talk to the neighbours,' Savage said. 'But be discreet. Spin them a story. Something to tease out any juicy details about the Parkers.'

They got out of the car and Calter ambled up the track to the next house while Savage pushed through the gates. A drive led to a standalone garage while a set of steps climbed to the front door. Large trees stood either side of the house and cast deep shadows over the building, preventing the sun from reaching the dark, moss-covered rockeries. If some of the trees had been cut back, the house would have had a great view across the cove and beyond to Bigbury-on-Sea and Burgh Island. As it was, huge clumps of rhododendrons served both to block the view and, Savage thought, prying eyes.

The door was answered by Mrs Parker, a woman in her early sixties. Dark, sombre clothing was from another era and consisted of a long black skirt and a black jacket with a starched white shirt beneath. Severe, Savage thought, the woman's grating voice as she spoke only reinforcing the fact.

'You must be the policewoman,' Mrs Parker said. 'You're not welcome and you'll get no tea. Frank's in the front room. See yourself in.'

Mrs Parker stood holding the door and made no effort to show Savage which way to go. Savage stepped in and onto bare floorboards. The boards creaked as she walked along the corridor. She stopped next to a door on the right and peered in. No, that was a dining room. On the other side was another door and Savage crossed over.

'In here.' A gruff command came from within, the voice similar to Mrs Parker's but an octave lower. 'You've got ten

142

minutes and I started timing from when you came through the front door.'

Savage entered the room. Like the hallway, there were bare floorboards, just a tattered hearth rug in front of the fireplace. A mantelpiece sat above, a silver framed photograph of a young boy on one side. The big bay window had its curtains drawn across, a gap only a hand's breadth wide allowing light in. The sun painted a strip on the floor which ran across to the fireplace, neatly bisecting the only furniture in the room: two high-backed armchairs. One was occupied by Frank Parker. Parker was older than his wife by a few years, his face lined and eyes sunken. He nodded at Savage and gestured at the other chair, a bony hand extending from his shirtsleeve. Like his wife, Parker wore a white shirt with black clothing, the trousers baggy around thin legs, a jacket buttoned tight on a similarly cadaverous frame.

'Sit down,' Parker said. 'Let's get on with it, you've used a minute of your time already.'

Parker had a strange way of speaking. He left his mouth hanging open after the end of a sentence, exposing his teeth. The mannerism had the effect of making it seem he was anticipating whatever Savage was going to say.

'Detective Inspector Charlotte Savage,' Savage said, bringing out her warrant card. 'I'm here about Woodland Heights.'

'I know who you are,' Parker said. 'And I can guess what you're here about.'

'You ran the home in the late eighties when Liam Hayskith and Jason Caldwell went missing. At the time, there were rumours, but most people believed they'd absconded. Only nearly thirty years later they've still not turned up. I'm here to find out what happened to those two boys.'

Parker's mouth opened, his grey tongue resting on his

143

lower teeth. He looked at the clock on the mantelpiece and then licked both lips in turn.

'Ridiculous. What do you expect to accomplish? When Liam and Jason went missing you lot came swarming. Every inch of the home was searched and nothing was found.'

'There were rumours of abuse at the home, Mr Parker, that much I do know.'

'Rumours are all very well and they can ruin lives, even lead to lynch mobs, but in the end they're just words. Hayskith and Caldwell ran away. Where they are now and what they are up to only God knows. If there are sinners in the story somewhere then I'm sure they will be judged.'

'I've spoken to a man who was a resident. He told me the home was like hell.'

'And did he tell you why he was there?' Parker sat back in his chair, appearing relaxed, but his hands gripped the arms, translucent skin tightening over his knuckles. 'They were delinquents, Inspector Savage. All of them. Liars, cheats, thieves, bullies, thugs. We even had a ten-year-old who'd stabbed his little brother to death.'

'Are you telling me you never saw or heard anything suspicious going on, that there was never violence?'

'Oh there was violence all right. Keeping order was nigh on impossible. They were always fighting amongst themselves. The most violent had to be restrained to prevent them injuring themselves or others.'

'Liam and Jason?'

'No, to be fair, they were good lads. When they went missing I was devastated. As you can imagine, the incident was both a professional and a personal tragedy. I couldn't understand why they'd run away. It was as if our love and care wasn't good enough.'

Savage saw Parker's eyes flick away from her for a moment.

She turned and saw Mrs Parker standing in the doorway, arms folded, a scowl on her face.

'Those boys were possessed by the devil.' Mrs Parker unfolded her arms and let them hang down by her sides, rigid, her fists clenched. 'By running away they rejected our affection, threw all our love back in our faces. I prayed they would be found so they could come back and be disciplined.'

'Disciplined?' Savage looked at Mrs Parker and then back at Mr Parker. 'You mean beaten?'

'The discipline always suited the offence,' Parker said, unapologetically. 'But not beaten. The word suggests something from the 1880s not the 1980s. I am not a tyrant.'

'No?'

'Not at all. I have lived simply, helped people when I can, forgiven my enemies. I will be judged, as all of us will be, when I have drawn my last breath.'

'Our peers can judge us harshly.'

'I'm talking about the Almighty, Inspector, not the tittle-tattle of the gossiping classes. Do you believe in God?'

'No. Not really.'

'God punishes. Both after death and in life too.' Parker reached for a cane which leant against the side of the chair. He picked the cane up in one hand and tapped the palm of the other with it. 'If those boys had turned to God for help most of their problems would have been solved.'

Savage gave an involuntary shiver as Parker pressed his lips together in an approximation of a smile. There was a tap, tap, tap. Not Parker with the cane, but his wife walking into the room and appearing at Savage's shoulder.

'Have you sinned, Charlotte?' Mrs Parker's bony hand shot out and grasped Savage's forearm. She leant over, Savage getting a waft of halitosis. 'Can you say you've led a blameless life?'

145

'I very much doubt she can.' Parker pushed himself up from his chair. He stepped forward, his spindly body looming over her. 'Let him who is without sin cast the first stone, Inspector. I did what was best for the boys back then and I'm not afraid to answer for my actions. Are you?'

'I'm warning you,' Savage said as she wrestled her arm free from Mrs Parker's grip. 'I could have you arrested.'

'I thought that's what you were going to do anyway.' Parker leered down and then pounded the cane on the floor in a series of staccato strikes which emphasised each word he spoke. 'Arrest. Us. For. Murder.'

'Well then, Inspector?' Mrs Parker touched Savage again, this time lightly on the shoulder. 'You can either arrest us or . . .'

'You can get the hell out of here.' Mr Parker rapped the cane on the side of Savage's chair. He turned sideways and looked at the mantelpiece. 'The ten minutes are up.'

Savage pushed herself to her feet and barged between Parker and his wife. They made no attempt to stop her. She turned at the doorway.

'I don't know what went on at Woodland Heights, but I can tell you I intend to find out.' Savage spun on her heels and went down the hallway to the front door. She flung the door open and scampered down the steps. As she opened the iron gate, she looked back up at the house. The Parkers had pulled the curtains open and stood like a pair of statues, staring down at her.

'Ma'am?' Calter was leaning against the car. She nodded up at the house. 'Everything all right? Those two look like a right couple of weirdos.'

'You could say that.' Savage slipped through the gate. 'Mr Parker all but threatened me with a cane.'

146

'Threatened?' Calter moved towards the gate. 'We should go back in there and arrest him then.'

'No.' Savage shook her head and took a deep breath. 'We need more evidence.'

'Well, the neighbours weren't much help. The Parkers keep themselves to themselves. They don't get involved in village life and callers apparently get short shrift.'

'Don't I just know it,' Savage said.

Chapter Sixteen

North Devon. Friday 23rd October. 1.23 p.m.

Riley and Enders left PC Sidwell bewildered, telling him only that they'd found a link between their case and the disappearance of Tim Benedict, the link being the use of a Taser weapon. There was no doubt, Riley said, that Benedict had been abducted. For the moment though he'd kept quiet about the link to the raft.

'Sidwell. He's in another league,' Enders said as they drove away. 'And you thought Plymouth detectives were backward.'

'Only you, Patrick,' Riley said. 'But Sidwell's right about one thing. That is, why Benedict?'

'Well you could say "why Sleet?" Two men, fifty miles apart, but there has to be a connection, right?'

'Exactly. Trouble is they're entirely disparate individuals.'

'Disparate?'

'Benedict's mid-sixties, Sleet twenty years younger. Benedict is a priest and Sleet an animal drug rep. I can't see them having crossed paths.'

'What about Sleet? He could have been up here visiting farms in the area.'

'Good point. We can check his schedule, though I'm not sure his patch goes this far north.' Riley stared through the windscreen as hedges and fields rushed past. 'We're a world away from Plymouth up here. Tiny villages, a few small towns, not much going on. I can't see anything Benedict could have got mixed up in which would tally with what Sleet's been doing.'

'This woman, Sarah. The one on the mobile. She could be the link. She's had an affair with both Sleet and Benedict and her hubby's got mad and taken both men out.'

'Now who's in another league, Patrick?' Riley laughed. 'No, I can't see it. Benedict is widowed, sure, but from what Sidwell told us he doesn't seem the bed-hopping type. Not that vicars are immune to temptation of course.'

'Something else then.'

'We need to start with the raft. Both men's initials were inscribed on the mannequin's arm along with two others. However, the chance of tracking the other two down using just their initials is minuscule. I mean CH and BP? That could be Christina Hendricks and Brad Pitt for all we know.

'Unlikely, sir.'

'Sure, but you get my point. What concerns me is that the mannequin was mutilated and came with an elaborate threat.'

'The Bible stuff?'

'Just so. My imagination might be running away with itself, but I don't think this is going to end well.'

After speaking to Parker, Savage found something was niggling at her. Back in her office mid-afternoon, she rifled through the statements from the boys at the home. Three of the boys had mentioned the cellar and Parker had hinted at corporal punishment. And the cellar was the one part of the house Savage hadn't searched. She'd planned to, she remembered, but Samuel's arrival had put paid to that. Short of obtaining a search warrant there was no way she was going to be able to return to the children's home officially.

Unofficially, however . . .

At a little after five p.m. Savage and Calter drove to Hope Cove again, this time in Savage's MG. Savage parked in the village car park, her vehicle one of only three sitting on the gravel expanse. Lights in nearby houses had begun to flare in the twilight and a gentle breeze wafted cooking smells from the inn across the way.

'Quite a day, ma'am,' Calter said, as they got out. 'Back and forth and back again, hey?'

Savage nodded. 'Yes. Thanks for coming.'

'You're lucky I'm available.' Calter zipped up her waterproof jacket. 'My Friday nights are usually sacrosanct. And there's this guy I've just met, a Marine.'

'If there was a problem you should have said.' Savage pulled on her own waterproof. 'I'd have come on my own.'

'No problem. I told him I was worth waiting for.' Calter moved on to her boots, lifting a foot onto the rear bumper of the MG and tightening the laces. She looked up. 'Are you sure we should be doing this?'

'Yes,' Savage said. 'There isn't any other option. Anyway, we're within our rights.'

'Well then why don't we just go in the front way and in daylight? And why come in your MG instead of using a pool car?'

'I don't want anyone to know we're searching the place again. As far as Samuel and Parker are concerned, I found nothing of interest. I'd like it to stay that way until we've got more evidence.'

'You think Samuel's involved?'

'He's involved somehow. I feel he told me too much to be implicated directly in the boys' disappearance though.'

150

Calter nodded and pulled on a pair of gloves and a black hat.

'Suits you,' Savage said. 'You look like a ninja.'

'I *am* a ninja, remember?'

Calter did a form of martial arts, Savage recalled. Ju-jitsu or something. More than once the DC had showed she wasn't to be messed with. Savage put on her own set of gloves and hat and hoisted the rucksack onto her back.

'Come on, let's get going. We need to leave the village before dark or it's going to look really odd.'

They walked down past the Hope and Anchor Inn and onto the coast path which skirted the beach. The wet sand glistened in the fading light and a set of footprints led down to the water's edge where a trio of dogs bounded round their owner. At the far end of the beach the local rescue boat sat in front of its boathouse. Several crew members stood around the RIB chatting.

'All right, girls?' one of the men said as they approached.

'Fine thanks,' Savage said as they turned to the right and began the steep climb up the coast path.

'He can rescue me any day, ma'am.' Calter looked back over her shoulder at the guy and smiled. 'Mind you, you know me and the sea. I get sick in a paddling pool.'

Steps led up from the beach and then the path curled out and round the top of the odd piece of land known as Bolt Tail. They had no need to head out onto the promontory so they cut across and rejoined the coast path as it ran along the clifftops in an easterly direction towards the children's home and Soar Mill Cove. They passed another dog walker, hurrying back to the village before the light gave out, but after that saw no one.

Dusk had well and truly fallen by the time they reached the point on the coast nearest Woodland Heights. Half a mile farther inland, lights from a cluster of houses marked the village of Bolberry. Overhead, the clear weather of the daytime had gone, replaced by dark clouds. Occasionally a smattering of stars glinted through a rift, but the clouds soon rolled across again, extinguishing the light.

'Now we wait,' Savage said, moving to one side of the path and finding somewhere dry and comfortable to sit. 'Until it's fully dark.'

'The home's not haunted, ma'am?' Calter said, as she plonked herself down alongside Savage.

Savage stared across to where the house stood sinister and looming. She wondered what sort of abuse had gone on there, whether the boys' screams had punctuated the still night air or whether, in fact, they'd been too scared to cry out.

'Haunted?' she said. 'Very probably.'

Within half an hour the last of the light had gone. Savage held a finger to her lips. Next to her, Calter's silhouette nodded. They pulled themselves up from the ground and padded away from the path and across an expanse of grass. The house emerged from the gloom, grey walls rising to where the roof touched a now formless sky, the upper windows nothing but black voids. At the bottom of the front steps, Savage stopped. In the distance a dog barked and she could hear the occasional car on the Salcombe road, a mile or so away. Behind them came the noise of the waves rolling in against the base of the cliffs. A brooding silence from the house.

'We go in,' Savage whispered. 'We stay together, take it easy, do this methodically, OK?'

'Yes, ma'am.'

They walked up the steps. Samuel had pulled the door

to, but the frame was warped and he hadn't been able to shut it enough to engage the padlock and hasp. Savage gave the door a gentle push and it scraped open.

'Can't see a thing.' Calter's voice hissed in the darkness as Savage pushed the door to. 'This is like being inside a coal scuttle. Oh!'

'Stay still.' Savage had reached out and touched Calter on the arm. Now she unshouldered her rucksack and rummaged inside, pulling out two small torches. She turned one on and handed the other to the DC. 'Use this, but keep the beam low and don't point it at the windows.'

Savage swept the torch down the corridor. The staircase rose into darkness.

'You want to check up there again?' Calter said.

'No, we're here for the cellar.'

'I was hoping you'd forgotten. Remember Harry and his cellar? I really didn't like that.'

Calter was talking about the serial killer, Matthew Harrison. He'd had a penchant for killing young women and then storing their bodies in a number of freezers which he kept in his basement.

Savage crept up the corridor towards the rear of the house. Debris crunched underfoot and on each side they passed rooms where shadows danced in the light from the torches. In one, a pair of red glowing eyes flashed for a moment before something scuttled off in the dust. When they reached the kitchen it seemed larger than Savage remembered. The oak table stretched across the space, pots and pans dangling from some kind of rack above. Against one wall stood a Belfast sink, the porcelain cracked, a tap dripping rhythmically into a broken mug.

'Nice,' Calter said. 'Just the sort of place to prepare school dinners.'

'This way.' Savage edged round the table and over to the far side of the room where one door led to a pantry and storerooms, the other to the cellar. She pushed the cellar door open. Uneven stairs fell away in utter blackness and a waft of dank and dirty air assailed her nostrils.

'Down there, ma'am?' Calter stood alongside Savage. 'You've got to be joking, right?'

'I'll go first,' Savage said. She stepped down onto the top stair, a huge granite slab, well worn and sloping left to right. She shone the torch at her feet and stepped down again. Each stair was a huge flag, rough and uneven. She continued on down, Calter just behind. At the bottom, her feet splashed into shallow water. She swung the torch around and the beam revealed puddles and debris.

A few metres in front of her a joist hung half fallen from the ceiling. The hole in the living room, she thought. Off to the right a narrow arch in a stone wall led to another chamber. She moved across towards it, trying as best she could to avoid the puddles.

'Ma'am!' Calter stood over by one wall, the light from her torch playing on the rough stones. 'Look here.'

Savage turned. Calter was examining a set of chains which hung from a hook midway up the wall. The chains were linked to a pair of manacles and in front of the wall stood a rusty old bed frame.

'I can't believe this,' Calter said. 'They brought the kids down here and tied them up as a punishment? Bloody animals.'

Savage said nothing. She wondered to herself how this had been missed. Surely the entire property had been searched when the boys went missing?

She went back to the arch and peered through. She flicked the torch round and the light revealed a small room just two or three metres across. The main part of the cellar had a stone

154

and earth floor, but in here the floor was concrete. The concrete had been roughly laid, little ridges here and there and a pronounced bowl in the centre where water had collected. Savage played the torch over the surface. In the right-hand corner there was some sort of scraping, a marking. She walked across, knelt, and pointed the torch down. Somebody had written a date on the surface before the concrete had hardened: 4/11/88.

Fourth of November, 1988.

The two boys had gone missing in August of the same year. The concrete had been laid a few months later. Why lay a new floor in this tiny room when the main part of the cellar was just as rough?

'I think we might have something else, Jane,' Savage shouted out. 'In here.'

There was a clanking as Calter released the chains. She came into the little room and Savage pointed down at the floor.

'Ma'am?'

'If the date on this concrete is correct, the floor was put down not long after Hayskith and Caldwell went missing. Suspicious, don't you think?'

'More than suspicious.' Calter peered down. 'But who laid the floor?'

'No idea, but they wouldn't have been able to mix this amount of concrete in secret.'

'And you really think they're under here? The two boys?'

'It's possible.' Savage stood and waved the torch round the room once more. 'Say someone killed them. They temporarily secrete the bodies elsewhere. A search takes place of the house and the local area. More than one search, according to the files. When everything is done and dusted, the bodies are brought back and buried in the cellar. Concrete is poured on top for good measure. The place has already been turned upside down, right? No way anyone is coming back again, and if they do, there's nothing to find.'

'Except those.' Calter swung her torch so the beam pierced the arch and shone into the next room. 'The manacles.'

'Yes, there's something not right about that. But it doesn't change the evidence here.'

'So what do we do now?'

'We get a warrant.' Savage waved her arm at the floor. 'To dig this lot up.'

'Really? Do you think there's enough—' Calter stopped. She glanced at the ceiling and then lowered her voice to a whisper. 'Did you hear that, ma'am? There's somebody up there!'

Savage followed Calter's gaze. She swung her torch upwards. A tiny shower of dust crossed the beam of light as the floor above creaked.

'Come on.' Savage moved from the little room into the main area, covering the end of her torch so only a tiny glow could be seen. 'Let's go upstairs.'

'This is the bit where you tell me the Force Support Group is on standby outside,' Calter said. 'Right?'

'Wrong, Jane. We're on our own.'

Savage began to climb the steps towards the rectangle of grey at the top. Halfway up she paused and listened. Nothing but the sound of the dripping tap. At the top she stopped again. There. Another creak, this time from somewhere on the first floor.

'They've gone upstairs,' Savage whispered. She turned to Calter. 'We go up. Once we see what they're doing, we announce ourselves.'

Calter nodded and followed Savage as she tiptoed from the kitchen and into the corridor. Plaster debris crunched under their feet and at one point a loud crack echoed through the hallway as Calter stepped on a piece of wood.

'Sorry, ma'am,' Calter said. 'I think we should rush them. Stealth mode's impossible.'

'OK, I'll go up, you stay here.' Savage indicated a door near the bottom of the stairway. 'Remain hidden, but if I shout, be prepared to tackle them, OK?'

'Yeah, but what about you?'

'I'll be fine, don't worry.'

Savage began to ascend the stairway. This was Elijah Samuel, she figured. He'd be furious that she was nosing around, but he'd hardly attack her, would he?

Every step she made brought a new noise: a creak, a rustle from a pile of newspaper, something dislodged which bounced down the stairs, clatter, clatter, clatter. On the landing she stood stock-still and held her breath. Whoever was up here had climbed to the attic and she could hear the scrape as one of the beds was being pulled across the floor.

She reconsidered her earlier judgement. Why would Samuel be exploring his own property in the middle of the night? If he was looking for intruders he'd surely have a big torch and he wouldn't be creeping around. She slipped along the landing and peered up the twisting stairway. An ethereal light painted the walls with a pale lustre. For a second she shivered, but then realised the clouds had broken and the glow was nothing more than the light from the moon.

Then she heard something.

A whisper.

Then another.

She placed a foot on the bottom stair and began to move up. Step by step she went, her back pressed against the wall so she could see as far round the curving stairwell as possible. A couple of steps from the top she hesitated. The whispering

157

was close now, just beyond the landing, probably inside the room where she'd found the bed with the writing scratched into the frame. She cocked her head in an attempt to decipher the words.

We'll be friends forever, won't we?

Yes!

Promise?

Yes!

Cross your heart and hope to die?

Yes! Yes! Yes! Especially the hoping to die bit.

Don't worry, the dying stuff is my speciality. But then you'd remember that, wouldn't you?

The whispers came one after another, some sort of conversation going on, only there was just the one voice, somebody talking to himself.

Savage took another step and as she did so a creak eased from beneath her foot. The whispering stopped, leaving total silence. She took shallow breaths, her heart pumping as she weighed her options. Moonlight flooded through a dormer to her left, illuminating the landing. Her shadow would fall across the entrance to the room and whoever was within would know she was coming. The surprise could cause an unnecessary confrontation.

'Hello?' she said. 'Who's there?'

Nothing.

And then something came from the room, a shadow sprinting across the landing and barrelling into her. She fell sideways, her body scraping down the wall. The dark form leapt past, taking several stairs in a single bound. Then they were gone.

Savage tumbled over, stair-surfing down several steps, her hands out in front of her, each bump knocking the wind from her lungs. She came to rest halfway down.

'Calter!' she shouted, a pain in her ribs coming as she yelled.

A screech came from the first floor. Not Calter, something else. Savage pulled her legs round in front of her and stood up. Nothing broken, thank God. She descended the rest of the stairs and as she ran along the first-floor landing she heard DC Calter call out from below.

'Ma'am? Are you all right?'

'Yes. Did anyone come down?'

'No.'

Savage groped in her pocket and found her torch. She flicked it on and illuminated the landing in front of her. Calter crunched up the stairs and they met at the top.

'Gone,' Savage said, feeling a cold draught on her face. She pointed the torch and a reflection flashed out a few metres away. A sash window, the bottom half pulled up. 'Through there.'

The two of them walked forward and at the window Savage peered out. Moonlight flooded a bare concrete yard; beyond lay a hedge and on the other side of the hedge nothing but empty fields.

Chapter Seventeen

Near Bovisand, Devon. Saturday 24th October. 10.29 a.m.

Saturday morning found Savage trying to run the *Curlew* investigation from her front room. Pete was out racing their little yacht, *Puffin*, so she was attempting to be both a mother and a police officer. She sat at a little desk in one corner while Samantha and Jamie played on Jamie's new Xbox. The device had been a birthday present from grandparents and had entered the household against Savage's better judgement.

'He'll grow up wanting to shoot things,' Savage had said to Pete.

'So?' Pete had replied. 'What's wrong with that?'

On the far side of the room a wail came from Jamie. Savage looked across to the screen where an innocuous and rather vacuous game appeared to involve nothing more than a furry monster jumping from platform to platform on an endless scrolling screen. As she watched, Jamie's avatar fell from a walkway into a pool of sharks and Jamie squealed again. Savage shook her head. Still, at least the thing was keeping him out of her hair.

Her mobile bleeped a tune and she picked the phone up.

'John, you've got it?' she said. 'The warrant?'

'Yes,' Layton said. 'At least it's all been OK'd. Just dotting the i's, etcetera.'

The flat tone suggested the outcome was never in doubt, but Savage knew different. The search warrant relied on there being reasonable grounds for believing an offence had been committed and there being material on site which would be of substantial value to the investigation. A complication was that the home had been searched before, albeit many years ago, so the police needed to argue this was either new evidence or something which had been missed previously.

'And you didn't mention my visit?'

'No, not the second one.'

'So how did you wing it?'

'The old "anonymous tip-off" routine. Worked a treat. Shall we say one o'clock at Elijah Samuel's place?'

Savage glanced at her watch. Pete wouldn't be back until one at the earliest and she needed to drive over there. 'Make it two, OK?'

Layton agreed and hung up.

She turned back to Jamie and Samantha. On screen, Jamie's furry creature had met yet another grisly demise, this time at the bottom of a rocky chasm. Luckily for Jamie and Samantha, the game had given them multiple lives. Savage smiled for a moment and then looked back at the *Curlew* papers, her mind returning to the two boys, Jason Caldwell and Liam Hayskith. They hadn't been so fortunate, she thought. They'd had just the one life each.

Elijah Samuel lived in a tiny thatched cottage in the village of Bolberry, just half a mile from the children's home. Savage stood in the lane as Layton and a uniformed PC went to the front door, Layton with the warrant in his hand.

The door swung wide and Samuel stood hunched in the

161

low porch. He nodded as Layton told him of their intention to search Woodland Heights.

'I won't bloody have it,' he said, gesturing over Layton's shoulder to Savage. 'I let her look round in good faith. If I'd known you'd hold it against me I'd have had her for trespassing.'

Then Samuel snatched the piece of paper from Layton's hand, retreated into the cottage and slammed the door.

With the warrant served, Layton led a procession of cars and vans to the home. He chatted to Savage as his CSIs unloaded the equipment.

'Shouldn't take long this, Charlotte,' Layton said. He pointed over to where two men were readying a compressor and a jackhammer. 'Unless the concrete is really thick, that'll break through it in no time.'

'Good. The sooner we can discover the truth about what went on here, the better.'

'Yes.' Layton gazed over at the house. 'Have you notified the coroner?'

'I've alerted him to the possibility we might find something. I've had Luke Farrell contact the relatives too. There'll be a lot of media interest when this gets out and I don't want them doorstepped.'

Layton nodded. 'Closure. That's what they want. The paradox is, only a positive result gives them peace. Anything else and they go on wondering.'

Closure. Savage had found some sort of closure for herself and her family, but it hadn't stopped her wondering.

Layton had moved over to one of the vans. More tools. Shovels, pickaxes, a couple of big dumpy bags to put the spoil in. Savage was glad everything was now official, that she was moving beyond the paper-chase Hardin had set her. There was no more hiding, no more covering things up. If they found something, there'd not only be the chance of criminal prosecutions, there would also be major repercussions across a number of agencies.

She got suited up in her PPE gear and followed Layton into the house. The CSIs had located the compressor outside the back door and a long hose snaked into the kitchen and down into the cellar. The motor on the compressor chugged rhythmically, a slight hiss audible.

She descended into the cellar, where the darkness had been banished by a white glare from several sets of lights on tripods. Layton cast a black shadow on one wall as he examined the bed and the manacles.

'You said you thought there was something odd about these, right?' Layton said. He held up one of the cuffs. 'Well, you're correct. They aren't thirty years old.'

'How can you tell?' Savage said, moving across to Layton.

'Look.' Layton held out the piece of metal. 'It's not tarnished or rusty, although the cellar is as damp as anything. Then there's where the chain is fixed to the wall. The mortar has been disturbed recently.'

Savage peered at the iron ring holding the chain. Where the shaft of the bolt penetrated the wall, the cement was a lighter colour. The surface layer had crumbled away as somebody had fixed the bolt in place.

'How long?'

'A couple of weeks, a few months. Sorry to be so imprecise, but I can tell you we're not talking years. The bed probably comes from one of the rooms upstairs. What's more, both the shackles and the bed have been wiped over. Whoever put them down here made sure to cover their tracks.'

'So they've been left as clues. Like the writing I found upstairs.'

'Perhaps.' Layton gestured over to the arched doorway. 'Come through here, there's more weirdness.'

Layton led the way through to the little room. Inside, one of the CSIs was making an adjustment to the jackhammer before he started on the floor. There was a low throbbing sound and the hiss of air escaping. The room was lit by another set of halogen lights on a stand, the glare unbearably harsh.

'Over here.' Layton moved across to the left-hand side where a broom leant against the wall. A pile of dirt had been swept away from the concrete into a little pile. 'Jim was just clearing the floor when we found this.'

Layton tapped the concrete with his foot and then pointed, circling the area with his finger. Savage could see that on the outside of the area the concrete was white. However, the patch which Layton was indicating was a darker colour.

'I'm sorry, John,' Savage said. 'I'm not big on ready-mix, you'll have to explain.'

'The white concrete was laid years ago. The date you found over in the corner is probably accurate. The darker area, although hard, hasn't fully cured yet. It's months old at the most.' Layton shrugged apologetically. 'I reckon somebody's beaten us to it.'

Layton hadn't been kidding about the length of time it would take to dig up the floor. Within ten minutes several square metres had been broken into large slabs. The sound had been unbearable and Savage, not having ear defenders, retreated upstairs to the kitchen. A little while later, Layton called her back down. She descended into a miasma of dust, the air thick with particles of concrete and a smell Savage knew from experience was anything but wholesome.

In the little room, the broken concrete had been piled into

164

one of the dumpy bags. The halogen lights shone into the resultant hole, illuminating a thick tar-like gloop.

'You can smell it, yes?' Layton said. 'Unmistakable.'

Savage sniffed the air and nodded. Adipocere. A substance formed from the body's fat during decomposition in wet and anaerobic conditions. Sealed under the concrete, the adipocere had persisted for over two and a half decades.

'Anything in there?' Savage leant forward and stared at the dark liquid. The liquid had an almost mirror-like quality, the white lights reflecting on the black surface.

'One of the lads has gone to get a pump. We'll get a hose in here. Won't take long to drain the water.'

Again Layton was right. Once the pump had been brought in, the liquid was soon sucked out.

'Got a filter on the end,' Layton said as he knelt at the hole and moved the hose around in the rapidly diminishing puddle at the bottom. 'Haven't come across anything yet though.'

The hose made a slurping sound as the last of the black gloop disappeared. Layton positioned the hose to one side of the hole, where it continued to gurgle away. He leant over and braced himself with one hand on the other side of the hole. He reached down with the other hand, feeling around in what was now just mud. He pulled out a handful of debris and one of the other CSIs held out a bucket.

Savage tried not to show her disappointment as the bits of stone and concrete splattered into the bucket. Maybe the smell was just a broken sewer pipe. Maybe she'd got this completely wrong. She sighed.

'Don't worry, Charlotte.' Layton turned his head, precarious above the hole. He smiled at her. 'We'll take this outside and sieve it. You know my motto. We'll find something, we always do.'

Savage nodded and left Layton to it. She went outside to

find the sky darkening. A persistent drizzle swirled in the air, almost as if the dank weather was mimicking the atmosphere in the cellar. She returned to her car and waited as the CSIs brought out bucket after bucket of sludge from the house. After a while, Layton came over and tapped on the window. Savage opened the door.

'There was more than at first sight,' Layton said. 'Kept bubbling up from the bottom of the hole. Probably some sort of watercourse down there. A spring maybe. You want to come across? We're going to start sieving the material now.'

Savage got out of the car and followed Layton to where the sludge had been poured into two large plastic builder's trugs. Someone had rustled up a length of hose and connected one end to an outside tap and now two CSIs were beginning to process the black goo. Bit by bit they scooped the sludge from the trugs onto a sieve and one of them worked the hose back and forth, washing the mud away.

Savage's heart jumped as she saw bits of white reveal themselves in the mud. Layton shook his head, explained the bits were pieces of concrete. The work continued, the CSIs painstaking in their attention to detail. As they reached the bottom of the first trug, Layton lowered his shoulders and shook his head.

'Maybe I was wrong,' he said. 'Maybe we won't find anything this time.'

'Never mind, John—'

'Ma'am?' One of the CSIs was sieving the last of the material from the trug, washing dirt from yet another piece of concrete debris. Only this wasn't concrete. He pointed down to the sieve where the clear water swirled over something brown. 'Here we go.'

'What is it?' Savage peered down. The thing looked like a little stick.

'Bone.' Layton picked the stick from the surface of the sieve. 'At least, a fragment of bone.'

'Human?'

'No idea, we'll need to get it to Nesbit.' Layton held the fragment between his thumb and forefinger. 'But given the circumstances, I'd say it might well be, don't you think?'

Savage left Layton to his work and drove the short distance to the village. Now there was potential evidence, Elijah Samuel had some questions to answer. The property was his, after all. Since he had been a resident at the home, then the caretaker and now the owner, it seemed inconceivable he didn't know at least some of what really went on there.

A knock on the oak door of the thatched cottage brought Samuel out into the drizzle. He stared beyond Savage towards the home, something like hatred in his eyes.

'You again,' he said, continuing to gaze into the murk. 'I told you before that you'll get nothing from me.'

'We've found a bone, Mr Samuel. In the cellar. My chief CSI reckons it's human. Given your connection with Woodland Heights, that puts you in the frame.'

'In the frame for what?'

'Murder, Mr Samuel.' Savage glanced back at the house. 'You told me it was hell in there. You need to explain what you meant by that. You can invite me in or you can come down the station and make a statement. Your choice.'

'Fine.' Samuel pushed the door wide and gestured for Savage to enter. The door opened directly into a living room. A large inglenook held a wood burner, an orange glow visible through the glass door. Two armchairs and a sofa sat arranged around the room, a TV in one corner. On one wall hung a number of photographs. Blokes in army gear on mountain tops. Some on a beach with palms in the background, a blue

167

ocean looking a lot warmer than the sea off the Devon coastline. A group shot with a desert and ruined buildings in the
background.

'You said you were in the army,' Savage said, indicating
the pictures. 'When was that?'

'After the home closed down.' Samuel seemed to relax
slightly. He indicated that Savage should sit and took the
armchair closest to the fire for himself. 'Four Two Commando.'

'Right.' Four Two Commando were based at Bickleigh
Barracks, not far from the Shaugh Prior tunnel where Liam
Clough's body had been found. Savage pointed to the desert
picture. 'Iraq?'

'Yeah. My last tour.'

'And then?'

'Property development. Being handy means I can do up
places myself. Started with just one, but I've got several properties now.'

'Including Woodland Heights?'

'Not for long. I had dreams of renovating it, now I just
want shot.'

'You said it was hell there, Mr Samuel. What did you mean?'

'What I said. It wasn't a pleasant place. Parker was a right
one. Ruled with a rod of iron. And I mean that literally.'

'So why did you stay on and become the caretaker? I
mean, if it was as bad as you said, why didn't you leave?'

'You wouldn't understand, love. Family, weren't they?
Maybe not Parker, but the others. His wife, the boys.' Samuel
turned to the fire and held out his hands to the warmth.
'Besides, I had nowhere else to go. It seemed as good an option
as any. I went to college a couple of days a week and learnt
a trade. Carpentry. Turned out to be useful back then, and
now. When the home closed, I found a new family in the army.
There were tyrants there too, but you stick with your mates

and look out for one another. I guess that's why I stayed at the home despite Parker. I was looking out for my mates.'

'Right.' Savage pulled out her notebook and flicked over the pages. 'Liam Hayskith and Jason Caldwell. They went missing on the night of twenty-sixth of August 1988. I believe you were called to the home on the following morning to repair a window in one of the storerooms. The glass had been smashed, right?'

'Yes.' Samuel nodded. 'I lived in a house in the village just up from here. Me and two of the teachers. The boys had used a can of baked beans to break the pane.'

'Because all the doors and windows were locked and this was their escape route. Makes sense. And yet checking the witness statements has brought up one or two anomalies. The first of these is the fact that, although you say you were summoned to the home, none of the other statements corroborates this. Nobody else remembers ringing you and asking you to come in on the Saturday. Mr Parker's statement says, "I might have, but I honestly can't remember." Aside from him there's no one.'

Samuel stared at the glowing door on the wood burner. 'People were running around like crazy. It was hectic that morning.'

'I'm sure it was,' Savage said. 'But no crime had been committed, had it? The police were only called because these two boys were runaways.'

'And later, when they couldn't be found. Then there were more questions.'

'Yes, but by then the exact details of what happened on the morning had become blurred. For instance, although the baked bean can lay on the grass outside the window, the glass itself had somehow mysteriously fallen inward. And the housekeeper, Miss Bickell, said she hadn't stocked a tin that

169

small. She insisted the larder only contained catering-size tins. I'm trying to get my head around what might have happened to Liam and Jason and I've come up with a theory, specifically concerning you. Would you like to hear it?'

Samuel continued to stare at the fire as he made an almost imperceptible nodding movement.

'I believe you smashed the window. For some reason you came to the home early in the morning and broke the pane with a tin of baked beans you'd brought with you. You hadn't thought through your actions clearly, so when the glass fell back into the storeroom you left the tin on the ground outside as a visual clue to reinforce the idea that someone had been breaking out. Now, do you want to tell me why you smashed the window?'

'How . . .?' Samuel turned from the fire. 'I can't tell you. Anyway, what does it matter now? Those boys never turned up, did they? They're dead. Long dead. I liked them, you know? I was a good few years older, of course, but we had some fun. They used to help me out with odd jobs. Them and Parker's son. We built things like bird boxes, a bench for round the back, compost bins for the veg garden. We made a go-cart one year. Powered by an old moped engine. The thing got out of control and smashed through a fence, but the lads put it all back good as new. Most of the boys were helpful in that way. You'd get the occasional trouble-maker, someone born wrong, but the majority were at the home through circumstance. Bad luck can strike anyone, can't it?'

'Yes,' Savage said, trying not to think on her own piece of bad luck. 'But that's not how Mr Parker tells it.'

'I'm sure it isn't. 'Despite the warmth from the fire, Samuel shivered. 'The thing was, whatever misfortune brought the boys to the home, it was compounded when they got there. Parker was a cruel and strict disciplinarian, but that wasn't the worst of it.'

'Are we talking abuse, Mr Samuel?'

'I couldn't say. All I know is Liam and Jason wanted out of there.'

'Why on earth didn't you report the situation? You could have gone to the police, education authorities, the newspapers or somewhere else. Instead you did nothing.'

'I didn't do nothing, did I?' Samuel paused and took a deep breath before continuing. 'On the night they vanished I made sure the front door to the home was unlocked last thing. I let Liam and Jason know so they could slip out in the middle of the night. I was guilty of not being brave enough to confront Parker, but I tried to make amends by giving the boys a chance of freedom.'

Savage stared at Samuel. She wondered if this was the truth of what had happened on that August night. Could there be some other explanation for the bone in the cellar? Perhaps Layton and his team of CSIs were wasting their time.

'And you saw Liam and Jason leave the home?'

'No, I didn't.' All of a sudden Samuel was aggressive. 'But where would they be if they hadn't escaped?'

'You tell me.'

'I can't because I've told you the truth.'

'So you never saw either of them again?'

'I . . .' Samuel paused. 'No. They vanished. Into the waves down at the cove.'

'The sea story is all too convenient. I believe the reason Liam Hayskith and Jason Caldwell never turned up is because they were murdered, Mr Samuel. And you helped cover up the murders, didn't you?'

'No!' Samuel stood, towering over Savage, his head almost touching the oak beams. 'No! No! No!'

171

'Are you saying they weren't murdered or that you didn't cover up the crime?'

'I told you, they disappeared! Parker rang me about three in the morning. Instructed me to get round to the home and make it look like somebody had broken out. He had no idea I was the one who'd left the door unlocked.'

'So you didn't worry about covering for him because it obscured your own tracks.'

'Exactly.'

'You did as he said and kept your mouth shut.'

'You don't understand.' Samuel jabbed a finger at Savage.

'Oh but I do,' Savage said. 'In my job you get to hear all the excuses under the sun. "They made me do it," "She led me on," "It was a long time ago," "I'd been drinking." I could go on but I won't, because I'm sick to death of excuses. What I want is answers.'

'Well I've given you the only ones I know.'

'Maybe you have.' Savage stood. 'But I can tell you I'm going to find out the truth.'

Savage made to leave. At the front door she stopped and turned.

'Think on it, Mr Samuel. You can come clean and be on the right side of the law or you can go down for conspiring to pervert the cause of justice. Your choice.'

Samuel held her gaze until she turned again, opened the door and left the cottage.

The sound of the stone being moved woke Jason from a fitful slumber. He blinked in the darkness. He had no idea how long it had been since the man's last visit. A day? Two days?

'Are you there, boy?' the voice from above said. 'Are you ready to be friends yet?'

Jason pushed himself into a sitting position, but didn't

answer. He wondered if keeping quiet was the right thing to do. He'd watched enough movies with Ned Stone to know the best way out of a kidnap situation was to befriend your abductor. And wasn't that exactly what the man at the top of the tube wanted?

'Hello?' Jason said, moving closer to the tube. 'Will you let me out if I do become your friend?'

'Yes I will!' The voice sounded pleased. 'Not just yet, but soon, I promise. I hope you'll want to stay with me and Smirker and have some fun. It'll be just like old times.'

Jason swallowed, feeling sick. He had a pretty good idea what the man wanted. His mum had warned him to be wary and his nan was always going on about the world being full of perverts. There'd been lessons at school too. Stranger danger, the teacher had said. This was the ultimate stranger danger, Jason thought. Some anonymous weirdo had captured him. He was plainly a psycho straight from one of Stone's horror movies.

'What's your name?' Jason asked, thinking that finding out who the man was might be a start. 'It's hard to be friends when I don't know what to call you.'

'Can't tell you. You see, once you know somebody's name you have to know their secrets as well, so I can't tell you. Not yet. Once I can trust you I can tell you. *Can* I trust you?'

'Yes,' Jason said. 'I'm very trustworthy. My mum says so.'

'OK then!' Silence for a moment. 'But we need to shake on it. Put your hand up the tube. I'd reach down but my hand is too big.'

Jason hesitated. He looked at the tube where a dim light cast a pale circle on the wooden floor. The man was right, the tube was probably too small for an adult's hand. He crouched next to the tube and twisted himself to one side. That allowed him to thread his arm into the tube, his hand grasping upward.

173

'Got ya!'

Something wrapped into place around Jason's wrist, some sort of leather material. He tried to pull back but the strap bit into his skin.

'Let me go,' he shouted. 'We had a deal!'

'There we go.' A hand held Jason's palm and shook it. 'The deal is done. I trust you and you need to trust me for a second. This won't take long, so don't struggle. I've got you well secured with my belt and if you move around I'll be forced to pull the belt tighter.'

'No!' Jason ignored the instruction and wriggled and yanked down, putting all his weight on his arm. It was no good. 'Don't hurt me!'

'I'm afraid there will be a little pain.' A hand tugged at his wrist and then a sharp pinch came just below the second joint of his pinkie. 'You see somebody has stolen one of Smirker's fingers and I promised I'd find him a replacement.'

'Noooooo!'

'Hold still will you?' Crunch. 'There we go!'

Jason screamed as something sliced through his little finger. Even with the pain, he noticed the sensation of the warm blood flowing over his hand. He yelled again.

'Don't be such a crybaby. Keep still, I'm going to clean you up.'

Up above, the man was doing something to Jason's disfigured hand, applying some sort of dressing, but Jason could hardly focus. He hung on his arm, thrashing around and screaming and screaming and screaming until a wash of nausea overcame him. He vomited over himself and then, mercifully, he slipped into unconsciousness.

Chapter Eighteen

Another Friday. I no longer look forward to the weekends since I discovered what Bentley is up to. He visits once or twice a month, but for the boys that is all too often. Especially for Jason, who's his favourite. The lad has gone downhill recently. He's lost weight and is sullen and withdrawn. Liam tries to buoy him up, but I don't think it makes much difference.

The routine is pretty much set in stone now. Bentley arrives and if my mother is here he spends an hour or two with her while Father retreats to the downstairs living room. After Bentley has finished with Mother he heads for the cellar and waits while one of the staff members fetches his choice of boy. By this time I'm already in place at the airbrick. As much as I hate it, I force myself to watch. Tonight it wasn't Jason and I breathed a sigh of relief as Bentley set to work.

The man is something else. At first I thought it was his size and strength which gave him his power, but his physicality is only part of his presence. The power comes from within, a self-belief which makes him feel he has a right to take whatever he desires.

And why not?

The boys have nothing society wants. No one cares about them. When they go to the village shop, the postmistress hovers hawk-like. 'No more than two of you in here at a time,' she

says. Parents in the playground pull their little ones away.
When something is damaged or goes missing, the finger is
pointed towards the home. A policeman comes and gives a
lecture, a talking-to. A clip round the ear isn't unheard of.

I think Bentley plays on this sense of isolation. I heard him
whisper to the boys that they were special, that he loved them,
that he wanted to look after them. Everyone else thinks them
runts, dregs, outcasts or delinquents, but he calls them his
treasures. Treasure is valuable, the boys know, treasure is worth
something.

So why not?

Father and the rest of the staff are all in on it and there
doesn't seem to be anyone who can do anything to help.

I guess that means it's down to me.

The Shepherd stands outside the barn and listens to the last
of the bell's tones fading into the night. Sunday – *God's day*
– is here. He needs to get to work.

Inside, he moves to the cells and stands in front of the
doors for a moment. The choice hasn't been an easy one to
make but Benedict's looking weak. Given the age and state
of the man, he could well die before he faces justice. That
would never do.

'It is time,' the Shepherd says as he slides back the two
bolts and opens the door. 'Time for you to face the altar.'

Inside, the hunched form of Benedict stirs. The man
straightens and then begins to stand.

'No,' Benedict says. 'Please, have mercy.'

'Mercy?' The Shepherd pulls the Taser into view and fires
the weapon at close range. The barbs strike Benedict in the
side and there is a burst of electricity. Benedict reels backwards and falls to the floor quivering. 'There's no mercy
here. Feel the power of the Lord God Almighty!'

As he enters the cell, Benedict is having some kind of fit, his arms and legs jerking back and forth. The Shepherd doesn't care. He kneels beside Benedict and rolls the man over.

'The kindness of our Lord is a wondrous thing,' he says as he works. 'Forgiveness, penance, and the promise of His love. Who could want for more?'

Benedict has regained some form of consciousness now. The twitching stops and the Shepherd lifts him to his feet. Benedict rises meekly, as if under some kind of spell or hypnosis. The Shepherd pushes Benedict from the cell and down the long corridor. He slides open the metal door and his voice echoes in the vast chamber.

'Behold, God's altar. Shortly you will prove to Him you are repentant and then you will receive the gift of everlasting life.'

Benedict's knees buckle at the sight of the huge machine, but the Shepherd pushes him forward. He moves him to the stainless steel table and stands him before it.

'You must mount the altar yourself,' the Shepherd says. 'Your penance must be voluntary for the act to have any meaning.'

'What?' Benedict looks at the Shepherd, his eyes only half open. Then he understands. 'No, I won't. I've done nothing wrong.'

The Shepherd sighs. He was expecting this. Luckily the barbs from the Taser are still embedded in Benedict's side, the wires curling to the weapon. The Shepherd operates the trigger and God's pure force courses through Benedict once more.

This time the Shepherd catches the man and slides him onto the altar, face to heaven. Benedict twitches and then is still.

'Put your hands in the shackles.' The Shepherd speaks flatly and this time Benedict complies in a daze. The hasps close automatically around Benedict's wrists, a second set clamping his ankles. 'So, we are ready. Do you, Tim Benedict, have anything to say?'

'Please!' Benedict shouts, the meekness gone. 'Why are you doing this?'

'You don't know your crime, do you?' The Shepherd is disappointed. How can Benedict repent if he doesn't understand what he has done? 'Cast your mind back and examine your conscience.'

'I . . . I . . .' Benedict shakes his head. 'No, my conscience is clear. I don't know who you are, but I'm sure I've done nothing to harm you.'

'Really? Remember your days as a curate over near Salcombe? Somebody came to you but you ignored their plea for help. Just like the priest in the parable of the Good Samaritan, you passed by on the other side of the road.'

'Passed by . . .? I wouldn't. Never.' Benedict begins to shake his head again. Then he stops. His mouth drops open. 'Oh God, no!'

'Oh God, yes.' The Shepherd leans over Benedict. 'You pretended to have faith and swore to serve God but you became corrupted by evil. You took an oath to protect the meek and the mild but caused untold suffering. Now you too must suffer.'

'I couldn't know! Please forgive me. The bishop told me to keep quiet.'

'And you, being a coward, obeyed.' The Shepherd places his face close to Benedict's. 'I *hate* cowards.'

'Please forgive me!'

'Forgiveness is not for me to give. You, of all people, should know that. God is the arbiter here.'

178

'Yeeesss! Of course!' Benedict's voice is almost a scream. 'Forgive me, God. I have sinned, but I beg for forgiveness. Please, I know I did wrong, but I'll make amends, I promise I will.'

'Good. God has heard your plea and now we'll see what He thinks of it.'

'Thank you. Thank God!' The emotion in Benedict's voice is palpable.

The Shepherd turns from Benedict and walks away, his heels clicking on the concrete floor as he leaves the chamber. He closes the sliding door and locks it. Then he stands next to a large red button on the wall. The button starts the countdown sequence and sets things in motion. Once pressed nothing can stop it. The Shepherd's been waiting for this, waiting for the day when the wrongs could start to be set right. He pauses for a moment and then reaches out and pushes the button.

He nods to himself and then moves down the corridor and enters a small room. There's a desk and chair, a computer and monitor on the desk. The monitor shows Benedict lying on the stainless steel altar, his voice coming through the speakers.

'Hello?' Benedict struggles against his bonds. 'I thought I was forgiven? When are you going to set me free?'

The Shepherd sits at the desk and leans forward. He pulls a microphone from one side of the monitor and speaks, his voice booming out through a powerful PA system.

'You *are* forgiven, Tim. God loves you and soon you will know that love.'

'Hey?'

'But first you must be punished. And the punishment must fit the crime. Are you ready to perform your penance?'

'What? I don't understand.'

179

'Never mind. Now make your peace with God.'

'No!' A shout comes from Benedict and now the man is blubbering. 'Please noooooo!'

'GOD IS WITH YOU, BENEDICT! FEEL HIS LOVE FOR YOU!' The Shepherd's voice echoes throughout the building. 'OPEN YOUR HEART TO HIM AND LET HIS SPIRIT FILL YOU!'

'Noooooo!' Along with Benedict's pleas, a mechanical noise is growing in intensity, the man's voice barely audible against the clatter of metal. 'Noooooo!'

The Shepherd moves the mouse and clicks and a burst of organ music blares out. He begins to sing, the words resounding through every room in the barn.

'THE LORD'S MY SHEPHERD, I'LL NOT WANT. HE MAKES ME DOWN TO LIE. IN PASTURES GREEN HE LEADETH ME. THE QUIET WATERS BY.'

In the chamber, pieces of machinery are moving, a huge hydraulic arms hisses into action, an electric saw begins to revolve, a drill spins up to speed and lowers. Over it all the sound of Benedict screaming.

Chapter Nineteen

Near Bolberry, South Hams, Devon. Sunday 25th October.
8.35 a.m.

Savage returned to Woodland Heights first thing Sunday morning. Overnight developments in the *Curlew* case had come in an email sent by Nesbit late on Saturday. The pathologist's few short words brought a whole lot of consequences for the investigation: the bone from the cellar was definitely human and what's more it belonged to a child.

A child.

Whether the bone belonged to Liam Hayskith or Jason Caldwell didn't matter. *Curlew* had now become a murder investigation.

She parked up and strolled across to where a patrol car sat on the gravel track near the front steps, the officers inside bleary-eyed from overnight guard duty.

'All quiet?' Savage asked as one of the officers slid down his window.

'As the proverbial, ma'am,' the officer said. He gestured to where the house stood in the grey light. 'Not a dicky bird. The seal on the cellar door's still intact. At least it was fifteen minutes ago. Can't say it was a pleasant night though.'

Savage thanked the officers and then walked over to the

entrance steps, turning as she heard a vehicle approaching. The Freelander eased into the car park and stopped. Inside, the bulky shape of DSupt Hardin remained stationary for a good minute before the door swung open and he climbed out.

The drizzle of yesterday had given way to a bank of grey cloud which hung overhead almost unmoving and Hardin lumbered over towards her, shuffling his feet as if the clouds above were pressing down on him. Not for the first time Savage wondered what was wrong. Hardin looked as if he was in a bad way. His mood didn't improve as he reached her and glanced up at the house.

'You found something then.' His eyes flicked from window to window and then to the front door. 'House of horrors.'

'Yes, sir. Nesbit sent this through.' Savage pulled out her phone and handed it to Hardin. 'It's a computer reconstruction using the fragment we found. A metatarsal, apparently.'

'You mean metatarsal as in footballers?'

'Yes. Only this isn't a footballer's, it's a kid's.'

'Fuck.' Hardin stared down at the photo on the phone, almost as if he was willing the image to disappear. Nothing doing; after a few seconds he handed the phone back and looked at Savage. 'So, who's in the frame for this? The owner? Staff? I need something, Charlotte. You know how it is. Heldon will want this to end quickly. The force doesn't need any more publicity, not so soon after the stuff with Simon Fox.'

'The situation is complicated, sir. We don't have much to go on. To my mind it looks as if there was a body, or bodies, buried under the concrete shortly after the two boys went missing. However, somebody returned to the scene recently and dug up the remains. They did a pretty good job at removing everything.'

'Apart from that.' Hardin pointed at Savage's phone and then shook his head. 'Problems we don't need.'

'Sir? Where are you going with this? I don't understand.'

'To be honest, I hoped we weren't going anywhere with it. Dredging up old memories, old bitterness, never pleasant.'

'Those two boys were probably murdered. It's likely there was widespread abuse going on at the children's home. Are you saying we should just forget those crimes?'

'Not at all. If I'd wanted that I'd have made sure somebody else was on the case. I know you, you're tenacious, once you get the scent something is wrong you don't give up. I was just hoping you wouldn't find anything.'

'Well I have. *We* have. This can't be put back in the bottle now. A piece of the bone has gone off for DNA analysis. Of course, we don't have any DNA for Liam Hayskith or Jason Caldwell, but we can match them through familial relationships. We'll know within a day or two what we're dealing with here, but either way this is almost certainly murder. *Somebody* was buried in the cellar. Whether or not it was one of the two boys doesn't really matter.'

'No.' Hardin said nothing for a few seconds. He delved in his inside jacket pocket and half pulled out an envelope. Then he appeared to change his mind and shoved the envelope back down out of sight. He shook his head. 'You're right, of course. It doesn't matter.'

'You want to see?' Savage gestured towards the front door. 'The cellar?'

Hardin peered past her, his face creasing with a pained expression. 'Go on then, show me.'

Hardin stared down at the water bubbling up from the hole in the concrete. The water appeared black in the glare from the arc lights. A fat green hose rose from the morass to a pump by the side of the hole. The outlet hose snaked across the floor, through the doorway and up the stairs. Despite the pump's best efforts, it couldn't keep up with the flow and one end of the cellar was flooded to a depth of several inches.

'Layton says there's a spring down there,' Savage said. 'If we're going to dig up the rest of the cellar we'll need specialised equipment.'

'Whatever.' The DSupt bit his lip and continued to gaze into the pool of ink as if the bubbles rising to the surface might tell him the story of what had happened years before.

'As I said, there's just one bone so far.' Savage looked around at the cellar, but Hardin seemed interested only in the hole. He's miles away, she thought. Lost in the past, possibly blaming himself for what happened. 'You couldn't have done anything, could you, sir? I mean everyone was convinced they'd run away.'

'Yes.' Hardin shook his head, the movement not matching his answer. His tongue poked over his bottom lip and he sighed. Then he moved over to one side of the cellar, sat down on one of Layton's plastic crates and put his head in his hands.

'Conrad?' Savage whispered Hardin's first name. She hardly ever addressed him like that, but something was very wrong. 'You can tell me, sir.'

'I was here, Charlotte.' Hardin looked up. 'Woodland Heights.'

'I don't understand? I know you were here.'

'The day after the boys went missing. Me and a lad from Kingsbridge nick. We came up to the home in a squad car to assist the detectives from Plymouth. There was a right flap on. Search and rescue crews along the coast, Plymouth and Salcombe lifeboats out at sea, volunteers scouring the nearby fields.' Hardin shook his head again. 'I thought I was unlucky, but that's nothing compared to what happened to these boys.'

184

'Unlucky?' Savage said. 'But you didn't find anything, did you?'

'I'm not talking about when the boys went missing. I mean before.'

'Before?'

'A few weeks before. There was some vandalism in the nearby village. Graffiti. Lewd stuff. Residents pointed the finger at the home. I was the local PC so I went to investigate. I questioned some of the boys but they were tight-lipped, wouldn't give anything away. I'd cycled out here and propped my bike round the side. When I got back to my bicycle, I found this stuffed under the rear mudguard.' Hardin reached into his jacket and pulled out the envelope he'd been fiddling with earlier. 'Back at the station I took a photocopy before I handed it over.'

Hardin opened the envelope and extracted a piece of paper. He held it out for Savage. She moved across and peered down, tilting the paper to examine it in the light from the halogens. It was a copy of a photograph and of low quality. Still, she could make out the image well enough: two men sitting in armchairs. A half-finished bottle of whisky on a small table between them. A clock on the wall. One of the men was a much younger Frank Parker, the other instantly recognisable to anybody who knew much about politics.

'He's dead, sir, isn't he? But I still don't understand. I know who these two men are – Parker and the politician – but what's the picture got to do with the disappearance of the boys?'

'That photograph was taken in the little snug upstairs. In the Parkers' apartment. He was visiting.'

'And that was a problem?'

'The man from Special Branch put it exactly the same way.'

185

'Special Branch?'

'I took the picture straight to my superior, the inspector at Kingsbridge Police Station. Bernie Black.' Hardin smiled. 'He was a good copper. I thought it best to go to him. He'd know what to do.'

'And he phoned Special Branch?'

'Yes. An officer arrived the next day. He asked me why there was an issue. The man in the photograph was in the Home Office. Woodland Heights was a type of young offenders' institution. He told me there was nothing unusual about the visit.'

'And you didn't believe him?'

'If there was nothing suspicious, then why did Special Branch need to send an officer down to speak to me? And why had "HELP" been handwritten on the back of the picture?'

'Help? You think—'

'Look at the clock on the wall, Charlotte.' Hardin pointed down at the picture. 'Tell me the time.'

'Half past three. I still don't . . .' Savage examined the photograph again. Whisky. A slab of cheese on a board. Some crackers on a plate. 'An afternoon snack?'

'The window.'

Savage looked to one side of the image. A sash window, curtains open and drawn to each side. And through the window she could see nothing but black.

'Night-time,' Hardin said. 'In the original, which was much better quality, the time of day was obvious. To my mind there could only be one reason for the man to be there relaxing in the early hours of the morning.'

'And you put this to the man from Special Branch?'

'No. He took the photograph and assured me there was nothing wrong. Ordered me to say no more of the affair, not even to my superiors. Back then I was just a young PC and all this abuse stuff hadn't come out.'

'But now?'

'The man in the picture's dead, isn't he? And presumably the powers that be up in London know all about him.'

'I wouldn't be so sure, sir.'

'Do you think I did wrong, Charlotte?' Hardin reached for the piece of paper and put it back in the envelope. 'I was obeying orders. The wife and I, well, she'd just had the nipper. We had a house with a mortgage. Money was tight. When the boys went missing, I asked Bernie Black about the photograph again. I remember his face, stern, troubled. "In hand" he told me and I left it at that. I made a mistake, didn't I?'

'I don't know, sir. You were—'

'Naive. That's the word. I assumed the chain of command worked. That the people at the top knew what they were doing.'

'They do, sir.' Savage half smiled. 'Sometimes.'

After the confines of the cellar, they escaped outside and walked westward along the coast path and away from the home. The clouds had slipped away and now a weak sun moved steadily higher, promising a fine day. The light lit up Hardin's face and Savage could see he was still burdened by something.

'There's more, sir, isn't there?' Savage said as they reached a viewpoint. To one side of the path a railway sleeper perched atop two large stones. She gestured at the makeshift bench. 'Shall we?'

Hardin lowered himself onto the bench and Savage sat beside him.

'I must get out here more often, Charlotte.' He looked at Savage for a moment and then swept his arm in the direction of the sea. 'Not here, not Woodland Heights. I mean the coast. I sit in my little bungalow with the missus. We're quite happy. We go to the shops, take a walk in the park, have a night out from time to time. But we don't do this.'

'I know what you mean, sir. We don't appreciate what's right on our doorstep, do we?'

'I used to like being a PC in this area. Exploring the countryside. It used to be a gentler way of life out here. At least that's what I thought until I saw the photograph. It unsettled me and after the boys disappeared I wasn't the same. I applied to be a detective and moved into Plymouth. I wanted to bang heads.'

'I can understand. That's the way I felt too.'

'About Clarissa?' Hardin shifted his gaze from the sea to Savage. Raised an eyebrow. 'Oh yes, Charlotte, I can read you better than you think. And I know more than you think, too.'

'More?' Savage swallowed, wondering exactly what Hardin meant. Did he know about Matthew Harrison, the serial killer she'd left to burn alive in his upturned car? Or was it Simon Fox and his son Hardin was hinting at? Savage had put a gun to Owen's head and had been close to pulling the trigger. 'Are you talking about—'

'Never mind.' Hardin raised a hand and jerked his thumb back in the direction of the children's home. 'There's more pressing business, and if you've been concealing things from me, then I'm guilty of the same. You're right, there *is* something else.'

'About Woodland Heights?'

'Indirectly.' Hardin paused and reached into his jacket again. This time he pulled out a couple of sheets of paper, flowing handwriting on one, some sort of drawing on the other. 'I received these letters. The first one came the day Jason went missing. That's Jason Hobb, not Jason Caldwell. The second came last Thursday. It was the second letter, along

188

with the coincidence with the names, which spurred me to action. I knew then I needed to investigate Woodland Heights. Of course, when I assigned you to the case, I had no idea what you would find. The letters could well have been a hoax.'

Savage took the pieces of paper from Hardin and read through. The first letter was plain weird, filled with descriptions of abuse and violence. Towards the end there were a number of accusations aimed at Hardin. Something about the DSupt not doing his duty, of overlooking crimes committed.

'So the letter writer is blaming you for the disappearance of the boys?' she said. 'Because nothing happened to stop the abuse after you received the photograph?'

Hardin shrugged. 'I guess so.'

She moved to the second piece of paper and shook her head as she took in the information. The drawings were unambiguous. 'A box? So Jason Hobb *is* still alive?'

'I've no idea,' Hardin said. 'We can only pray.'

'I'm struggling to get my head around this, sir. You suggested to me that the names of the two sets of boys being the same was no coincidence and these letters prove it, right?'

'Yes.'

'But you've had this one since Thursday.' Savage waved the second letter. 'You knew Jason Hobb was alive but you did nothing to try and save him.'

'That's not fair, Charlotte. You've seen the picture with the government minister. The letters may well have been part of some prank. I needed to be sure before I took this any further. There are consequences.'

'Consequences?' Savage pushed herself to her feet and walked away a few paces. She turned back to Hardin. 'Jesus! Of course there are fucking consequences. You've probably signed Jason Hobb's death warrant. What the hell were you thinking?'

'Operation *Lacuna* hasn't wanted for resources. We've thrown everything at it.'

'Yes, but these letters are *evidence*. Who knows where the investigation would be now had Garrett and the team had sight of them last week. You've put personal issues before operational ones. That's bang out of order, sir.'

'Really? And you've never done that?' Hardin shook his head. 'I remember telling you once about a line one shouldn't cross. My advice fell on deaf ears, didn't it?'

'I did what was bloody right at the time.' Savage spat out the words. She realised she was getting dangerously close to being insubordinate. 'I never compromised anyone's safety the way you've done.'

'Matthew Harrison?'

'Harrison deserved to die. You can't compare him to Jason Hobb. To be honest, sir, you're in a whole lot more trouble than I ever was.'

'Thanks for your candid assessment, Charlotte, but what's done is done. Right now we need to focus on what went on here and see if the historical case can help us find Jason.'

'What about the man in the picture? The minister?'

'Heldon. This will be in her in-tray first thing tomorrow morning.'

'And if she behaves in the same manner as your old boss, Bernie Black?'

'I don't want to think about that possibility.' Hardin shrugged and shook his head. 'Because if she does, then I reckon we've lost. Not just you and I, but all of us. The whole bloody human race.'

Chapter Twenty

Well, I tried my best. I didn't dare approach Father or Mother because I'm pretty sure they wouldn't do anything. Bentley has so much control over the both of them that I can't see either would betray him. Instead, I went to the village to see my friend Perry. He's a year older than me and he's clever and wise. I told Perry about Father and Bentley and the things which went on in the cellar. I asked him to tell his parents. He seemed unsure, but eventually he agreed he would.

The following week I was summoned to Father's office. He said he was disappointed with me for spreading lies and gossip. I wasn't to leave the home without permission nor to speak to any of the boys in the village. I wasn't to see Perry again. He also said I would receive discipline. Ten strokes of the cane each day for the next week.

Perry, it seemed, had let me down.

A few days later I summoned up the courage to speak to the new curate. He comes to the home and runs a Sunday school. There's a short service and then the boys have to study the Bible. Mr Benedict always seemed like a nice man to me, so on Sunday, as he was leaving, I followed him as he went down the front steps. I walked with him across the fields and as we strolled I told him about Bentley.

He was very concerned. At the gate he said the matter was

extremely serious and he would talk to me on the following Sunday. The week went by and after Sunday school was over I once again walked with Mr Benedict. He said he'd thought long and hard about the matter. He'd even approached the bishop. I could see he was uneasy and somewhat reticent. When I pressed him as to what to do, he told me the solution was to pray. I was to pray for myself and all the boys and to pray for Bentley and Mother and Father too. My prayers would be answered, he assured me. It might take some time, but God would see to it that everything turned out OK in the end.

So I tried praying, honestly I did. I prayed in the evening before I went to bed. I prayed in the morning when I woke. I prayed in break time when I was at school. I ended up praying ALL THE BLOODY TIME! Not one prayer was answered. Every weekend Jason was being dragged down to the cellar with Bentley. Either God wasn't listening or He didn't care.

By this time I was exasperated. Then, this morning, I saw a bicycle parked at the bottom of the front steps. I recognised the bike as belonging to a local policeman, PC Hardin. It turned out he'd come because of some minor incident in the village. For a moment I thought to speak to him exactly as I'd spoken to Tim Benedict. Then I remembered the caning. If Father found out, the ten strokes a day would be nothing. I needed to try another way.

In the dining room in our private apartment there's a display of photographs relating to the home. The day Bentley came for that first visit. Some pictures of various old boys. One of Father shaking hands with some local dignitary. The photographs are in a glass display cabinet above the sideboard. Mother insisted on the cabinet because there are dozens of photos and she was fed up of them cluttering up the room. The one of Bentley standing on the front steps isn't the only one of him. There's another taken in the little snug. Bentley and Father sitting in armchairs. I think Mother must have taken the picture. You'd think with the things Bentley has done Father would remove all evidence of the man, especially such a personal picture. But Father's vain. He hates Bentley but he likes the kudos the man has. Besides, this particular photograph is tucked round the back. I expect my parents have quite forgotten it's there.

I went to the dining room and retrieved the photograph. On the back I wrote one word: 'HELP'. Then I took the picture and slipped it under the mudguard of the policeman's bicycle.

It's late now. Past midnight. I'm writing this beneath the covers using my little torch for light. For the first time in a long while I'm hopeful. You see, I think PC Hardin's a good man. He talks to the boys here as if he cares. Once he gave us an interesting lecture all about police work, about how crimes are solved. At the end of the lecture he told us how he wanted to become a detective.

Well, now's his chance.

The Shepherd isn't happy. After singing Psalm 23 to Benedict he'd headed outside to get some fresh air, leaving the altar working away. A nearby tor had been tempting and he'd walked and clambered his way up, kneeling at the very top and raising his face towards heaven where the stars shone with a brilliance like diamonds. He prayed for guidance and then went back to the farmyard, got in his car and drove home, leaving Benedict in the arms of God.

He'd slept fitfully, a bad dream troubling his sleep.

In the morning, upon returning to the barn, he'd realised why. The altar had stopped working. The nightmare had been a message from God telling him something was wrong.

Now, the Shepherd stands next to the stainless steel table and stares down at Tim Benedict. The man is still alive when he should be lifeless and long dead. His body is a mess of cuts and drill holes. Blood is oozing from a dozen wounds. Yet he is still breathing.

A miracle.

That's all it can be, the Shepherd thinks. Then he looks up at the gantry overhead. A broken belt hangs loose. The belt has fallen and jammed in one of the hydraulic rams. The machine has shut itself down to prevent further damage.

Not a miracle, a malfunction.

For a moment the Shepherd wonders about fixing the belt and starting all over again. But that wouldn't be what God wanted, would it? God had seen fit to allow the belt to break. God had stopped the machine. God had sent a message to the Shepherd in the form of a bad dream. God had forgiven Benedict.

Now the Shepherd is confused. Forgiveness isn't something he's factored into his plans. People need to be punished.

The man with the skull . . .

Yes, of course. Forgiveness for the boy who digs in the grubby soil would be unthinkable.

The Shepherd sighs. This isn't what he wants at all. Still, if God has willed it, who is he to argue?

He shakes his head and begins to tidy up. He releases the manacles holding Benedict's arms and legs. Then he goes over to the far side of the room where there is a large green council bin. He wheels the bin across to one side of the table. There's a gurgle from Benedict as the Shepherd heaves the body into the bin. The body goes in head first, but the man's shoulders are too wide. Where the bin narrows about halfway down, the body becomes jammed. The Shepherd tips the bin back and forth in the hope the sheer weight of the body will cause it to sink down further.

The Shepherd steps back. The scene is faintly ridiculous. The legs are poking out from the top of the bin, the left hanging one way and the right the other. This won't do. He needs to transport the body to the sea. He looks around and spots a number of heavy fence posts leaning against the back wall of the barn. He goes across, selects the meatiest, and returns to the bin. He clambers up onto the altar and then begins to use the post as a battering ram.

Benedict gurgles again as the Shepherd bashes down with the fence post, pounding the body until bit by bit he pushes the whole bloody pulp down into the bin.

There, job done. God may have seen fit to stop the machine halfway through the cycle, but, the Shepherd thinks, justice has still been well and truly served.

Chapter Twenty-One

Monday morning and Riley was wondering how much longer he'd have to spend on the Sleet/Benedict case. Both men were missing, sure, but there'd been no new developments over the weekend. The Taser confetti at Benedict's house and on the road near Sleet's car suggested a crime had been committed, but there was little else. Nothing had come from the forensic analysis of the car nor the search of the surrounding moorland. He'd had a preliminary response from Taser International in the US, but even that wasn't good news: the original purchaser had sold the weapon on several years ago and it didn't appear to have been re-registered. The paper trail was dead. With that avenue of investigation closed, was there enough evidence to continue to investigate? So far his lurid thoughts on the journey back from North Devon had proved unfounded and the threatened violence implied by the disfigured mannequin didn't appear to have been carried out.

As he sat at his desk staring at his screen, Riley allowed his mind to wander. Up to now they'd had a couple of lucky strokes on the case: Phillips miraculously spotting that Tim Benedict's and Perry Sleet's initials matched the ones on the box on the raft; his own realisation about the vacuum cleaner and the good fortune the machine hadn't been emptied. Luck, though, could only get you so far; what they desperately needed was a decent lead. And a decent lead, short of tracing the mysterious Sarah, felt a very long way off.

He glanced across to where Gareth Collier was badgering the two young DCs working on the pet grooming parlour drugs investigation. Riley wanted to get back to the case. That was a chance to bash some lowlifes and, just possibly, take out one or two of the main dealers too. He pushed himself to his feet, intent on having a word with the office manager. He'd suggest spending the rest of the day on the Sleet and Benedict case and then shelving it.

Riley went over to Collier and was about to interject when Enders came through the double doors at speed. He narrowly avoided colliding with DC Calter who was carrying three cups of coffee across the room.

'Steady, tiger,' Calter said. 'I paid good money for these.'

'Tim Benedict!' Enders shouted across to Riley, almost breathless. 'He's turned up.'

'Where?' Riley said.

'The River Erme. You know, up from Mothecombe Beach?'

Riley shook his head. He didn't know. It was left to Enders to explain the river lay a little way west of Bigbury-on-Sea, a few miles south of the town of Modbury.

'There's a long lane which leads from the village of Holbeton down to the estuary. The estate manager for the Flete Estate spotted a car parked near the bottom. He didn't recognise the car so went to check. He walked down to the water and saw a raft with a bloke in a ski mask doing something with a wheelie bin.'

'A raft?'

'Yes.'

'So Dan Phillips was right.'

'Yes. Anyway, the estate manager figured somebody was fly-tipping, so he shouted out. The man ran off, so the manager investigated the wheelie bin. Would you believe, Benedict was inside?'

'*Inside?*' Riley shook his head, not liking where this was going. 'Are you telling me he's dead?'

'No, sir.' Enders cast a glance heavenward. 'He's critically ill, but by some miracle he's still alive.'

'Still alive' was a relative term. Tim Benedict had been rushed to Derriford Hospital and was now in the ICU.

'Not surprised he needs intensive care,' Enders said as Riley drove them east towards the Erme estuary. 'He was head down in the bin and half drowned in his own blood.'

'What?' Riley took his eyes from the road just long enough to stare at Enders, but the DC shrugged. Said he didn't know any more than what he'd been told.

'Here!' Enders gestured off the main road as they came up fast on a turning, a little lodge house on the right. 'Holbeton's that way.'

They turned off and followed a tortuous route up a hill and through patches of woodland and lanes with high banks and gnarly old hedges. Then they slowed and entered a pretty village with a pub and a post office and not much else. They took a lane which passed between thatched cottages and the village primary school. Once they were out of the village, Riley pressed his foot down again even though the road narrowed further. The lane wound this way and that down a valley and into woodland, the first sign they might be approaching the estuary, a huge bed of rushes on their left.

Riley slowed as they approached a gate in the road, a sign on a fence to one side warning the area beyond was a private estate. In a pull-in sat a pickup truck, a patrol car and John Layton's Volvo. Two uniformed officers were standing with a man in a green Barbour.

Riley stopped the car and got out. Layton had already gone on down to the scene, one of the officers explained.

'Quite a sight.' The officer nodded to the man in the Barbour. 'As Mr Johnson here will tell you.'

Johnson, the man in the Barbour, was mid-fifties with a weathered face, bushy eyebrows and a calm manner. Beneath the coat he wore a chunky sweater, combat trousers and stout boots. Every now and then he stomped one or other of his feet down in the mud to emphasise a point.

'Adam,' he said, extending a hand to Riley. 'Estate manager.'

Riley shook the man's hand. 'Sorry to make you go through it again, but can you tell me what you found?'

'Eight this morning I was doing my regular round. See, I like to take a circuitous route into the estate office and check everything looks OK. Anyway, I'd come down from Holbeton – the way you just did – and was about to turn north up the estuary when I spotted a car parked just beyond the gate here. By rights it shouldn't have been there so I thought I'd take a look. I walked down towards the water and on the foreshore I spotted this bloody great contraption on top of which was this bloke in a ski mask wrestling with a wheelie bin. Never seen anything like it.'

'So what did you do then?'

'First thing I thought was this idiot was dumping something. Fly-tipping. I ran along the track and shouted at him. As soon as he heard me he jumped off the platform and began running towards me with this thing in his hand. A Taser, I think you call it. I know a thing or two about weapons and I knew the Taser didn't have a great range so I left the track and went a little way into the woods. He ran past me to his car. I gave chase, but he drove off. Didn't think there was much point in following in my vehicle so I went back to the water to see what was in the bin. Soon as I saw the guy inside, I ran back to my car and used one of the estate walkie-talkies to call the office and told them to phone for an ambulance. No mobile coverage down here, see?' Johnson shook his head. 'Then I went back to the bin. Christ, I wish I hadn't. That poor bloke. He was making this goddamn awful wheezing sound but I couldn't do anything for him but wait until the ambulance came.'

Johnson shook his head again, stomped his feet and stared down at the ground. Riley thanked the man and told him he could go. Somebody would take a full statement later.

'One other thing,' Johnson said, stopping halfway to his pickup. 'Not sure if it's relevant or not, but while I was waiting for the ambulance I was standing up on the raft. I could see a couple of hundred yards downstream and there was this pot boat drifting about in the deeper water. Little fifteen-footer with a small cuddy and a load of dan buoys sticking up at the back, a rough-looking chap with a beard and a roll-neck fisherman's sweater just standing and staring at me.'

'So?'

'Up here? You wouldn't place a lobster pot this far up. Not if you want to catch anything.'

'And the boat – what happened to it?'

'Disappeared round the corner.' Johnson turned his palms face up. 'Might be nothing, but I thought you should know. The guy might well be a witness.'

Riley thanked Johnson again and then retrieved his wellies from the boot of his car. He put them on and then stood for a moment.

'What are you thinking, sir?' Enders said. 'Something to do with that fisherman?'

'Johnson said this guy might be a witness.' Riley turned and looked through the trees towards the estuary. 'I'm thinking it's more likely he's an accomplice.'

Come Monday, Savage found she was back on the *Lacuna* case. DCI Garrett had been struggling with a severe flu bug over the weekend, which gave Hardin the excuse he needed to make her deputy SIO and shift the DCI to something less taxing.

'Can't having Mike popping his clogs on his last month,' Hardin said. 'Besides, we now know these investigations are linked. You'll bring your knowledge of the children's home side of things into the hunt for Liam Clough's killer and the search for Jason Hobb.'

Savage nodded. She'd become so wound up in the mystery surrounding Woodland Heights that she'd almost forgotten about the Clough boy. Now the memory of the body came back to her. The poor kid lying in the dark tunnel. Asphyxiated. Did the same fate await Jason Hobb? She gave an involuntary shiver, excited to be back on the case but nervous of the outcome.

She went to the crime suite to review the entire operation. Collier had done his best, but as she looked through the policy book with him, she was shocked at how little the investigation had proceeded over the past few days. As SIO, Hardin should have been pushing the investigation forward, but there was a distinct lack of leadership evident. She wondered if, due to his personal connection to the case, he was up to the job.

'Crap, right?' Collier said. 'But you can't really blame Hardin or Garrett. The only real forensic lead was the grease on Liam Clough's body. Came back from the lab that it was

201

a Castrol car grease. Could have come from a garage, but you can buy the stuff at Halfords. Dead end.'

'Anyone have any suggestions as to why the killer smeared it over the boy?'

'No, Charlotte.' Collier looked at Savage as if she should know better than to ask. 'He's a fucking nutter, isn't he? Nothing these loons do makes sense.'

'Clough wasn't sexually assaulted, otherwise I'd say it was some kind of sex game. Still, you don't go to the trouble of preparing the body like that unless it means something.'

'Well, it beats me. The other problem is we've found no connection between the disappearance of Hobb and the murder of Clough. To be honest, without that, we're floundering.'

'Try these.' Savage pulled out photocopies of the letters Hardin had given her and put them on the desk. 'I think they might help.'

As Collier examined the letters, Savage explained about Operation *Curlew* and what was going on over at the children's home. She told him about the history of the place and her interviews with the Parkers and Elijah Samuel. For now, under orders from Hardin, she left out the exact details of the picture taken at the home.

'It's not surprising you found no link between the boys because there is none,' she said. 'They were chosen by chance. If Liam had been named Paul and Jason called John they'd still be alive.'

'So this nutter's only motive was to draw attention to the children's home?'

'Looks that way.'

'But he's something to do with the home, am I reading that right?'

'He must be.'

'Then we might be getting somewhere. You see, Ned Stone was a resident at the home for a short time.'

'*What?*'

'Yes. Only for a few months, and a year or so before the disappearance of Hayskith and Caldwell. He was eleven years old at the time and went to a foster family when he left.'

'When did you discover this?'

'It only came to light this morning when an indexer entered all the boys who'd been resident since the home opened in the seventies. The computer spat out the match.'

'If he wasn't before, he must now be the number one suspect. Any news on his whereabouts?'

'No. We've got a list of his friends and associates and they've all had multiple visits. Not a dicky bird so far. Problem is his mates are not exactly amenable to cooperation.'

'Well, finding him is a priority. This simply isn't good enough, Gareth. We should be on top of everything by now. We need to trace and eliminate the rest of the boys and staff and then concentrate on Stone.'

'In hand.' Collier gestured over to one corner of the room where a couple of civilian researchers were working hard, heads down over their keyboards. 'I've already got a full list of names from the council of everyone connected with the home and we're going through them now.'

'Good. Next, we need a plan for finding Stone.'

'Right.' Collier was silent. Something was bugging him. After a moment he jabbed a finger down at the copies of Hardin's letters. 'But do you think Ned Stone wrote these?'

Savage looked at the letters too. The spaghetti-like writing was beautiful while at the same time had a touch of madness about it. Huge letters curled back on themselves with unnecessary flourishes and unfathomable squiggles. In contrast, the plan and elevation showing the coffin-box had been done in pencil. Neat perpendicular lines spanned the page. Areas of shading had been painstakingly hatched in. Each element had been shown in fine detail and overall the drawings were a work of perfection. They'd been created by somebody with draughting skills. An architect or somebody who'd studied technical drawing at least.

'What's your point, Gareth?' Savage said.

'Neither letter seems like anything Stone could have produced.' Collier paused and looked first at the letters and then at Savage. 'And if Stone didn't write these . . .' He left the sentence hanging and shook his head.

'Somebody else did,' Savage said.

Riley left Enders with the officers and walked down the track, heading for a slash of beach visible through the trees. Layton had already run out several lengths of blue and white tape to ensure no one used the little path at the edge of the estuary, so Riley was forced to make his way through the undergrowth. Brambles snagged at the legs of his trousers and more than once a low branch caught him in the face. At the bankside he clambered down onto soft sand. The estuary was a couple of hundred metres wide and the water curled seaward in two distinct streams. Between the streams, the raft lay marooned on a sandbank and atop the raft, lying on its side, was a green wheelie bin.

'Darius.' John Layton, fully suited in a white coverall with blue bootlets and gloves, was on his hands and knees on the raft beside the bin. He shouted across. 'We've got a right mess in here. Come and take a gander. To the left of the tape, please.'

Riley moved to the water's edge, paused for a second, and then waded in.

'Bloody hell!' Cold water rushed up the sides of his wellies and several dollops found their way inside. 'Give me a simple shooting in a nice dry London tenement any day of the week.'

'Stinking of piss and with the local youth chucking stuff at you?' Layton waved his hand at the surroundings. 'Prefer this little paradise with the fresh sea air and utter tranquillity myself, but each to his own.'

Layton was correct about the tranquillity. The estuary ran between banks of woodland set on steep hillside, the sandy strip disappearing round a bend a few hundred metres away. Tranquil didn't begin to describe the isolated nature of the place. There was nothing here. Aside from the raft, the only thing attributable to humans was an aircraft contrail drifting in the sky.

'Footprints?' Riley waded across the stream and stepped out onto the sandbank. A series of deep indentations ran from one side of the raft into the water.

'Yes, but the outlines are blurred. Won't get much from them, I'm afraid.' Layton pointed at a pile of wood on the raft beside the wheelie bin. 'Still, there's more than enough here.'

'He was trying to assemble that?' Riley looked at the pieces of wood, something like a flat-pack wardrobe. 'A box. Exactly like the coffin thing we found on the raft at Jennycliff. The raft looks identical too.'

'Just so. He must have brought everything down here in his car – raft, barrels, the coffin and the wheelie bin. Getting the whole lot in place and putting it together would have taken a while. I reckon he started well before first light.'

'But he didn't finish the job.'

'No. I don't think he factored in the terrain. Moving all the stuff from the car to here would have been tricky. Luckily for our victim time ran out.' Layton gestured into the bin. 'Had the estate manager not come along when he did, I doubt very much he'd have been found alive.'

The bin was facing away from the bank so Riley had to

edge round in the soft sand. He bent and peered into the bin. His first impression was of a mass of dark red smeared over the sides. Down the far end, a pool of blood spread towards him and had coagulated in a frozen waterfall at the edge. In amongst the blood, little pieces of pink poked above the liquid like atolls in a red sea.

'I see what you mean.' Riley swallowed. Stared at the inside of the bin. 'I'm trying to get my head around what happened here.'

'The bin was upright when Mr Johnson found it. As soon as he realised somebody was inside, he tipped the bin over. The blood which had collected in the bottom flowed out. The man inside was, quite literally, drowning in the stuff. Mr Johnson's quick thinking saved his life.'

'This is . . .'

'Beyond belief?' Layton nodded. 'Yeah. Perhaps you're right about that tenement job you mentioned earlier.'

'Yes.' Riley straightened and gazed at the scenery for a moment, thinking there was a terrible contrast between the beautiful estuary and the awful fate of Tim Benedict. He stared down at his feet where the river gurgled around his wellingtons. Noticed the blue floats. 'The chemicals, John. The stuff in the barrels at the boatyard. These barrels look identical.'

Layton moved to the edge of the raft and peered over. 'They do, don't they?' He shook his head. 'But I haven't got the results back yet. I'll hurry the lab along.'

'Do that, would you?' Riley turned his attention back to the raft and the huge bloodstain. 'Be nice not to have to witness anything like this ever again.'

Chapter Twenty-Two

Riley was back in the station early Tuesday morning. The Benedict and Sleet case was no longer simply about a couple of mispers. The discovery of Tim Benedict in the wheelie bin had crystallised what they were dealing with and Hardin had summoned Riley to an emergency meeting. On his way to the DSupt's office he bumped into DI Savage in the corridor. Riley nodded a greeting.

'Alright, ma'am?' He stopped as Savage moved to the side and leant against a noticeboard. 'I hear your cold case has turned hot.'

'Not as hot as yours, Darius.' Savage shook her head. 'Unbelievable. Who would do such a thing?'

'At the moment we have no idea. Thing is, we've got another man missing and we could do with finding him before our nutter decides on a repeat performance.'

'Sound like our case. One dead, one missing. Only there's more than one dead now.'

'Right.' Riley wanted to stay and chat, if only because Savage looked as if she needed to unburden herself of something. There was Hardin though. Riley could imagine him pacing back and forth, glancing at his watch, and cursing. 'Got to go. Catch up later, right?'

'Sure, Darius,' Savage said. 'Good luck up there.'

Riley turned and ran down the corridor. He bounded up the stairs to the DSupt's office and knocked on the door. Hardin opened the door himself, standing there with a phone pressed to his ear. He waved Riley in and pointed at a chair facing his desk. As Riley sat, Hardin continued with his call. The conversation was distinctly one-sided, with the DSupt uttering a succession of 'Yes, ma'ams' and trying to get a word in but failing. The call over, Hardin paced back behind his desk and crashed down into his chair.

'Bloody woman.' Hardin put his mobile on the table and stared at the phone as if the device actually held the source of all his troubles. Something like a bottle with a genie inside, the stopper temporarily back in place. 'To say she's becoming a pain in the backside is an understatement. She's now decided to pay us a royal visit. At least Foxy knew when to give a man some space to think.'

Riley kept his mouth shut. Simon Fox had lost it. Become a criminal himself. As bad as Maria Heldon might be, she had nothing on the old Chief Constable.

'The vicar chappie, what's the latest?' Hardin looked at Riley, expectant.

'Tim Benedict?' Riley thought it fitting the man should at least be given a name. 'He's still in a critical condition.'

'Unconscious?'

'Yes.'

'Time frame?'

'The consultant said it's still touch-and-go. When and if Benedict regains consciousness he may well be brain damaged.'

'Bugger.' Hardin considered the phone again. He reached out and pushed the sliver of black to one side of the desk.

'As you can imagine, the CC is not in a good place right now. We've got the missing boy and the murdered kid. That would be bad enough, but this attack on the vicar is another order of magnitude more serious.'

Hardin continued. The media, he said, would be all over this. The fact Benedict was a vicar provided a tasty angle, while the attack symbolised a complete breakdown of moral values. The casual placing of Benedict in the bin only added to the horror.

'I don't think it was casual,' Riley said. 'Quite the opposite. The raft is identical to the one we found at Jennycliff. The attacker planned this and he'd have needed some skill and foresight to carry out the kidnappings and to build the raft.'

'Skill?' Hardin said. 'Whoever did this is a complete psychopath. A nutter. I've read the report on Benedict's injuries. Simply horrendous.'

Riley said nothing. Hardin didn't understand that being crazy and clever were by no means mutually exclusive.

'Now then, you've done well, Darius. Commendable work. However, from here on in I need a senior officer up front. The Taser suggests to me a link with organised crime and that, as you know, is DI Phil Davies' area of expertise. He's going to be taking over up front. Now, where are we with this? I want to know what you've got, however slim. Leads, suspects, witnesses.'

The assignment of Davies to the SIO role was disappointing but expected. A high-profile case like this was never going to be led by a detective sergeant. Still, he could earn himself some brownie points by showing the DSupt the progress the investigation had made so far. He peered down at the notes he'd prepared and began to fill Hardin in. He went through all the preliminary details and then told him about the first raft and their meeting with Dan Phillips over at Jennycliff. It was Phillips, he explained, who'd alerted them to the disappearance of Tim Benedict and the fact there might be a link between Sleet, the raft and Benedict. Hardin was unimpressed.

'Toerag.' Hardin jabbed a finger at Riley. 'I wouldn't be surprised if he knows more about this than he's telling. Sounds a bit unlikely he just came on the names like that.'

'Phillips has a nose like a sewer rat,' Riley said. 'I can well believe he did.'

'Well.' Hardin paused and then changed tack. He pointed at the map on the wall, his finger aimed at the patch of sea south of the Erme estuary. 'I get the torture of the mannequin, but what's with the raft? And also, where the hell's Perry Sleet?'

Riley shrugged his shoulders. His notes had nothing in them which might help answer Hardin's question. 'To be honest, sir, I've no idea. I'm hoping we'll get some forensic evidence from the Benedict crime scene.'

'Hope, Sergeant Riley, is something we resort to when we're desperate.' Hardin leant forward. Sneered. 'Now, please tell me we're not desperate?'

To Savage's immense disappointment, Monday had seen no new developments in the *Lacuna/Curlew* case. The CSI team at Woodland Heights had pretty much concluded and Layton had produced a brief written report. First thing Tuesday, Savage sat in her office with a cup of coffee and digested the bad news: the ground physics had come up negative and, short of demolishing the entire structure, there was nothing more to be found in the house. If she wanted to, Savage could meet him there at noon, by which time he'd be finishing up.

The morning squad meeting was short but not sweet. Hardin was annoyed by the lack of progress and took his frustration out on the *Lacuna* team. Savage could see the pressure was getting to him. One high-profile op was bad enough, but Devon and Cornwall Police now had two head-line-making cases to deal with.

'We've got until the weekend,' Hardin said, as he wrapped the meeting up. 'After then, Maria Heldon is going to send in her pretty boys from Exeter to help us. You know, the ones who think officers west of the moor smell of either a herd of sheep or a bag of kippers and enjoy fucking either.'

Hardin's remarks were greeted with a roar and Savage smiled to herself. At the last moment the DSupt had turned the bollocking into a pep talk. If anyone needed an incentive – which they shouldn't – the thought of interference from force HQ at Middlemoor would provide them with one.

After giving her own briefing, which focused on the importance of finding Ned Stone, Savage headed over to Woodland Heights to liaise with John Layton. When she arrived, she found him standing next to his old Volvo, a Tupperware box of sandwiches sitting on the roof.

'Bit behind schedule, Charlotte,' Layton said as he peeled the lid from the box. 'Down to yesterday's discovery on the Erme. Never seen anything like it. The bloke had been tortured and then dumped in a wheelie bin, the bin hoisted onto a raft. I think the aim was for the whole caboodle to float out to sea. What the poor fellow had done to deserve such a thing, I've no idea. The only silver lining is he's still alive. Just.'

Savage nodded. 'I'm worried Hardin's going to prioritise that investigation over this one.'

'Might do,' Layton said, extracting a thick wholemeal sandwich from his box. He waved the sandwich at the home. 'But time's on your side. The case has taken the best part of thirty years to get this far, another month or two won't make any difference.'

'Not to Jason Caldwell, no, but to the other Jason it will. Time isn't on his side at all and I don't want to think what his kidnapper might be doing to the boy.'

'Crazy fucker.' Layton took a bite of his sandwich. 'I'm glad you understand these nutters, Charlotte, because I confess I don't.'

'I don't know what's going on here either.' Savage turned towards the house. 'Which is why I really needed you to find something in there which can help. Anything.'

'I see.' Layton followed her gaze. 'Well, we've done the cellar and stripped some of the floorboards up. Plus we've managed to get behind all the panelling in the loft. And the GPR operative's been over the garden and car park. I'll take you inside and show you what we've been up to, but I'm sorry to say we've scored a blank so far.'

'Shit.'

'Yes, shit.' Layton nodded and then looked away from the house towards the coast. 'To be honest, why would you put something in the home when you've got all this around? And I'm sorry, but we can't start digging up the surrounding countryside. I wish I could be more positive.'

'You do your best, John. You always do.'

Layton reached into the car and picked up his Tilley hat from the front seat. Plonked the hat on his head. 'Let's hope that's enough, hey?'

Within the hour the Benedict case had burgeoned into something resembling a serious investigation. The operation had a name – *Caldera* – and the team had grown to include a receiver, a document manager, indexers, several DCs and various ancillary staff. There had also been a promise from Hardin that they wouldn't have to fight for resources with *Lacuna*.

'You know Hardin,' Enders said to Riley as together they

supervised the initial set-up of the incident room paraphernalia under the watchful eye of the operation's SIO, DI Davies. 'For every column inch of front-page news, we get an extra officer. Slip to the inside pages and we'll be lucky to retain a three-legged police dog and a PCSO.'

The chance of the story dropping from the front pages became minimal when they received the bad news mid-morning: Benedict had passed away despite the sterling efforts of the ICU team.

'Blood loss,' the consultant said when Riley spoke to him on the phone. 'And the shock. The body can only take so much, see? Although many of the injuries were superficial, put together they amounted to more than he could take. I counted thirty-seven different puncture points on his torso alone.'

'Made by?'

'No idea. You'll have to ask the pathologist. Benedict's on his way down there now.'

No, Riley thought as he hung up, Benedict wasn't on his way anywhere. A husk which once contained him was heading down to the mortuary, sure, but the real Benedict had either ceased to exist or was in a better place. Riley wondered if death had come any easier to the man, seeing as he was a vicar. Perhaps his belief had faltered at the last minute.

The notion was a depressing one, but when he put the options to Enders, hoping he might make a joke of it, the DC wasn't much help.

'Not necessarily a better place, sir,' he said. 'Tim Benedict might be going to hell for all we know.'

'Hell? He's a vicar, don't they get a VIP service?'

'Depends. Say he's done something to deserve this. Say him and Sleet are mixed up in some funny business.'

'Funny business? What are you talking about, Patrick?

213

We've nothing to link the two men and I fail to see what sort of business could justify torturing Benedict and chopping him up.'

'Well, there's one thing I can think of.' Enders nodded his head over towards where several members of the *Lacuna* team were standing round a whiteboard. 'Abuse. Kiddie fiddling. Child pornography. I'd say that would justify topping Benedict.'

'He's a member of the clergy for God's sake!'

'My point exactly.'

'You're jumping to conclusions with no good evidence.'

'Still, don't you think it might be a good idea to get Benedict and Sleet's computers in to Hi-Tech Crimes? Wouldn't take Doug Hamill more than an hour or two and then we'd know.'

Riley sighed. 'OK. Just to keep you happy. Get on to that PC Sidwell and ask him to send Benedict's laptop down here. And then you're coming with me to Derriford. We've got to pay our respects.'

'Hey?'

'The last rites. Tim Benedict's post-mortem.'

Layton's tour of the house convinced Savage that Woodland Heights had given up all its secrets and any further work would be pointless. She drove away from the place feeling dejected. Forensic evidence in both the *Lacuna* and *Curlew* investigations had been in short supply, neither having provided a decisive lead which could take them to the killer or killers. Finding Ned Stone was now the top priority. When she got back to the station, she'd suggest to Hardin that they needed to pile all their available resources into tracking him down.

In Bolberry she turned left and headed parallel with the coast towards Hope Cove. DC Calter was down in the village with two local officers, going door to door trying to jog old memories. Savage had arranged to rendezvous with Calter at the pub for a quick lunch and afterwards she fancied a walk on the beach to clear her head.

The lane left the village and threaded between tall hedges. The car crested a small rise, off to the left open fields rolling to the coast. Savage pulled the car to the side of the road and into a gateway, intending to take one last glance at Woodland Heights from a distance. She got out of the car and moved to the gate. The home lay a mile away across the fields and she realised she was looking at the rear of the house. The other night her assailant had jumped from a window into the backyard and he'd have run across fields to the west. She traced an imaginary line away from the house until her eyes came to a small clump of trees and scrub surrounded by farmland, perhaps half a mile distant. Had the man gone to ground there? Was it even possible he'd run on past, ending up at Parker's house?

Savage remembered Parker. He used a stick and had appeared frail. She couldn't see him being able to shimmy down a drainpipe and sprint across open countryside.

She climbed over the gate and began to walk across the fields towards the wood, her mind working overtime. The concrete in the cellar had been laid in 1988, just over two months after the disappearance of the boys. Recently, the cellar had been disturbed and human remains removed. Yet at some date between the boys going missing and the date written in the concrete, a body or bodies had been brought to the cellar after having been hidden somewhere else first.

She reached a hedge with a fence, the fence topped with barbed wire. She scouted to the right until she came to an open gate. Beyond, a field of corn stubble stretched to the wood. Was it possible the remains had been hidden there and brought back once the initial search had finished?

Five minutes later she stood under a huge oak at the edge of the copse where a broken fence marked the boundary. Within lay a dense thicket of hazel coppice, gangly ash trees, small pines and a mass of brambles and other scrub plants. In the field a stiff breeze had been sweeping across from the south-west. Here nothing moved, the tangle so impenetrable it shielded what was within from the rest of the world.

For a moment she paused, enjoying the peace and solitude. The week since the inquest into the death of Simon Fox had flown by and she'd barely had a minute to reflect on the outcome. Nor had she spent much time with Pete and the children, something she had promised herself she'd do once the inquest was done and dusted. Work had, as usual, got in the way. Damn it, she thought, life passed so quickly. It seemed only yesterday that Clarissa and Samantha were starting school. Now Jamie himself was in primary school and Samantha three years into secondary. Her daughter was a typical teenager: moody, headstrong, reactive. There were days when anything Savage or Pete said seemed to cause her great consternation. And yet, Savage reflected, her own behaviour at that age had been similar. 'I blame your family's hair,' Pete often joked. 'Red and fiery and does exactly what it says on the tin.'

Savage smiled and then blinked herself back into the present. She stepped over the broken fence and moved into the wood. She wondered if any reports of the searches from years ago remained in the files. Even if the reports were there, she doubted if exact details had been logged. Still, the woodland would have been searched, she thought.

The copse covered an area about the size of a couple of football pitches. She could call out a police search advisor and a search team, but it hardly seemed worth the bother. In half an hour she could quarter the woodland and satisfy herself there was nothing here.

Ten minutes later, on her hands and knees as she crawled beneath the bough of a fallen beech, she realised she'd vastly underestimated the time needed. She pushed herself up from the ground and ran a hand through her hair. A couple of leaves and a twig tumbled to the ground. She peered down to where the twig lay at right angles across a small depression. She bent to get a closer look. Not a depression, a trail.

A little way to her right, the trail skirted a patch of brambles. She straightened. The track had probably been made by rabbits or pheasants. Still, it might make her progress a little easier, might even lead to the edge of the wood where she could reconsider whether to continue the search.

She followed the trail to the brambles and beyond to where it wound into a stand of hazel. An animal had been digging at the base of the hazel and a scattering of rabbit droppings on the fresh soil hinted at the culprit. Savage moved forward and then looked down to where a pristine Mars bar wrapper sat plumb centre on the rabbit's spoil heap. She bent and pinched the wrapper between her fingernails so as not to touch the surface, and lifted it to her nose. The chocolate smell was distinct. Somebody had been here recently.

All of a sudden she felt a little nervous. The hazels crowded overhead, a thicket of bramble all around. Running anywhere in this would be impossible. She patted her jacket pocket for her phone. Nothing. She'd left the bloody thing on the passenger seat of the car.

She told herself not to panic. She was in a woodland in the English countryside. John Layton and several officers were not more than half a mile away. Nothing to worry about.

A few more steps and she'd rounded the hazel. On the other side she expected to find the edge of the woodland; instead, standing several metres tall, stood a wall of laurel. Savage moved closer. This was no manicured garden hedge and within it boughs tangled this way and that, twisting in the dark shadows. Unlike the hazel and ash trees, the laurel was evergreen and the denseness of the leaves stopped the light from penetrating. Still, the lack of light meant nothing grew at ground level. She could slip through the clump, duck under a couple of the larger branches, and find her way to the other side. Then she'd call it a day.

Savage moved under the canopy, her feet scuffing in the leaves shed from the laurel. She blinked. This place, she thought, was like some huge cave, a túnnel perhaps. She stepped forward and swatted at a solitary fly which buzzed at her face. A few more strides, most taken at a crouch, and she realised she'd come to some sort of dead end. The laurel here was tangled around a small clearing and there was no way out. She looked closer. No, not tangled, the branches had been woven together like a willow plait. Some of the larger ones had even fused into an almighty knot of wood. The process had taken years, decades perhaps. To one side of the clearing a house brick lay on its side, while nearby something else had disturbed the soil.

She examined the ground more closely. She bent and knelt in the leaves and mulch and swept the leaves with her hands, pushing away the loose material. Soon she'd cleared a patch of ground. Somebody had moved the leaves to conceal where they'd been digging. She began to scrape in the soil itself. By rights the entire area should be thick with laurel roots. Back home at Bovisand, she and Pete had spent a whole weekend removing a laurel bush and the roots had made the job near to impossible. Here though, the soil was soft and she was able to dig easily.

Savage's hands grew dirty as the soil began to pile up at one side of the clearing. Earth gathered beneath her nails and she felt damp seep through to her knees. Within a couple of minutes she'd dug several inches down and came up against a piece of slate. She worked her way across until she found the edges and then lifted the slate.

For a second she stared at what was underneath, unable to comprehend what she was looking at. A hemisphere. Round, white, shiny and the size of a small football. A couple of lines crazing their way across the surface. She reached out a finger and then stopped, her finger hovering in mid-air, suddenly aware she was shaking slightly.

Bone.

She realised she was looking at the top of a skull, the whole thing sitting in a neat hole capped by the piece of slate.

Savage moved backwards. Not only because she was frightened, but also because the clearing had become a crime scene. Everything she did from now on could compromise the work of Layton and his CSIs. She cursed. She should have gone with her gut instinct and called the PolSA at the outset. She stood and edged back some more, trying to leave the clearing the way she had come. She remained in a crouch and placed her feet in the prints she had made.

Then she heard a sound. Something in the undergrowth. She turned around in the tunnel of laurel stems to see a dark shape pressing forward, hunched over. In the gloom she could tell the figure was male, but his face was swathed in a black scarf and the hood of an anorak covered his head. For a moment the eyes held still, gazing straight at her. Then the man came charging forward.

Savage didn't have room to turn around so she backed up as fast as she could. She tripped on a root and fell over, immediately turning herself to try to scrabble away.

'Arrrggghhh!'

She curled herself into a ball as the man yelled and leapt on her, fists pummelling into her back. She tried to shout herself, but a hand grabbed her hair and slammed her face down into the soil. Then he was sitting astride her as she lay on her front. Something brushed against her neck and then she felt a piece of thin material slide around her throat. She put her hands up but it was too late. The man shifted his position, a knee now pressing down in the small of her back. Savage turned her head. She could see the man's hands pulling on a strip of leather, choking the life out of her. She tried to kick out and then to turn herself, but the ground beneath was soft and provided no purchase. She blinked, aware of the world beginning to fade away. She realised there was something she should remember. Her husband, her children – Jamie and Samantha. And Clarissa of course. Poor. Dead. Clarissa.

For an instant, Savage pictured her daughter, Clarissa's face framed with hair like her own.

Red hair like her own . . .

Red?

Savage flicked her eyes towards the hole in the ground. Beyond the skull, out of focus, *was* something red. She stretched her fingers out, scrabbling past the hole and reaching for the red blur, reaching for the one thing which could save her. Her fingers grasped the rough surface, but now the red colour was dissolving into grey. Everything was becoming grey. The green leaves, the flecks of white sky visible through the canopy above, the brown soil. Colour sloughed away, leaving a world leached of contrast, of life itself.

She stopped struggling and let herself go limp. For a split second she felt a change in her attacker as he reacted to her apparent death.

Which was when she rolled onto her side and swung her arm backwards, bringing the brick in her right hand up and round so it slammed into the side of the man's head.

Chapter Twenty-Three

Near Bolberry, South Hams, Devon. Tuesday 27th October.
1.31 p.m.

'Charlotte!'

Savage opened her eyes to see the skull lying a foot away from her nose. The mouth wore a wide grin and the right eye blinked at her, a light in the eyeball flashing like a drop of water caught in a sunbeam.

'Hello!'

The skull spoke again and the eye blinked. The other socket remained unseeing, empty and black.

'Charlotte!'

The voice was insistent, the smile appearing to get even fuller along with the accent. Female. A West Country drawl.

'Ma'am, where the bloody heck are you?'

Not the skull. DC Calter.

'In here, Jane,' Savage said as she pushed herself up into a sitting position, nausea sweeping over her as she did so. She rubbed her neck and gulped. 'I'm OK.'

The skull lay next to the hole she had dug. There was no sign of her attacker or the brick she'd hit him with. The man must have pulled the skull from the ground, perhaps intending to take it with him. For some reason he hadn't.

Then she saw why.

An area of disturbed ground stretched away from the hole for a metre or so and several brown and stained objects poked above the soil. Bones. Whoever had attacked her had intended to retrieve not just the skull but the bones as well. Calter's arrival must have scared him off.

'Ma'am?' Calter's voice came through the dense laurel from a few metres away. 'What are you doing in there?'

'It's a long story, Jane.' Savage swallowed again and tried to blink away the fuzziness which clouded her vision. 'Have you got your phone?'

'Yes, ma'am. But you haven't got yours. When you didn't turn up at the pub, I called John Layton. He said you'd left Woodland Heights some time ago, so I drove up from Hope Cove to see where you'd got to. I found your car and spotted the phone on the front seat. Thought you'd nipped into the field to take a wee. Only you hadn't, had you?'

'No.' Savage shook her head and, despite the grim surroundings and her injuries, smiled to herself. She could well imagine Calter leaping a gate and squatting in a field with her knickers round her ankles. 'Call Layton again, would you?'

'Right.'

Savage turned and half stood. In a crouching position, she moved from the clearing and through the laurel tunnel. She found Calter standing next to the clump of hazel, phone in hand.

'Did you see anyone?' Savage straightened and let out a groan as a spasm of pain shot up her back. She gestured at the woodland. 'In here or in the fields?'

'No, ma'am.' She handed Savage the phone, but not before taking in Savage's dishevelled appearance. 'Why?'

'John?' Savage waved a hand, dismissing Calter as Layton answered. 'I think I've found one of the boys.'

The post-mortem lasted several hours and it was well after lunch before Riley and Enders emerged into the daylight. The ordeal had been made worse by the fact that the pathologist had been a stand-in for Nesbit. Gone were the dry jokes, intelligent repartee and amusing anecdotes. Instead Riley had to endure a conversation almost entirely focused on the man's passion for wine, a subject Riley knew next to nothing about.

'I was going to mention the nice white I bought at Lidl the other day,' Enders said as they walked to their car. 'Three ninety-nine. A little sharp, but a dash of lemonade cured that. Lovely.'

Riley shook his head. He was still thinking about the state Benedict had been in even before the pathologist had started his work. In the end his verdict had pretty much matched that of the consultant. Benedict had died from exsanguination and traumatic shock. How that had happened wasn't in any doubt as the pathologist had painstakingly noted every cut and slice and blow. There had been some conjecture as to how each individual injury had been caused, but the attack had likely involved a variety of workshop devices, including a drill, a circular saw and a router.

Outside, Riley glanced up at the sky where the sun was already heading towards the horizon, an autumn chill in the air to match the cold of the mortuary. He remembered his own close shave with power tools – an angle grinder wielded by Ricky Budgeon, a crook he'd once crossed. He'd walked away, unhurt, thanks to DI Davies and DI Savage. Benedict hadn't had Davies and Savage on his side though, he'd relied on God and God hadn't showed up in time. What had the man done to deserve to be put through such terror? And what about Perry Sleet? Was he still alive and awaiting the same fate as Benedict?

On the short drive back to the station, one avenue appeared to be closed. Riley took a call from Doug Hamill, their Hi-Tech Crimes guru. Benedict's laptop had been driven down from North Devon in a squad car and Hamill had made a preliminary examination.

'No porn,' he said. 'Either of the legal or illegal kind. Not much on there at all to be honest. Some sermons, part of a book Benedict was writing, emails, some family snaps.'

'Nothing dubious there? No pictures of kids?'

'Kids, yes, but the kind of pictures you'd happily get printed at Boots. I think they're of various relatives. I've also checked for hidden and deleted files and analysed his internet use, but there's no suggestion he was involved in anything remotely dodgy.'

'OK,' Riley said. He was relieved Enders' hunch hadn't played out. The case was bad enough as it was without making it more sordid. Still, he felt guilty about wasting Hamill's time. 'Sorry to trouble you, Doug, but it was worth a look.'

'Worth a look?' Hamill chuckled down the line. 'It was more than that. You see, I *did* find something on Tim Benedict's laptop.'

'I thought you said—'

'I said I didn't find anything dodgy, but I did find something *interesting*. Being a vicar meant he had a lot of contacts. Hundreds of them. He had them all in a spreadsheet. I had a quick scan through to see if I could pick anything out.'

'And?' Riley held up his hand as Enders pulled the car to a stop in the station car park and made to get out. 'Have you got something or not?'

'I've got a name.'

'Related to the enquiry?'

'Definitely. There's a phone number in the spreadsheet which we've already got in our system.'

'Doug, I haven't got time—'

'The number's the same as the one on Perry Sleet's mobile. The one which belongs to the woman we know as Sarah. Only now we know her full name. She's Mrs Sarah Hannaford.'

'Have you contacted her?'

'Her mobile's still switched off, but I've managed to find and get through on her home number. She's meeting a friend in Plymouth this evening so I've arranged for her to drop in. Sweet, huh?'

More than sweet, Riley thought as he hung up, this was surely the breakthrough they'd been waiting for.

The noise from the chainsaw reverberated through the copse for a good half an hour before Layton was satisfied with the safe route in.

'Is there any type of tool you don't have access to, John,' Savage said as Layton examined the new path which tunnelled beneath the laurels.

'A time machine.' Layton stood at the edge of the clearing and indicated to one of his juniors where a set of stepping plates should be placed. 'Would simplify everything if I could go back and view the scene as the crime was taking place.'

'I thought that's what you did?'

'Nice of you to say so, Charlotte, but I do get it wrong. Sometimes.'

'Could that be Jason?' Savage pointed into the clearing at the skull. Next to the skull, a CSI was beginning to remove the earth from where the other bones lay in an approximation

225

of a skeleton. 'I mean, he's only been missing for a week. How on earth could he get in that state?'

'Boiling.' Layton didn't say anything for a moment. Then he cocked his head up at Savage. 'The killer could dissect the body, pull the bones apart and then boil them up to remove the flesh.'

'Shit, no.'

'However, those other bones are brown and aged. I'm not sure they belong to Jason Hobb.'

'But the skull might?' Savage stared down to where the right eye socket twinkled in the light. 'Will we have to wait for DNA evidence?'

'Not necessarily.' Layton hopped onto the line of stepping plates and moved across to the skull. He bent over. 'Look in the mouth. There's a filling in one of the teeth. Nesbit's bringing the dental record for Jason. I believe it could provide some relief for Mrs Hobb.'

'Providing it's a negative.'

'That goes without saying.'

'So the other bones, they're from the cellar, right?'

'Would make sense if they were.' Layton stood, his head pressed up against the roof of the laurel chamber. 'Somebody dug them up a month or so ago and brought them here, probably because the house was put up for sale.'

'Only I come along and disturb the dump site and mystery man attacks me.' Savage pointed to where the CSI was using what looked like a giant paintbrush to sweep soil from around a thighbone. 'We fight and while I'm unconscious he starts to retrieve the bones, only he hears DC Calter coming and has to leave in a hurry.'

'He's certainly audacious. We're only half a mile from the home.'

'Well, you said yourself we couldn't go digging up the

surrounding countryside. He probably felt quite safe here. And perhaps that's part of the rationale behind this particular site. It could mean something.' Savage glanced around at the tangled undergrowth. Adults would struggle in this terrain, bashing their heads on low branches, having to crouch and crawl, getting their hands dirty and their clothes snagged. 'I could imagine boys from the home coming here and building dens and playing games.'

Layton nodded and then turned at the sound of somebody coughing. 'Nesbit.'

Savage shifted her position. Andrew Nesbit was trying to fold his beanpole-like figure so as to pass beneath several low branches.

'I knew I should have trained as a GP,' Nesbit said, his head and neck contorted to one side. 'A warm and dry consulting room, nice old ladies with heart flutters, little Jimmy with a nasty rash on his twinkle which no amount of nappy cream can shift.' Nesbit came into the clearing, took one look around and then lowered himself to sit on a stack of stepping plates. He stared across at the skull and bones. 'Not this. Christ not this.'

'It's grim, Andrew,' Savage said. 'Very grim.'

'Well, let's try and make it a little less grim. I've got the boy's dental record.' Nesbit opened his bag and pulled out a piece of paper. Stared down. 'Three, seven. The left mandibular second molar.'

'Thank goodness,' Layton said, gesturing at the skull. 'It doesn't match. That's not Jason Hobb.'

Savage felt a moment's relief. 'But the skull didn't come from the cellar, did it? This could be a third person.'

'No. The bone's been polished, true, but once the surface had been stained like the rest there's no way it could be brought back to that white state. However, is there any reason

227

why the skull couldn't belong to these bones? Perhaps the head was removed from the body. Since it didn't remain underground for all those years, it wasn't stained.'

'Bloody hell, John,' Savage said. 'I thought we were going down the "less grim" route. Are you saying the victim was decapitated?'

'Happens doesn't it?'

'Yes.' Savage glanced across at the skull where the right eye sparkled. The glint, she now knew, came from a marble which had been wedged in the socket. The skull, she suspected, had taken on a life of its own, perhaps been part of some kind of ritual. Such abominations weren't uncommon, particularly amongst serial murderers. 'But if he did that to this victim, then what about Jason Hobb?'

Nobody said anything and the only sound was the scrape, scrape, scrape of the CSI brushing the dirt away.

'People.' Nesbit extracted his kneeling cushion from his bag and now he moved forward and joined the CSI. 'Hypothesis, yes. Speculation, no. OK?'

Savage nodded and then extracted herself from the laurel clump, leaving Nesbit and Layton to complete the forensic examination. She walked to the edge of the wood. At one side of the copse a line of officers were fingertipping the ground while a search dog and its owner worked a patch of brambles. So far nothing had been found other than a set of bootprints.

An hour later Layton came to find her. Nesbit had finished.

Back in the laurel chamber the bones lay spread out on a sheet of plastic. The skull had been placed at one end with the rest of the bones arranged in their correct positions. A CSI knelt to one side firing off a series of photographs.

'Remarkable,' Nesbit said as Savage ducked in. 'Nearly every bone is present. If this is the body from the cellar, then whoever dug it up took a lot of care in making sure they got everything.'

'But they didn't,' Savage said. 'They missed the metatarsal.'

'Quite correct. On the right foot, part of the fifth metatarsal is missing. And one of the fingers.'

'So if this is the body from the cellar then it's almost certainly Liam Hayskith or Jason Caldwell.'

'Yes. Familial DNA will prove it one way or another.'

'Any notion as to cause of death?'

'With the body in this form it would usually be difficult, if not impossible, but in this case I'm pretty sure I have the answer.'

'And?'

'The boy was stabbed.' Nesbit pointed at the skeleton. He picked up three pieces of backbone. 'Here, you can see striations on the surface of the lumber vertebrae. L2, L3 and L4. Multiple knife wounds penetrating deep into the abdomen, likely hitting the aorta. From the number of marks on the bones, I'd say he was attacked in a frenzy.'

'Jesus.'

'There's worse. You see, I made a detailed examination of the skull. While doing so I noticed something loose inside.' Nesbit put the vertebrae down and moved his hand to a series of plastic petri dishes which held various small bones. 'You know I said a finger bone was missing?' Nesbit picked up one of the dishes.

'Yes.'

'Well, the thing is, Charlotte, I've found this.'

Savage moved closer as Nesbit held the dish out for her to see. Sandwiched between the two circles of plastic lay something like a thin, pink sausage, red sauce at one end, a semicircle of white at the other. For a moment she was confused. Was

Nesbit playing some sort of trick on her, an optical illusion? He'd said a finger bone was missing but he was showing her . . . a finger?

'Oh my God!'

'I think we can probably say this might well have belonged to Jason Hobb, yes?'

Chapter Twenty-Four

Crownhill Police Station, Plymouth. Tuesday 27th October.
6.10 p.m.

Back at Crownhill by six o'clock, Savage attended a hastily convened meeting with Hardin. The CC, he told her, was on her way over. And she wasn't coming to hand out medals.

'But does she have anything for us?' Savage said. 'I mean relating to the photograph of the minister?'

'Heldon tells me it's in hand.' Hardin turned from the coffee machine. 'A team in London have apparently been investigating the man for some time. We're not to release anything though, not yet. It could jeopardise a number of live cases.'

'You don't think she's fobbing you off?'

'No, Charlotte, I don't.' Hardin plonked his cup of coffee down on his desk. 'Talking of fobbing off, she's due here within the hour. Be nice if I could have something for her, hey?'

Hardin raised a hand to his mouth and bit a nail. A sign of tension, Savage thought. She knew this was tough for Hardin. Even if he hadn't been personally involved, this case was every senior officer's worst nightmare. A kid dead, another one missing, and now a heap of bones. Maria Heldon

231

would want answers from Hardin or else she'd want scape-goats.

'This finger you found.' Hardin took his hand away from his mouth, peered at a hanging nail for a few seconds, then made the connection and snapped his arm down. 'If it does belong to Jason Hobb then he must be still alive. There wouldn't be much point to this charade otherwise.'

'Perhaps, but I'm not sure you can tell that to the Chief Constable.'

'Nonsense. All she wants is something to feed to the press, something to make her look better. Listen, Charlotte, Operation *Lacuna* is becoming a plaything for this nutter. We can't let it continue, so we need to take the initiative.' Hardin paused. He stared down at a piece of paper on the desk. 'So far we've, what? One suspect?'

'Ned Stone, yes. At least for the present-day case. But Stone had left the children's home when the boys went missing in 1988 and at the time he was twelve years old.'

'Wherever he was and whatever age, work up a scenario which could link him to *Curlew*. And I want some action points for Heldon when she arrives, right?'

Savage was about to protest. Nesbit had suggested she take herself off to A&E to have the bruises on her neck checked out. At the very least she needed to go home and rest.

'Well?' Hardin waved at the door. 'Get bloody moving!'

Savage nodded, stood and left Hardin biting his nails.

Down in the crime suite, Collier was keen to show her that he, at least, was up for brownie points from the CC.

'Operation *Lacuna* and Operation *Curlew*,' he said. 'Not parallel investigations any longer, more like sequential. The finger from Jason Hobb buried in the copse along with the bones of Jason Caldwell. No longer any question about it.'

'It's him?'

'I've just had the lab on the phone. The blood type of the finger is the same as the Hobb boy and we've got a DNA result on the metatarsal from the cellar. There's a familial match to one of Caldwell's uncles. We'll still need to wait for a DNA test on the rest of the bones, but I don't think there's much doubt now.'

'So the killer is one and the same. I was thinking the killer of the boy in the tunnel wanted us to investigate what went on at the children's home because he was angry the murders hadn't been solved. The finger of Jason Hobb at the dump site suggests to me there's only one killer, two or three victims, murders nearly thirty years apart. I've never come across anything like this before.'

'We're jumping to conclusions,' Collier said. 'Dangerous. We stick to procedure and follow this through.'

Sticking to procedure meant the continuing rounds of interviews. Detectives had been dispatched to speak to the boys – now men – from the home who lived in the UK. Telephone interviews were being arranged with those abroad.

Then there were the other staff members. One of the teachers had committed suicide and the other had died of a heart attack. Miss Edith Bickell, the housekeeper, had vanished without trace, which left Elijah Samuel and the Parkers and their son.

'You'll do him?' Collier said, his ubiquitous marker pen held at the ready. 'He teaches DT over at Ivybridge Community College. If what you tell me about the Parkers is true, then he might have some interesting stories about his parents.'

'And by implication, the home, is that what you are suggesting?'

'Vested interests, Charlotte. The boys, the staff members, the Parkers. It's just possible this guy could give you an impartial viewpoint.'

Savage nodded. Frank Parker was tied up in all this certainly, but would his son be willing to spill the beans?

'Shit,' Collier said, eyes wide as he stared over Savage's shoulder. He held his marker pen up as if in self-defence. 'It's the bloody Hatchet, thirty minutes early.'

Savage swung round. DSupt Hardin was holding the door for Maria Heldon and it appeared as if he was having trouble breathing. Heldon swept into the room and made a beeline for the whiteboard. Collier tried to slink away but Savage reached out and grasped him by the arm.

'DI Savage,' Heldon said. 'I might have known you were involved in this farce somewhere along the way.'

'Ma'am?' Hardin had caught up with Heldon. He tried to mediate. 'DI Savage found the body and the finger. The finger suggests Jason Hobb is still alive.'

'Suggests?' Heldon half turned to Hardin. 'And that will be some comfort to the mother, will it? Her son's finger on ice while we wait for the rest of him to turn up, possibly piece by piece? I'm surprised, Conrad, you of all people should see how this one is going to play out. A head, a heap of bones and the poor lad's finger. The press will have an absolute field day. We've got at least two children dead, four if we're unlucky. Plus the vicar.'

'The *Caldera* case is completely separate. It's an unfortunate coincidence. Bad luck.'

'Bad luck? I'll tell you what's bad luck.' Heldon jabbed a bony hand towards Hardin and then swept her arm around. 'This is bad luck. An unfortunate coincidence that so many poor-calibre detectives have gathered in one place. How else to explain the complete lack of progress? You know, Conrad, rotten apples are slippery underfoot. Best kick them out of the way before you stumble on them, yes?'

'We're closing in on the killer, ma'am. An arrest is imminent.'

'Really?' Heldon brightened. Something for the nine o'clock news was always going to be welcomed. 'And when can I expect this?'

'DI Savage?' Hardin half turned, as if he was back in his rugby days and about to make a dodgy offload. 'Could you brief the Chief Constable on those action points you prepared earlier?'

Hours passed. Days perhaps. Jason had lost all track of time. Despite the ministrations of the man, his right hand had swollen badly. In the dim light from the torch he could see blotches of dark red on the white bandage where the blood had seeped through. On one side something yellow had stained the material. Pus, Jason thought.

At first the pain had been excruciating. Now, though, the sensation was more of an itch. Even though he knew his finger had been amputated, there was a feeling of pins and needles which seemed to come from the very tip of his pinkie. He desperately wanted to scratch the itch, but that would mean taking the bandage off and he didn't want to do that. And anyway, there was nothing to scratch.

He dozed and ate and drank. At some point he entered a dream-like state where his mother was there in the box with him reading him bedtime stories as if he was still a little kid. After that he slept for what seemed like a long time.

When he woke, he felt better physically, but the thought of his mother brought tears to his eyes. Was he ever going to see her again? What would she be doing now? She'd be worried to death, no doubt.

Jason pushed himself up from his lying position with his left hand.

His left hand . . .

That was the only piece of good fortune. When the man had told him to put his arm up the tube he'd used his right hand because that was the hand you used to shake with. However, he was left-handed. Cack-handed, his grandfather had always said, before adding, 'Just like I am.' He'd then reel off a long list of famous people who were left-handed to show Jason that the affliction was nothing of the sort.

Jason sat and flexed his fingers. Sure, he had one hand which *was* working, but what good was that? He groped for the torch in the dark, and pressed the switch. He swung the torch around, illuminating the plywood box. He was now pretty sure he was buried underground, but even if he'd been above ground he couldn't see a way of escaping. For one thing, he didn't have any kind of tool. He moved the torch to the empty cans of Coke. For a moment he wondered whether he could fashion something from one of the cans, but no, the aluminium would be way too soft.

He sighed, absent-mindedly using his left hand to rub his right wrist. The man's belt had cut into the flesh and the rawness was still bothering him.

The man's belt . . .

Jason moved his hand to his own belt. The thing had a big metal buckle and the prong was thick and long with a sharp point.

Back in the crime suite after a canteen dinner, Riley found the Chief Constable had left a scene of psychological devastation behind her. The junior members of the *Caldera* team were particularly shaken, especially since their SIO had been absent.

'Where is he?' Riley asked one shell-shocked indexer. 'DI Davies?'

'Something about illegal Tasers, sir,' the woman answered.

'Said he had a contact who might know where to get one. Only . . . ' The woman appeared reticent.

'Go on.'

'It all came up rather sudden. No actions or anything. He left about a minute before the Hatchet arrived and, well . . . he took the stairs.'

Riley shook his head and patted the indexer on the shoulder. Davies was a crafty bugger. He'd obviously got wind Heldon was on the warpath and slipped out just in time.

He moved across to his desk and found a Post-it from Doug Hamill stuck to his monitor. Sarah Hannaford would be in at seven p.m.

At six fifty-nine a call came through. Hannaford was downstairs. A minute later, Riley was in reception, the sergeant pointing over to a woman in her early sixties sitting in a chair. Sarah Hannaford had black hair half gone grey, the hair framing an angular face with high cheekbones. The lean face was at odds with her figure, which was short and dumpy. As Riley came over, she looked up from the *Police* magazine she'd been reading and smiled.

'Sergeant Darius Riley,' he said, holding out a hand. 'I believe you might be able to help us with our enquiries concerning the Reverend Tim Benedict and Perry Sleet.'

'Yes, I might.'

The woman took Riley's hand, but rather than shaking it she allowed him to help her up from the chair. He thought the action rather quaint.

Riley showed Hannaford to an interview room while a junior officer procured some cups of tea and a plate of biscuits, by which time he'd discovered the woman lived in a village over near Salcombe. She explained she'd known both Tim Benedict and Perry Sleet when she was younger.

'Perry lived next door to me when he was a lad. He used to play with my son. They'd be in and out of my house and Perry's house, not really caring which was their real home.'

'And the Reverend Benedict?'

'The Reverend. It's funny to hear him called that.' Hannaford smiled for a moment. Then her expression changed to one of dismay. 'I was so shocked to see his name on the news. How could such a thing happen?'

Riley had no answer for the woman. He shook his head. 'You were telling me how you knew Tim?'

'Yes.' The smile was back again. 'Tim was in the final stages of his curacy – this would be getting on for thirty years ago – and he officiated at the wedding of my sister. He was a family friend back then, see? He moved away when he got his first proper parish, but we still kept in touch occasionally. You know, Christmas and the like.'

Hannaford was staring at Riley but her mind was elsewhere, her face perplexed. Regrets? Something else? Riley wasn't sure, but he wasn't here to provide a counselling service. On the other hand, this woman appeared to be the link between the two men. Why was there the subterfuge to do with Perry Sleet though? Sleet was forty-one. Was it conceivable he was having an affair with a woman over twenty years his senior?

'Sarah,' Riley said. 'Can you tell me some more about your relationship with Perry? Why, for instance, you called him last week?'

'It's not what you're thinking.' Hannaford moved her right hand on top of her left and touched a gold band on one finger. 'I'm happily married.'

'So the call . . .?'

'A month or so ago this man came to my house. He wanted to know if I had contact details for Perry. Well, I didn't – I hadn't seen him since he went off to college – and even if I had, I wouldn't have given them to this bloke. He was a ruffian. I know that's an old-fashioned word, but it's exactly what he was. A load of tattoos and nasty look about him. Not that the two go together, but you know what I mean?'

'Yes.' Riley felt a tingle of excitement begin to rise within. Here, at last, was a lead. 'So you contacted Perry?'

'No, not immediately. As I said, I didn't have any idea where he was. It wasn't until last weekend, when my son was visiting with his family, that I decided to get in touch with Perry. My son – Anthony – lives in London, and had been asking about old friends and people in the village he hadn't seen for years. I told him about the rough chap. He said it would be a good excuse to get in touch and he'd love to hear what Perry was up to. Anyway, the village grapevine is such that it didn't take long to find out about Perry and get his details.'

'So you arranged to meet?'

'Goodness no. I simply phoned and told him about this man. He couldn't think of anyone the guy could be, but he thanked me. Afterwards we chatted a bit – pleasantries, you know – and I promised my son would look him up next time he visited.'

'And this call was around lunchtime Tuesday last week?'

'Uh-huh, I guess so.'

'A couple more questions,' Riley said. 'One, why the secrecy? You called from a pay-as-you-go mobile and the thing has been turned off ever since.'

Hannaford looked askance. 'There was no subterfuge, Mr Riley. My mobile is for emergencies only. I don't generally use it, but on the Tuesday we had a builder in installing an extractor fan in the kitchen. The electricity was off and the builder was making an infernal racket drilling through the wall. I went for a walk and made the call while I was out. When I got home I turned the mobile off and it hasn't been switched on since.'

Shit. Riley shook his head. By such slim margins were cases made or broken. 'And you didn't think to contact us when Perry first went missing?'

'That's just it. I didn't know he *was* missing. It wasn't until I heard the news this morning about Tim and that police were linking the crime with the disappearance of another man – Perry – that I realised.' Hannaford raised one hand to her face and slid her forefinger across one eye and then the other. She moved the finger away and stared at the moisture on its tip. 'If I'd contacted you a month ago, Tim might still be alive and Perry wouldn't be missing.'

Unlikely, Riley thought. A call to the police about a man asking questions wouldn't have merited much more than a note in the log. Resources were stretched to the point where sending out officers to interview every concerned and well-meaning member of the public was unrealistic.

'You're not responsible, Sarah,' Riley said. 'Let's just concentrate on trying to find Perry, OK?'

'Yes.' Hannaford tried to smile, but the smile didn't come.

Back home, Savage found the house empty and dark. In the kitchen a note in Jamie's faltering handwriting informed her that he, Samantha and Pete had gone out to eat. 'BURGERS! Mummy!' Jamie had written, knowing Savage would be disapproving of the kids' choice of restaurant.

She went into the living room, but left the lights off so she could gaze through the big French windows at the night vista. Plymouth glowed off to the right, while ahead lay the Sound. Several large ships lay at anchor, their deck lights making them appear like spacecraft floating in a black sky.

Farther away, on the other side of the Sound, the twin villages of Kingsand and Cawsand twinkled as if they were from a twee Christmas card. To the left a white line of surf marked the breakwater. Beyond the breakwater the open sea.

She shivered and went across to touch a radiator. The radiator was hot, the cold psychological. It was those bones, she thought. Something terribly sad about seeing them lying in the soil. 'At least he'll get a proper funeral now,' someone had said as officers had stood as Layton solemnly carried the crate of bones from the copse. Great. A funeral. A decent burial would make everything OK, would it?

She moved to the sofa and slumped down in the gloom, feeling exhausted. She kicked her shoes off and brought her legs up onto the chair, feeling the bruises from the attack. She touched her neck and then lay back against a pillow. The assault had unsettled her and hours later the shock was beginning to hit home. And then there was Maria Heldon's visit to Crownhill. For all his shortcomings, Simon Fox had had a way with people. Heldon didn't. But Savage's mood went beyond Heldon's grating manner and, to be blunt about it, the CC had been right about the lack of progress. The investigation was moving forward, but it wasn't because Savage was in the driving seat. She had a real sense that somebody else had hold of the controls. They were pressing the accelerator; they were turning the wheel. All the police could do was hang on for the ride.

History was what this was all about. The mysterious letter writer blamed Hardin for what happened at the home years ago and somehow the DSupt was supposed to make amends. She sighed. She knew all about history and how one single moment could have consequences down the years. Was that the case here? Certainly, if abuse had taken place at Woodland Heights, then the victims had every right to be angry and

241

demand justice, retribution even. But the murder and kidnapping of two kids was no way to go about it.

A clatter from the front door marked the entry of Pete and the children. All three of them piled into the hallway. Savage called out.

'Mummy,' Jamie said as he came into the living room. 'Why are you sitting in the dark?'

'Good question.' Pete stood in the doorway. He reached for the light switch. 'Everything OK?'

'Yes, fine,' Savage said, blinking against the sudden glare. 'Tired. Hungry.'

'Well, prepare for everything to be better than fine then.' Pete held up two paper bags. 'We've got burgers and fries and Coke and we bought an extra lot for the cat.'

'We don't have a cat, Daddy,' Jamie said as he romped across the room to Savage and piled onto her lap. 'Do you mean Mummy?'

Pete cocked his head on one side and looked at Savage. He'd noticed the marks on her neck. For a second his expression turned to one of concern, but then he censored himself and nodded. 'I guess I must, Jamie.'

Savage put her arms round her son and hugged him. She closed her eyes and pushed her face into his soft hair. As she did so she saw the skull again. The white bones, the glint in the eye from a marble, the teeth formed in a chilling grin which wasn't anything like a smile at all.

Chapter Twenty-Five

It's Sunday and the most awful events have occurred this weekend. Nothing in my life has prepared me for this day. Nothing can ever be right again. No one can ever suffer enough for their sins and that includes me.

It started on Friday. By midnight I guessed that Bentley wouldn't be coming, but when I crept from my room I encountered Mother dressed up like a turkey for Christmas. I was wrong, Bentley was coming! I cursed PC Hardin for the umpteenth time. It had been weeks since I slipped him the photograph and he seemed to have done nothing at all. Anyway, I snuck from my room and climbed to the attic to warn Jason.

'Jason's gone,' one of the boys up there said. 'Jason and Liam.'

'No!' I shouted, feeling sick to the stomach. 'Where?'

'The cove.'

Of course, the cove. Sometimes in the summer we play down there and hide out in the cave.

I raced down the stairs and climbed out the window. Down the drainpipe and onto the yard. I ran round to the front of the house as headlights swept up the track.

Bentley!

I made for the coast path as fast as I could. At that point I didn't care if I should stumble and smash my head, all I wanted to do was find my friends. At the path, I turned left and made my way to where the land fell away down to the cove. I scampered past mounds of rock and skipped down the last part of the path. I staggered onto the beach and tripped and fell in the soft sand.

For a moment I lay there and listened to the beat of my heart and the surge of the waves way off down the beach. I raised my head and stared at the horizon where the stars slid from this world to the next. The sky was only slightly lighter than the inky black of the sea, but I could see something down there. Some sort of structure at the point where the beach and waves met. Then I heard voices.

Jason and Liam!

I pulled myself up from the sand and began to lope towards the sea.

'Jason!' I shouted. 'Jason! Jason! Jason!'

I arrived at the sea breathless and splashed into the surf to where Jason and Liam were standing next to a raft. Plywood sheets sat atop cross-beams, beneath which sat a dozen plastic barrels. The whole lot was lashed together with rope. Both boys were naked aside from underpants and wellington boots and in the pale light their skin glistened.

'What are you doing here?' Jason said. 'We don't need your help!'

'But . . . ' Jason didn't seem pleased to see me. Quite the opposite. Liam stood beside him and they shared the same scowl. 'I came to warn you. Bentley's here!'

'Warn us? What good is that? You could have stopped him but you did nothing.'

'Nothing?'

'You were watching at the airbrick. All those times. Why didn't you tell somebody?'

'I tried to help. I told the policeman. I told others too.' I put

244

out my hand and grasped hold of Jason's arm, but my hand slipped free. 'What . . .?'

'Grease,' Jason said, matter-of-factly. 'To keep us warm.'

'You're crazy!' I stared past the raft. Out there, beyond the breakers, the sea was piling up. The wind was increasing. The flimsy structure the boys had built wouldn't last long. Their attempt to emulate Channel swimmers, laughable. 'Come back with me and we'll go to the police.'

'The police?' In the dark I saw Liam shake his head. 'I thought you said you tried that? They won't do a thing.'

'Please don't go.' I slid my hand into my pocket and touched my flick knife. I was going to give the weapon to Jason so he could protect himself from Bentley.

'Leave us alone, traitor!' Liam said. He stepped between Jason and me. 'We're getting out of here and you're in our way.'

Liam flung out an arm and punched me in the chest. I stumbled backwards and fell to the ground as a wave swept up and washed over me. I flailed in the water and swallowed sea and sand. Then I pushed myself up.

The boys were manoeuvring the raft, guiding it seaward. Another wave rushed in and the raft rose to the crest and then slipped down the other side. Jason and Liam clambered onto the structure. They each had a paddle and they knelt and dipped them in the water as one.

'No!' I screamed.

I ran after them and the water quickly reached my waist. I launched myself at the raft and managed to grasp hold. I pulled myself up and stood on the platform, trying to balance in the swell. Liam turned and raised his paddle. He swung it and caught me in my midriff. I grabbed the paddle with one hand while the other pulled out the flick knife. The blade sprung open and flashed in the starlight.

'Don't leave me!' I was staring at Liam but the words were meant for Jason. 'I beg you! You're my only friends!'

Liam still had hold of the paddle and he stood. I slashed at him, and as he raised the paddle to protect himself, the knife sliced him on the hand. He fell backwards, dropping the paddle overboard.

'You idiot!' Jason screamed, as he crawled across the raft towards me. 'You're ruining everything.'

'But I . . . I . . .'

Jason pushed himself to his feet and came at me, hands outstretched. I tried to push him away, but my hand slipped on his greasy skin. Then he was at me, hands flailing and fists punching. I raised my knife to defend myself against the onslaught.

'Give me that.' Jason grabbed for the knife, the blade catching him first on one hand and then the other. He cried out, looking down at where blood oozed from his palms.

Then a wave destroyed itself on the front edge of the raft, the spray hissing backwards, the force heeling the makeshift craft at a crazy angle. Jason tumbled forward. I tried to catch him, but I overbalanced and we both plunged into the water.

For a moment the world was nothing but froth and roaring waves and screaming: Liam, Jason and myself. Then I was half swimming, half stumbling, trying to drag Jason to the shore. My hands clasped Jason's arms, but the grease on his skin prevented me from getting a good grip. I gave up and wrapped my own arms round his midriff and pulled him until the water gave way to pebbles and wet sand.

In the distance I could see Liam kneeling on the raft, raging at me and at the world. His paddle was gone and his one arm hung down limply. He could do nothing as the raft was caught in a rip and moved slowly towards the horizon.

I collapsed on the beach and held Jason close. I think he

must have knocked his head because he was barely conscious as he slumped back in my arms. I lowered him to the sand and examined him. The only visible wounds were to his hands where his palms were marked with deep cuts. I ripped my shirt off and tore it in two and then wrapped the material round the cuts.

'I'm going to get help,' I said, as I stood. 'You'll be OK?'

Jason nodded, the starlight overhead reflected in his pale eyes. I ran from the beach and didn't turn back.

Now, as I lie under my covers in the small hours of Sunday morning, I wish I had.

The Shepherd is beginning to lose faith. Things are going wrong. Very wrong.

He is sitting in the little room at the barn, staring at the security monitors. He's watching a recording of the altar taken as the machine worked on Benedict to see if he can understand what caused the malfunction. Perry Sleet is up next and this time everything must run smoothly.

He thinks about the debacle down at the estuary. Nearly getting caught. The raft failing to catch the tide. The mysterious appearance of the pot boat. Almost a disaster.

Perhaps, he thinks, the whole idea with the raft was foolish. A theatrical flourish he could have done without. But no, the symbolism is important to him. He is telling a story and the raft forms an integral part of the tale.

The boy who plays with the skull in the grubby soil . . .

Yes, him too. The Shepherd and the boy are two actors in a play. The raft is a prop which brings meaning to the Shepherd's actions. Launching Benedict and Sleet onto the ocean, watching their bodies drift out to sea, would have been cathartic. Now that's no longer going to be possible, but it doesn't mean Sleet will go unpunished.

On the screen in front of him, Benedict is suffering again and again as the Shepherd repeatedly replays the recording. There's nothing to indicate why the belt broke, but the Shepherd continues watching the drill bit drilling and the circular saw sawing. Each time the tools bite into Benedict's skin, the Shepherd feels a little better. Benedict has truly paid for his cowardice, but there are three more to come.

The man with the skull . . .

Yes, of course. The man with the skull must be made to pay, but confronting him will be for later. His trial will be the last one and his act of penance must be truly voluntary. Unlike Benedict, he must walk to the altar and submit of his own accord. There isn't much the Shepherd can do to force him.

The Shepherd stops the video playback. He's seen enough. He shuts down the security system and turns off the computer. He rises from the chair.

It's time to talk to Perry Sleet. Time to prepare him for what's to come.

Chapter Twenty-Six

Crownhill Police Station, Plymouth. Wednesday 28th October. 8.45 a.m.

Riley came into the crime suite on Wednesday morning to find DC Enders poring over a spread of newspapers. As Hardin had predicted, the general tone was one of sheer horror with a subtext around the loss of all Christian values. If crimes such as this could happen in sleepy Devon, then what hope for the rest of the country?

'They've gone to town on this one, sir,' Enders said. 'The *Daily Mail* cites the erosion of British values by immigrants, while the *Guardian* – would you believe it – has an op piece on whether second-homers are to blame. Apparently villages are becoming ethnically cleansed as you rich Londoners buy up all the cute cottages.'

'I'm not rich,' Riley muttered as he took in the headlines. 'And I'm not a Londoner. Not any more.'

'I wouldn't be so sure, sir. The way things are going, you might be moving back there and I might be off to my mam's folks in Derry.'

'What?' Riley looked up from the papers.

'Word on the grapevine is that Hardin's not happy.' Enders prodded one of the papers, his finger coming down on a

249

picture of Tim Benedict. 'Yesterday's visit from Heldon and now this. Apparently he wants a result pronto.'

'Bloody hell, *Caldera* has only been going twenty-four hours. What does he expect? Miracles?'

'Why not?' Enders tapped the picture again. Benedict standing outside his church. 'Considering our victim, you'd think we'd be due one, wouldn't you?'

Riley nodded. Leads, so far, had been minimal, and the only piece of luck had come from the mobile number. He moved away and made a phone call. The facial composite officer needed a kick up her backside. She'd sat with Sarah Hannaford the previous evening and worked on an EvoFIT image of the man who'd asked questions about Sleet and Benedict, but as yet nothing had come through. When she answered, the officer was apologetic; there'd been a rape in the town centre and she'd been at the SARC with a victim until the early hours. She'd send the material through in the next few minutes.

She was as good as her word and within five minutes Riley had the image. He printed out a few copies and slipped one onto Enders' desk.

'A generic Plymouth thug,' Riley said. 'Could be any one of a hundred scrotes.'

'Yes,' Enders said. 'But he looks familiar.'

'Well I don't think he's someone we've come across on this case.' Riley read through the notes accompanying the picture. 'The man apparently has a load of tattoos, including "F.U.C.K." on the knuckles of one hand. Sounds like a real charmer.'

'Tats?' Enders scanned the picture again. 'Hang on, sir! I *do* know this man.'

'You do?'

'Only through passing. Spotted him on one of the round-robin morning bulletins.' Enders held up the picture and turned to where DS Collier was sorting through a pile of paper on the other side of the crime suite. He shouted across to him. 'Gareth, who's this?'

Collier stared at the picture and then ambled across.

'Well blow me.' Collier pointed at the *Lacuna* whiteboard. 'That's the mother's squeeze. Ned Stone.'

Collier had arranged for Savage and Calter to visit Brenden Parker – Frank Parker's son – early Wednesday. The man, he said, was on a long-term sickie from his teaching job. He'd be at home all morning. Home turned out to be a modest semi on a 1980s development in the town of Ivybridge. The estate was already beginning to look tired and dated and Savage spotted more than one agent's board on the road in. Still, the place was handy for the college where Parker taught.

A brick path led between two small patches of lawn to a dark oak door with an obscured glass panel. The bell brought a man to the door, a tentative smile showing on a face similar to his father's: thin, puckered-in cheekbones, a Roman nose, and mousey hair. The hair had been thickened with wax in a vain attempt to provide much needed volume. Parker raised a hand and fluffed the hair on one side of his head, self-conscious of his appearance.

Savage introduced herself and Calter and Parker showed them in. The layout of the house was bog-standard. Stairs on one side of the hall and a living room on the other. At the back, a kitchen-diner. She stood at the threshold to the living room. The layout may have been standard but the furnishings were not. Parker had inherited his father's taste for a sort of Puritan minimalism. There were three chairs in the room, all of them wooden with no cushioning. There was no sign of a television or any means of playing music. A newspaper lay on a small occasional table next to one of

251

the chairs. The place seemed somewhat spartan, but from the records, they knew Parker was single. Men living alone, Savage thought, were diminished. They either compensated by purchasing all manner of gadgets and hi-tech equipment or, like Parker, they let things slide.

Savage and Calter sat and exchanged glances while Parker made some tea. The man seemed a sensitive soul and it didn't take much of a leap to imagine him mentally battered and bruised by having such domineering parents.

Parker served the tea in a rather grand silver teapot, the milk, bizarrely, condensed from a can. When Savage showed interest, he explained the pot belonged to his mother. She nodded, wondering how to reconcile the stern Mrs Parker with such a beautiful item. She also wondered about Parker's accent. His voice had a strange sing-song lilt to it that seemed familiar.

'I hope this doesn't come as a shock to you,' Savage said. 'But we've found human remains in the cellar at Woodland Heights. The original missing persons investigation has now become a murder enquiry.'

'I see.' If the news came as a surprise, Parker didn't show any reaction. He nodded, the expression on his face more one of resignation than alarm. 'Jason?'

'Why do you say that?' Savage cocked her head. 'It could be either of the boys. It could even be someone else.'

'You don't believe that.'

'Look, Mr Parker, I—'

'Please call me Brenden. I prefer to be on first-name terms.'

'OK, Brenden. You're right, I don't believe it. We're sure the remains belong to Jason Caldwell. What I'm not sure about is what went on in the home. I'm hoping you might be able to help me.'

'Help you?' Parker stared at Savage, unblinking. His face

was a picture of despair. As if what Savage had asked was utterly impossible. 'I can't. Nobody can help now. It's all too late.'

'It's too late for Liam and Jason,' Savage said, shaking her head. 'But there's more to this than them. If no one is prepared to open their mouth and tell me the truth about what went on, then whoever committed this crime is going to get away with it. And I can tell you, Brenden, I hate it when people get away with things.'

'But that's just the point. They do get away with it. Always.'

'They won't this time. Don't you want justice for the boys?'

'Justice?' Parker cocked his head almost as if he didn't believe such an outcome was possible. 'Yes, I do. Very much. Jason and Liam were my friends. My very best friends.'

'Well then.' Savage paused. She let the silence build for a few moments. 'Why don't we go back to the night when Jason and Liam disappeared? Start from there?'

'The night . . .?' Once more, Parker's face dropped. Savage thought she saw a shiver pass through him.

'August twenty-sixth, 1988. You remember the day?'

'Not the day. Only the night.'

Savage glanced at Calter. The DC shrugged.

'So the night,' Savage continued. 'Jason and Liam escaped, right? Why did they want to do that?'

Silence. And then Parker let out a long sigh and leant back in the chair. The wood creaked in response. He sat there, shrunken, as if when he'd breathed out half his spirit had been expelled at the same time as the air.

'Excuse me a moment.' Parker pushed himself up from the chair and stumbled from the room. He returned a few moments later with a glass of water and a foil strip of pills. 'Sorry, I've got the most awful headache. Must be the stress.'

'Brenden?' Savage said. 'You were telling us why Jason and Liam wanted to run away.'

'Yes.' Parker popped three pills from the foil and washed them down. He took several more gulps of water and put the glass on the table. 'Father was a bully. Bullies seek positions where they can gain easy power. Woodland Heights was just such a place.'

'Did he beat you?' Savage shifted her position, moving a little closer to Parker. 'Did he beat the boys?'

'Beat us?' Parker met Savage's eyes and then Calter's. Then he hung his head low and stared at the floor. 'Oh, he did so much more than simply beat us. He allowed things to happen.'

'To Jason and Liam?'

'To all the boys. Not me, of course, I wasn't a victim of abuse. There was this man. He was in the government. He . . . he . . .'

'OK.' Savage nodded. She didn't want to go into the finer details. Not here. That would be for specialist officers who could take things slowly and get any accusations properly recorded. Right now she needed to know about Jason and Liam. 'August twenty-sixth. You were telling us what happened?'

'Was I?' Parker glanced at Savage and then turned his head to the window. The back garden had a neat little lawn, a large metal shed up against the rear fence. 'They'd borrowed tools, Jason and Liam. From Elijah Samuel's store shed. I didn't know at the time, but they'd hidden the tools in the cave down at Soar Mill Cove so they could build a boat. On the night, Samuel let them out through the front door and they made, their way to the cove. I found they'd gone and followed them. On the beach I . . .'

Parker stopped and paled visibly, like a TV picture with the colour reduced to near zero. His hand reached across

254

the glass table and touched the teapot, as if he was trying to draw some comfort from the warmth of the metal.

'Brenden?' Calter. Doing her friendly act. 'Tell me what happened.'

'I had an argument with Liam.' Parker came out with the line straightaway, but then he paused for a few moments, as if he was struggling to think of what to say. Finally, he continued. 'In the confusion, I slashed him on the hand with my pocketknife. Then Jason became involved and I cut him too. Liam disappeared into the darkness but Jason sat on the sand, bleeding from a gash on both palms. I begged him to stay put and ran back to the home. When I got there, I told Father. He sent me to my room and said he'd deal with it.'

Calter leant forward. 'And?'

'He . . .' Parker collapsed, his upper body folding until his head rested on his knees. He uttered a huge sob. 'He . . .'

'It's OK,' Savage said, taking over once more. She tried to contain her excitement. They were so close now. So close to discovering the truth which had remained hidden for near on thirty years. She shifted her position, moving a little closer to Parker, and then spoke in not much more than a whisper. 'You can tell us.'

'He returned a few hours later and told me Jason was dead.' Parker turned his head and peered out from his hands like a child would. 'Father had gone down to the beach and found him. He'd died by the time Father got there. I'd killed him. Murdered him. Father said I'd go to prison for a hundred years if anybody found out.'

Parker covered his face again and hunched down. Savage glanced across at Calter. The DC nodded, plainly believing the veracity of Parker's story. Savage wasn't so sure. According to Nesbit, Jason Caldwell had likely died from a frenzied knife attack and the weapon had had a long blade. There

255

was no way a pocketknife could have caused the marks Savage had seen on Caldwell's skeleton.

'So you didn't tell anyone?' Savage said.

'I wanted to.' The face peered out again. 'I wanted to admit the crime. I loved Jason, you see? But Father said if I did own up, then the home would close down. All the boys would be thrown into an adult prison.'

'And you believed that?'

'Yes. He told me I wasn't to be selfish. God, he said, knew what I'd done. There was no need to involve the police.'

'God?'

'Yes.' Parker emerged from behind his hands and sat up. He rubbed his eyes. 'My father is a very religious man. He thinks God alone has the authority to punish those who sin. He told me I must live with my sin until the day God decided to act.'

'I'm sorry to ask, Brenden, but what happened to Jason's body?'

'Father and Elijah Samuel took the body somewhere and hid it. A couple of months later they brought Jason back and buried him in the cellar. They laid a new concrete floor on top. Of course, the cellar had already been thoroughly searched by then, but I knew.'

'You wrote the date in the concrete.'

'Yes. While it was still wet.'

Savage nodded. Brenden's story was tragic. A thirteen-year-old boy forced to live with the guilt of a crime that may have been an accident. The real offender here was Frank Parker. He'd almost certainly concealed Jason's death to prevent attention being drawn to the home, to protect the minister. And perhaps he'd done more than just that. If Jason's injuries were as superficial as Brenden had described and Nesbit's assessment was correct, then it was possible

Parker Senior had gone down to the beach and murdered Jason Caldwell in cold blood.

Savage sat in silence for a moment. Then she sighed inwardly. She had one last line of enquiry to deal with.

'Brenden, you may or may not be aware that two boys went missing last week. Their names are Jason and Liam. The boy named Liam is now dead.'

'Oh no! You mean . . .' Parker faltered. He tried to speak, his voice overcome with emotion. 'Are you saying . . . it can't be . . . my God!'

'The person or persons sent the police two letters which called on us to investigate the disappearance of the original Jason and Liam. Do you think your father could be involved in some way?'

'But why?'

'Your father is – how shall I put this? – a little crazy. Suppose he's re-enacting what happened, trying to get history to repeat itself. He's chosen these new boys as part of a weird game. Do you think that's possible?'

'I couldn't say.' Parker shook his head. His eyes filled with moisture again and he wiped away a tear. He stifled a gulp. 'No, I really couldn't say.'

Savage raised a hand. She didn't need to hear any more. Frank Parker had at the very least conspired to prevent the burial of a body, but Savage hoped to get him for much more and they had plenty enough to arrest him on suspicion of murder. The best thing they could do now was get Brenden into the station and make this official. They needed officers who knew how to care for victims of sexual abuse and violence, who could take Brenden back to the awful days of his childhood without causing any more damage.

'Thank you, Brenden,' Savage said. 'You've been very helpful in what must be difficult circumstances.'

'You're not arresting me then?' Parker raised his head, visibly less cowed. 'For murder?'

'No.' Savage glanced at Calter. The DC shrugged her shoulders in agreement. Theoretically they could bring Parker in and charge him, but he wasn't the villain here and there was no way Savage wanted to cause the man any more suffering. She looked back at Parker. He'd brightened, but his demeanour was still that of a frightened child. 'If what you've told us is true, then it's possible you may face some charge, but given your age at the time I don't think that's likely. We'll need to get the full story as soon as possible though, so I'm going to arrange for a couple of specialist officers to visit this afternoon and take a statement. Would that be OK?'

Parker nodded, but appeared nervous once more. Savage told him he needn't worry, there'd be support for him throughout the process. He had nothing to fear from his father any more.

Outside, Savage and Calter stood by their car for a moment. The suburban estate was the epitome of normal. A mother pushed a baby in a buggy while a toddler trotted along beside her. Three doors up, a Tesco delivery driver was unloading the crates from his van while chatting to an elderly woman. Who could possibly know that inside number seventeen was a man who'd been part of such an appalling set of events?

'I could do with a coffee and a bite to eat, ma'am,' Calter said. 'Shall we?'

Savage turned back to the house, thinking of Parker alone in there with his memories. Why had he kept quiet for so long? Was it simply fear? Maybe there was a misguided sense of loyalty. Abusers often cast a spell over their victims and the situation was only compounded when there was a familial relationship. Brenden's father had dominated life at the home and dominated his son. He'd made the boy believe he was

258

responsible for the death of Jason Caldwell. Now it was time for him to pay.

'Sorry, Jane.' Savage shook her head. 'We've got unfinished business with Frank Parker.'

Finding Ned Stone, Riley thought, was going to be easier said than done. The guy was on the radar for the *Lacuna* case involving at least one child killing, and yet, so far, there'd been no sign of the man. Collier was philosophical about the lack of progress.

'He'll turn up,' Collier said as he studied the EvoFIT image. 'Jason's mother gave us the names of a few of Stone's mates and we've had officers round to visit them on several occasions. Nothing yet, but it's only a matter of time.'

'Right.' Riley nodded. He left Enders to get a list of Stone's friends from Collier and went out into the corridor.

Police work could be frustrating, especially when waiting for a known suspect to make an appearance. But Collier was right, short of sealing off the city and conducting a street-by-street, house-by-house search, there was little they could do.

Or was there?

Riley reached into his jacket pocket and pulled out his phone. He scrolled through his contacts until he came to a number labelled 'Car repairs'. He pressed 'Call' and a few seconds later someone answered.

'Darius,' a gruff voice said. 'How's life?'

The voice belonged to Kenny Fallon. The city's number-one gangster. A man who Riley had done business with before, as had DI Savage and DI Davies. Dealing with Fallon was going way over a line DSupt Hardin had drawn, a line, which if crossed, meant the end of your police career and quite possibly a prison sentence to boot.

'Kenny,' Riley said. 'I need a favour.'

At the other end of the line, Fallon chuckled. 'You know I'd do anything to help the police. Nothing like turkeys voting for Christmas, is it?'

'It's not criminal, not even dodgy.'

'Well, that's all right then. Wouldn't want to do anything *illegal*, would I? Not me. I'm one hundred per cent legit.'

'I need to find somebody urgently.'

'Really?' More laughter. 'I thought you were shacked up with that tasty bird who works with those kids on the Swilly? She's moved in with you, hasn't she? You'll be playing happy families soon, mark my words.'

'Not a woman, a bloke.' Riley cursed to himself as Fallon began to wind him up. Swinging both ways now, was he? Uncle Kenny didn't mind, Fallon assured him, but that was no way to treat the lovely Julie.

Fallon, it appeared, knew all about him and his personal life, but that wasn't surprising. Davies had told Riley that if a dog so much as cocked his leg outside of one of Fallon's clubs the man would know. He had a finger in every pie in the city and was on first-name terms with half a dozen police officers, several councillors and at least one MP. The dangers of dealing with him were obvious. He knew everything about you and, Riley suspected, with one word could bring your world crashing down.

'Ned Stone,' Riley said. 'We've marked his card as being involved in the murder of the vicar. We also want to question him about the death of Liam Clough and the disappearance of Jason Hobb.'

'And you can't find him, is that it?' Fallon tutted. 'You need the help of an upstanding member of the public.'

'He's a case, Kenny. You'll have heard what happened to Tim Benedict. As for the lads . . .'

'Not too fussed about the vicar, but the boys? He's well out of order there.'

'So you'll see what you can do?'

'I'll sort him, Darius. Don't you fret.'

'We need to question him, Kenny. No violence. I just need to know where he is, right?'

Riley waited for a reply, but none was forthcoming.

'Kenny?' Collier had just stepped out into the corridor, so Riley turned away and faced the wall. 'Kenny?'

Then he hung up.

As a tool, the belt buckle was pretty ineffectual, but it was all Jason had. He tapped around the sides of the box until he found a hollow sound on one wall, reasoning there might be some sort of void there. If the box was buried underground, he didn't want to break through the roof and cause a cave-in. Better to cut through on one side and then dig up from there.

At first he tried scraping away at the wood to see if he could make some kind of hole, but that didn't work. Next he began to score lines in a rectangle shape, the idea being to gradually wear through the wood until he could cut out a panel. Once the panel was removed he'd be able to dig his way sideways and then up.

The work was slow and tedious. He kept the torch off most of the time, only allowing himself a few seconds' light every now and then so he could check on his progress. After several hours he'd scored a deep gash on all sides of the rectangle but was still not through the wall. He worked on until tiredness overcame him. He slept fitfully for a while and then consumed another chocolate bar. With renewed energy he started again and after a while he felt the point of the buckle slip through the wood. He flicked the torch on and through the slit he'd made he saw soil.

Yes!

For the first time since he'd been captured, a glimmer of hope came over him. He switched the torch off and began to scrape again, this time working furiously at the wood. An odour of earth and decaying vegetable matter seeped into the box, but Jason didn't care. After another hour the panel split on one side and he was able to ease the wood inward until it broke away. A quick flash with the torch revealed a mass of soil and stones beyond.

Now the going was much easier. He used his hands to pull the earth and stones into the box and piled the debris up one end. Soon he'd excavated a chamber almost large enough to crouch in. A few more minutes' work and he'd be able to begin digging upward.

Jason clawed at the wall of soil, releasing a large stone behind which lay a plank of wood. For a moment he wondered what the plank was doing buried underground, but then he carried on. If he could get the plank out, he might be able to use it as a digging tool. His fingers worked their way around the edge of the plank and he yanked it free, one end of the rotten wood splintering as he did so.

There was a wash of air and the smell of something putrid. He gagged and then reached for the torch. The beam flicked on and he played the light where the wooden plank had been. A void lay beyond. This could be a way out, he thought. The passage could be some sort of tunnel to the surface.

He crawled forward, sticking his head through into the space, his hands pushing on something which cracked as it yielded. He pulled the torch to the front and shone the beam into the void.

In the white light the corpse appeared colourless, like a zombie from a black and white horror movie. Jason glanced down. His right hand had broken through the dried skin of the stomach and he felt something liquid ooze over his fingers. He gagged as the stench rose from the corpse and a thick vapour of decay reached the back of his throat. He scrabbled away as fast as he could, retreating into the box and huddling in the corner. Too late he realised he'd left the torch behind, aware of the light beginning to dim as the batteries died.

Chapter Twenty-Seven

Hope Cove, South Hams, Devon. Wednesday 28th October. 11.50 a.m.

The plan to confront Frank Parker was a simple one. Savage and Calter would go to the house while backup waited in a patrol car out of sight down the lane. Parker would be questioned and possibly arrested. Also in the patrol car was Luke Farrell, the FLO. He'd be staying with Mrs Parker if her husband was taken away, ostensibly to offer support. He'd also be finding out whether she'd been complicit in the abuse or in the murder of Jason Caldwell.

The weather had turned blustery. Out in the bay beyond Hope Cove the strong breeze whipped spray from the wave crests and foam streaked the surface of the sea. As they stood outside Parker's place, they felt the force of the wind.

'Nice view, ma'am,' Calter said, gazing out towards the horizon. 'But bleak, hey?'

Savage nodded and they went through the gate and climbed the steps to the front porch. A rap brought Mrs Parker to the door.

'You!' Mrs Parker peered through the gap, seemingly unwilling to open the door more than a couple of inches. 'We've told you everything. Go away!'

'We need to speak to your husband,' Savage said. 'Is he in?'

Mrs Parker pulled the door open. 'Same room as before. Same time. Ten minutes. OK?'

'This won't take ten minutes, Mrs Parker.' Savage walked in and down the hallway, swinging left into the living room. Parker was standing by the mantelpiece staring at the picture of the young boy. Savage could see the family resemblance now. The boy was Brenden Parker aged twelve or thirteen. As she moved across the room, she wondered if she'd missed something before. Should she have been able to deduce the boy's suffering from the cold look in his eyes?

'Inspector Savage?' Parker turned from the mantelpiece and slid across the floor towards her. 'Oh, I see you've brought a friend.'

'Detective Constable Jane Calter,' Savage said as Calter came and stood alongside. 'We've found human remains concealed at Woodland Heights. We have reason to believe you know how those remains got there.'

'I see.' Parker stood stock-still in the middle of the room. 'And might I ask what leads you to such a conclusion?'

'We'll come to that later. Do you deny burying Jason Caldwell in the cellar?'

Parker turned and gazed back at the mantelpiece. He appeared to be studying the picture of Brenden once more. Then he retreated to one of the armchairs and sat down.

'No,' Parker said. 'To be honest, I'm glad you've found out. I've had to keep the secret for all these years.'

'Why, Mr Parker?'

'For my son.' Parker glanced at the picture on the mantelpiece again. 'You see, *he* killed Jason Caldwell.'

'Brenden?' Savage tried to act surprised, as if she didn't already know. 'I think you'd better explain, Mr Parker. Tell us the whole story.'

265

'Yes. The whole story.' Parker sat rigid in the chair for several seconds before letting out a long breath. 'The night the boys went missing was no different than any other. It was summer, so most of them had been out playing until dusk. The boys went to bed and I did my rounds. There was nothing amiss. I think I read a little and then we – that's my wife and I – went to bed. The first I knew of any trouble was a knock at the bedroom door at some time after two in the morning. Brenden stood there with blood all over him. He was dripping wet.'

'He'd been down at the cove?'

'Yes. He told me Liam and Jason had been down there too and there'd been an argument. He said Liam had stabbed Jason.'

'Liam?'

'Yes, but I'm afraid to say I didn't believe him.' Parker hung his head for a moment. 'You see, Brenden is a habitual liar. He takes after his mother. I could see the blood on his clothing, I could see the pocketknife in his right hand. I knew he'd been the one doing the stabbing.'

'So you covered up for him?'

'Not just for him. For the good of everybody. To save the home. It was about reputation, Inspector. This sort of thing could have closed us down. I decided no good would come from reporting the incident. The boys at the home were very fragile. Any kind of disruption to their way of life would have caused them problems.'

'But there was disruption. A huge search for the boys.'

'Yes, but nothing like what would have happened.'

'So how did the body get in the cellar?'

'I enlisted the help of Mr Samuel. At first he was reluctant and wanted to go to the police. I told him that the home would be closed, that he'd lose his job and that the boys would be taken away and the group split up. That won him round. We retrieved the body from the beach and took it to some woodland nearby. Wrapped the corpse in plastic and bound it with parcel tape. Several months later we brought the body back and buried it in an old sump in the cellar. We used the fact the place was prone to flooding as an excuse to lay concrete down there.' Parker shook his head. 'I can still remember the feel of the body through the plastic. Swimming in liquid it was. Foul-smelling. And the flies. Jesus, I'll never forget the flies. It was November, but unseasonably warm, and thousands of them filled the cellar.'

'And nobody else at the home knew?'

'Everyone knew about the concreting, obviously, but not about the body. Only myself, Brenden, my wife and Samuel. We explained the flies as being a result of a fractured sewer pipe. On the night of the disappearance, Samuel suggested the tale about the boys swimming out to sea and drowning, since that's what appeared to have happened to Liam. If his body was ever found, it would lend credence to the entire story. To be honest, I didn't hold out much hope everything would work out, but after the initial search, the investigation seemed to mysteriously wind down and from then on the police only made perfunctory visits.'

Hardin needed to hear this, Savage thought. When he'd shown the photograph of the minister to his superior, a train of events had been set in motion. As soon as the boys had gone missing, calls had been made, favours called in and the case had been put on the back burner. The end result was that Operation *Curlew* had been doomed to fail from the outset.

Frank Parker's story was plausible, but she didn't buy it. She guessed what had actually happened was that Parker had gone down to the cove and been presented with a terrible dilemma: if he'd brought Jason back to the home and taken him to hospital, questions would undoubtedly have been asked. Jason may well have spilled the beans about what was going on at the home. The other option was far less risky. He could simply kill the boy, leaving his son to believe he alone was responsible.

'I'm sorry, Mr Parker, I don't believe you.' Savage nodded at Calter and the DC moved forward extracting a pair of handcuffs from her jacket pocket.

'Frank Parker,' Calter said. 'I'm arresting you on suspicion of the murder of Jason Caldwell. You don't have to say anything, but it may harm your defence if you don't mention something which you later rely on in court. Anything you say may be given in evidence.'

Parker shook his head, but he turned round when Calter asked him to. He cupped his hands behind his back and they led him out into the corridor.

Mrs Parker hovered near the front door. 'Frank?'

'Don't worry,' Parker said. 'We'll have this nonsense sorted in no time.'

'No!' Mrs Parker moved to the centre of the corridor, hunched forward with a back arched like a cat about to spring into action. 'This isn't your fault. You tried to do your best by the boy and now look what's happened.'

'Edie! Silence, woman!'

Mrs Parker cowered and slumped to one side of the corridor as if Parker had kicked her in the ribs. Calter pushed Parker forward and Savage followed. As they traipsed down the steps, a scream came from behind them. Mrs Parker stood on the threshold with her hands reaching towards the sky.

'God, I beseech you, what have you done? Frank is innocent!'

Luke Farrell was waiting at the gate and as Calter put Parker in the back of the squad car he came across to Savage.

'Ma'am?' Farrell glanced up the steps. 'Should I?'

'No,' Savage said, following his gaze to where Mrs Parker clawed at the air. 'I don't think you can help her. We'll question Mr Parker first and then see about bringing her in.'

'Your call.' Farrell shook his head. 'But in my book it's a good one.'

En route to the custody centre at Charles Cross Police Station, tailing the patrol car with Frank Parker in, Savage took a call from DS Riley. Ned Stone, apparently, was now implicated in the murder of Tim Benedict. She listened as Riley told her about the new evidence surrounding Stone and then made a judgement call.

'Let them book Parker in,' she said to Calter, gesturing at the car in front. 'We need to talk to Darius.'

At Crownhill, she met Riley in the crime suite. Collier hovered in the background, voicing his concern about the congruence of the two investigations.

'You've got Stone pegged for this vicar killing?' Savage asked Riley.

'He's definitely implicated in the disappearance of Perry Sleet, which means he connected somehow with Tim Benedict's death.'

Riley explained about the use of a Taser in both kidnappings and how Stone, Benedict and Sleet were linked together through Sarah Hannaford.

'Benedict was a curate where she lived and Sleet a neighbour's son.'

'Where was this?' Savage said.

'Somewhere over near Salcombe.' Riley glanced at his notes. 'Bolberry.'

'*Bolberry?* Shit, Darius, that's next door to the Woodland Heights children's home. Ned Stone was a resident at the home, albeit before Jason Caldwell and Liam Hayskith went missing. Why didn't you make the connection to Operation *Curlew*?'

'Sorry, ma'am.' Riley turned his hands up in guilt. 'It was only this morning Stone became a suspect in our case. I guess we haven't correlated all the information yet.'

'OK, let's leave that for a moment and try and get our heads around what's going on here. We'll start at the beginning and go through the events sequentially. One, Jason and Liam disappear in 1988. Nothing is found until Layton digs up the cellar and discovers a bone which belongs to Jason Caldwell and we find the rest of the boy's skeleton is buried in a wood near Woodland Heights. We now suspect Frank Parker of killing Jason to cover up the abuse at the home. Fast-forward to the present day. Tim Benedict and Perry Sleet go missing. Next, Jason Hobb goes missing and Liam Clough is murdered. Finally, Benedict turns up critically injured and dies a day later.'

'And you're suggesting Stone is the link between these crimes?'

'Stone was a resident at the home, he was enquiring about Perry Sleet and he had contact with the Hobb boy through Hobb's mother, Angie.'

'What about the raft?' Riley said. 'The one Tim Benedict was found on is identical to the one which washed up on the beach at Jennycliff. Do you think Stone could be involved with that too?'

'I doubt it. I can't see Stone having the nous to build such a thing. He can barely cobble together a sentence, let alone a complex woodworking project. And even if he could, where did he construct the thing? He lives in a bedsit.'

'The same place he's holding Jason?' Riley said.

'I don't buy it. Stone has three brain cells. If he *is* our man, then he doesn't have the wits to cover his tracks. Which

270

means we should get something from his house or car. His place has already been looked at but I think it's time it was searched properly.'

Savage told Riley that she'd despatch a team of CSIs over to Devonport to rip up Stone's bedsit and examine his Corsa. A week ago, DC Calter had suggested just that; Savage hoped her decision not to proceed back then hadn't been the wrong one.

'This is getting much too complex for my liking,' she said. 'We've got Stone and Parker as suspects in linked investigations, but the PACE clock is running on Parker, so it would be nice to find Stone before we have to release him.'

That wasn't the only clock which was running, Savage thought, as she remembered the drawing Hardin had been sent. The drawing depicted a stick-figure representation of Jason Hobb imprisoned in a box. Scared, alone and buried underground, time was almost certainly running out for him too.

After speaking to Riley, Savage and Calter rendezvoused with an interview advisor at the custody centre. The advisor, a small thin man in his thirties, looked as if he was about to have kittens. When Parker had been booked in, he'd been asked about legal representation, but he'd rejected the offer.

'He's refused a lawyer.' The advisor shook his head. 'Apparently the only thing he needs is a Bible. It's bloody inconvenient, I mean, he's a nutter, isn't he? This God and damnation stuff. All he needs to add is he's hearing voices and we're bloody knackered. If he's got mental issues, then any sense we're cajoling him could lead to all sorts of problems down the line.'

'Are you telling me we need an appropriate adult?'

'If not a lawyer, then yes. If he'll wear it.'

'I can put it to him, but no, I don't think he will.'

Half an hour later, armed with copious notes from the advisor, Savage and Calter moved to the interview room where Frank Parker awaited. Savage wanted to know if Parker was still refusing a lawyer and if he'd accept an appropriate adult.

'No. God will judge me,' Parker said as Savage pulled out a chair and sat. 'His love and protection are enough. His will will be done and there is nothing you or I can do to alter that fact.'

'Fine,' Savage said. She was fed up with Parker's religious talk. Whether it was put on or genuine, she wasn't going to let his preaching stand in the way.

Calter conducted the preliminaries with the audio and video equipment and then they were off. Savage ran through the events of the 26th August as described by Brenden Parker. She then asked him if he agreed with that version.

'Yes, all true.' Parker sat as straight as a broom, one hand extended rigidly across the table and resting on a hastily rustled-up Bible. 'I went down to the cove and found Jason lying in the sand, blood all over him. Brenden had dragged him up the beach away from the water and into the shelter of a cave. I think Jason had been alive at that time, but looking at the state of the body I knew there was nothing anyone could have done. It was a sickening sight.'

Savage said nothing for a minute. Silence, she often found, revealed the veracity of any statement. In this case she thought Parker's words were a pack of lies. She let Parker sit a little longer and then spoke again.

'Except there was plenty which could have been done, wasn't there?'

'No, Inspector. Jason had bled to death. Brenden had stabbed him repeatedly.'

272

'Not at all. The wounds were superficial. Brenden cut Jason with a pocketknife. The blade was perhaps two inches in length. According to the pathologist, the weapon used to kill him was much larger. Something like a kitchen knife.'

'Patholo . . .' Parker blinked rapidly and then clasped the Bible with both hands. 'I thought there were only bones left?'

'Jason Caldwell's bones have told us a lot. There's no way a pocketknife could have caused Jason's death.'

'Brenden must have had a different blade then.'

'Well, coincidentally a kitchen knife was reported missing by the housekeeper, Edith Bickell.' Savage looked down at her notes. 'The knife vanished from a locked drawer and she was sure she'd used it earlier that evening.'

'There you go. Brenden must have used that.'

'Later, though, Miss Bickell retracted the statement, saying instead the knife had been missing for months. Odd, huh?'

'Not at all. Her memory must have played tricks on her. Edie's like that, even now she—'

'Edie?' Savage stared at Parker, something clicking in her brain. She cast her mind back a few hours to when they'd arrested him. He'd shouted at his wife as they'd led him away: *Edie! Silence, woman!* Edie, Savage thought. Not Deborah. Of course. She had it now. Mrs Edie Parker was none other than Miss Edith Bickell. The change of name explained why Collier had had trouble tracking her down. Savage nodded and then smiled. 'And Edie Bickell is your *second* wife, right?'

'What of it?' Parker snapped. 'Edie and I got together after the home closed. Deborah, my first wife, left me. She took Brenden and ran off. Turned the boy against me.'

'Right. Seems to me back then Edith might have been doing you a favour in changing her story about the knife because she was in love with you. Or perhaps, afterwards, you owed her.'

'Complete and utter nonsense.'

Once again Savage let Parker's words hang for a minute. Then she tried a new tack.

'You know why the investigation wound down, don't you, Mr Parker? The real reason you didn't report Jason Caldwell's murder.'

'I've told you why I didn't report it. I didn't want to implicate my son and I didn't want the home to close.'

'And I don't believe you.' Savage reached into the folder once more. She brought out the photocopy of the picture Hardin had given her and slid the image across the table. 'Might this not have played a part?'

'My God! Where did you get that?'

'You didn't want anyone poking their noses in too deeply, did you?'

'I . . .'

'As you said, a murder investigation would have caused massive disruption. There would be more than just a few questions. This man's name would have come out and you would be implicated in the abuse as well.'

'You don't understand. This isn't what you think.'

'But it is, Mr Parker. Next you're going to tell me some story which provides a justification for what went on in the home. You're a sad, pathetic excuse for a human being. You hide behind your religious rhetoric, but underneath you're nothing but a pervert and a murderer. You went down to the cove and you discovered Jason. He was cut badly on his hands but he wasn't dying. You'd brought the kitchen knife with you and you decided there'd be fewer questions if you killed Jason. I bet the poor boy looked up from the sand, pleading for help. Instead of help he got a blade in the stomach.'

274

'*STOP!*' Parker spat the word at full volume. He leant forward and stared at Savage. Then his bottom lip began to quiver. His eyes filled with tears and he collapsed face down on the table with his hands on top of his head.

Savage glanced across at Calter. The DC shrugged. This wasn't what Savage was expecting at all.

'I can understand why you did it, Frank, but I can't understand why you told Brenden he was guilty. A thirteen-year-old boy. He's spent his life thinking he killed Jason Caldwell. What a burden for him to carry.'

Parker continued to sob, his face pressed against the Bible. Savage opened the folder again. She pulled out two more photographs.

'We need your help, Frank,' she said. 'You can put things right.'

Parker looked up as Savage pushed the pictures across the table.

'The left-hand one is Liam Clough. He was murdered, his body dumped on the Drake's Trail cycle path. The other boy is Jason Hobb and we believe he's being held captive. He's buried in the ground in a makeshift coffin. If we don't find him soon then he'll die.'

'Jason?' Parker stared at the pictures. 'My God, no, what is this?'

'You know what this is, Frank. It's history repeating itself. Somebody playing a deadly game.'

'Mr Parker?' Calter spoke using an even lighter tone than Savage. She reached across the table and pointed at the picture of Jason. 'That little boy is scared. He needs your help, Frank. Where is he?'

Parker turned from Savage to Calter. 'I've got nothing to do with this. Are you crazy? Why would I hurt these two?'

'Come on, Frank, you killed Caldwell.' Calter extended

her arm a little farther and touched the Bible beneath Parker's hands. 'It's a fantasy, isn't it? These two boys are standing in for the two boys in the past. I'm sure God will forgive you if you tell us the truth.'

'You're crazy.' Parker snatched the Bible from underneath Calter's hand and drew the book across the table. He clutched it to his chest. 'What happened on the beach was awful, but I was trapped. The minister threatened me and I had no choice, but ever since, I've lived a blameless life. I swear to Almighty God I'm innocent of these crimes.'

'Mr Parker.' Savage decided to go formal again. 'We believe there's a link from these contemporary crimes to the missing boys from the home. It seems beyond doubt whoever abducted Jason Hobb and Liam Clough is connected with Woodland Heights.'

'Maybe you're right, but the connection isn't me.'

'So who is it then?'

'Why don't you ask Brenden?' Parker said the words with venom. 'He's the cause of all this. If he hadn't got into a fight with Caldwell, then none of this would have happened. I will confess to killing Jason Caldwell and I'll make a statement to that effect. I will not admit to anything else because, by God, I'm innocent of any other crime.'

Savage nodded. Parker, it appeared, was done. She nodded to Calter to pause the interview and they left the room. In the corridor, Savage asked the DC what she thought.

'A charmer, our Mr Parker,' Calter said. 'Happy to diss his own son when the blame lies with him all along.'

'Well, somebody's telling porkies,' Savage said. 'Let's see what progress the sexual offence liaison officers have made with Brenden and then re-evaluate the situation. Depending on what they've found out, we may need another word with him.'

'You think he could be in the frame?'

'Well, I'm pretty sure that between the pair of them the Parkers are responsible for this whole thing.'

'What have you done!' The voice came in the pitch-black. 'You abomination! Not only are you trying to escape again like you did all those years ago, you've also disturbed Mother.'

Jason flinched in the darkness and cowered back into the corner as he heard the sound of a spade clanging on stone. Somebody was digging down from above. He reached out in the dark and found a long thin piece of the planking he'd dug out earlier. The end had splintered and left a sharp point

'Well, I won't have it. You're staying here with me now, whether you like it or not. I don't know. I thought Smirker was mischievous. You're in another league entirely. Wait until I get down there, my boy, I'll give you a taste of discipline you'll never forget.'

'No, please!' Jason called out. The corpse had been one thing, but now the nutter was coming for him. 'I'm a good boy really. Ask my mum.'

'What's that you say?' The digging stopped. 'A good boy?'

'Yes. Honestly. And I'll be your friend.'

'How can I believe you? Boys lie all the time. The other Jason lied to me. He said he was my friend and then he ran off. Later he came back and I put gems in his eyes. He was a good boy for years, but now he's run away again.'

'I won't run away, I promise. Cross my heart.'

'Ah! How do I know you're crossing your heart?'

'Look down. I'm right beneath the tube.'

Silence. And then a shaft of bright light. The beam from a powerful torch.

'OK, show me.'

'Drop the torch down so I can light myself up.'

Silence again and then the sound of the torch sliding down. Jason caught the torch as it fell from the bottom of the tube. He glanced up the tube and saw a face press down, an eye moving into place at the end. He pulled the piece of wood to him and selected the sharp end.

'Are you looking?' he said.

'Yes. Show me.'

'OK.'

Jason rammed the piece of plank up the tube with all his might, connecting with something soft and squishy at the other end.

Chapter Twenty-Eight

I haven't written anything for over two months. Two months!
My world has fallen apart since that night on the beach, but
it's time to put pen to paper and record what happened.

As Jason lay in my arms, I knew I had to get help. Liam had
disappeared out to sea, so my only hope was to run back to the
house. I lowered Jason to the sand and ran for all I was worth.
Back at the house, my father was coming down the front steps
with Bentley. At my approach the two of them looked up, Father
concerned. I blurted out what had happened and Father at once
made to come with me. Bentley said something to Father, but
I didn't catch it. He then got into his car and drove away.

Father then set off for the beach. I wanted to come, but he
changed his mind and insisted I remained behind. It wasn't
until several hours later that Father returned. He stomped
upstairs to the apartment and barged into the living room. I
was lying on the settee, my head on Mother's lap. I raised my
head. Father was covered in dirt. Sand – of course – but mud
and leaves too.

I asked him where Jason was but he only started to shout.
It was all my fault, he said. And my mother's. I began to cry
and asked him again about Jason. You killed him, he said. You
stabbed him and left him dying in the surf.

Then Father hit me. Not a smack but a full-on punch which

knocked me down. As I lay on the floor, I thought of what had
happened at the cove. I'd cut Jason on the hands, but could I
have killed him?

'No,' I said as Father walked away. 'Noooooo!'

What had I done? What awful sin had I committed? Had
I blacked out in a rage and stabbed Jason?

Now, over two months later, I've at least managed to work
out what happened to Jason's body. You see, Father and Mr
Samuel have been in the cellar tonight. I watched through the
airbrick as they carried a bundle down the steps and through
into the adjoining room. The bundle had to be Jason's corpse.
They must have hidden him somewhere away from the home.
Now everything had calmed down, they'd brought him back.
I couldn't see what Father and Mr Samuel were up to, but I
could hear. They were digging and then afterwards they were
mixing concrete.

Once they'd gone off to bed, I made my way down to the
cellar. The place smelled of cement and other odours. And the
flies, there were masses of them. In the little room next to the
cellar, I found an area of freshly laid concrete. I knew Jason
was down there. Sleeping. He could only be sleeping because
he couldn't be dead. I couldn't have killed him. Not me.

I'd brought a number of night lights with me and I placed
them around the room. On one side were a set of scaffold
boards Father had used to tamp down the concrete. I took a
couple of the boards and slid them across the wet concrete. I
scrabbled across the boards and began to dig. It took ages as I
flung lumps of wet concrete to one side. The more I dug, the
more the concrete tried to flow back into the hole. Eventually
the cement dried somewhat and I managed to clear an area a
few feet across. Beneath the concrete was soil and rubble. I
picked out dozens of pieces of brick and stone and put them
in a tin bucket. Each time the bucket became full, I dumped

the contents to one side. Eventually I saw something golden in amongst the earth: hair!

It took me a while to understand what they'd done. All I could see was the top of his head. Then I realised they'd buried him vertically in an old well, with huge lumps of stone all around him. I leant over and tried to remove some of the stones, but the task was impossible. Jason was wedged in place.

I think it was then I lost it. I figured that there was no way to get him out. I began to cry as I thought of his beautiful face, his welcoming smile and his sparkling eyes.

And then a thought came to me: I didn't need to get him out. Not all of him, anyway.

The Shepherd blinks and finds himself sitting in the rocking chair. The light has gone from the day, hours gone from his life. He turns to the clock. Five thirty. He shakes his head. He must have been asleep since lunchtime, but once again a series of bad dreams means he doesn't feel rested. An ache spreads across his shoulders and he flexes his muscles to try to relieve the tension. Then he pushes the floor with his feet, setting up that comforting rhythm which enables him to think.

He'd dreamt of cellars and concrete and bodies rotting in the ground. He'd dreamt of a cane swishing through the air, punishment administered without rhyme or reason. He'd dreamt of abuse carried out by the powerful with the co-operation of the weak and cowardly. Finally, he'd dreamt of the cove again. The sea tumbling over itself, the wind howling, salt spray in the air, screams in the darkness.

That night, he thinks, God was absent from the world, for what God would send a storm to punish three innocent children?

Two innocent children . . .

Two innocent children, yes. The boy who plays with the

skull wasn't innocent. Not then and not now. The other two boys, though, had done nothing to deserve such wrath. Yet come the dawn, one was dead and the other swept out to sea.

The Shepherd shakes his head. His faith these days is absolute and unbreakable. The questions which come from his dreams are there to tempt him to stray from the path he has set out upon, but the certainty of scripture provides all the answers.

Trust in the Lord with all thine heart; and lean not unto thine own understanding. In all thy ways acknowledge Him, and He shall direct thy paths. Be not wise in thine own eyes: fear the Lord, and depart from evil.

Yes, the Shepherd thinks, fear the Lord and depart from evil. For it is only by doing so the nightmare can be ended. He ceases rocking and listens. There. The voices once again. The sound of two boys singing.

Oh, for the wings, for the wings of a dove . . .

The Shepherd smiles to himself. He stares into the dark of the room and mouths the lyrics until he reaches the final line.

And remain there forever at rest.

Then he closes his eyes and sleeps again.

Chapter Twenty-Nine

When Savage phoned the sexual liaison officer to discuss Brenden Parker, she was shocked to discover that no interview had yet taken place.

'Out, ma'am,' the officer said. 'We knocked, spoke to the neighbour, hung round for a good half an hour in case he'd gone to the shops. Nothing. I guess, from what you told us, he could be so traumatised that he's changed his mind about wanting to talk.'

Savage hung up, thinking that wasn't it at all.

By six o'clock Savage and Calter were outside Parker's house in Ivybridge. Lights glowed in the windows of neighbouring properties, but Parker's place was dark. They got out and Calter went up to the front door and tapped on the glass panel.

'Still not here, ma'am,' she said as she bent to the letterbox and peered through. 'I reckon he's gone AWOL.'

'Right.' Savage paused for a moment and then made a judgement call. 'We bust it.'

'You sure about this, ma'am?' Calter said as Savage returned to the car and pulled out a wheel brace. 'Don't we need a warrant?'

'I've got my feeling.'

'About Brenden?'

'About the Parkers in general.' Savage glanced at the door. 'I think once we're inside we might find an answer. If we need an excuse, we can use Jason Hobb as a justification.'

'That's what I like about you, ma'am. You've got a way of making everything seem perfectly reasonable and above board.'

Savage gave Calter a half glance and then swung the wheel brace at the section of glass next to the lock. The glass crazed and Savage used the brace to knock the pieces out. She slid her hand in, undid the latch and pushed the door open. She moved into the house. Calter tiptoed in behind.

'Take a look at the post, would you?' Savage gestured at a shelf in the hall where a mass of envelopes and circulars lay in a pile. 'See if there's anything interesting. Brenden?' she hollered out down the hall. She moved along and into the bare living room. She reached for the light switch and as the light came on, her eyes were drawn to the paper she'd noticed on their earlier visit, an *Ivybridge and Salcombe Gazette* from late August. She walked across and picked up the newspaper. She flicked through the slim publication, stopping at a page within the property section where a picture had been roughly cut from the page. Beneath the picture some of the text for the advertisement remained.

. . . ideal for conversion to a boutique B&B, a small hotel, or a number of flats. Alternatively, the property would make a grand residence for an extended family. With breathtaking sea views and easy access to the yachtsman's paradise of Salcombe, this property . . .

284

Savage moved her eyes to the top of the page. Marchand Petit was the agent's name. The same name as on the board at Woodland Heights.

On its own, the fact Brenden Parker had shown enough interest to cut out the picture of the children's home was unremarkable. Parker Junior had lived in the home for a number of years. He may have cut out the advertisement simply to show to a friend. On the other hand, the date, August, was around about the time the concrete in the cellar had been disturbed and partly relaid. Was it possible Parker or somebody else had become alarmed at the thought the property might be redeveloped? Redevelopment would almost certainly see the cellar inspected. Bearing in mind the dampness down there, a surveyor or architect may have advised that some sort of remedial work should take place.

'Ma'am?' Calter leant into the room, wanting to know what Savage had found. Savage showed her the newspaper and explained her theory.

'The property was going to be sold,' Savage said. 'Which is why somebody came and retrieved Jason Caldwell's body. Only they didn't get it all.'

'The fragment of metatarsal?'

'Yes. Though I daresay the bone would have been missed had the floor been dug up by builders.'

'Probably.' Calter nodded and then passed Savage a greetings card. 'I found this amongst the mail. It might explain Brenden Parker's extended sick leave.'

There were flowers on the front of the card, 'Condolences' written in gold script. Inside was a sickly-sweet poem from the card designer and a one-line written note.

SORRY TO HEAR YOUR MUM HAS DIED . . .

'She's dead? Frank Parker never said anything when he mentioned her.'

'Maybe he doesn't know Deborah Parker's dead.' Calter pointed to the signature. 'And look who it's from: Ned Stone.'

'Stone? Bloody hell. I wouldn't have thought he was the type of bloke to have sympathy for anyone.'

'He was there though, wasn't he, ma'am?' Calter pointed to the blank hole in the newspaper. 'At the home?'

'Yes. Before the two boys went missing. He must have been friends with Brenden. Close friends. Get on to Collier and double-check the dates, would you?'

Calter nodded and pulled out her phone. Savage, meanwhile, made her way to the back of the house and the kitchen. The fridge had been emptied and cleaned, switched off and the door held open with a rolled-up tea towel. The oven was spotless. The cupboards held not much other than a few tins of stew and some bottles of still spring water. She went to the sink and turned the tap. Nothing other than a slight hiss of air. The water had been turned off at the mains. Likewise the gas.

Parker had pulled a fast one on them, Savage thought. He hadn't been living permanently in the house for weeks, but for some reason he'd come back earlier in the day. The empty fridge explained why he'd been forced to give them condensed milk. It had been pure good fortune he'd been in when they visited.

Savage looked around the kitchen again. To the left of the back door a key hung on a hook. She stared through the glass. In the gloom, she could see a small patio and an area of lawn. At the edge of the lawn stood a shed. Not a common or garden shed, but a substantial metal workshop. She unlocked the back door, walked across to the shed and tried the key from the hook. The key slotted perfectly into the heavy padlock.

The lock clicked open and she swung the door outward. Inside, there was a smell of sawdust and wood oil. Against one wall stood a workbench with a vice. Nearby, a router table sans router. Above the workbench there was a rack with hooks and slots for tools, a place for everything. Only nothing was in its place, for the rack was empty.

Brenden Parker was obviously a keen woodworker. So keen that wherever he'd gone to he'd taken his tools with him.

Savage moved to the bench and ran her hand over the surface, picking up sawdust on her fingertips. She raised her hand to her nose. The sawdust smelt fresh. Parker had been making something recently.

She brushed the sawdust from her hands and watched as the flecks floated to the floor, several alighting at her feet next to a large tub with a red lid. She stared down at the tub for a moment, trying to understand why it might be important. Then, with a growing sense of unease, she realised. Liam Clough's body had been covered with some sort of sticky substance which had turned out to be grease. She bent and read the label on the tub, feeling a frisson of excitement as she took in the brand name: *Castrol*.

As Savage came in through the kitchen door, she turned back and looked at the shed again. She wondered when Parker had taken up his woodworking hobby. Then she remembered he was a teacher at a local secondary school. What was it Collier had said, DT?

Design and Technology.

This wasn't a hobby at all, this was Parker's profession. Shit, Savage thought. The drawings of the box in the ground had been created by somebody with draughting skills. Parker obviously had those skills as well as the equipment to construct such a thing.

There was a creak from the ceiling. Calter was up there exploring the bedrooms. Savage went into the hallway and shouted up the stairs.

'We've got this totally wrong, Jane,' she said. 'Brenden Parker is the killer of Liam Clough and Jason Hobb's kidnapper. He was right under our noses and we've let him slip through our fingers.'

'Uh-huh. Makes sense, ma'am.' Calter's voice floated down from above. Her voice sounded flat and unsurprised. 'Come up here.'

Savage took the stairs two at a time. On the landing a door stood open to a bathroom.

'In the bedroom, ma'am.' Calter's voice came from a room at the back. 'We're too late.'

Savage moved along the landing to the master bedroom. She stepped inside. A double bed was positioned between a set of built-in wardrobes, high-level cupboards spanning the space above. Her eyes were drawn to the mirror on the ceiling above the bed.

'Wow,' she said.

'That's what I thought. Bit kinky for a suburban semi.'

Savage glanced around. A double duvet on the bed had been scuffed back and a pile of clothes sat on a chair. She could see nothing amiss.

'I thought you'd found him. Parker.'

'No.' Calter gestured across to the bed. 'But somebody else has.'

Savage moved across to where Calter was standing. The DC pointed down at a small dark stain.

'Blood?' Savage said. 'But not much more than from a minor cut. A nosebleed perhaps.'

'Not the blood, ma'am.' Calter waved her hand in a circle. 'Those.'

Scattered across the bed were a number of small pieces of paper. Confetti. Only the confetti looked like none Savage had ever seen. Yellow and pink and each with an identical sequence of numbers on.

'Shit,' Savage said. 'Brenden Parker's been Tasered.'

Riley received a text message from Kenny Fallon at a little after six thirty p.m.

Flat A, 25 Emma Place

Ten seconds later, Riley was talking to somebody in the control room and within ten minutes he had confirmation from officers on the ground over in Stonehouse that Stone was in handcuffs in the back of a squad car on his way to the custody centre.

'Result,' Riley shouted to Collier, who was fixing a picture of a forty-something man to one of the *Lacuna* whiteboards. 'We've got Ned Stone.'

'Great.' Collier tapped the picture and smiled. 'If you could just round up this guy as well, I'd be very grateful . . .'

'Sure thing.' Riley laughed. 'But after I've dealt with Stone, OK?'

He left the crime suite and went in search of Enders. Once he'd found the DC they went over to the custody suite in the centre of town, where an hour went begging while Stone sorted a lawyer. While they were waiting, a call came through from DI Savage. Brenden Parker was now the main suspect in *Lacuna*, she said, leaving Riley free to question Stone under the auspices of Operation *Caldera*. While he was doing so though, he should try to connect Stone with Parker. Stone apparently knew Parker well enough to send him a condolence card.

When Riley and Enders entered the interview room, Riley caught a whiff of pine disinfectant mixed with a heavy perfume. Neither did anything to disguise the fact somebody had recently urinated in one corner.

'Really, mate,' Stone said, shaking his head. 'I've been grilled over the disappearance of Angie's boy and now you're trying to pin a murder charge on me. It's out of fucking order.'

'We'll see.' Riley approached the table where Stone was sitting, the source of the perfume, his brief, Amanda Bradley, perched on a chair alongside. Bradley was one of the area's top lawyers. She had a preference for Chanel suits worn with low-cut tops and push-up bras. Riley had long suspected her attire was designed to win over male clients and distract male officers, but he wondered why she bothered; with her encyclopedic knowledge of the law and shrewd argumentative powers, she was a formidable opponent whatever she was wearing. Riley nodded a greeting to her and then turned back to Stone. 'Once you've answered our questions.'

'I'm not answering—'

Bradley put out her hand to silence her client. She smiled at Riley, her teeth glinting like diamonds. 'I'm sure Mr Stone will be happy to answer your questions.'

'Let's hope so.' Riley pulled out a chair and sat down. 'Otherwise he's in deep shit.'

Enders prepared the interview equipment and conducted the preliminaries. Stone was suspected of being involved in the murder of Benedict and the abduction of Sleet. In addition, there were still questions regarding the disappearance of Jason Hobb.

'So you see, Ned,' Riley said, 'You are, to all intents and purposes, fucked.'

'No way!' Stone said. 'I didn't do any of those things.'

'Really?' Riley picked up his notes. 'You went to see Sarah Hannaford about Perry Sleet. First, Sleet goes missing and then Tim Benedict turns up critically injured. He dies a day later.'

'You can't fucking pin all that on me.' Stone spat the words out, phlegm on his lips. 'I never went near Sleet or the vicar.'

'Do you deny you visited Mrs Hannaford and asked questions specifically about the whereabouts of Sleet?'

'That old bint?' Stone grinned. 'She should keep her mouth shut.'

'So you admit you did visit her?'

'Might have.'

'Why did you want to know where Perry Sleet was?'

'He's an old friend. We go way back.'

'Right. Would that be back to the Neanderthal age then?' Riley shook his head. He took a piece of paper and slid it across the table to Stone. 'Here's a picture of Sleet to remind you. Where do you know him from?'

'I told you, he's an old friend.'

'And one morning you suddenly decide to look him up. This after how many years?'

'Be twenty, twenty-five years. More. And yeah, that's about how it happened.'

'And you and Perry Sleet . . .' Riley gestured at Stone. 'You've got a lot in common, have you? Him with a good job, loving wife, nice family and house. You with, what? A pile of clothes on the floor of some stinking bedsit? Come on, Ned, you can do better than this. At least spin me something believable.'

'I just fancied meeting up with him, all right?'

Riley sighed. This wasn't going well. 'You knew him from

the home, didn't you? Woodland Heights? You were a resident there.'

'So what if I was?' Stone shook his head. 'I was eleven fucking years old. Perry lived in the village. I guess he must have been my friend.'

'You guess? And that was good enough for you to try and make contact after nearly three decades? "Hello, Perry. I was a little tyke in the children's home and you were a middle-class kid in the village. We might have been friends. Aren't you going to invite me in?"' Now it was Riley's turn to shake his head. 'Come on, Ned, we're in fantasy land. Tell us the truth.'

'Fuck off.' Stone turned to Bradley. 'It's no wonder people don't come forward if this is what happens when they do.'

'No, you're right.' Bradley, silent until now, scented an in. She bared her teeth. 'I think it's entirely unreasonable to expect my client to discuss events surrounding the children's home with you when he's under arrest. These are sensitive and possibly distressing matters we are talking about and he was only eleven years old. Nothing which happened back then can be relevant to this investigation, therefore I ask you to desist from that line of questioning.'

'We're trying to get to the bottom of why Mr Stone was interested in reacquainting himself with Perry Sleet,' Riley said. 'A man he just said was a friend. Let's start with what happened when you met him, Ned.'

'Met him?' Stone stared deadpan across the table. 'I didn't meet him. Scout's honour.'

'And you expect me to believe that?'

'I think you should,' Bradley said, leaning back in her seat and shifting her shoulders to emphasise her cleavage. 'If my client says he doesn't know . . . well, he doesn't know. Remember, Mr Stone is possibly a victim himself and I keep hearing from the police that victims are to be believed in all circumstances.'

'Bollocks.' Riley leant forward. 'We'll soon have evidence from your bedsit and car, Ned. Our CSI guys are so good that if Sleet or Benedict have even breathed in your general direction they'll find something. It will be too late for explanations then, so you best tell us now what happened.'

'Look, you thickos.' Stone leant over the table too, his face just inches from Riley's. 'I never met Sleet, OK? I tried to find out his details but failed. Then I thought better of it. Like you said, me from the scrote end of Plymouth, and him all married with kids and a new house and all. Not compatible, were we?'

'Where were you on Sunday night, Monday morning, Ned? You've been AWOL for days. What have you been up to?'

'I was with Angie. Went round there Saturday night and stayed until yesterday.' Stone smiled. 'She needed comforting, didn't she? I'm sure she'll back me up.'

'Angie?' Riley half turned to Enders. The DC hunched his shoulders. This wasn't what they needed to hear. If Stone really was over at Mrs Hobb's house in Torpoint in the early hours of Monday, then he couldn't have been dumping Tim Benedict in a bin on the Erme estuary. 'Can anyone else confirm you were there?'

'Yeah, as a matter of fact I reckon they can.' Stone was grinning now, realising he was off the hook. 'I ran out of fags Sunday night, so first thing Monday I snuck round to the local shop. The guy there'll remember me because we had a natter about the Pilgrims. We won away at Luton on Saturday, didn't we? Top of the league, by a mile. Reckon we'll—'

'There.' Bradley tapped Stone on the shoulder and motioned for him to be quiet. 'I'm sure you can verify Mr Stone's account, but I don't think my client could have put it plainer or been more helpful. Any more questions?'

Riley cursed to himself. Things weren't going to plan. The elation he'd felt when Collier had identified Stone from the EvoFIT had long gone. Riley was about to wrap the interview so they could take a break and reassess when he remembered Savage's request.

'One more question,' Riley said. 'When did you last see Brenden Parker?'

'Bren?' Now it was Stone's turn to be wrong-footed and he appeared to be lost for words for a few seconds. Then he smiled. 'Oh, yeah, I bumped into him a while back. Went for lunch. Brenden, Angie, and me.'

'What did you talk about?'

'Old times. Jobs. Plymouth. You know. After lunch we went to the park for a kickaround.'

'A kickaround?' Riley raised an eyebrow, trying to imagine Stone larking about, having fun. 'What, you and Brenden?'

'Yeah. Me, Brenden and the kid. We had a right laugh, especially since we'd had a couple of jars. Three and in. Penalties. One v two. Angie even had a go. Brenden loved it. You could see he wished he had kids of his own. Funny thing was, it reminded me of when I was back at the home, playing footie on the fields out the back. Good times in amongst all that crap.'

'By "the kid", do you mean Jason Hobb?'

'Hey?' Stone cocked his head. 'Yes, of course. Why do you ask?'

Chapter Thirty

Savage returned to Crownhill, leaving Brenden Parker's house swarming with police. Layton and his team of CSIs were going through every room while a team of locals checked a patch of scrub at the back for any evidence of Jason Hobb. Up in the crime suite, she found Gareth Collier finishing off some admin.

'Any sign of the boy?' Collier said.

'No,' Savage said. 'He's not at Parker's place.'

'Well I've put the Dartmoor search and rescue teams on standby and made sure the force helicopter is available. I've informed the RNLI too. Wherever Jason is, I'm confident we can be there within the hour. Oh, and I've let Derriford know they might be dealing with a medical emergency as well. I wanted to make sure all the bases are covered.'

'Good work, Gareth.' Savage stared at one of the whiteboards where little red stickers adorned a map of South Devon and wished she was as positive about finding Jason Hobb alive as Collier.

At half nine, DS Riley called through from the custody suite.

'Two points, ma'am,' Riley said. 'One to do with Stone, the other Frank Parker. First, Stone's come over. He seemed genuinely shocked when I said Brenden Parker had probably kidnapped Jason Hobb. Turns out that Stone, Angie Hobb and the boy met up with Brenden a few weeks ago. That's how Brenden knew about Jason. Anyway, Stone's pretty much changed his tune now. Says he'll do all he can to help.'

'And you don't think Stone's got anything to do with killing Tim Benedict?'

'No, ma'am, I don't. He's got a cast-iron alibi.'

'So if not Stone, then who?'

'Brenden Parker. Stone said he spoke to Sarah Hannaford about Perry Sleet and then passed the info on to Parker. I believe that was the extent of his involvement.'

'That doesn't ring true. We've just discovered Taser evidence in Brenden Parker's bedroom. Parker's not the killer. At least not *Brenden* Parker. I'm leaning towards Frank Parker being responsible for everything.'

'Perhaps, but that leads me to my second point. Parker Senior has been ensconced with a duty solicitor for the past two hours and together they've come up with a written statement. Not being on the case, I don't get much of it, but the good news is he's admitted to killing the Caldwell boy. The bad news is he's going "no comment" until he's charged with an offence.'

'Shit.' With a confession they had enough to charge Parker, Savage thought, but it didn't help with the search for Jason Hobb. 'Thanks, Darius. Send the statement through, would you?'

Savage hung up and went across to a nearby terminal. She logged into her email account and five minutes later an email pinged into her inbox. She read the statement. The fact Parker had coughed to the Hobb murder was good.

What was not so good was he was now blaming the minister for putting him up to it. Parker's first wife, Deborah, had apparently been having an affair with the minister and he'd used his relationship with Deborah to get close to the boys. Parker had tried to stop the abuse but he was in too deep. The sordid triangle had left Parker on the verge of a breakdown, but in the end, the death of Jason Caldwell had pulled Parker to his senses. He escaped from his wife's clutches and left the home with Edith Bickell, the housekeeper. Six months later, Parker filed for divorce from Deborah, citing irreconcilable differences.

'Problems?' Collier had taken his jacket from a nearby chair. He pulled it on. 'Or can I go home?'

'Nothing I can't deal with.' Savage smiled at the office manager. 'You can go. Goodnight.'

With Collier gone, Savage focused in on the details about the minister again. What part had he played? Whatever it was, she needed to speak to Hardin right now. She pulled out her phone, aware there was a text she'd missed.

Urgent. Call me now. CH.

She cursed. *CH?* Conrad Hardin. Savage pressed call and Hardin answered after a single ring.

'Charlotte, thank God! Everything's turning to ratshit. When I got home there was a letter waiting. The wife picked it off the front doormat mid-afternoon. Hand-delivered for Christ's sake!'

'Sir?'

'Are you listening, Charlotte? The bastard knows where I live.'

'The letter, sir, what does it say?'

'The nutter wants me to go to Soar Mill Cove. Tonight.'

'Shit, you're joking?'

'No.' There was silence for a moment. 'I'll sort out some backup, but I want you to meet me there in forty-five minutes. Can you come?'

Savage was already on her feet. She crossed the room and pushed through the doors into the corridor. 'Yes, sir, I can.'

'I'll see you in the coast path car park then. Soonest.'

Five minutes later and she was in her car heading away from the station and towards the dual carriageway. The streets were quiet, just the occasional set of headlights reflecting on roads slick with drizzle. At Soar Mill Cove, she thought, there'd be nobody at all. Nothing but the sea and the cliffs and the wind and the rain.

She arrived at the coast some thirty-five minutes later, the shape of Woodland Heights looming black against the night sky. She ignored the track to the home and instead followed the road round to the National Trust car park where a solitary vehicle stood near the entrance. Inside the car the interior light illuminated the bulky figure of DSupt Hardin. As she pulled up alongside, he opened his door and got out.

'Sir?' Savage said as she got out of her own car. 'Where the hell's the backup?'

'Not coming, Charlotte.' In the darkness, Savage couldn't make out the expression on Hardin's face, but she heard him exhale a sigh. 'This is personal. I wasn't stupid enough to come here on my own, but I needed someone I can rely on, not a load of grunts. We're different, Charlotte, you and I. I usually do things by the book. Bullet points. A click of the mouse. One, two, three. You're a maverick, you act on impulse, make it up as you go along. I guess the clue's in your name. Savage. The name comes from the French, doesn't it? Doesn't mean aggressive or nasty at all. It means wild. That's your nature.'

'Sir?' Savage was lost. She'd never heard Hardin talk like this before. 'What did the message say?'

'Here.' Hardin reached into his jacket and pulled out a scrap of paper. He passed the paper across to Savage.

Savage leant into the car so she could use the interior light to see. The handwriting had the same distinctive curls as the first letter, but there was just one line.

DO YOUR DUTY, PC HARDIN. SOAR MILL COVE. TONIGHT.

'This doesn't make sense,' Savage said. 'With the evidence we found at Brenden Parker's place, it looks like he's the killer of Liam Clough and the person who's got Jason Hobb.'

'So?'

'But somebody's Tasered Parker. They've abducted him. The same person who took Perry Sleet and killed Tim Benedict has now got Brenden Parker.'

'But why . . .?'

'Something to do with the home. Something those men have done. Sir, I really don't think we should be going down to the cove without backup. This could be dangerous.'

'Nonsense. I'm going to do my duty. Just like the letter said.' Hardin went round to the rear of his car and sprung the hatch. He pulled out a set of walking boots and a couple of torches. He handed one to Savage. 'Take this and if you've got any gear then get it on.'

'But, sir—'

'Shut it, DI Savage. That's an order. If you don't want to come, then fine. Otherwise let's get moving.'

Savage shook her head, but took the torch. She went to her car, retrieved her waterproof and in the boot found a pair of wellingtons. Not ideal for walking the coast path, but they'd have to do.

They kitted up and set off. The path was level for the first half a mile and then dropped sharply away down to the cove. They trudged along, little pools of light from the torches the only thing to focus on.

'So Brenden Parker's out of the picture now, is he?' Hardin said as they walked. 'He kidnapped Liam and Jason and killed Liam Clough. However, the tables have been turned. But if somebody *has* captured Parker and he's the killer, then how did he hand-deliver a note to me this evening?'

'That's why I said it's a trap, sir.'

'So who did it? Parker Senior is in custody, as is Ned Stone.'

Savage left the question unanswered and they walked on in silence, taking care on the steep path which zigzagged down the hillside. The going wasn't easy in daylight, and now, with only torches and in the wet, the path was treacherous. Finally, they reached the bottom, where a slippery concrete ramp led down to the beach. Savage could hear the waves in the distance, a line of white surf punctuating the darkness.

The cove felt very different at night. The beach sloped down to the sea, bisected by a stream which tumbled over little stones and made a constant low gurgle to complement the rhythmic noise from the waves. To either side, the cliffs rose like black curtains. Above, rain floated down from dark clouds, becoming silver speckles as the drops were caught in the torch beams.

'Here we are,' Savage said as they stepped onto the beach. 'What now?'

'We split up.' Hardin played his torch on the stream. 'You've got wellies so you take the right side. Save me getting wet, won't it?'

Savage was going to protest, but Hardin had already set off into the darkness, moving across the beach to the eastern

300

side, the beam from his torch sweeping back and forth as he went. She turned and plodded through the stream, the water surging up the side of her boots.

She reached the far bank of the stream and trudged over an area of wet sand and seaweed. Hardin appeared to think they'd find something down here, but what? Some kind of message, a cryptic clue, a bad joke? Suppose there was nothing to find, suppose he'd got it wrong and she'd got it right? Suppose somebody was going to find them?

She turned her torch off to make her presence less obvious and then criss-crossed the beach, going from the stream to the cliffs and back again and working her way down towards the sea. Her night vision improved with every passing minute and before long she found she'd covered most of her side. Now she reached a rocky outcrop which she needed to climb over.

'Charlotte!' Hardin's voice boomed out across the cove. Light reflecting on the cliffs marked his position at the far edge of the beach. 'Anything yet?'

Jesus, Savage thought. Talk about keeping a low profile. She shouted back that she was still looking and then began to edge over the rocks. The wellingtons, useful for keeping her feet dry as she'd crossed the stream, were now a liability, the last sort of footwear she wanted when clambering over wet rocks. She moved slowly round the outcrop, using the torch intermittently to guide her way. On the other side, she knew there was a fissure in the cliff face, a crack which turned into a cave. Beyond, the cliffs jutted round to another beach which could only be reached at low tide. She wouldn't go there, not without Hardin.

As she eased herself off the rocks onto a finger of sand, her heart missed a beat. Something lay in the sand. She switched her torch on. A shoe. Black leather with a flat heel, a woman's style. She peered along the finger to where the sand ran between two outcrops and into a pool of water which led into the cave. She shone the torch on the water. Tiny fish darted away from the beam and on the bottom of the pool a crab moved sideways across the sand. The water was too deep for her wellingtons and she didn't fancy clambering across the seaweed-covered rocks. She flicked the torch beam beyond the pool and into the cave. The light penetrated the darkness and what had been a gaping hole leading to the underworld was revealed as not much more than a crack in the rocks leading back just a few metres. There was nothing in there other than a few pieces of flotsam and jetsam: a couple of plastic fishing buoys, some pieces of wood, a tangle of netting.

Savage turned to go back the way she'd come, but as she did so she slipped on a patch of seaweed. She put her hand out to brace herself as she dropped to the sand, at the same time letting go of the torch. The torch fell into the pool, the light extinguished immediately.

Blackness. She closed her eyes for a second, trying to regain her night vision. When she opened them, the black had changed to grey. She pushed herself up, aware of her damp clothes covered in sand. She wondered how she was going to get back around the outcrop without a torch. She could call Hardin, she supposed, but she never liked to ask for help unless absolutely necessary. For one, Hardin would assume he was coming to her aid because she was a woman.

Savage glanced around. The shadows were making her uneasy; her night vision had partially returned, but overhead the clouds had thickened, the rain now heavier. She peered up to see if there might be any chance of a respite. Above the cliffs dark shapes scudded across the sky, the wind sweeping in from the south-west. A gust tore at her hair and she reached up to tuck a strand back under her hood. As she did so, something bumped against her hand. Savage ducked, thinking she had got too close to the cliff face. She turned and looked up to see a naked foot swing past her eyes.

Savage stepped back and tripped over again. Dangling there in mid-air hung the body of a woman, her hands and feet bound together, one foot bare, the other foot wearing a black shoe. There was a noose around the woman's neck and the rope from the noose disappeared up into the darkness of the night, the body slowly rotating in a grotesque parody of a dance.

Chapter Thirty-One

A lot's been happening since I rescued Jason from the cellar. The home is going to close down on orders from the Home Office. According to Father, it's all to do with some government initiative, but Bentley is involved somewhere, I'm sure. The incident with Jason and Liam brought too much attention on the place and shutting the home was the best option. The upheaval has finally brought to light the problems in Father and Mother's relationship. They're splitting up and Mother is leaving. Surprisingly she's taking me with her. She sat me down and told me she had been a bad parent, but that she would make it up to me. Of course, with the home closing, it means we're moving. And when I say 'we', I mean Mother and Smirker and I.

Smirker is my new friend. My only friend. He's perfect. He always listens and he always wants to play. For the record, I guess I need to explain how Smirker came into being. You see, when I retrieved Jason's head from the cellar I realised I couldn't keep him. Not in his present state. Still, I didn't want to lose him, not again. I stole a large pot from Miss Bickell's kitchen and that night I took it down to the cove. I gathered driftwood and at the entrance to the cave I built a fire. I filled the pot with seawater and set it to boil. Once the water was bubbling, I delved into my rucksack and brought out Jason's head. I dropped the head in the pot and boiled it for several hours, at some point falling into a deep sleep. A strange light woke me and I blinked my eyes open to see a dawn sky of deepest crimson. I drained the water from the pot and found the skin had sloughed away from the skull. I pulled out the skin and put it to one side, thinking I might dry the scalp and make some kind of wig from it. Then I lifted the skull from the pot. I found that the brain had softened and it was a simple matter to extract everything using a fork. Next, I took the head down to the shoreline and washed it until there was nothing left but gleaming bone.

As the waves ebbed and flowed over the hunk of bone in my hands, I realised Jason had long gone. Perhaps his soul had been carried out to sea and he was with Liam. Perhaps he was in Heaven. Perhaps he was gazing down at me through the eyes of one of the gulls which swooped in over the breakers. Really, I had no idea. But when I looked at the skull I understood it didn't matter. Here was a new friend, a friend who'd be true, who'd stick with me through any adversity. Tim Benedict was right all along. Praying DID work and God HAD answered my wish. He'd taken his time, but the wait was worth it.

I took the skull back to the cave where I sat it on a rock. I groped in my coat pocket and found two large marbles. I placed one in each eye socket so the skull could see who'd rescued him. My new friend grinned at me and it was at that very moment I knew his name had to be . . . SMIRKER!

The wait is over. The Shepherd goes to Sleet's cell and opens the door. The man is trying to hide in one corner, crouching like a mouse cowers from a cat.

'Get up,' the Shepherd says. 'It is time for you to do penance. To atone.'

Sleet hunkers down, but the Shepherd is in no mood for

wasting time so he pulls out the Taser and fires the weapon. The barbs hit Sleet in the thigh and he rolls away from the corner, his body in spasms as thousands of volts of electricity surge through him. He opens his mouth and a guttural roar spews forth.

The Shepherd steps forward and grabs Sleet. He pulls the man to his feet and leads him from the room. In the corridor they pass a large mirror on the wall. Sleet glances at his reflection and creases his face as if he can't believe what he's seeing.

In the next-door chamber the glare from the lights shines down on the altar. Sleet flinches as he spots the stainless steel table and the glint from the power tools.

'Behold the altar,' the Shepherd says. 'Where you will atone for your sins.'

'That guy in the cell next to mine,' Sleet says. 'You put him on here? Tortured him?'

'No.' The Shepherd leers in close. 'The Reverend Tim Benedict tortured himself the day he decided to become a coward. From then on his path was predestined. This was always how it was going to end for him.'

'But I haven't been a coward.' Sleet struggles to remain upright. 'I haven't *done* anything.'

'I think that's the point, Perry,' the Shepherd says. 'You didn't do anything. That's what cowardice is.'

'Do I know you from somewhere?' Sleet turns to the Shepherd. 'You look familiar.'

'Familiar? Your memory fails you now as your conscience failed you back then.'

'Back when?' Sleet staggers forward as the Shepherd pushes him. 'You can't do this without telling me what I've done, without establishing my guilt.'

'The altar establishes the guilt. The guilty place themselves upon it and receive God's punishment.' The Shepherd pushes Sleet onward. When they reach the altar, he puts his hands out and touches the manacles. 'These cuffs, they're self-locking. The same with the foot irons. A penitent man can, should he so wish, secure himself to the altar.'

'You're crazy.' Sleet stands upright now. 'Why on earth would anyone wish to do that?'

'Regrets, Perry. Atonement. Perhaps you don't feel guilt for what you've done, but put yourself in the place of somebody who might. The altar offers a way to receive the punishment one feels one deserves. After you, I have two more guests; the final one will, I hope, comply with humility and without argument.'

'And once this person is in place, you're saying they can operate the machine?'

'I set this up so it could be self-operated, yes.' The Shepherd knows Sleet is stalling, but he's happy to explain. After all, he took months constructing all this and is rather proud of his labours. 'Just outside the door to this room there's a button. Press the button and you have five minutes to get yourself locked in place. Once pressed, the altar is entirely automatic.'

'And supposing you change your mind?' Sleet looks at the Shepherd. 'Is there some way of shutting everything down?'

'Change your mind?' The Shepherd laughs. He knows Sleet is trying to find out how to turn the altar off. 'The whole point is you can't change your mind. Once the altar has been started nothing can stop it.'

'There's no need to go through with this, you know?' Sleet says. 'Whatever I've done, I'm sorry for. I'll make amends.'

'Yes, you will. Climb up.' The Shepherd waves the Taser. As with Benedict, the barbs are still in Sleet's skin. For a second, Sleet pauses, but then he complies. 'Lie facing the ceiling and click your hands into place.'

'No.' Sleet is up on the altar, but he's sitting up, not lying down. 'You can't make me.'

'There's no escape, Perry. Not for the coward who didn't tell.'

'Hey?' Sleet stares at the Shepherd. Finally there's a hint of recognition in his eyes. 'My God, no! Please, I'm sorry. Let me go. Please let me—'

The Shepherd shakes his head and squeezes the trigger on the Taser.

'Aaarrrggghhh!' Sleet's body goes rigid and he cries out. As he does so, the Shepherd pushes him backwards until he is prone and then clicks the man's wrists and ankles into place. 'Noooooo!'

'There, all done.' The Shepherd places the Taser on the floor. 'Now we begin.'

Chapter Thirty-Two

Savage's shout brought Hardin stumbling out of the darkness, his feet wet from where he'd waded through the stream. He flashed his torch in Savage's face.

'What is it, Charlotte?' Hardin stood next to her, gasping for breath. 'Found something?'

Savage didn't answer. Instead she reached for Hardin's hand and guided his torch beam up into the darkness.

'Oh fuck!' Hardin took several gulps of air. 'Please, not Jason.'

'No, sir.' Savage played the beam of light on the woman's face, now recognising the thin, haggard features. 'This is an adult female. It's Edith Parker, Frank Parker's second wife.'

'Thank God.' Hardin reached out a hand and pushed Savage's arm down. 'I don't need to see any more. This is sickening. To be honest, Charlotte, I'm not sure I can cope with it any longer. Those boys . . . this . . . I . . .'

'Sir?' Savage turned to face the DSupt, aware of a snuffling sound. Was Hardin crying? 'I understand. You know I've had my own problems. You can talk to me.'

'No.' Hardin coughed, trying to cover his emotions. 'We

309

need to call this in. Get on top of the situation. Re-establish control. Understand? Just tell me what we need. Personnel. Agencies. Resources.'

'Yes, sir,' Savage said. She took a deep breath and tried to focus. 'Andrew Nesbit, John Layton and his CSIs, a search advisor and additional officers to check the whole area. Gareth Collier to coordinate things from Crownhill. The coastguard clifftop rescue team to retrieve the body, the helicopter, the RNLI. Traffic officers to take care of road-blocking the lanes. The coroner and—'

'Well get on it, woman. Now!'

Hardin swung around and stomped off across the beach, leaving Savage with the sound of the waves and the body of Edith Parker for company.

It was forty-five minutes later when the first groups began to arrive. The team leader for the coastguard rescue came down to the beach and stood alongside Savage. He guided his crew into position at the top of the cliff using a high-powered torch.

'Ten minutes to get themselves anchored,' the man said. 'Then they'll be able to descend.'

John Layton appeared before the ten minutes were up. He took one look at the sheer rock gliding up into the darkness and dismissed any chance of a detailed examination of the area at the top of the cliff until daylight.

'You don't often get to call me a jobsworth, Charlotte,' Layton said, craning his neck to see what the rescue team were up to. 'But in this instance health and safety take priority. Sorry.'

'Fine, John,' Savage said. 'If you're worried, then there's something to be worried about.'

'We'll get a look at the body and the rope when they lower her down. Is Dr Nesbit on his way?'

'Yes. Someone's walking him in at the moment. Shouldn't be more than a few minutes until he gets here.'

'Looks like they're ready.' Layton nodded upwards to where one of the coastguard rescuers was dangling on a rope near the body. 'We'll need to hold them up until Nesbit arrives.'

Layton moved across to talk to the coastguard team leader as Savage watched the man on the rope tie a second line a little way above the noose.

'They'll cut it,' Layton said returning to Savage's side. 'Let the whole thing down slowly. Nesbit will want to get a look at the body before the noose is removed. Talk of the devil.'

'Charlotte. John.' Nesbit's silk-like voice slipped from the darkness as his lanky form emerged into view. In one hand he held his black bag, in the other a tiny penlight. 'I left my chaperone at the edge of the beach. Told him I would have no trouble finding you. Somewhat foolhardy of me since I ended up wandering around in a stream.'

Nesbit shone his little light down at his feet. He was wearing a pair of brogues and white chinos. The trousers were sodden up to the knees.

'Talk about sensible footwear, doc,' Savage said. 'Didn't anyone tell you where the body was?'

'Woodland Heights was the message I got. Nothing about walking half a mile along the coast and then descending a treacherous path to a beach where I'd have to ford a raging torrent to get to the scene.'

'Sorry, Andrew. Can you make it over the rocks?'

'Without braining myself and ending up on my own slab?' Nesbit peered across to where Layton had erected some battery-operated lights to illuminate the area beneath the body. 'Faint heart, Charlotte, faint heart.'

The three of them clambered across the rocks and stood

311

at the entrance to the cave. Layton nodded across to the coastguard team leader and gave him the go-ahead. Savage looked upwards. The man dangling in mid-air said something into his lapel-mounted radio and then took a knife and began to cut the rope a metre or so above the noose. The rope parted and the strain was taken up on the second line which ran up into the darkness. The rescuer made a second comment into his radio and then the body began to descend as those above lowered the rope. He fended off from the cliff and then was in the open space of the cave mouth.

'Stop half a metre from the ground please,' Nesbit shouted. He turned to Savage and Layton. 'I want to check the ligature and the body before the weight is taken off.'

The corpse slid down, spinning slowly until Layton was able to reach up and steady it. The coastguard rescuer abseiled down on a separate line and then unclipped himself and jumped clear.

'Woah!' Layton shouted out.

The body stopped descending, the feet just a few centimetres from the ground. Nesbit walked forward. Layton was still holding the body steady.

'She didn't die from being hanged,' Nesbit said within seconds of examining the woman's neck. 'Look, there's signs that a separate ligature was used. See the marks here, and here on the neck well below where the noose is.' The pathologist reached up with one hand and gently lifted an eyelid. 'Yes, petechiae are present. In addition, subconjunctival haemorrhaging. Blood-red eyes in layman's terms. The capillaries have ruptured in the sclera.'

'Meaning?' Savage said.

'There was a struggle.' Nesbit lowered the eyelid and then moved his hand down to the neck again, where there were a series of red lines. 'Look at these scratches. Not made by

312

the killer, but by the victim in a vain effort to try to loosen the ligature. The poor woman put up a hell of a fight.'

'Jesus.' Savage cast her mind back to when she herself had been attacked in the copse, thinking how lucky she'd been. 'It makes sense she wasn't killed here. Any kind of a struggle up at the top of the cliff would have been very dangerous.'

'And in the dark as well,' Layton said. 'I wouldn't have fancied dancing around up there whether the victim was alive or dead.'

'No,' Savage said. She looked up into the darkness once more, thinking of the man she'd seen on her first visit to the cove. 'He knew the area. He certainly would have had to reconnoitre before he lowered the body down. From up there, you'd never know the location of the cave. To my mind the fact the body was hanging in the entrance wasn't a coincidence.'

'A message?' Nesbit turned to Savage. 'Using the body as some kind of marker?'

'Jason Caldwell was murdered at the entrance to the cave by Frank Parker. Parker's son, Brenden, was obviously so affected by what happened here at Soar Mill Cove that he is now driven to leave this kind of signature. That could also point to the boy being dumped in the tunnel as being significant, the tunnel doubling for the cave.'

'I thought you didn't have much time for this kind of psychological mumbo-jumbo?' Nesbit said. 'Not that I'm saying you're wrong. Sounds highly plausible to me.' Nesbit moved back to the body. 'However, for the moment we must deal with the facts as we have them here. Let's have the body down.'

Two of Layton's officers had laid a body bag on the floor. The coastguard gave another order into his radio and the body slipped down some more. The CSIs manoeuvred the corpse and gently laid it atop the bag. Nesbit bent over and spent a couple of minutes examining the body.

The pathologist shook his head. 'I think I've seen enough for the moment. We'll examine her more fully at the mortuary. For now, let's get the bag closed up and give this poor woman some dignity.'

Chapter Thirty-Three

Sleet is lying in the altar room, secured to the altar. Everything is ready to go. The Shepherd says a final few words to him, but he's screaming, not listening at all. The Shepherd walks from the room and slides the heavy metal door shut. The latch clicks and self-locks. There. Sleet is safe now, ready to be delivered to God and absolved of all his sins.

The Shepherd moves to the control room. He walks across and slumps down in the seat. On one of the monitors there's a close-up of the altar, Sleet's head and shoulders filling the frame. The man is frothing at the mouth, drool spilling down his cheek and accumulating on the shiny surface beneath him. The Shepherd watches for a couple of minutes and checks everything is OK. Sleet is babbling now, begging for his life and crying like a baby.

Time to begin.

The Shepherd stands and makes his way from the control room. He stops in the corridor. Brenden Parker is talking. The Shepherd can't believe what he is hearing. The man is asking to be pardoned.

'This isn't right,' Parker says. 'Your plan is flawed. It's based on inaccuracies.'

The Shepherd stands rigid and stares at Parker. This won't

do. He hasn't time to listen to pathetic excuses. He needs to get on and deal with Sleet.

'You watched the abuse and did nothing,' the Shepherd says. 'Down at the cove you killed Jason Caldwell. You must suffer the consequences in the same way that Tim Benedict did. In the same way that shortly Perry Sleet will.'

'I didn't kill Caldwell,' Parker says. 'The police have arrested my father for the crime. You've got the wrong man.'

'I see.' The Shepherd considers Parker's words. All these years he'd assumed Brenden was guilty. This is something he needs to think about. He can't just dismantle the edifice he's built and throw away decades of hatred. 'You must understand you remain accused of saying nothing, of being a coward like the others. If you'd stood up to be counted, things might have been very different.'

'No. The minister would still have got away with it. Those type of people always do and they always will. I would have been beaten. I may even have ended up buried in the cellar like Jason. Besides, I was just a child. A kid. You can't blame kids for the actions of adults. Kids can't stop wars or stuff like that.'

'Right.' The Shepherd shakes his head. He can see where this is going. 'I must say you've changed your tune since the last time we spoke.'

'Yes. Since the police visited me I've been reconsidering. They made me see that I'm innocent in all of this. I'm as much a victim as Jason was, as Liam and the others.'

'A victim?' The Shepherd nods and bows his head for a moment. 'And these others, you mean the boys, don't you?'

'Yes, of course. The boys weren't to blame. Suffer the little children.'

'Suffer the little . . .' Parker is taking the biscuit now, the Shepherd thinks. Who's the religious expert around here?

He shakes his head. 'No, they weren't to blame. But Tim Benedict? Did you approve of what happened to him?'

'Oh yes. Very much.' Parker grins. 'He deserved *everything*.'

'And what about Perry Sleet?'

'Oh, he was privileged, wasn't he? Not at the home. I don't think he has any excuse, so he should still face the altar. He should still be punished.'

'Interesting.' The Shepherd nods. 'And PC Hardin? What about him?'

'I really can't understand why you haven't brought him here.'

'You can't understand . . .' The Shepherd tuts to himself. The arrogance of the man. 'I had a plan to bring him here, but you've been interfering, haven't you? You've stirred things up so much that I'm not sure it's possible any longer.'

'Well then, I was wondering if I might be permitted to deal with him?'

'You?'

'Yes.'

'But that would mean releasing you.' The Shepherd stares hard at Parker. 'And although the police may have absolved you of the murder of Jason Caldwell, there are your other actions to take into account.'

'But they don't concern you, do they?' Parker grins again. 'They are, how should I say, outside your remit?'

'Outside my . . .' The Shepherd doesn't much like Parker's tone, but the man is factually correct. The Shepherd's remit had been to bring to justice the cowards associated with the abuse at the children's home and to punish the murderer. Once that was accomplished, the task was done. 'Yes, I suppose technically you're correct.'

'So release me and I'll deal with Hardin. If I get a chance, I'll deal with Father too.'

'So be it.' The Shepherd bows his head once more. He doesn't want to see that stupid grin again. 'But get out of here before I change my mind.'

The Shepherd walks off down the corridor towards the altar room. To the right of the door to the room is the big red mushroom-shaped button on the wall. He moves his hand up to the button and rests his palm on the rounded surface.

Brenden Parker's words have unsettled him deeply. The man, apparently, is innocent, and all the Shepherd's hard work has been meaningless. In the last few months he's felt himself pulled back and forth as he tried to reconcile the two sides of his psyche. The good and the bad. The light and the dark. The altar was designed to be the ultimate arbiter of that, but God, for some mysterious reason, appears oblivious. For one awful, horrific, blasphemous moment, the Shepherd wonders if God really exists, if all there is is a universe of swirling atoms. It appears as if men like Frank and Brenden Parker, like the minister, control the world, leaving people such as the Shepherd powerless to make any kind of meaningful decisions.

Anger wells up inside him. He's not going to let this happen. He's not going to let Brenden Parker decide how this ends. There's one small thing he can do. He can refuse to go along with Parker's missive. He'll let Sleet live. The final joke *won't* be on him.

He removes his hand from the button and turns and walks away from the door, aware his life as the Shepherd is over.

I'm starting to write again. Yes, again! This time it's not been months, it's been years and years and years. The cowboy pres-ident is long dead, as is Nelson Mandela. The England football team haven't improved much, but a few years ago Great Britain actually held an Olympic Games in London. We did rather well.

Some things don't change though. I'm still here. Just. It's been a struggle to survive, but I guess Mother helped me to cope. She took me to live with her in a grand house in the country. I suspect some of the money to purchase the place came from Bentley. Talking of Bentley, he died of a heart attack on Christmas Eve 2001. Strangely enough, he was on a visit to a secure boys' unit where he was a trustee when it happened.

Father was broken after the home closed. He got together with Edith Bickell, the housekeeper, and became even more religious. I saw him on and off to start with, but every time we met he'd quote great lengths of the Bible at random. We haven't spoken now for years, although I do think his beliefs rubbed off on me to an extent.

Mother tried her best to make up for the lack of love in my early days. I daresay she mollycoddled me rather too much, because I've found it hard to go on without her. Forming relationships has always been difficult ever since Jason died and Mother and Smirker were my only friends. I moved out for a while, but when she became ill I returned to look after her. I guess the morning she died was the start of all my troubles.

Enough of the past, where are we now?

Well, it's been crazy, really crazy, and I've been busy, busy, busy. Early this afternoon I went to see Father. I wanted to know what was going on, what he'd told the police, but Father wasn't there, he'd been arrested. Edith, the bitch, blamed me of course. She started ranting and raving and telling God all sorts of nasty things about me. Well now, I couldn't have that, and it wasn't long before she was face down on the floor and I had my belt around her neck. Struggle, struggle, struggle. Pull, pull, pull. Her arms flailed around and her legs kicked out for a good couple of minutes before she gave up. I never liked her. She took the place of my mother and turned my father against me. Anyway, I bundled her into the car and took her to the cove. I strung her up and swung her out. After that I hurried back to Ivybridge to pick up some gear, which is where the crazy stuff started for real.

You see, this weirdo has been tracking down people who were responsible for not speaking out about the abuse at the home. Apparently I'm one of them!!! I walked into my bedroom and the nutter Tasered me, took me to his secret hideout and threatened to torture me to death. The situation was looking grim until I told him I was completely innocent.

Now, that doesn't make much sense, how could I be completely innocent? I killed Jason Caldwell, didn't I?

NO I DIDN'T!!!

You see, earlier, two police officers came round. They wanted to know all about the children's home and what went on there. I told them everything I knew. All about Bentley, my father and the others. I even told them about the night down at the cove and how I cut Jason with my knife. How, by the time Father returned, he'd died. In short, I admitted to Jason Caldwell's murder.

They were very sympathetic and said I shouldn't blame myself. They didn't even arrest me. Unbelievable!

So, back to the nutter. I was able to explain to him that I was no longer in the frame. I was, in fact, innocent in the eyes of the law. He was concerned about my other activities, but I argued my case. Said his role was only to deal with the crimes at Woodland Heights. He fell for it! Which was lucky. Lucky too the police don't know about those other activities and the truth about Jason and Liam. The NEW Jason and Liam. They don't realise that I'm the one who kidnapped Jason and buried him in a box in the ground and they don't know about the things which have gone horribly wrong. The way I played a *game with Liam, forcing him to strip and cover himself with grease and then taunting him with my knife. How, once I'd cut him on the hands, he wouldn't stop screaming. I tried to explain to him that the game was just make-believe, a re-enactment of something which had happened years ago. I told him we could still be friends, but he wouldn't listen so I knocked him to the ground. Then I used my belt to shut him up for good, pulling it tighter and tighter and tighter (perhaps I learnt that from watching Bentley). To be honest, the power rush was like nothing else I've experienced, so if the new Jason doesn't want to be my friend . . . well, there's a silver cloud.*

Two silver clouds, actually. You see, the police managed to find my secret place and they stole Smirker from me. I miss him terribly. I thought the new Jason would step in and be a real friend, but it hasn't quite worked out. So I've been thinking, why not make a NEW Smirker?!!! Smirker never argued, never spoke back, never became violent. He never, ever poked me in the eye with a sharp stick. He always listened attentively and I'm beginning to think he was the best friend a boy could have. I don't think the task will be difficult. First the belt, then the saw and then the big pot. Yes, that's it! No more chances for the lad, I've decided the NEW Jason is going to be the NEW SMIRKER!

Chapter Thirty-Four

Riley groped for his mobile to silence the buzzing of the alarm. Struggled to understand why the blasted thing wouldn't shut up.

'Darius?' Julie's voice came out of the darkness beside him. 'It's the door, love, not your phone.'

Riley shook the sleep from his head and pushed himself from the bed. He grabbed his dressing gown from the back of the door and headed down the corridor. He pulled the front door open.

'Morning, sir.' Enders. One hand about to ring the buzzer again, the other holding a half-eaten pasty. 'Sorry it's so early.'

'Early? It's not even late yet, is it?'

'Six thirty. DI Davies sent me to pick you up.'

'Davies?'

'Yes, sir.' Enders held out a piece of paper. 'You know the stuff in the barrels? Well, Layton got a result back yesterday. The chemicals from both rafts are identical. They are an organophosphorus compound, in this case sheep dip.'

'So the barrels come from a farm. Do you know how many farms there are in Devon, Patrick?'

322

'Lots. But we've had a bit of help from the animal health company Sleet worked for. Apparently, as soon as Layton knew he was dealing with sheep dip, he got on to them. According to Layton, they've had their chemists hard at work overnight and they've identified the brand as one of their own. What's more, because the formula has changed, they've managed to work out the batch number. The last delivery of the relevant batch was made over four years ago.'

Riley took the piece of paper. A list of addresses in two columns. No more than ten.

'They could have been stolen or picked up from a tip, anything.'

'Yes.' Enders pointed at the sheet of paper. 'But whoever captured Perry Sleet has also got Brenden Parker and Parker knows where Jason Hobb is. Davies thinks it's worth a shot and, with your experience on the Agri Squad, he reckons you're just the man for the job.'

Savage had finally crawled into bed at around two thirty a.m. The tide had come in at the cove and put paid to any more forensic analysis. The CSIs were planning to take a look at the area at the top of the cliff at first light, but in the dark, with wet conditions underfoot, they too had called it a day.

She was at the station by nine the next morning, complaining to Calter she'd had little sleep.

'Sleep?' Calter said. 'You should ask John Layton about that. Apparently he's been up all night.'

Calter was right.

'Busy as a bee,' Layton said when she called him up. 'We need to set up an emergency chinwag with Hardin and the rest. *Curlew*, *Lacuna* and *Caldera*.'

Twenty minutes later that's what they had. A hastily convened meeting in the briefing room. Everyone present looked expectant. Layton, the rumour was, had played a blinder overnight. He'd not only come up with evidence which might help locate Perry Sleet, he'd also made a major step towards solving all three cases.

'Now then, folks,' Hardin said, full of life and considerably more perky than he had been the night before. 'You all know there's been a development. At this moment we're not sure quite what it means. To sum up what we know so far: yesterday DI Savage established that Brenden Parker is the most likely suspect in the Liam Clough/Jason Hobb case. Unfortunately Parker's gone missing, apparently abducted by the same person or persons who killed Tim Benedict and kidnapped Perry Sleet. Brenden Parker is the son of Frank Parker. Parker Senior ran the Woodland Heights home and, we believe, killed Jason Caldwell way back in 1988. Sleet lived in a nearby village at the time and Benedict was a curate in the area. In addition, last night we discovered the body of Edith Parker – Brenden Parker's stepmother – at Soar Mill Cove. There's more though. John?'

'Thanks.' Layton stood. He moved to the whiteboard where he'd pinned a number of photographs. 'To summarise the forensic findings, this is what we know: in the cellar at Woodland Heights we unearthed evidence a body had been buried there. We only discovered a fragment of a fifth metatarsal, but this was matched to the skeleton which was later discovered in a nearby copse. Missing from the skeleton was the previously mentioned metatarsal and a little finger. The skeleton was likely dug up from the cellar at Woodland Heights a couple of months ago and reburied at the copse. However, at the copse we also found a finger, recently severed, which we now know belonged to Jason Hobb. Having also got the familial DNA results, I can confirm the identity of the skeleton is the other Jason, Jason Caldwell. Everyone with me so far?'

Layton paused and allowed the information to sink in. A few detectives shook their heads, unable to follow. The majority nodded. Layton looked around at the room and then he went to the desk and picked up one of his polygrip bags. Inside was something resembling a small brown twig.

'Moving on now to Operation *Caldera*. DS Riley examined a raft we found over at Jennycliff and retrieved a small finger bone and a patch of skin with biblical writing on it. The skin was actually from the head area, a scalp.' Once again Layton stopped. He reached forward, picked up another polygrip bag and waved it around. 'I can tell you now that the skin in this bag and the bone in the other bag belong to the skeleton we found in the copse near Woodland Heights.'

There was silence for a few seconds and then the room exploded, everyone talking at once and shouting over each other. Hands gestured and fingers pointed and it was left for Hardin to thump the table and bring the room to order.

'Eyes on the prize, people, eyes on the prize!' Hardin banged the table again, this time once for each investigation. '*Curlew*!' Bang. '*Lacuna*!' Bang. '*Caldera*!' Bang.

For a moment Savage thought her fellow detectives might repeat Hardin's staccato outburst as a sort of weird war cry or football chant, but they didn't. Instead, there was a moment's silence before everyone began talking again.

Collier spotted Savage and sidled over. 'What do you reckon then, ma'am?' he said over the noise. 'What the hell is this raft guy up to?'

'Gareth, my head's still spinning. I'm trying to work out the implications.'

'Me too, but I'm thinking this is a process. It started with a demonstration – the raft at Jennycliff. The mannequin had been mutilated and clues had been left in the box. Namely the skin and the bone. There were also several sets of initials carved into the arm of the dummy which matched those of Tim Benedict, Perry Sleet and Brenden Parker. They're all being made to pay for something which happened back in 1988 when the three of them were associated with the children's home.'

'But there were four sets of initials, yes?'

'Yup. TB, PS, CH and BP.'

Savage nodded slowly, thinking for a moment. Then she pulled out her phone and accessed her text messages. She highlighted one she'd received the previous evening and showed Collier.

Urgent. Call me now. CH.

'CH?' Collier said. 'Who was that from?'

'Him.' Savage turned and looked across the room to where the DSupt was in conversation with John Layton. 'Conrad Hardin.'

After the briefing, Savage tried to speak to Hardin about her worries. The DSupt was having none of it. He was a target, he said, sure, but what did that matter in the grand scheme of things? The boys were the issue. The boys in the past and the boys in the present. Nothing should divert their attention from that.

Exasperated, she left Collier to deal discreetly with sorting out some protection for Hardin and his immediate family and headed for her office. She sat and stared at her terminal screen where she had a mass of documents open. Maps, crime reports, suspect profiles, press stories from way back. Despite the optimism engendered earlier by John Layton's hard work, she remained pessimistic. She tried to cling onto some sort of hope the situation would end well, that they'd find Jason Hobb, but the longer he remained missing, the more that seemed an unlikely outcome.

She pulled up a map screen and panned around. Zoomed in on a couple of places. She had no idea what she was looking for. Inspiration. A miracle. Some sort of handle on where Brenden Parker might have hidden the boy.

'Ma'am?' A young DC she didn't know knocked and peered round the door. 'There's a bloke for you. Some sort of bearded tramp in a coat. Smells of fish. Refuses to speak to anyone but you. Says it's important. I've put him in a room downstairs.'

'Uh-huh.' Savage nodded, only half listening, her mind still on the search for Jason. 'OK, thanks.'

Downstairs, she found her visitor in an interview room, the stench of fish apparent as she opened the door. As the DC had said, the man wore a huge black coat and had a full beard which covered every inch of the bottom half of his face. He sat on one side of a desk, a mug of tea in his huge hands, a plate in front of him containing nothing aside from a few biscuit crumbs.

It was the guy from the houseboat over at Torpoint, Larry something.

'Mr . . . ' Savage couldn't remember the man's surname.

'Told you afore, Larry's the name. Larry Lobster.'

'Larry, yes.' Savage moved over to the desk and sat. Close to, the stench was awful. Fish, diesel and bilge water over a hint of tobacco. 'What can I do for you?'

'Seen you guys out looking for the lad,' Larry said. 'Dartmoor. The coast. The estuaries. Some crazy fucker's got you lot all stoked up like a lobby stuck in a pot, hasn't he? Can't find the way out, can you? Trapped.'

'Jason?' Savage tried to breathe through her mouth. 'Do you know something?'

'Tides is what I know.' Larry put the mug down and raised a hand to his head. Tapped his right temple. 'That first raft. The one found over at Jennycliff. I've been working these waters for years and I tell you it likely came from the River Erme.'

'It could have come from anywhere, Larry,' Savage said, thinking the man had picked up the location from the news reports on the second raft, the one with Tim Benedict on. 'Besides, the Erme is ten miles to the east. I can't see the raft having drifted all that way. It's an interesting theory, but—'

'Not a theory, fact.' Larry reached for the mug again and took a gulp, drops of tea left in his beard when he put the mug down. 'One of my buoys gets cut by a passing yacht, I know exactly where to find it. Eddies, currents, rips, tidal streams. They push back and forth, this way and that. Appears random, but in the end those oceanwhatnofors can map them years in advance. And the second raft, that *was* on the Erme, wasn't it?'

'Yes, but the man didn't manage to launch it. He'd spent so long assembling the pieces that he ran out of time and the craft became marooned on a sandbar.'

'That's where you're wrong.'

'Mr . . . Larry. I'm sure you mean well, but we're pushed here today.' Savage tried to be polite, but she needed to get shot of Larry and get back to work. Quite why he'd come in, she didn't know. Perhaps he was lonely. 'Jason Hobb is our concern now, not the tides.'

'Sure he is, girl, but you're looking not listening. Trapped, I said. Like the boy. The lobster, you see. The poor fellow sniffs some bait and then takes a wrong turn. Tries to back up, only the way a pot works he can't find the exit. Lobster pot one minute, cooking pot the next.'

'Larry, if you've got some information then please stop

talking in riddles. Otherwise I could put you in contact with social services, sort you out some help. You shouldn't be living out on that—'

'Fuck social services! Bunch of tossers, the lot of them. And it's not me who needs help, you do.'

'Me?'

'Hot water getting hotter. Cooking you up so you're nice and tender.'

'Larry, I—'

'THE BOY! JASON!' Larry swept his arm across the table, catching the mug and sending it flying. The mug tumbled to the floor and smashed into several pieces, tea splashing everywhere. Larry shook his head and wrinkled his nose. 'Sorry. Tryin' to tell you, aren't I? I can get you out of the pot. I know where he is.'

Savage stared at Larry. Took in the black coat smeared with fish oil. The full beard. The right hand – the one with no thumb and the crab claw fingers which scissored back and forth. How could this man possibly know anything about Jason unless he'd been directly involved in his disappearance?

Larry blinked at her and his eyes sparkled like silver sand at the bottom of a rock pool.

'Tell me,' she said, all of a sudden beyond caring where the information came from.

'That bloke wasn't launching the raft when he got caught Monday morning. He was trying to retrieve it.'

'Retrieve it?'

'Yes. See, he'd launched it from farther up the river in the middle of the night. With all this rain the water was plenty high enough. He hoped the raft would come down and meet the tide and be carried off. Only there wasn't enough height in the tide and the raft got stuck on a sandbar. When he was discovered, he was down there taking the thing apart, not putting it together.'

'So how does this help us find Jason?'

'The raft was launched from the Erme for a reason, and that's because of what's upstream. See, Brenden's mother's there.'

'Brenden's mother? You mean Deborah Parker? We understood she was dead.'

'Alive or dead she's the key.'

'How do you—?'

'I know, that's all. You don't need the whys or wherefores. You just need to find a way out of the pot, understand?' Larry pushed himself up from the chair. 'He was mad Brenden, back then when we was kids. Weird like his dad. Reckon, from what he's been up to recently with them boys, he ain't improved much either.'

'Larry.' Savage stood too. 'You stay right there. We need to get a statement.'

'I'm not staying anywhere.' Larry shuffled to the door. 'I've told you all I know. The mother, understand? I'll be on my boat if you needs me.'

The fisherman slipped into the corridor, leaving Savage staring at the broken cup, the pieces surrounded by a puddle of steaming tea. Brenden Parker, she remembered, had sought comfort from the warmth of a silver teapot which had belonged to his mother. At the time, they hadn't realised she'd died nor did they know the story behind her relationship to Brenden.

That was it. Savage turned and dashed from the room. Half a minute later and she was in the crime suite confronting Collier.

'Deborah Parker. Frank Parker's first wife and Brenden Parker's mother,' she said.

'Who?' Collier raised a marker pen in defence. He turned to his whiteboard and examined a list of names. 'Not on the radar.'

'No, because she's dead.'

'Dead?' Collier shook his head. 'So where are you going with this? Ghosts?'

'No, Deborah Parker's not coming back.' Savage pointed to a map on another board. 'But it's what she left behind I'm interested in.'

Savage explained to Collier what she wanted and went to find Calter. Five minutes later and she returned with the DC in tow.

'Well?'

'I'm confused,' Collier said, waving a piece of paper at Savage. 'I can't find a record of Deborah Parker's death, but I've got her address. She lives over in the countryside near Modbury.'

'Lives?' Savage took the address. 'That can't be right. We found a condolence card at Brenden Parker's house.'

'Whatever. The property's right on the Erme, upstream from where the second raft was found.'

'Find a car,' she said, turning to Calter and shooing her from the room. 'We need the PolSA, a search team, John Layton and his CSIs. Alert the air ambulance too, we might need a medevac.'

'Yes, ma'am!' Calter had already pulled out her phone and she was punching numbers as they ran down the corridor.

Chapter Thirty-Five

Near Modbury, South Hams, Devon. Thursday 29th
October. 12.38 p.m.

They sped along the A38, Savage topping a ton for most of
the way. After the dual carriageway they had no option but
to take minor roads and progress was torturous. While
Savage concentrated on keeping the car on the road, Calter
made call after call on her phone.

Near Modbury, Savage turned off onto a tiny lane which
climbed a hillside before dropping down a steep hill.

'Here, ma'am,' Calter said.

Savage slewed the car round and took a track which led
through a couple of fields towards a large house. Behind the
house a field ran down to a line of trees, the blue of the
River Erme beyond.

The place may have once been home to a local doctor or
solicitor, Savage thought. Now it lay abandoned, broken glass
in the windows, a full-length veranda partly collapsed at one
end, an old rocking chair next to a small cast-iron table
sheltering under the porch.

They bounced down the track and pulled up in front of
the house. An iron fence ran around a small plot, the grass
long and almost waist-high. To the back, a paddock lay thick

with docks and nettles and off to one side sat an orchard with wiry apple trees badly in need of pruning.

'The drawing showed a box buried in the earth, so check the grounds first.' Savage leapt out of the car as they stopped. 'Come on.'

She ran up to the gate and pushed it open. A stone paved path hugged the right-hand side of the house. She went along the path, Calter close behind.

'You reckon he's here then? Jason?' Calter said.

'Got to be.'

They rounded the house and crossed through an area of long grass to the orchard. A post and rail fence surrounded the trees and a gate stood open to the plot. In places, the grass had been trampled. Someone had been here recently.

'There!' Savage said, pointing to an area of disturbed ground, a pile of soil still dark brown with moisture. She moved across to the pile and felt a sudden lurch in her stomach when she saw the hole alongside. 'He was in here.'

She stared down into the hole. The sides plunged down through the dark earth and at the bottom sat a large box perhaps a metre or so wide by two long and maybe a metre or so deep.

'The lid, ma'am,' Calter said, pointing to a large sheet of plywood on one side of the spoil heap. Next to the plywood lay a short section of tubing, something like a drainpipe. 'Jesus, I can't imagine what it must have been like trapped down there. Horrible.'

Savage nodded. Several cans of Coke and the wrappers from numerous packets of biscuits and chocolate bars had been pushed into a corner. To one side of the box, fresh soil showed through a rough opening in the plywood.

'But where is he now?' Savage peered closer. The opening led through to a neighbouring hole, narrower than the first.

In the bottom, Savage could see the outline of a wooden coffin, the lid splintered and pulled aside, a plain wooden cross thrown down on top.

'Ma'am?' Calter stood alongside Savage. 'If Jason was in the first hole, who or what was in this one?'

'No idea, but the hole was dug today as well.' She pointed at the spoil heap and then scanned the orchard. The rest of the grass was long and untrampled. 'There's nothing out here, let's try the house.'

Back round the front, Calter stopped as she stepped onto the veranda. She knelt on the wooden boards.

'Blood, ma'am.' The DC pointed to several dark splotches near the front door. 'Fresh, by the look of it.'

'OK,' Savage said. 'Let's see what we can find inside.'

Calter nodded, stood, and reached for the door handle.

'Gloves!' Savage said, reaching into her own pocket and pulling out a pair. 'Here, have these.'

'Thanks.' Calter took the gloves and put them on. Then she reached for the door handle once more, turned it, and pushed the door open.

A narrow hall stretched away in front of them, a door to the right and left. A staircase ran up to the first floor on one side of the passageway. Calter moved into the house and Savage followed. The draught from the open door had disturbed a layer of dust on the floor and motes swirled in the air. There was something else in the air too. Steam, drifting from the rear of the house.

'Empty, ma'am,' Calter said. She pointed into the room on the right. Bare floorboards, an old rocking chair, a monk's bench, a huge but plain dresser, some moth-eaten velvet curtains. 'Just a load of ancient furniture. I reckon whoever lived here is long gone.'

Savage took a glance into the room to the left. It was the

same story. Empty. Peeling wallpaper on the wall next to the window where the rain had come through a broken pane.

'Somebody's here.' Savage sniffed the air and pointed down the hallway. 'In the kitchen.'

She moved along the hall to where a glass-fronted door stood half open, beads of moisture streaming down the pane. She pushed and the door swung to reveal a farmhouse kitchen. To one side stood an Aga, steam hissing from beneath the lid of a large pot.

'Careful,' Savage said. 'We don't know who we're dealing with. They could be armed with a Taser. Whatever, they're very dangerous.'

Calter strolled across to a door, but there was nothing behind except a small larder. She shrugged and then looked to the ceiling.

'Right, there's nothing here.' Savage gestured back the way they had come. 'We'll try the first floor.'

She moved back down the hallway to the stairs and began to climb. Beneath her feet the treads creaked in protest, but otherwise appeared sound.

'More blood, ma'am.' Calter pointed to another dark stain as she followed Savage up the stairs. 'Let's hope it doesn't belong to Jason.'

Every few steps there was another spot of blood. On the landing the trail turned left and led into a large double-aspect bedroom.

'Careful, ma'am.' Calter reached out and grabbed Savage by the shoulder. 'No floorboards.'

'Thanks.' Savage's attention had been drawn to the ceiling which was covered in hundreds of pages of tiny print. She peered up. The pages were thin, like cigarette paper. 'These are pages from the Bible.'

'What the hell is this, ma'am?'

'No idea.' Savage turned her gaze to the floor. Or rather, the lack of one. The floorboards had been removed, leaving only the joists. Beneath the joists she could see the slim wooden wattles running back and forth. They wouldn't be that strong. Step in the gap between the joists and your foot would go right through the plaster. 'But let's be careful, OK?'

Unlike the rooms downstairs, this one had furniture. A huge cast-iron bedstead straddled the joists, the bed's feet carefully positioned on two floorboards which had been left in place. On the far side of the room, beside the window, stood a tall, heavy wardrobe.

'Christ Almighty!' Calter leant in through the doorway and pointed across to the bed. 'What the heck . . .?'

Savage stepped into the room, making sure she planted her feet firmly on the joists. She walked across half a dozen of them until she stood alongside the bed. Someone was lying there, the bedclothes pulled up to the person's neck. Grey hair tumbled over the pillow, spread in a fan-like fashion and framing a face of cracked skin. The nose had gone, the nasal bone exposed. Likewise the lips had dried to nothing, revealing white teeth, a golden flash of filling top right.

'From the grave in the orchard,' Savage said. 'She's obviously been dead for a while.'

'She?' Calter tiptoed across the joists. 'I know it's got long hair, but how do you know it's not a man?'

'There's a photograph on the pillow.' Savage pointed to a picture in a small gold frame which lay to the right side of the head. A woman with a mass of long blonde hair was sitting in a chair, a small boy of eleven or twelve on her lap. 'I think that's her.'

'So who's the boy?'

'Brenden Parker, of course. This woman must be his mother.'

'Bloody hell.' Calter shook her head. 'Sleeping Beauty, she isn't.'

'The question is, where's Jason? Check the wardrobe, would you?'

Calter nodded and worked her way across to the huge piece of furniture. She fiddled with a key which was in the lock, and then opened the door.

'Oh God!' Calter turned her head away from the wardrobe for a moment. 'You'd better come and look at this, ma'am.'

Savage stepped across the joists until she stood alongside Calter. The DC pointed inside. At the bottom of the wardrobe a pile of clothes lay in a jumble. A dark navy cag with a matching inner fleece. A pair of jeans and an Argyll shirt, tie-dyed with fresh red blood. Above the clothes, several dresses hung on wooden hangers.

'Looks like Jason's coat and shirt. From the amount of blood on the shirt and the trail on the way up here, I'd say he's seriously wounded.'

'But where?' Calter spun on her heels, almost losing her balance on the joists. 'The trail of blood leads into this room.'

Savage turned too. The bed and wardrobe were the only pieces of furniture in the room. There was no loft hatch and both windows were closed. The bed was high off the ground and Savage didn't have to lean over far to be able to see right underneath. Nothing. She stood upright and stared at the bed again. A tingle spread from her fingertips all the way along her arms. The tingle became a chill which washed across her chest. The thin corpse was too bulky. There was something else beneath the bedclothes.

She stepped back across the joists until she reached the bed. Atop lay a crocheted blanket, beneath another blanket, this one wool. Beneath that, and turned over at the top, was a white sheet. The whole lot was tucked in neatly down the sides and at the end of the bed. Savage grasped the linen up near the pillow and pulled the material out from beneath the mattress. With a flick she threw the whole lot back.

'Oh fuck!' Calter stood, mouth open. 'No!'

The corpse was unclothed. Skin, aged and dry and yellowing, hung in crumpled folds. Here and there, white bones protruded through cracks in the skin. It was hard to believe this thing had ever been living, Savage thought, that the corpse wasn't some alien zombie creature about to rise from the dead. Harder still to realise the woman wasn't alone in the bed. That her shrivelled arms were cradling the naked, headless body of a child, hugging the poor creature close to her dried and barren breasts.

The shock of seeing the corpse of Deborah Parker was as nothing to the realisation that the body she was holding in her arms had no head. As the horrific vision sunk in, a chill slipped down Savage's back.

'Ma'am!' Calter put a hand to her chest. 'Oh God, ma'am . . . I've never . . .'

'Easy, Jane.' Savage moved from the bed and tiptoed her way across the rafters. 'Back downstairs, quick.'

'Was that him, ma'am?' Calter said when they'd made it down to the hallway. The DC shook her head and took several deep breaths. 'Poor Jason Hobb?'

'Yes, I think so.' Savage paused for a moment. She wondered whether Calter had recovered sufficiently for what she had in mind next. 'If you're up to it, then with me, OK?'

'Sure, ma'am.' Calter took one long breath. 'Never better.'

Savage turned and went down the hallway towards the kitchen, Calter close behind. The kitchen was much as they'd left it. The larder door still half ajar, the pan on the stove still bubbling away.

'Ma'am?' Calter said. 'What is it?'

'That.' Savage gestured over towards the Aga. 'The pot.'

'Hey?' Calter moved past her and strode into the room. 'The pot? I don't get it.'

'You don't want to know.' Savage came in and walked over to the stove. She reached for an oven glove which was wrapped round the cooker rail. 'Here, take this.'

'What do you want me to do with it?' Calter said as she took the glove.

'I want you to lift the lid on the pot. Look away when you do so. There's no need for you to see.'

'Oh Christ, ma'am. You're fucking joking me, right?'

'No, Jane, I'm not. Now just lift the lid.'

Calter slipped the glove onto her right hand and reached across the stove. Her hand curled as she grasped the handle on the lid. As she lifted the lid a whoosh of steam rose upward like a mushroom cloud and she stepped back to avoid being burned.

Savage moved closer. Inside the pot the water was on a rolling boil, bubbles tumbling over and over. And in amongst the turbulence, Savage could see a mass of blond hair swirling back and forth.

'Sickening,' Hardin said. 'The worst possible news imaginable.'

Savage stood with Hardin and DC Calter on the track leading to the house. The garden, orchard and house were out of bounds. John Layton's territory. No argument. He'd already investigated a lean-to at the side of the house and found a whole host of woodworking tools and now he was up in the bedroom with Nesbit and a photographer. He'd commented that the joists wouldn't take any more weight.

'Wouldn't want the whole lot to come crashing down into the living room, would we?' he'd said.

Hardin was off on one of his rants about managing media expectations. They'd played this wrong, he said. The pressure arising from the discovery of Tim Benedict had meant they'd taken their eyes off the ball. The grisly discovery of Jason's body would refocus the media's attention. When it came to light that the police had questioned the killer but done nothing, all hell would break loose.

'Fucking nightmare.' Hardin shook his head and then stared at Savage. 'You were there. At Brenden Parker's place. How come you never twigged? You, of all people, Charlotte. Hunting killers was in your blood, you said. You had a track record, you said. Well, I never should have listened to you. Get this – Parker admitted to you that he killed Jason Caldwell, but you didn't think to take it further. Sussing out Parker was the only chance we had of finding Jason. Except now we've bloody found him, haven't we?'

Savage tried not to stare at the ground. This wasn't her fault, she thought. Hardin was out of order. Brenden Parker hadn't killed Caldwell, it had been his dad. Sure, the incident must have affected the boy and the guilt he'd carried all these years had probably led to his current mind state, but was there any way she could have known?

'Sir?' Savage decided to try to calm the DSupt down. 'If it hadn't been for a member of the public coming forward, we'd never have found this place. It's off the radar, not in any of our evidence.'

'Well, why the bloody hell wasn't it in any of our evidence?' Hardin swept his arm around and jabbed at the house. 'One look at the house and even the dimmest DC would realise this is the lair of some fucking nutter. If somebody had an ounce of brains, Jason Hobb would still be alive.'

'Presumably the killer chose his mother's place because he thought we'd never discover it without his help.'

'Don't get clever with me, DI Savage. If we start waiting for criminals to help us out, we may as well pack up and go home now. Pathetic.'

Savage was about to say something else when Layton and Nesbit came out of the house. It was the signal for the mortuary attendants to go in. Savage shivered, thinking of having to separate the two bodies from each other and pack the dried, shrivelled corpse into a body bag. And then there was the pot with the head in. She didn't even want to think about how they'd deal with that.

'A stab wound in the stomach,' Nesbit said as he approached. 'Went deep enough to sever the aorta. Jason Hobb likely died in a similar manner to Jason Caldwell.'

'Like father like son,' Hardin said. 'Brenden Parker is one fucked-up individual.'

'Quite, Conrad.' Nesbit half smiled. 'Anyway, the trail of blood you saw was superficial. My hypothesis is Jason Hobb died from massive internal bleeding. His head, thank God, was almost certainly removed after death. We'll know for sure after the post-mortem.'

'And the woman?' Savage said. 'Natural causes?'

'Much trickier to know. There aren't any visible signs of death. Maybe the post-mortem will throw up something, maybe not. To judge by the state of the corpse, she's been dead for a good few months. Assuming the grave in the orchard was dug at the time of death, we may be able to get something from that. What do you think, John?'

'Yes. Soil samples and bugs,' Layton said by way of explanation. 'We'll check out the rest of the orchard and blitz the house as soon as the bodies have been removed.'

'Charlotte,' Hardin said, pulling Savage away to one side and lowering his voice. 'The minister, what do we know of his connection to this woman?'

'According to Frank Parker, Deborah Parker had some form of relationship with the minister. Obviously when the boys went missing the heat became too much and he never came back to the home. Anyway, the place shut down not long after.'

'But here?' Hardin glanced back at the house. 'Could there be anything we could use?'

'I doubt it. The place has been stripped. There might be something at Brenden Parker's house in Ivybridge.'

'Talking of Parker, where is he? I thought he'd been Tasered by the nutter who'd captured Sleet and Benedict?'

'I don't know, sir. I think we're close to the endgame though. Perhaps Parker knew he was in danger himself, knew his time was up. That could be why he killed Jason Hobb and placed him in the arms of his mother, almost as if she would protect him from any further harm.'

'Jesus.' Hardin shook his head. 'So, taking stock, Brenden Parker is still somewhere out there. There are two dead boys, a dead woman, a dead clergyman and a man who's still missing. Not to mention the historical abuse and murder and the involvement of a top government minister. Quite how I explain this to Heldon, I really don't know.'

With that, Hardin wheeled about and headed towards several officers who were smoking next to the gateway. When he reached them he laid into the group with a torrent of expletives.

'It's getting to him,' Calter said as Savage went over. 'Think I'll try and keep my distance for the rest of the day.'

'It's getting to us all,' Savage said. 'But this is personal not professional.'

'Personal? You mean he's connected to this somehow?'

'Way back, yes.' Savage turned to face the house. 'When he was a young PC.'

Calter nodded, as if Savage had explained everything. She hadn't, though. The burden of a secret, she thought. She of all people should know what that felt like.

She turned to the house where the two mortuary assistants had reappeared at the front door, a body bag slung between them. From the ease with which they were carrying the bag, she guessed it contained the old woman. Dry skin and bone and not much else, apart from Deborah Parker's own secrets which she'd carried with her to her grave in the orchard.

Chapter Thirty-Six

Crownhill Police Station, Plymouth. Thursday 29th October. 4.15 p.m.

Savage was back at Crownhill by late afternoon. Hardin had called a press conference for five p.m. and already the vultures were gathering in the car park at the back of the police station. TV vans, local and national hacks, Dan Phillips amongst them.

'Charlotte!' Phillips shouted out as Savage climbed from her car. 'Bad news, huh?'

'There's going to be a statement, Dan,' Savage said as Phillips came over. 'Five o'clock.'

'You've found him, haven't you? And he's dead. No doubt in my mind, I can read it on your faces.'

'No comment.' Savage walked towards the entrance and pushed through the doors into the station.

In the crime suite the sombre mood which Phillips had spotted was evident. No jokes or wisecracks or larking around. Officers either stood in small groups talking in hushed tones or were heads down over their keyboards. Some of them, like Savage, had been to this place before. It was a place of press conferences with grieving families, flashes of light from the cameras illuminating tear-stained faces, words stuttered out by the mother or father or brother or sister. A place of soul-searching, where the silence was punctuated only by the ticking of the watchful clock as the errors were written into the policy book for a review team to pore over at a later date. Careers were broken by events like this, people too. It was, Savage had found, a place of utter darkness and despair where, unless one was very careful, emotions could take over from professionalism.

Gareth Collier was in his default position at one of the whiteboards, a marker pen in one hand. Savage went across.

'I've been over the stuff we've got on Brenden Parker,' Collier said. 'I'm pretty sure we couldn't have worked this one out without the help of your informer friend.'

'Thanks, Gareth. If we can . . .' she paused. Three desks away, Calter had just answered a telephone. Her manner had gone from professional and friendly to monosyllabic, her face from flushed with the heat of the room to white. In that instant, Savage knew the darkness and despair were about to get a whole lot worse.

Calter hung up. She placed both her elbows on the desk in front of her and clasped her hands together. Closed her eyes for a moment, head bowed.

'Jane?' Savage said. 'What's the matter?'

Calter opened her eyes and sighed. 'Two boys have gone missing, ma'am. Modbury Primary.'

'No.' Savage felt her legs turn to jelly. 'Go on.'

'Some terrible mix-up. Their absence wasn't noticed first thing this morning because they were supposed to be on a school trip. It was only when the coach returned this afternoon the teachers realised a mistake had been made. They double-checked with the parents but the boys had set off first thing this morning. A witness saw someone pick them up.'

345

'Please tell me it wasn't—'

'It was, ma'am. We've got a description and it's pretty much a ringer for Brenden Parker.'

Riley peered through the windscreen at the Dartmoor landscape. A narrow lane twisted between mossy banks. A strip of green in the centre of the tarmac. Potholes. Not many people came this way, Riley thought. Walkers, perhaps, maybe a family with a car full of screaming kids looking for a place for a picnic.

The lane ended abruptly, a set of tall wooden gates blocking the way, a chain wrapped several times around the gates, with a 'Private Keep Out' sign added for good measure. Neither walkers nor picnickers would get any further.

'This is the last one on our list, Patrick,' Riley said. 'Probably be the same as all the others.'

'Probably.' Enders made no effort to move. 'We're somewhere between Cadover Bridge and Sheepstor, but it might as well be the high moor. There's nobody here.'

Riley couldn't blame Enders for feeling fed up. They'd received the news about the discovery of Jason Hobb a couple of hours ago and now the search felt almost academic. Plus they'd been at it since early morning and this was the tenth farm they'd been to. The previous nine had all checked out. No sign of Brenden Parker, no sign of Perry Sleet. Every farmer they'd spoken to had confirmed that they'd had deliveries of the specific brand of sheep dip in the past, but they'd also assured them no containers had ever gone walkabout. Empty barrels had been returned to the manufacturer for reuse, or rinsed out and stored, the residue disposed of along with the used dip.

Riley climbed out of the car and approached the gates. A heavy padlock secured the chain. They had a few tools in the boot of the car, but nothing which could get through this. He turned and moved to the bank at one side of the gates. He used one of the gateposts to pull himself up. Standing on the bank, he could see over the hedge. The security was an illusion. A field bordered the farmyard, a drystone wall running between the two. He looked back down the road. Fifty metres away a five-bar gate marked an opening. They could walk back down the lane, climb over the gate and go through the field. The wall wouldn't be much of a problem.

Enders was standing next to the car when Riley returned. He didn't fancy it.

'I'd rather not, sir,' he said. 'We'll get muddy.'

'Not a problem.' Riley sprung the hatch. Next to his own pair of boots there was a carrier bag. He'd almost forgotten it was there. 'Davies' wellies. Left over from the last op we did together on the Agri Squad. Bit of luck, no?'

They donned their boots and walked to the entrance of the field. They opened the gate and went through into an area of poor pasture dotted with clumps of rushes. They crossed the field and arrived at the wall. Enders took a couple of strides towards the wall and then heaved himself up, his boots scrabbling to gain purchase. He swung one leg up, then the other and slipped down the other side, knocking a large coping stone from the top of the wall. Riley jumped out of the way as the stone thudded into the earth at his feet.

Enders huffed and then muttered something from the other side as Riley took a couple of steps back and then ran at the wall and vaulted up and over in one clean movement. He landed with a squelch, ankle-deep in farmyard muck.

'Well,' Enders said. 'We're truly in the shit now.'

'Over there.' Riley pointed across to a set of low metal hurdles arranged in something of a maze. 'A sheep race.'

Two years ago, when he'd still been in London, Riley

would have thought a sheep race was some weird country-side sport played by perverted farmers. Now he knew a race was a series of hurdles used to confine and shepherd sheep for the purposes of shearing or foot trimming. Or, more pertinent to their investigation, in order to corral them into a sheep dip. The hurdles looked rusty and weeds grew up within the pens.

'Nobody's dipped here for a while, sir,' Enders said. He peered down at his feet. 'And this is cow shit, not sheep.'

'Four years, remember?' Riley said as he walked across to the hurdles. 'This place isn't in use any more other than as a watering spot for cattle.'

'So why are we bothering?'

Riley stopped next to the sheep race. On the far side the weeds had run out of control and dock and nettle a metre or so high lay in a forest up against a stone wall.

'There.' Riley pointed along the wall to where the weeds gave way to an area of earth and yellowing plants. Three blue barrels stood against the wall, but it was obvious from the virgin soil that many more had recently been removed. 'That's why we're bothering.'

'They're the same ones used on the rafts,' Enders said. He turned and looked to where an old farmhouse stood in another patch of scrub, the windows boarded over. A little way beyond, a U-shaped configuration of buildings nestled against the hillside. 'You think . . .?'

'It's worth a look.'

A stone byre sat on the left, open-fronted, several pieces of rusting farm machinery inside. Ahead of them was a long low building, the slate roof in need of repair, a gaping hole at one end. To the right there was a large stone barn with a corrugated cement roof. The structure was in a much better state. The stonework had been freshly pointed, the roof was clean of moss with several new sheets and a nice new health and safety sign advising the use of crawlboards. Stone steps led up to a substantial wooden door.

They plodded across to the buildings and climbed the steps. The door had a large hasp and padlock, but the hasp hadn't been closed and the padlock hung unlocked.

'Looks like somebody left in a hurry,' Riley said. He pulled the handle on the door.

Inside, it was dark. Riley reached in and flicked a light switch to the right of the door. A series of fluorescent tubes sprang into life and illuminated a corridor.

'Half finished.' Enders nodded at the white walls and concrete floor. 'A full-scale barn conversion. Must be worth a bit, I reckon. Maybe as a holiday home.'

Riley stared down the corridor. Enders had it wrong. This wasn't any prelude to turning the building into a dwelling. The fittings were all too industrial. Bulkhead lights, electric cables in armoured trunking, a concrete floor and, above their heads, a ventilation tube.

'I don't think it's a house.'

'Post whatsit. *Grand Designs*. Kevin bloody McCloud. I shouldn't be surprised if at the end of this passage there's a kitchen with half an acre of stainless steel worktop.'

Riley shook his head. This wasn't a house, more like a factory.

They walked a few metres down the corridor to where there was another door. Riley opened it. There was a small square hallway beyond. Two doors close together on one wall, and a door in each of the other walls.

'Here.' Riley went across to the pair of doors. The left door stood open and inside he could see a small room just a couple of square metres in size. Straw covered the floor and when Riley examined the door he saw two large bolts on the outside. 'Some sort of cell. I reckon Benedict or Sleet was in here. We've found him, Patrick, found the guy with the raft.'

For the second time that day, Savage sat in a car haring west along the A38, this time with Calter at the wheel. Confusion still reigned, but what facts they had spoke for themselves. The boys had definitely been taken.

They'd left home at eight twenty for the short walk to the school. The teacher organising the trip had heard the boys were both ill, while staff remaining at the school thought the boys had gone on the trip. A witness had seen the pair get into a vehicle with Brenden Parker. Recognising Parker as one of her teenage children's teachers, albeit from a different school, she hadn't thought anything of it.

Savage shook her head, her own feelings as a mother over-whelming her need to concentrate. This was every parent's nightmare. An ordinary day turned into a day to remember for the rest of your life. She'd had just such a day herself of course, and the memories had never left her. Even now, with the mystery surrounding Clarissa's death cleared up and the man ultimately to blame gone, she struggled to accept the fact that she was not responsible. Deep down there was a part of her that thought she was a bad mother, that she and Pete had failed as parents. By any definition, losing a child proved that.

A squeal of brakes as Calter came into a corner a little too fast brought her back to the job in hand. They were on the final straight. Everything speeding up. She thought on the timings. Parker had been Tasered on the Wednesday, but whoever had attempted to kidnap him had plainly failed because today he'd gone to the house in Modbury, dug his mother from her grave and killed Jason. Afterwards he'd kidnapped the two schoolkids. Or perhaps the events had happened the other way around. Whatever, he was losing focus, beginning to act irrationally. They could only hope the frenzy of activity would lead to Parker making a mistake.

Modbury was chaotic. A queue of cars sat in a jam, a police roadblock stopping further progress. Calter overtook and was flagged through. The primary school was on the outskirts, an old Victorian building. Half a dozen squad cars sat alongside the stone boundary wall and the mobile incident room van had been parked in the playground. As Savage got out of the car, she heard a buzzing overhead and looked up to see the black and yellow police helicopter circling above.

The police search advisor stepped down from the incident room van as Savage approached.

He shrugged. 'I'm doing my best, but to be honest I don't hold out much hope.'

Up in the van, Hardin sat staring at a screen showing the countryside from the air, the whole lot spinning and sliding this way and that. For a moment Savage couldn't understand what the DSupt was looking at. Then she had it. A live feed from the helicopter. A map spread on the desk in front of him had been scribed with red lines: the PolSA's search grids.

'We're fucked,' Hardin said without turning to acknowledge her. 'The PolSA has just told me the boys are dead. He reckons they'll be under a hedge somewhere within a couple of miles of here.'

'He's wrong, sir.'

'Bloodlust, Charlotte. He's killed once today already, so it stands to reason those boys are next. You saw what the weirdo did with Jason and the dead woman at the house. He's a grade-one nutter and he intends to go out in a blaze of glory.'

'They're still alive, I know it. We need to find out who the man with the Taser is, now more than ever. He knows something we don't and I believe it's important.'

'What the bloody hell are you talking about? He's no better than Parker. Look what he did to Tim Benedict.'

Savage had no argument with that. She stared at the footage from the aerial camera. The helicopter had moved away from Modbury and followed the main road before turning towards the old house. The aircraft banked sharply and the land slid sideways, the horizon slipping in from the top of the screen. Light blue sky, a dark azure sea beneath. Then the helicopter righted itself, the view once again coming from directly beneath.

Hardin was making some comment about widening the search parameters, bringing in outside help in the form of the army.

'A lot of ground to cover,' he said. 'The PolSA reckons anywhere between the sea and the A38. Bloody nightmare.'

Savage zoned out the DSupt's words. There was something she'd seen in the aerial footage, something important. She looked again at the screen, which now showed the house, the helicopter hovering directly above. Layton's Volvo was still parked on the track, several white CSI vans alongside. Ant-like figures swarmed in the orchard, while an officer with a dog worked along a nearby hedge. To one side of the picture, the estuary curled seaward.

'A waste of time,' Savage said, not really knowing why she'd vocalised her thoughts. 'They're not there. Not at the mother's house.'

'What the hell are you talking about, woman? Got a feeling, have you? Female intuition? Time of the fucking month?'

Savage ignored him. Hardin's rudeness and old-style sexism always came to the fore when he was under pressure.

Considering the circumstances, she could forgive him that. She tried to focus on what she'd just seen. The fields, blue sky, the estuary. And what had Hardin just said? *The PolSA reckons anywhere between the sea and the A38.*

'The PolSA is wrong, sir. Not *between* the sea and the A38.'

'If not there, then where?'

'Not *between, at.*'

'At the sea? He's not taken those boys for a day out at the beach, Charlotte. No bucket and spade trip this. No ice cream. He's going to bloody kill them.'

'*Two* boys, sir. It's obvious. Parker has to be returning to Woodland Heights. He's taking the boys back there to re-enact or relive what happened. Possibly to go to Soar Mill Cove where Jason Caldwell was killed by Frank Parker. He *has* taken them for a day out at the beach.'

'What?' Hardin turned and stared at Savage for a second. Then the penny dropped. 'Oh my God.'

'We need to get over there,' Savage said, already moving.

'Yes. I need to redeploy.' Hardin reached for his mouse with one hand, his mobile with the other. 'All our efforts need to be focused on the coast. The helicopter, the search team, the army.'

'No, sir. Softly-softly. Just the two of us. We don't want to scare him. On our way we can call an armed response unit and a few extra officers. That's all we need for now. Too much commotion and Parker will panic.'

'Just the two . . .?' Hardin met Savage's eyes. Usually he'd call for the works. Do things by the book. 'Yes, you're right. We'll take my car.'

Savage stepped down from the incident room van and hit the ground at a trot. Hardin bleeped open the doors to his Freelander and they got in. He started the engine and pulled out onto the main road, leaving DC Calter standing open-mouthed as they roared past.

The second door led to an identical cell and a search left Riley with no room for doubt. On one wall a name had been scratched into the stone: *Sleet*.

'Home sweet home,' Enders said as he looked around. 'Not even a bucket to crap in. Nice.'

Riley ignored Enders. If Sleet had been in the right-hand cell, then Tim Benedict or Brenden Parker must have been in the other one. He moved back around to look. There was just a chance one of the men had left some sort of clue as to the identity of their captor. At the far end, the straw had been piled up, so Riley went across and pulled some of the material away. He soon regretted his action.

'Here's your shit.' Riley stared down at the clumps of brown. 'Whoever was in here had the sense to do the business in one place.'

'Like a cat?'

Riley nodded while thinking something was wrong. 'I'm beginning to wonder if Brenden Parker was here at all. DI Savage and DSupt Hardin discovered a body – supposedly a victim of Parker's – in the evening. Yet earlier it appeared as if he'd been Tasered in his home some time that afternoon. How could that happen?'

'You're talking about a nutter, Darius. Anything's possible. Perhaps he escaped.'

Riley nodded. He had to concede it didn't make much sense. There had to be another explanation.

'Let's check the rest of the building.'

One of the other doors in the hallway opened onto a narrow passage. Concrete block walls led deeper into the barn, bulkhead lights every few metres, a full-length large mirror hanging incongruously halfway along. At the end, a heavy metal door stood blocking their way.

'It slides, look,' Enders said, pointing to the tracks in the floor and ceiling. 'I should think this switch opens the door, no?'

To the right of the door a big red button sat halfway up the wall. The button was the circuit-breaker type you could hit with your palm. A wiring conduit ran from the button up to the ceiling where the tubing disappeared through a hole. Enders reached out.

'Wait!' Riley said.

Enders pulled his hand back, but it was too late. He'd already pressed the button.

Chapter Thirty-Seven

Near Cadover Bridge, Devon. Thursday 29th October. 5.48 p.m.

Nothing happened. Riley glanced at the door, aware for the first time of a small domed light on the wall above. The light glowed red, almost as if it signified something was happening beyond the door. Something which could not be interrupted.

'It should be opening.' Enders pointed to the tracks in the floor and ceiling. 'But it's not.'

'Let's backtrack,' Riley said, gesturing along the corridor. 'Try the other door.'

Enders nodded and they returned along the corridor to the anteroom. The remaining door was locked and a tentative shove by Riley did nothing to change the situation.

'I'm going to bust it,' Riley said. 'This one's only wooden. No sense in wasting any more time.'

He stepped back and then leapt at the door, raising one leg and kicking the wood next to the lock. The frame splintered away and the door slammed open. Enders reached in and went for the light switch.

Inside, a bare concrete floor and block walls contrasted with a leather executive chair at a desk. A large computer monitor sat on the desk, a keyboard and mouse in front of the screen. Beneath the desk a small tower unit rested on the floor.

Riley walked across, reached down and turned the switch on the base unit. There was a low hum and then the monitor flickered into life. A couple of minutes later the system had booted up. There was no login or password required and some sort of program had begun running already.

'Security cameras,' Riley said, as he pointed to a row of thumbnails. 'Look, there's some archive material.'

'How do you know?'

'The timestamp. This is from the anteroom with the cells. There must be a movement sensor that activates the camera.' Riley clicked the thumbnail and the footage began to play. A man stood facing the mirror which hung on the wall in the corridor. He appeared to be gesturing at the mirror, talking to his own reflection. Then he walked away.

Riley jerked back upright in the chair, not believing what he was seeing. It didn't compute, it didn't compute at all.

'What is it, sir?' Enders stood at his shoulder. 'What's the problem?'

'He's the problem, Patrick.' Riley pointed at the screen. He clicked again to move the video back a few seconds. The man turned and walked away from the mirror again. This time there was no doubt in Riley's mind. 'Him.'

'Who is he?' Enders bent and squinted at the screen.

'He's the main suspect in the *Lacuna* case. Collier showed me a picture of him yesterday. His name's Brenden Parker. He's the man who kidnapped Sleet and Benedict.'

Dusk was falling when Savage and Hardin arrived at Woodland Heights. The sea was flat calm, a huge glossy mirror, pinpricks of emerging starlight reflected on the surface. As they pulled up, Hardin jabbed a finger in the direction of the house.

'Not the beach, Charlotte,' he said. 'Brenden's in there with them.'

They got out of the car. The ground- and first-floor windows stood dark and impenetrable, but in the attic rooms light flared into the night. Hardin was right. Brenden Parker was up there.

'I was wrong,' Savage said. 'I didn't consider the tide, and neither did Brenden. It's high now. There is no beach. We might be too late.'

'Let's pray not,' Hardin said. He looked over towards the front door. 'What do we do now? Go in or wait for reinforcements?'

Savage was tempted to say that he was the boss, he should decide, but there was something holding Hardin back. She could see it in his eyes, the way they jumped around. He was nervous, his bluff, overbearing manner gone. And then there was the matter of the initials found on the raft: *CH*. Parker wanted Hardin up there. It would be foolish to give him what he wanted.

'*I* go in,' Savage said. 'On my own. He knows me and I don't suppose it will be much of a surprise when I come up the stairs. I think he wants this, wants his guilt to be discovered.'

'Yes, Charlotte. But does he want to be arrested? I doubt that very much. He's got some idea for the denouement and at the moment he holds all the cards. Your plan's much too dangerous, I say we wait.'

'The boys, sir. We can't just leave them.'

'They might already be dead. If you go up there, there will just be somebody else to worry about. Down here I'll be none the wiser.'

'No.' Savage took her mobile out from her pocket. 'You call me now and I'll answer and then conceal the phone. It

358

won't be a brilliant line, not as good as a wire, but you'll get some idea of what's going on. When backup arrives you'll have some valuable information.'

Hardin stuck his tongue out over his bottom lip. He paused to weigh the options and then nodded. 'Go on then, but Charlotte?'

'Yes, sir?'

'Be careful.'

Savage smiled. 'Of course.'

It took a couple of minutes to set up the trick with the phone and then Savage moved towards the steps. At the top the door stood ajar. Savage pushed the door open and then waited there for a moment to allow her eyes to adjust to the darkness. After a minute or so the interior of the hallway revealed itself, a wan, ghostly light filtering down from the first floor. She stepped across to the foot of the stairs, debris from the fallen plaster ceiling crunching underfoot.

Climbing the stairs in silence was impossible and each tread creaked as she moved up to the first floor. But then Parker knew they were coming, knew they would have figured it out, so total surprise was unlikely anyway.

On the first-floor landing there was more light, a pale glow washing down from the attic rooms. Savage walked to the foot of the attic stairs. Cocked her head. There was movement up there, someone sobbing, a voice and a creak of floorboards. She began to ascend the twisting stairway. Half a dozen steps further up, the stairs turned left and reached a small half landing. Above that they curled back on themselves and came to a larger landing area, off which were the bedrooms. Savage moved up slowly, each step she took accompanied by a little creak. Light poured from one of the bedrooms, the same one in which she'd found the inscription on the bed. She reached the top of the stairs and edged forward. Her feet scraped on the rough boards, but the sound was masked by a moaning from above.

She peered round the doorjamb. Before she had a chance to assimilate the situation, a voice rang out.

'Detective Inspector Savage. I knew it wouldn't be long before you joined us.'

Riley fiddled with the mouse and closed the archive video. He brought up one of the menus.

'What are you doing, sir?' Enders said. 'We haven't got time for this. We've got to let the others know about Parker.'

'The CCTV clip was recorded,' Riley said. 'I'm looking for the live feed.'

He clicked a menu item labelled 'Cameras' and the screen split into four sections, each with a separate picture. Above each feed, a title: 'Cells', 'Driveway', 'Farmyard', 'Altar'.

'Sir!' Enders jabbed at the screen labelled 'Altar'. 'That's Perry Sleet!'

Riley looked at the screen. A half-clothed man lay face up on some sort of stainless steel bench. The camera view was from above and to the side and the man's head was turned towards the camera. The face, while no longer grinning as in the holiday snaps Riley had seen, unmistakably belonged to Perry Sleet.

'This is now,' Riley said. 'See the timestamp? For some reason Parker hasn't touched him.'

'What's that thing he's lying on?'

Riley stared at the screen and wondered if Enders hadn't been spot on all along. In the centre of the room there was an island out of an expensive kitchen. Stainless steel, three metres by two, some sort of lighting gantry hanging above. Except it wasn't a lighting gantry, more like a disturbing modern art installation. There were coils of wire up there

360

and something which looked like a robotic arm. Riley could see an electric drill attached to a vertical pillar. On the far side a hinged contraption bore a circular saw blade. There were rods, levers, gears and hoses. A knife had been welded to one end of a metal bar attached to a hydraulic ram.

'A torture machine,' Riley said. 'Think about Tim Benedict's injuries.'

'Shit.' Enders shook his head. 'We've got to get Sleet out of there, sir. Wherever "there" is.'

'The metal door. He must be behind that. But there's no hurry, Parker's long gone.'

'Really?' Enders pointed to the screen. 'So why is that lot moving?'

Enders was right. The robotic arm attached to the overhead gantry had begun to swing down. Something on the end rotating at high speed. On the other side of the gantry the electric drill began to descend. Atop the table, Sleet moved. He rattled the cuffs around his hands. Then he opened his mouth. Muffled by the walls of the building though it was, Riley could still hear Sleet's long, drawn-out scream. He watched, both fascinated and horrified as the process continued. Knives began to move back and forth and the circular saw was now a blur of spinning metal.

'We'll never break down the door.' Riley pushed back the chair. Enders had already made for the exit, his phone in his hand, but Riley stood for a moment. There was something he'd seen on the side of the barn as they'd crossed the farmyard. The health and safety sign warning about using crawlboards. 'The roof, Patrick. We can smash our way through the roof!'

Chapter Thirty-Eight

Near Bolberry, South Hams, Devon. Thursday 29th October. 5.59 p.m.

The two beds in the room had been pulled away from the wall and turned on their sides, bisecting the space and creating a low barrier. Beyond, Brenden Parker sat in an old armchair which had been placed up against the window. The window was a dormer, a double-opening casement. The sill was some way above the back of the armchair. Sitting on the windowsill, facing out with their legs dangling in space, were the two boys. Parker blinked at Savage with one eye. The other squinted out, the eyeball bloodshot and surrounded by a mass of bruised and swollen skin. A scab sat on the side of his head a little way back from his right temple. When Savage had interviewed him before, his hair had been fluffed up to cover the injury. She berated herself; if she'd been more observant she might have realised that this was the man who'd attacked her in the copse.

'As you can see,' Parker said, 'it would be very dangerous to try anything stupid.' He gestured at a pair of ropes which had been tied to the bed frames and ran from there in a gentle curve up to each boy's neck. The ropes had been tied in a noose. 'One push and it's all over.'

'It's all over for you anyway, Brenden. There's no escape, so you may as well give yourself up.'

'I don't want to *escape*. In case you missed it, I wanted you to catch me. I gave you numerous clues but you failed.' Parker gestured at one of the overturned beds. 'I carved a message under there. I placed the manacles down in the cellar. I sent Conrad Hardin the messages. I wanted you to work out what had happened here and why. But what you worked out wasn't what I was expecting. It turned out I *hadn't* killed Jason Caldwell, that it was my father. Unfortunately the revelation came much too late. Father was in custody and out of my reach and I . . . well, I'd already gone too far.'

'You killed Liam Clough and Jason Hobb.'

'The thing with Liam was an accident. I wanted to play, but he wouldn't stop screaming.'

'So you choked the life out of him and left him in the tunnel half naked and covered in grease.'

'You don't understand. I was trying to bring closure to that part of my life. To resolve my issues. I also hoped Jason and Liam would be my friends. I've never had many friends.'

'Friends? You butchered Jason. For Christ's sake, you boiled his head in a pot.'

'I had to, I lost Smirker, you see? After he died, I buried his skull in the wood where we used to play. It was his favourite place in the whole world. I used to go there and talk to him. He was my confidante, my best buddy. Then, when I heard the house was up for sale, I went and retrieved the rest of his bones from the cellar. Everything was great until you lot interfered and stole him away from me. With Smirker gone, I thought Jason could be his replacement, but he didn't want to play ball, so Jason had to become the new Smirker. Not before he poked me in the eye though. Funny, I now look like Smirker. Ol' one eye. Ha, ha, ha!'

363

'Right.' Savage shook her head. She didn't know what the hell Parker was going on about.

'None of this was my fault, you know? Somebody else was to blame.'

'Not so, Brenden. Your father may have been responsible back then, but you're the guilty party here.'

'NO!' Parker pushed himself up from the armchair. Now Savage could see he held a small plastic weapon in one hand. A Taser. 'I was thirteen!'

'My God!' The revelation came as Savage stared at the Taser. 'You're the guy who kidnapped Perry Sleet, who killed Tim Benedict.'

'Of course.' Parker appeared surprised at Savage's reaction. 'I call myself the Shepherd, when I'm in character. To be honest though, the Shepherd is a bit of a bore. He doesn't know how to have fun. I much prefer being plain old Brenden.'

'But . . .' Savage shook her head, tried to understand the contradictions. 'You Tasered *yourself*?'

'Give the Shepherd some credit. He did the Tasering, I just stood there and took it. I must say it wasn't pleasant. Quite the most painful thing I've ever experienced. The thing about a Taser though – the whole point of them – is the effects are only temporary. Within a few minutes I was back to normal. Well, as normal as I'll ever be. I had to do it because I thought I was guilty of the murder of Jason Caldwell. Luckily I managed to convince myself otherwise.' Parker smiled. 'Or should I say, you managed to convince the other me otherwise. Or is it me who convinced I otherwise? The whole thing is so terribly confusing.'

Savage glanced up at the boys hunched on the windowsill. This was worse than she thought. Parker was a complete nutcase, Looney Tunes, bonkers. The death of Jason Caldwell when he was but a boy, along with an abusive father and growing up in the awful environment of the home, must have affected him deeply. The loss of his mother had pushed him over the edge and now he'd flipped completely. The gruesome way he'd disposed of the Hobb boy was proof of that. At any moment he could lose control and push the boys to their deaths. She had to keep him talking.

'But your father killed Jason Caldwell; why punish Benedict and Sleet?'

'I wanted to punish the cowards who let all this happen. I went to Perry for help and he blanked me. Likewise Benedict. I told him what was going on at the home, but he ignored my pleas. Can you believe he told me to pray? And PC Hardin acted no better. I left a message for him, a clue in the form of a picture. I even wrote "HELP" on the back. Ultimately it was Hardin who killed Clough and Hobb, in the same way he killed Caldwell. If Benedict, Sleet and Hardin hadn't been cowards complicit in the covering up of the minster's abuse, none of this would ever have happened.'

'Hardin wasn't complicit. He reported the matter, but his superiors told him to drop it.'

'And it was up to him to decide who should face punishment and who should be let off scot-free, was it? Concentration camp guards are usually found guilty, so why not Hardin?'

Savage shook her head. She had no answer for Parker. Hardin had done his best, but should he have done more? And how many others had done as Hardin had? In every corner of the country there were people who'd looked away or chosen not to take things further. Nothing could excuse Parker's own behaviour, but might he have turned out different had Hardin insisted on being heard?

'I want Hardin up here with me,' Parker said. 'I'll exchange him for the boys. Hardin's the final person on my list.'

'That's not going to happen, Brenden. You're mentally ill and you need help. Release the boys and I'll see this ends in the best possible way. I know you don't want to kill them.'

'WRONG! You don't know anything about me. Killing started this whole thing and killing can finish it. I tried to control myself by becoming the Shepherd. I looked to God to see if He had the answers. He fucking didn't.'

Savage held out her hands and made a calming gesture. Parker was staring at the ceiling, sucking air in and out, the Taser swinging back and forth. She let the silence build and then lowered her voice and spoke again.

'Why Jason Hobb? Why Liam Clough?'

'Why?' Parker lowered his head, his eyes rolling down until they met hers. 'I had to have boys with those names for my game with Hardin to work. I also wanted them to be my friends. Jason, Liam and me. Best buddies. It could have been perfect.'

'So it was just luck you picked them?'

'With Liam, yes, but I was having trouble finding a young boy called Jason, the name's not so common nowadays. If Ned Stone hadn't been going out with Angie Hobb, he'd never have come to my attention.'

'And you met Stone so you could ask him to help you find Sleet and Benedict?'

'He was at the home. He suffered too. Everyone did. Originally I was going to have Stone help me capture Benedict and Sleet, but then I came across this.' Parker waved the Taser. 'A wonderful piece of equipment. Once I managed to get one in my hands, I became all powerful, God-like.'

'But these boys.' Savage gestured at the window. 'They're as innocent as Hobb and Clough.'

'Innocent? Now there's a word.' Parker raised a hand and tapped a finger to his temple. 'But that's all it is, a word.

Who is truly innocent? The corollary to the question being, who is truly guilty? Your Hardin pretended to be blind to the facts all those years ago. Even though he knew the minister was abusing boys, he still did nothing. Now he's got another roll of the dice. He can come up here and save these two, or . . .' Parker half turned and gave the pair of ropes a little tug. 'Or he can kill them.'

'You'll be responsible, Brenden. Not Hardin.'

'NO!' Parker moved towards the windowsill. He placed a hand on the back of one of the boys. 'I'm fucked up because he did nothing. And if he does nothing now, then both these children will die.'

'OK, OK.' Savage held up her hands. 'Take it easy. We can work this out. Hardin is down in the car park.'

'Really?' Parker cocked his head on one side but then smiled knowingly. 'No, I put my head above the parapet and get a bullet in the brain for my troubles.'

'Even if there was a sniper down there, do you think they'd risk shooting you when you're so close to the boys? They could hit one of them or you could fall from the window, knocking them down. Presumably that's why you got them up there in the first place?'

Parker nodded. 'Clever, aren't I? All right then, I'll take a peek.' He turned and climbed up on the armchair and peered out of the window. After a couple of seconds he ducked back inside and dropped down into the chair. 'Seems you're right. Is there anything you don't know?'

'I don't know why you're doing this, but we can talk about that when you've released the boys.'

'I told you, I want Hardin.'

'Fine, I need to make a call, OK?' Parker nodded and Savage reached into her pocket, slowly withdrew her phone and held it to her ear. 'Are you getting this, sir? Parker wants

to exchange you for the boys . . . yes . . . yes . . . I think so
. . . yes . . . really? Hang on, I'll ask him.'

'Well?' Parker said as Savage looked up from the phone.
'What's the score?'

'He'll do the exchange, but downstairs. We have to be
sure the boys are safe.'

'No, you'll set a trap. I release the boys and then some
SWAT team comes rushing in. Stun grenades, tear gas, and
before you know it there's a gun to my head, the trigger
pulled in self-defence.'

'No SWAT team, Brenden. Conrad is suggesting we call
the BBC out to Woodland Heights, get the whole thing down
on camera. You can make a statement about the events which
took place and then we do the swap. The BBC won't send
their reporter up here, so the interview needs to take place
on the front steps. Once the interview is concluded, you
release the boys and go back inside with Hardin and myself.'

'The BBC?' Parker moved his hand from the boy's back
and considered Savage's words. 'An interview? That could
work, yes. I like it! But I want to be allowed to tell them
everything, understand?'

'Did you hear that, sir?' Savage nodded at Hardin's
response and then ended the call. She looked at Brenden.
'He's going to phone the news crew now, we just need to
wait until they arrive.'

'Wait?' Parker smiled. He reached up and wiped a tear
from his good eye. 'Oh yes, I've waited nearly thirty years
– I think I can handle a few more minutes, don't you?'

At one corner of the barn a substantial drainpipe hugged
the stonework. Riley glanced down at his wellies. Hardly the
best footwear to climb in, but perhaps the rubber would give
his feet purchase. He placed his hands around the drainpipe

and gave an experimental pull. The pipe appeared solid enough so he began to climb. It wasn't far, perhaps four metres to the guttering. The hardest part was hauling himself over the lip of the roof, but he managed to wriggle up and then lie prostrate on the corrugated surface.

'Are you there?' Enders' voice floated across the farmyard in the darkness.

'Yes.' Riley began to crawl towards the apex. As long as he stayed near the edge, the roof would probably hold his weight. In the centre of one of the cement sheets, without any structure to support his weight, the roof would almost certainly give way.

He reached the top without incident and sat astride the ridge. Down in the farmyard, Enders stood in the gloom, the light from his phone illuminating his face. Riley shouted to him.

'Any news?'

'Help is ten minutes away, minimum,' Enders said. 'And then we've still got to break down the door.'

'Perry Sleet doesn't have ten minutes.' Riley shook his head. Cursed inwardly. 'I'm going in.'

'Be careful, sir.'

Riley wasn't listening. He'd already begun to move along the ridge, trying to work out where the corridor was. He'd need to go beyond that point in order to be above the room Sleet was in. In the dark it was hard to judge the distance, but he stopped when he thought he'd gone ten metres. He moved down from the apex a little. Beneath his hand he felt the smoothness of a Perspex panel, but when he put his face to the panel he could see nothing through the crazed material. He moved to one side and started feeling for the little boltheads which protruded above the sheets. The bolts indicated where the sheets were secured to the rafters. He soon found a pair and sat between them. He braced himself as best he could with his hands and then stamped hard with both feet. The roof shuddered, but didn't break. He tried again and this time was rewarded with a cracking sound. From below he heard Sleet cry out. A scream followed by a plea for help.

Riley stamped again and again. Pieces of roof began to fall inward, clattering down onto the floor inside the building. A few more kicks and Riley had created a hole big enough to get through. He peered down into the gloom, a pale glow below. Something mechanical whirred and Sleet let out another scream.

Damn it! Riley calculated the distance to the floor. Four metres for the wall and then another three for the pitch of the roof. He moved to the edge of the hole and felt down for the rafter beneath the broken roofing sheet. He lowered himself as much as he dared and then let his body fall, grasping the top of the rafter with both hands. He swung into space and hung for a moment. Now or never. He let go and dropped to the floor, landing awkwardly on the hard concrete, a burst of pain shooting up his ankle.

'Heeelllppp meeeeee!' Sleet screamed off to Riley's right. 'Arrrggghhh!'

There was a high-pitched whine and a rush of air. Riley pushed himself up from the floor. Bulkhead lights on the walls provided a low illumination and he could see Sleet lying on the stainless steel table beneath a huge gantry, a trellis of tubing supporting various pieces of machinery. A circular saw on some sort of mount. A drill attached to a vertical bar. A huge piston thing with a knife attached.

Riley ran forward. Sleet lay face up, his torso sliced skin and muscle, blood oozing from dozens of cuts.

'Urrrgggghhh!' Sleet gurgled, spitting red mucus. 'Arrrggghhh!'

Riley stood at the side of the table looking for some sort of stop button. The saw began to descend again, the blade flashing in the light. Riley put his hands out and grabbed the metal arm the saw was attached to. For a moment he thought he'd stopped it, but the power of the hydraulic arm was too much and the saw moved down, the teeth ripping into Sleet's legs.

'Arrrggghhh!'

The cacophony of whining and drilling and pumping and whirring seemed to rise in pitch along with Sleet's screams. Riley hauled himself up onto the table using a corner of the gantry. He stood and reached for a loom of cable which rose from the gantry and then looped across to some sort of junction box high on one wall. He pulled with one hand and then used both, hanging in mid-air for a moment before there was a loud bang accompanied by a shower of sparks as the cable ripped itself from the junction box and Riley fell to the floor. The noise from the machine tools ceased and the only sound was a faint gasping from Sleet.

Then the lights went out.

Savage's mobile buzzed in her pocket. She pulled the phone out and looked down at the text message. 'They're here,' she said.

'Let's go then.' Parker pointed with the Taser. 'Downstairs. Everyone. You first, then the boys and then me. Go on.'

'We're coming down!' Savage shouted out. 'Keep clear!'

The two lads swivelled on the windowsill and Savage saw their faces for the first time. Tear-stained, white with fear, on one of the boy's cheeks a nasty bruise. They clambered down as best they could, their hands bound together in front of them.

'Don't worry,' Savage said, trying to smile. 'Everything's going to be OK.'

She walked out onto the landing and edged down the stairs. The two boys followed, the ropes running limply from their necks back to Parker. Parker had the Taser and the rope in one hand and in the other he held a flick knife.

'I'm warning you, Savage,' Parker shouted. 'I could slit their throats in half a second.'

'Nobody's going to try anything, Brenden. Just stay calm.'

'Oh, I'm calm all right.'

They made it to the top of the main stairs and then began to descend. Bright light illuminated the hallway, and through the front door, Savage could see a woman standing on the porch. Beside her, a cameraman hunkered behind a camera on a tripod. Both the woman and the man wore padded jackets, 'BBC' emblazoned on the front pockets.

Savage edged forward, the two children following.

'Wait!' Parker shouted from behind. He had the knife held out. 'We stop here and Hardin comes across.'

'Release the—'

'WE DO AS I SAY OR WE GO BACK IN!' Parker screamed. He waved the Taser at Savage. Then he smiled and whispered, 'OK, send Hardin over, I'll make a statement, I'll release the kids and then I get to go upstairs with you and PC Plod.'

'I'm coming in.' In the darkness beyond the lights a bulky figure moved and Hardin lumbered from the shadows. He climbed the short flight of steps to the porch and nodded at Savage. 'The boys all right, Charlotte?'

'Yes, sir.'

'Good, good.' Hardin half turned and raised a finger.

The reporter edged slightly to the left and held out a microphone. Everything beyond the lights was black. Like looking into a torch beam. The reporter had begun to say something but Savage wasn't hearing her. Her attention was held by the cameraman. Or more succinctly his boots. Hi-Tech Magnums. Not the sort of footwear she'd expect a BBC employee to be wearing. And there was something very wrong with the camera. No way the guy was going to get any usable footage with the lens cap on.

Parker didn't appear to have noticed anything amiss. He moved forward and his bad eye squinted against the lights. He gestured to Hardin to stand to one side and then used the Taser to push the boys in front of him, the knife held horizontally as if ready to slash the blade across both their throats. The reporter extended her arm further, the microphone like a carrot to tempt a donkey. Parker took another step and the slightest hint of a smile spread on the woman's face. Except now Savage realised she wasn't a reporter at all. She was DC Becky Miles from the Covert Operations Unit.

'None of this was my fault,' Parker said. 'There has been a catalogue of errors. PC Hardin should have—'

From out of the black, Savage thought she saw a tiny flash of light, heard an almost indiscernible *phut*.

Parker stood still for a moment, a growing circle of blood on his forehead. Savage leapt forward and grabbed Parker's knife arm, pulling the blade away from the children as he slipped to the floor. One of the boys started screaming and then, from behind the lights, emerged Luke Farrell and a female FLO.

'It's over,' Luke said as he and the woman officer gathered up the boys and led them away. 'Let's get you back to your mums and dads. They're waiting over here.'

Once they'd gone, the TV cameraman stepped from behind his tripod. His jacket slipped open, revealing a chest holster beneath. He moved to Parker and checked for signs of life. He glanced up at Savage and shook his head. Then he made a signal out into the blackness.

All at once the TV arcs went down to be replaced by a softer glow from a set of lights atop the mobile incident room van. Inspector Nigel Frey, the head of the Force Support Group, stood next to the van alongside Chief Constable Maria Heldon. Savage took a final look at Parker and then she and Hardin walked over.

'Well done, DI Savage,' Maria Heldon said. 'Excellent work.'

'Parker,' Savage said. 'He never stood a chance, did he?'

'A chance?' Heldon said. 'No, we couldn't take the risk.'

'I gave the order to fire as soon as it was safe to do so,' Frey said. 'The sniper was off to the left. Twenty metres. The walls to each side of the steps shielded the children. There was no possibility of hitting them. As a backup the cameraman was an armed officer and Becky was there too. The risk to you and the DSupt was minimal.'

'Minimal, yes.' Savage glanced at Frey. She knew she should thank him – this was the second time Frey and his officers had come to her rescue – but inside she was strangely devoid of emotion. If this was a victory, it was one where the winning came with a price attached. She half smiled at Frey as he walked off towards the house.

'I guess you were right, DI Savage,' Heldon said. 'Parker didn't stand a chance. But we couldn't let him have one, could we?'

'He wanted to tell his story,' Savage said. 'About the minister and what went on here. Will that still come out?'

'Oh yes, I'm sure it will,' Heldon said. She smiled. 'Eventually.'

The Chief Constable turned on her heels and walked away to where an officer held open the door to her car. Savage stood for a moment and then spotted DC Calter standing beside a pool Focus parked at the side of the house. She walked across.

'Ma'am?' Calter reached out a hand and touched Savage on the arm. 'You all right?'

'Yes,' Savage said. 'I could do with a lift though.'

'Sure.' Calter clicked open the driver's door. 'To the station?'

Savage turned back to Woodland Heights. The building stood stark and grey in the glow from multiple sets of lights. Two CSIs were working at the front door where Brenden Parker's body lay slumped on the steps. Rain had begun to fall and a low wind moaned against the distant cliffs.

'No,' Savage said as she shivered. 'Home.'

Chapter Thirty-Nine

It took the best part of the weekend for the meetings, paper-work and debriefs to subside. Savage lost count of the number of forms she had to fill in and the number of statements she had to make and sign. Monday morning, thinking she was at last getting on top of everything, she went to the crime suite to find three officers from the Professional Standards Department poring over an array of documents DS Gareth Collier had laid out for them.

'Vultures,' Collier whispered as he stood next to Savage. 'Scavenging for easy pickings.'

PSD, it turned out, were interested in discovering if mistakes had been made in the *Curlew/Lacuna* investiga-tions. Their arrival coincided with the news that Angie Hobb was taking legal action against Devon and Cornwall Police and her brief was Amanda Bradley. The lawyer had neatly segued from representing Ned Stone into what could be a nice little earner. She'd linked the historical *Curlew* case with the present-day *Lacuna* one and indicated she intended to show gross negligence and/or conspiracy in both. Maria Heldon, in countermove, had self-referred the force to the

IPCC. Savage thought it unlikely either the PSD, the IPCC or Amanda Bradley would get anywhere near the truth of what had happened all those years ago.

'The words "shit" and "fan" come to mind.' Collier took a cloth and scrubbed something from the whiteboard. He stared at the smudge of black he'd made and then wiped again until all remnants of the marker pen had gone. 'We did our best though, didn't we?'

Savage didn't answer, aware the question was rhetorical, the tone in Collier's voice enough to show he, at least, didn't think they had. She wasn't sure either, but in the end she remembered a maxim her old boss, DCI Walsh, had often used when things had gone wrong: *Don't beat yourself up; it's the criminals who commit the crimes.*

Who the criminals in the *Curlew/Lacuna* case were, Savage wasn't sure. The government minister, obviously. Brenden and Frank Parker, yes – and Parker Senior would be going down for murder. Elijah Samuel? The CPS were talking about charging him for helping Frank Parker to conceal Jason Caldwell's body, but Savage thought a successful prosecution remote. Ned Stone, a criminal if she'd ever seen one, looked like he was getting off scot-free, for telling Brenden Parker where he could find Perry Sleet was hardly a crime. Bernie Black – Hardin's old boss – had died years ago so his actions would also go unpunished. Then there was the man from Special Branch. His identity was a mystery and looked likely to remain so. Finally, there was Conrad Hardin. Would the man who'd been at the bottom of the chain of command end up taking the flack? Savage hoped not.

In the canteen for a late lunch, she found Hardin sitting at a table on his own. A cup of milky coffee stood on the table and the DSupt was dunking a ginger nut as she pulled up a chair, put down her food, and sat.

'Charlotte.' Hardin looked up and then took a bite of the biscuit. 'You want a word?'

'Yes.' She hadn't had a chance to speak to Hardin one-to-one since the events at the home. She poked the tuna salad in front of her with her fork. 'About last Thursday.'

'Right.' Hardin finished his biscuit and then took a sip of coffee. He made a face. 'Go on.'

'The Chief Constable said she couldn't take the risk with Brenden Parker. If I was a cynic, I'd say she meant she wasn't keen to hear what Parker had to say. The end result suited her.'

'You need to understand that the Home Secretary had called her earlier in the day. Impressed upon her the need to handle the incident carefully. The situation was, in all senses of the word, volatile. Still is, to be honest. Apparently the *Herald* have got wind of something. Dan Phillips is pretty shrewd and I bet it won't be long before he joins the dots. This isn't going away, Charlotte, even if some people up in London wish it would.'

'Has Dan got the whole story?'

'I don't know. You'd better ask him.'

'I mean, does he know about the photograph?'

'Of course not.' Hardin went for another ginger nut. 'But Heldon knows. And she's aware I told you.'

Savage nodded. She moved a piece of lettuce from one side of her plate to the other, not really interested in her food.

'You deceived me, sir. On the phone. There was never any chance the BBC were going to turn up at the children's home, but I believed you and so did Parker.'

'I didn't tell you the whole truth, but the deception was necessary.'

'It was clever, sir, I'll give you that. You offered to give Parker exactly what he wanted all those years ago and he

378

fell for the trick because he simply wanted to be heard.'

'I would have gone up there to save the boys, but he'd have killed both of us. The ploy seemed like the best option.'

Savage bent to her food. The tuna tasted dry and the coleslaw on the side was tart with vinegar. She gave up and reached for her own coffee as Hardin took another gulp of his. For a moment the noise and bustle of the canteen intruded and then Hardin spoke again.

'You should know that *I* approved the use of lethal force, Charlotte. Not the Home Office, not the Chief Constable, not Nigel Frey. Parker's death may have suited others, but the decision was mine. It was the only way to be sure of the boys' safety.'

'But—'

'I let Jason Caldwell and Liam Hayskith down all those years ago. My actions led directly to the deaths of Jason Hobb and Liam Clough.' Hardin shook his head. He took a handkerchief from his pocket. Savage could see his eyes were laden with moisture. 'In my mind the risk wasn't Parker exposing some elite paedophile ring, the risk was that another two boys might die. I couldn't have their deaths on my conscience, do you understand?'

Savage thought back to Thursday night. She remembered the boys' faces as they'd climbed down from the window and again as they'd been returned to their parents. Then she thought, inevitably, of her own children, of how she'd do anything – *anything* – to protect them from harm.

'Yes, sir,' she said. 'I guess I do.'

Riley didn't return to work until the end of the following week. He tried to enter the crime suite discreetly, but his crutches put paid to that. A rousing cheer went around the room and the regular wags shouted out abuse.

'Hopalong! Jake the Peg!' The best came from Enders who came across to Riley as he hobbled across to his desk.

'Puts a whole new meaning to your career path, doesn't it, sir?' Enders grinned and patted Riley on the back. 'Fast-tracked, you ain't!'

The banter was well meaning and the cheering came with official backing: Maria Heldon was putting Riley forward for a commendation for bravery, his actions almost certainly having saved Perry Sleet's life. However, when Riley had dropped through the roof of the barn he'd fractured his ankle. Adrenaline had kept him on his feet for long enough to give Sleet first aid for a few minutes, but once medical help arrived, he'd collapsed in agony.

'He's a lucky boy,' Enders said once the commotion had died down. Riley sat at a terminal browsing Sleet's Facebook page. Catherine Sleet had posted some pictures of Sleet in hospital as well as a 'thank you' for messages of support. There was another picture of Catherine herself, bedside. 'Rescued by you, and Mrs Gorgeous to tend to his every need.'

Sleet *had* been lucky. His injuries were similar to those Tim Benedict had sustained but, being younger, it looked as if Sleet would pull through. Plus he hadn't had to endure being stuffed upside down in a wheelie bin.

Brenden Parker's actions were plainly those of somebody with serious mental issues, but behind the monster image which the media chose to highlight, there was an explanation, albeit one with considerable controversy attached. Parker, some psychologists were arguing, had a form of dissociative identity disorder, better known as a split or multiple personality. In his time off work, Riley had read up on the subject. As far as he could make out, it was likely Parker's experience in childhood had caused the affliction. The traumatic events surrounding the death of Jason Caldwell had led to the suppression of some memories and the development of an alternate personality. The death of his mother had caused a complete mental breakdown in Parker and led to the emergence of this alter ego – a new personality intent on punishing the people who had let Parker down in his childhood, even though that included Parker himself. Part of him wanted to expose what had happened at the home and part of him wanted vengeance. Where kidnapping and killing Jason Hobb and Liam Clough came into it, Riley had no idea, but it seemed likely that Parker was trying to recreate some aspect of his childhood. The raft had been part of that too and Parker's alternate personality had seeded the first one with two chilling artefacts which pointed to a crime having been committed all those years ago: the finger bone and the piece of scalp belonging to Jason Caldwell.

Later in the morning he tried to explain dissociative identity disorder to Enders, but the DC wasn't having any of it.

'You're joking me, sir, aren't you?' Enders said. 'You're saying none of this was Parker's fault?'

'No, merely that DID is an explanation for his behaviour.'

'Crap.' Enders shook his head. 'It's the way of the world these days, isn't it? Always some excuse. Blame this, blame that, but don't take responsibility for your actions. Doesn't wash with me. You don't cut an eleven-year-old boy's head off and boil it up in a pot because of something that happened in your childhood. You do it because you're a fucking nasty piece of work. End of.'

Riley smiled to himself as Enders stomped off, thinking the DC had pretty much nailed it.

By the weekend the weather was set fine, a light breeze from the north cooling the air, but bringing a blue sky and a strong winter sun. When Pete suggested a trip out on *Puffin*,

Savage jumped at the chance. Jamie was as keen as ever and Samantha perked up when a pub lunch was added into the equation.

The sail across to Cawsand Bay took an hour, the yacht gliding through a flat sea with Savage at the helm. They dropped anchor and went ashore to eat and then afterwards sat on the beach while Jamie larked around at the water's edge and Samantha played on her phone. Savage zipped her waterproof up against the cold and leant against Pete.

'OK, love?' he said, putting his arm around her.

'Sure. Never better than this.'

'No.' Pete nodded out to where *Puffin* swung at anchor surrounded by a glittering sea. 'Who needs exotic places, hey?'

'You miss it, don't you?' Savage looked at Pete and shielded her eyes from the sun. 'The Navy.'

'I'm still in the Navy.'

'You know what I mean. The travel, the ocean.'

'Of course.' Pete turned back and gestured at Jamie and then Samantha. 'But it doesn't mean I'd swap you and the kids for that life again.'

Savage said nothing. She was touched, but deep within she wondered if Pete was telling the truth. Since he'd relinquished his command, she'd seen a change in her husband. He'd been better with the kids, more sociable, but something was missing inside. A passion, a spark.

Half an hour later they dinghyed back to the boat and clambered on board. Pete hauled the anchor up while Savage took the helm. They motored out of the bay into the gentle north-easterly.

'We'll not bother with the sails,' Pete said. 'Be tacking back and forth forever to get home.'

Savage turned to look over her left shoulder. The sun

hung above the Cornish shoreline. Dusk was a couple of hours away.

'Can we take a detour?' Savage said. 'To Torpoint? We can cut inside Drake's Island. It'll only take us twenty minutes.'

'Why . . .?' Pete started to ask the question and stopped. 'Sure. But if we're on police business then I'll be submitting an expense form for the diesel.'

'No, not police business.' Savage stared ahead. Wondered whether she was the one now being dishonest. 'This is personal.'

After a few minutes, Savage swung the wheel to port and they passed between Drake's Island and Cornwall. Not long after, the estuary narrowed and Royal William Yard appeared on the right and beyond it Mayflower Marina. Now the river opened out on the left, a vast expanse of mudflats, to the north of which lay Torpoint. Savage slowed the boat and studied the mud. Fingers of water had begun to invade the mud as the tide came in. Before her eyes, tiny veins became trickles, became streams.

'I'll need the dinghy,' Savage said. 'You could potter up to the Navy yards and pick me up on the way back.'

'Right . . . ' Pete cocked his head. 'Where are you off to then?'

'Ashore.' Savage pulled the throttle into neutral and the boat slowed. 'Ten minutes once I get there.'

'And where is there?'

'That.' Savage pointed to the ramshackle collection of wood which marked Larry the Lobster's houseboat.

She killed the outboard motor a few metres from shore and the dinghy drifted in and beached where the mud turned to gravel. She jumped from the dinghy, bowlined the painter to one of the uprights on the gangway which led to Larry's boat, and walked out. When she reached the end of the walkway, she realised something was different: the space where the pot boat had been tied alongside was now occupied by a small, wooden yacht. The yacht stood nestled in the soft mud but would float once the tide rose. A tap, tap, tap echoed from the innards of the craft.

'Hello!' Savage stepped onto the houseboat and edged round to the rear. 'Larry?'

A mess of tools and cans of paint and varnish lay strewn about the cockpit, along with the innards of what appeared to be a diesel engine. Up on the foredeck, several coils of rope looked new, as did a set of bright white fenders.

The banging ceased and somebody huffed from below. The steps to the companionway creaked and Larry's bearded face popped out.

'I knew it be you,' Larry said. 'Heard someone on the gangway and said to myself, "It'll be that Inspector Wotsit."'

'Charlotte,' Savage said. 'I'm not on duty, I was just passing.'

'Passing?' Larry clambered out into the cockpit. He gazed across the water to Plymouth. 'Out for a swim, was you?'

'No, I came by yacht and by dinghy. I—'

'Never mind.' Larry picked up a rag from the floor and wiped his hands. 'You're here now. What do you want? I thought you got the man who killed Jason?'

'Yes we did. Both of them.'

Larry raised an eyebrow. 'Both of them?' He spat into the rag. 'How's that then?'

Savage explained as best she could. She told Larry about Brenden Parker and his deluded mission to reveal what went on at Woodland Heights. How he'd killed Liam Clough and Jason Hobb and sought revenge on those he held responsible for allowing the historical abuse at the home to continue. Then she moved on to tell of how Frank Parker had tried

384

to cover things up by killing Jason Caldwell down on the beach and making his son believe that he was responsible.

'I guess I wanted to thank you for your help,' Savage said. 'And to fill you in on what happened.'

'And why would you want to do that?'

'I thought you'd want to know.' Savage stared at Larry and held his gaze. It was obvious now that beneath the weather-worn face and hidden under the beard was a much younger man. 'Liam.'

'Liam?' Larry chuckled and shook his head. He used the hand with five digits to wipe the other hand, smearing grease from the knuckle where the thumb had been. 'No, the name's Larry now. Liam's long gone. Better forgotten. Way past the time to move on.'

'But you were out there, I saw your pot boat when I was at Soar Mill Cove. I didn't twig at the time.'

'When I read about that raft at Jennycliff and heard about them boys going missing, I knew something was keel up. I kept searching the coast looking for answers. I nearly found them up the Erme estuary but the guy ran off. I had my suspicions, but I never twigged it were Brenden until I heard on the news that you lot were looking for him. By then it was too late. Too late for Jason Hobb anyway.'

'You tried. We all did.' Savage half turned towards the shore, remembering the night Jason had gone missing. She said nothing for a moment and then turned back and gestured at Larry's hand. 'You told me you lost that at sea on a fishing boat.'

'Well, I was at sea.' Larry's beard parted in a smile. 'Just.'

'Brenden cut it off, didn't he? As he tried to prevent you from sailing off, you struggled and he lashed out.'

'Well, Parker's dead now and I did sail off. And as I said, I've moved on.'

'And are you going to again?' Savage ran her eyes along the lines of the wooden yacht. 'Lovely boat.'

'Aye. She is. She was chocked up ashore for years, but now there's just a few more things to fix and then I'm off.'

'Where?'

'I'll cross the Channel and head south. Hole up in a Spanish *ría* for the winter. Potter round to the Med in the spring.'

'Why now?'

'I'll not get any younger, so I thought I'd take a year or two off. I've sold my pot boat and I've got a bit stashed away. I don't need much to survive on. Never have.'

'Can I ask you something, Larry?'

'Sure. But I might not answer.'

'Why did you stay hidden all these years? You'd done nothing wrong. You could have come forward. Certainly when you were eighteen.'

'They'd have thought of something to keep me quiet. Look what happened to Jason. When the minister popped his clogs I considered telling my story, but by then I was in the Merchant Navy. Excuse the pun, but I didn't want to make waves.'

'But what about your parents? Wouldn't they want closure?'

'They got closure when they abandoned me to the care system. I owe them nothing. After I left the home, I had to fend for myself. For the first few years, I was begging and thieving and up to all sorts. Later, appropriately, I turned to the sea for answers. Got a berth on a deep-sea fishing boat. Discovered I loved it out there.' Larry paused and then turned to look over his shoulder. A few hundred metres away, *Puffin* was circling in deeper water, Pete at the helm, Jamie and Samantha waving from the bow. 'They're waiting for you. Your family.'

'You'll be OK?'

'Of course. Why wouldn't I?'

'Look me up when you get back from the Med.' Savage gestured at Larry's yacht. 'I'd like a sail in her. She's a fine boat.'

'I might do that. If I come back.'

Savage walked back along the gangway to where the dinghy now bobbed at the end of its painter. She climbed aboard, started the engine and manoeuvred round the houseboat. Larry stood watching her from the stern of his yacht.

'Good luck,' Savage shouted as she passed.

'Luck?' Larry shook his head. He raised a hand to the sky and pointed at the high cirrus clouds. 'There's no such thing. Just the wind and the waves.' He laughed. 'And the tides of course. Don't forget the tides.'

Savage gunned the outboard and the dinghy rose on to the plane. She headed for Pete and the kids. When she arrived at *Puffin*, Pete tied the dinghy on and helped her aboard.

'All right?' Pete said as he engaged the engine and they began to move off.

'Fine.'

She walked forward and stood at the bow with Jamie and Samantha as Pete steered them through the Narrows and turned for home. Out in the Sound a lone yacht slipped towards the breakwater, the genoa full with the northerly wind. She wondered where the boat was headed. A late afternoon sail around the bay, or perhaps, like Larry, bound for somewhere farther afield?

MISSED
THE FIRST BOOKS
IN THE
DI CHARLOTTE
SAVAGE SERIES?

*'Harry likes pretty things.
He likes to look at them.
Sometimes that isn't enough.
He wants to get closer.
Naughty Harry.'*

Introducing DI Charlotte
Savage: woman, mother
and crime fighter.

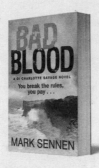

'We're going to find them, sort them, pay them back . . .'

DI Charlotte Savage is back chasing a killer with a very personal grudge . . .

'He could be out there right now. Passing you on the street. You'd never know . . .'

DI Charlotte Savage is back, chasing a killer who was last at large ten years ago, a killer they presumed dead . . . Now he's back and more dangerous than ever.

'*Four murders in not much more than a week. Was that acceptable?*'

DI Charlotte Savage is back. And this might just be her toughest case yet . . .